PRAISE FOR
THE TEMERAIRE SERIES
BY NAOMI NOVIK

"Enthralling reading—it's like Jane Austen playing Dungeons & Dragons with *Eragon*'s Christopher Paolini."
— *Time*

"This book is for anyone who's read one of Patrick O'Brian's nineteenth-century-set naval adventures and mused: *You know what would make this better? Dragons.* A completely authentic tale, brimming with all the detail and richness one looks for in military yarns as well as the impossible wonder of gilded fantasy."
— *Entertainment Weekly*
(Editor's Choice, grade of A)

"Patrick O'Brian with dragons, and it works like a charm . . . an amazing performance."
— *Chicago Tribune*

"Temeraire remains one of the most interesting dragons to ever grace the printed page."
—*Romantic Times BOOKclub*

"Just when you think you've seen every variation possible on the dragon story, along comes Naomi Novik to prove you wrong."
—Terry Brooks

"A joy of a first novel, a wonderful take on dragons, on those who fly them, and on the relationship that unfolds."
—*The Magazine of Fantasy & Science Fiction*

"A splendid novel. Not only is it a new way to utilize dragons, it's a very clever one and fits neatly into the historical niche this author has used. The plot was excellent, extraordinary in that the reader has no idea where it's leading—which is always fun. Let's hope this is the first of many from Naomi Novik. She'll be one to watch."
—Anne McCaffrey

THE TEMERAIRE SERIES BY NAOMI NOVIK

His Majesty's Dragon
Throne of Jade
Black Powder War
Empire of Ivory
Victory of Eagles
Tongues of Serpents

EMPIRE OF IVORY

TEMERAIRE · BOOK 4

NAOMI NOVIK

BALLANTINE BOOKS · NEW YORK

Empire of Ivory is a work of fiction. All incidents and dialogue, and all characters with the exception of some well-known historical and public figures, are products of the author's imagination and are not to be construed as real. Where real-life historical or public figures appear, the situations, incidents, and dialogues concerning those persons are entirely fictional and are not intended to depict actual events or to change the entirely fictional nature of the work. In all other respects, any resemblance to actual events, locales, or persons, living or dead, is entirely coincidental.

A Del Rey Mass Market Original

Copyright © 2007 by Temeraire LLC

Published in the United States by Del Rey Books, an imprint of The Random House Publishing Group, a division of Random House, Inc., New York.

DEL REY is a registered trademark and the Del Rey colophon is a trademark of Random House, Inc.

ISBN 978-0-345-49687-4

Printed in the United States of America

www.delreybooks.com

OPM   9

To Francesca,
may we always flee lions together

I

Chapter 1

"SEND UP ANOTHER, damn you, send them all up, at once if you have to," Laurence said savagely to poor Calloway, who did not deserve to be sworn at: the gunner was firing off the flares so quickly his hands were scorched black, skin cracking and peeling to bright red where some powder had spilled onto his fingers; he was not stopping to wipe them clean before setting each flare to the match.

One of the little French dragons darted in again, slashing at Temeraire's side, and five men fell screaming as a piece of the makeshift carrying-harness unraveled. They vanished at once beyond the lantern-light and were swallowed up in the dark; the long twisted rope of striped silk, a pillaged curtain, unfurled gently in the wind and went billowing down after them, threads trailing from the torn edges. A moan went through the other Prussian soldiers still clinging desperately to the harness, and after it followed a low angry muttering in German.

Any gratitude the soldiers might have felt for their rescue from the siege of Danzig had since been exhausted: three days flying through icy rain, no food but what they had crammed into their pockets in those final desperate moments, no rest but a few hours snatched along a cold and marshy stretch of the Dutch coast, and now this French patrol harrying them all this last endless night. Men so terrified might do anything in a panic; many of them had still their small-arms and swords, and there were more than a hundred of them crammed aboard, to the less than thirty of Temeraire's own crew.

Laurence swept the sky again with his glass, straining for a glimpse of wings, an answering signal. They were in sight of shore, the night was clear: through his glass he saw the gleam of lights dotting the small harbors all along the Scottish coast, and below heard the steadily increasing roar of the surf. Their flares ought to have been plain to see all the way to Edinburgh; yet no reinforcements had come, not a single courier-beast even to investigate.

"Sir, that's the last of them," Calloway said, coughing through the grey smoke that wreathed his head, the flare whistling high and away. The powder-flash went off silently above their heads, casting the white scudding clouds into brilliant relief, reflecting from dragon scales in every direction: Temeraire all in black, the rest in gaudy colors muddied to shades of grey by the lurid blue light. The night was full of their wings: a dozen dragons turning their heads around to look back, their gleaming pupils narrowing; more coming on, all of them laden down with men, and the handful of small French patrol-dragons darting among them.

All seen in the flash of a moment, then the thunder-clap crack and rumble sounded, only a little delayed, and the flare dying away drifted into blackness again. Laurence counted ten, and ten again; still there was no answer from the shore.

Emboldened, the French dragon came in once more. Temeraire aimed a swipe which would have knocked the little Pou-de-Ciel flat, but his attempt was very slow, for fear of dislodging any more of his passengers; their small enemy evaded with contemptuous ease and circled away to wait for his next chance.

"Laurence," Temeraire said, looking round, "where are they all? Victoriatus is in Edinburgh; he at least ought to have come. After all, we helped him, when he was hurt; not that I *need* help, precisely, against these little dragons," he added, straightening his neck with a crackle of popping joints, "but it is not very convenient to try and fight while we are carrying so many people."

This was putting a braver face on the situation than it deserved: they could not very well defend themselves at all, and Temeraire was taking the worst of it, bleeding already from many small gashes along his side and flanks, which the crew could not bandage up, so cramped were they aboard.

"Only keep everyone moving towards the shore," Laurence said; he had no better answer to give. "I cannot imagine the patrol will pursue us over land," he added, but doubtfully; he would never have imagined a French patrol could come so near to shore as this, either, without challenge; and how he should manage to disembark a thousand frightened and exhausted men under bombardment he did not like to contemplate.

"I am trying; only they *will* keep stopping to fight," Temeraire said wearily, and turned back to his work. Arkady and his rough band of mountain ferals found the small stinging attacks maddening, and they kept trying to turn around mid-air and go after the French patrol-dragons; in their contortions they were flinging off more of the hapless Prussian soldiers than the enemy could ever have accounted for. There was no malice in their carelessness: the wild dragons were unused to men except as the jealous guardians of flocks and herds, and they did not think of their passengers as anything more than an unusual burden; but with malice or none, the men were dying all the same. Temeraire could only prevent them by constant vigilance, and now he was hovering in place over the line of flight, cajoling and hissing by turns, encouraging the others to hurry onwards.

"No, no, Gherni," Temeraire called out, and dashed forward to swat at the little blue-and-white feral: she had dropped onto the very back of a startled French Chasseur-Vocifère: a courier-beast of scarcely four tons, who could not bear up under even her slight weight and was sinking in the air despite the frantic beating of its wings. Gherni had already fixed her teeth in the French dragon's neck and was now worrying it back and forth with savage vigor; meanwhile the Prussians clinging to her harness were all but drumming their heels on the heads of the French crew, crammed so tightly not a shot from the French side could fail of killing one of them.

In his efforts to dislodge her, Temeraire was left open, and the Pou-de-Ciel seized the fresh opportunity; this time daring enough to make an attempt at Temeraire's back. His claws struck so near that Laurence saw the traces of Temeraire's blood shining black on the curved edges as the French dragon lifted away again; his hand tightened on his pistol, uselessly.

"Oh, let me, let me!" Iskierka was straining furiously against the restraints which kept her lashed down to Temeraire's back. The infant Kazilik would soon enough be a force to reckon with; as yet, however, scarcely a month out of the shell, she was too young and unpracticed to be a serious danger to anyone besides herself. They had tried as best they could to secure her, with straps and chains and lecturing, but the last she roundly ignored, and though she had been but irregularly fed these last few days, she had added another five feet of length overnight: neither straps nor chains were proving of much use in restraining her.

"Will you hold still, for all love?" Granby said despairingly; he was throwing his own weight against the straps to try and pull her head down. Allen and Harley, the young lookouts stationed on Temeraire's shoulders, had to go scrambling out of the way to avoid being kicked as Granby was dragged stumbling from side to side by her efforts. Laurence loosened his buckles and climbed to his feet, bracing his heels against the strong ridge of muscle at the base of Temeraire's neck. He caught Granby by the harness-belt when Iskierka's thrashing swung him by again, and managed to hold him steady, but all the leather was strung tight as violin strings, trembling with the strain.

"But I can stop him!" she insisted, twisting her head sidelong as she tried to work free. Eager jets of flame were licking out of the sides of her jaws as she tried once again to lunge at the enemy dragon, but their Pou-de-Ciel attacker, small as he was, was still many times her size and too experienced to be frightened off by a little show of fire; he only jeered, backwinging to expose all of his speckled brown belly to her as a target in a gesture of insulting unconcern.

"Oh!" Iskierka coiled herself tightly with rage, the thin spiky protrusions all over her sinuous body jetting steam, and then with a mighty heave she reared herself up on her hindquarters. The straps jerked painfully out of Laurence's grasp, and involuntarily he caught his hand back to his chest, the numb fingers curling over in reaction. Granby had been dragged into mid-air and was dangling from her thick neck-band, vainly, while she let loose a torrent of flame: thin and yellow-white, so hot the air about it seemed to twist and shrivel away, it made a fierce banner against the night sky.

But the French dragon had cleverly put himself before the wind, coming strong and from the east; now he folded his wings and dropped away, and the blistering flames were blown back against Temeraire's flank. Temeraire, still scolding Gherni back into the line of flight, uttered a startled cry and jerked away while sparks scattered over the glossy blackness of his hide, perilously close to the carrying-harness of silk and linen and rope.

"Verfluchtes Untier! Wir werden noch alle verbrennen," one of the Prussian officers yelled hoarsely, pointing at Iskierka, and fumbled with shaking hand in his bandolier for a cartridge.

"Enough there; put up that pistol," Laurence roared at him through the speaking-trumpet; Lieutenant Ferris and a couple of the topmen hurriedly unlatched their harness-straps and let themselves down to wrestle it out of the officer's hands. They could only reach the fellow by clambering over the other Prussian soldiers, however, and while too afraid to let go of the harness, the men were obstructing their passage in every other way, thrusting out elbows and hips with abrupt jerks, full of resentment and hostility.

Lieutenant Riggs was giving orders, distantly, towards the rear; "Fire!" he shouted, clear over the increasing rumble among the Prussians; the handful of rifles spoke with bright powder-bursts, sulfurous and bitter. The French dragon made a little shriek and wheeled away, flying a little awkward: blood streaked in rivulets from a rent in his wing, where a bullet had by lucky chance struck one of the thinner patches around the joint and penetrated the tough, resilient hide.

The respite came late; some of the men were already clawing their way up towards Temeraire's back, snatching at the greater security of the leather harness to which the aviators were hooked by their carabiner straps. But the harness could not take all their weight, not so many of them: if the buckles stretched open, or some straps gave way, and the whole began to slide, it would entangle Temeraire's wings and send them all plummeting into the ocean together.

Laurence loaded his pistols fresh and thrust them into his waistband, loosened his sword, and stood up again. He had willingly risked all their lives to bring these men out of a trap, and he meant to see them safely ashore if he could; but he would not see Temeraire endangered by their hysteric fear.

"Allen, Harley," he said to the boys, "do you run across to the riflemen and tell Mr. Riggs: if we cannot stop them, they are to cut the carrying-harness loose, all of it; and be sure you keep latched on as you go. Perhaps you had better stay here with her, John," he added, when Granby made to come away with him: Iskierka had quieted for the moment, her enemy having quitted the field, but she still coiled and re-coiled herself in sulky restlessness, muttering in disappointment.

"Oh, certainly! I should like to see myself do any such thing," Granby said, taking out his sword; he had forgone pistols since becoming Iskierka's captain, to avoid the risk of handling open powder around her.

Laurence was too unsure of his ground to pursue an argument; Granby was not properly his subordinate any longer, and the more experienced aviator of the two of them, counting years aloft. Granby took the lead as they crossed Temeraire's back, moving with the sureness of a boy trained up from the age of seven; at each step Laurence handed forward his own lead-strap and let Granby lock it on to the harness for him, which he could do one-handed, that they might go more quickly.

Ferris and the topmen were still struggling with the Prussian officer in the midst of a thickening clot of men; they were disappearing from view under the violent press of bodies, only Martin's yellow hair visible. The soldiers were near full riot, men beating and kicking at one another, thinking of nothing but an impossible escape. The knots of the carrying-harness were tightening, giving up more slack, so all the loops and bands of it hung loose and swinging with the thrashing, struggling men.

Laurence came on one of the soldiers, a young man, eyes wide and staring in his wind-reddened face and his thick mustache wet-tipped with sweat, trying to work his arm beneath the main harness, blindly, though the buckle was already straining open, and he would in a moment have slid wholly free.

"Get back to your place!" Laurence shouted, pointing to the nearest open loop of the carrying-harness, and thrust the man's hand away from the harness. Then his ears were ringing, a thick ripe smell of sour cherries in his nostrils as his knees folded beneath him. He put a hand to his forehead slowly, stupidly; it was wet. His own harness-straps were holding him, painfully tight against his ribs with all his weight pulling against them. The Prussian had struck him with a bottle; it had shattered, and the liquor was dripping down the side of his face.

Instinct rescued him; he put up his arm to take the next blow and pushed the broken glass back at the man's face; the soldier said something in German and let go the bottle. They wrestled together a few moments more; then Laurence caught the man's belt and heaved him up and away from Temeraire's side. The soldier's arms were spread wide, grasping at nothing; Laurence, watching, abruptly recalled himself, and at once he lunged out, reaching to his full length; but too late, and he came thumping heavily back against Temeraire's side with empty hands; the soldier was already gone from sight.

His head did not hurt over-much, but Laurence felt queerly sick and weak. Temeraire had resumed flying towards the coast, having rounded up the rest of the ferals at last, and the force of the wind was increasing. Laurence clung to the harness a moment, until the fit passed and he was able to make his hands work properly again. There were already more men clawing up: Granby was trying to hold them back, but they were overbearing him by sheer weight of numbers, even though struggling as much against one another as him. One of the soldiers grappling for a hold on the harness climbed too far out of the press; he slipped, landed heavily on the men below him, and carried them all away; as a tangled, many-limbed mass they fell into the slack loops of the carrying-harness, and the muffled wet noises of their bones cracking together sounded like a roast chicken being wrenched hungrily apart.

Granby was hanging from his harness-straps, trying to get his feet planted again; Laurence crab-walked over to him and gave him a steadying arm. Below he could just make out the washy seafoam, pale against the black water; Temeraire was flying lower and lower as they neared the coast.

"That damned Pou-de-Ciel is coming round again," Granby panted as he got back his footing; the French had somehow got a dressing over the gash in the dragon's wing, even if the great white patch of it was awkwardly placed and far larger than the injury made necessary. The dragon looked a little uncomfortable in the air, but he was coming on gamely nonetheless; they had surely seen that Temeraire was vulnerable. If the Pou-de-Ciel and his crew were able to catch the harness and drag it loose, they might finish deliberately what the soldiers had begun in panic, and the chance of bringing down a heavy-weight, much less one as valuable as Temeraire, would surely tempt them to great risk.

"We will have to cut the soldiers loose," Laurence said, low and wretched, and looked upwards, where the carrying-loops attached to the leather; but to send a hundred men and more to their deaths, scarce minutes from safety, he was not sure he could bear; or ever to meet General Kalkreuth again, having done it; some of the general's own young aides were aboard, and doing their best to keep the other men quiet.

Riggs and his riflemen were firing short, hurried volleys; the Pou-de-Ciel was keeping just out of range, waiting for the best moment to chance his attack. Then Iskierka sat up and blew out another stream of fire: Temeraire was flying ahead of the wind, so the flames were not turned against him, this time; but every man on his back had at once to throw himself flat to avoid the torrent, which burnt out too quickly before it could reach the French dragon.

The Pou-de-Ciel at once darted in while the crew were so distracted; Iskierka was gathering herself for another blow, and the riflemen could not get up again. "Christ," Granby said; but before he could reach her, a low rumble like fresh thunder sounded, and below them small round red mouths bloomed with smoke and powder-flashes: shore batteries, firing from the coast below. Illuminated in the yellow blaze of Iskierka's fire, a twenty-four-pound ball of round-shot flew past them and took the Pou-de-Ciel full in the chest; he folded around it like paper as it drove through his ribs, and crumpled out of the air, falling to the rocks below: they were over the shore, they were over the land, and thick-fleeced sheep were fleeing before them across the snow-matted grass.

* * *

The townspeople of the little harbor of Dunbar were alternately terrified at the descent of a whole company of dragons onto their quiet hamlet, and elated by the success of their new shore battery, put into place scarcely two months ago and never before tried. Half-a-dozen courier-beasts driven off and one Pou-de-Ciel slain, overnight became a Grand Chevalier and several Flammes-de-Gloire, all hideously killed; the town could talk of nothing else, and the local militia strutted through the streets to general satisfaction.

The townspeople grew less enthusiastic, however, after Arkady had eaten four of their sheep; the other ferals had made only slightly less extravagant depredations, and Temeraire himself had seized upon a couple of cows, shaggy yellow-haired Highland cattle, sadly reported afterwards to be prize-winning, and devoured them to the hooves and horns.

"They were very tasty," Temeraire said apologetically; and turned his head aside to spit out some of the hair.

Laurence was not inclined to stint the dragons in the least, after their long and arduous flight, and on this occasion was perfectly willing to sacrifice his ordinary respect for property to their comfort. Some of the farmers made noises about payment, but Laurence did not mean to try and feed the bottomless appetites of the ferals out of his own pocket. The Admiralty might reach into theirs, if they had nothing better to do than sit before the fire and whistle while a battle was carrying on outside their windows, and men dying for lack of a little assistance. "We will not be a charge upon you for long. As soon as we hear from Edinburgh, I expect we will be called to the covert there," he said flatly, in reply to the protests. The horse-courier left at once.

The townspeople were more welcoming to the Prussians, most of them young soldiers pale and wretched after the flight. General Kalkreuth himself had been among these final refugees; he had to be let down from Arkady's back in a sling, his face white and sickly under his beard. The local medical man looked doubtful, but cupped a basin full of blood, and had him carried away to the nearest farmhouse to be kept warm and dosed with brandy and hot water.

Other men were less fortunate. The harnesses, cut away, came down in filthy and tangled heaps weighted by corpses already turning greenish: some killed by the French attacks, others smothered by their own fellows in the panic, or dead of thirst or plain terror. They buried sixty-three men out of a thousand that afternoon, some of them nameless, in a long and shallow grave laboriously pickaxed out of the frozen ground. The survivors were a ragged crew, clothes and uniforms inadequately brushed, faces still dirty, attending silently. Even the ferals, though they did not understand the language, perceived the ceremony, and sat on their haunches respectfully to watch from a distance.

Word came back from Edinburgh only a few hours later, but with orders so queer as to be incomprehensible. They began reasonably enough: the Prussians to be left behind in Dunbar and quartered in the town; and the dragons, as expected, summoned to the city. But there was no invitation to General Kalkreuth or his officers to come along; to the contrary, Laurence was strictly adjured to bring no Prussian officers with him. As for the dragons, they were not permitted to come into the large and comfortable covert itself at all, not even Temeraire: instead Laurence was ordered to leave them sleeping in the streets about the castle, and to report to the admiral in command in the morning.

He stifled his first reaction, and spoke mildly of the arrangements to Major Seiberling, now the senior Prussian; implying as best he could without any outright falsehood that the Admiralty meant to wait until General Kalkreuth was recovered for an official welcome.

"Oh; must we fly again?" Temeraire said; he heaved himself wearily back onto his feet, and went around the drowsing ferals to nudge them awake: they had all crumpled into somnolence after their dinners.

Their flight was slow and the days were grown short; it lacked only a week to Christmas, Laurence realized abruptly. The sky was fully dark by the time they reached Edinburgh; but the castle shone out for them like a beacon with its windows and walls bright with torches, on its high rocky hill above the shadowed expanse of the covert, with the narrow buildings of the old medieval part of the city crammed together close around it.

Temeraire hovered doubtfully above the cramped and winding streets; there were many spires and pointed roofs to contend with, and not very much room between them, giving the city the appearance of a spear-pit. "I do not see how I am to land," he said uncertainly. "I am sure to break one of those buildings; why have they built these streets so small? It was much more convenient in Peking."

"If you cannot do it without hurting yourself, we will go away again, and orders be damned," Laurence said; his patience was grown very thin.

But in the end Temeraire managed to let himself down into the old cathedral square without bringing down more than a few lumps of ornamental masonry; the ferals, being all of them considerably smaller, had less difficulty. They were anxious at being removed from the fields full of sheep and cattle, however, and suspicious of their new surroundings; Arkady bent low and put his eye to an open window to peer inside at the empty rooms, making skeptical inquires of Temeraire as he did so.

"That is where people sleep, is it not, Laurence? Like a pavilion," Temeraire said, trying cautiously to rearrange his tail into a more comfortable position. "And sometimes where they sell jewels and other pleasant things. But where are all the people?"

Laurence was quite sure all the people had fled; the wealthiest tradesman in the city would be sleeping in a gutter tonight, if it were the only bed he could find in the new part of town, safely far away from the pack of dragons who had invaded his streets.

The dragons eventually disposed of themselves in some reasonable comfort; the ferals, used to sleeping in rough-hewn caves, were even pleased with the soft and rounded cobblestones. "I do not mind sleeping in the street, Laurence, truly; it is quite dry, and I am sure it will be very interesting to look at, in the morning," Temeraire said consolingly, even with his head lodged in one alley-way and his tail in another.

But Laurence minded for him; it was not the sort of welcome which he felt they might justly have looked for, a long year away from home, having been sent halfway round the world and back. It was one thing to find themselves in rough quarters while on campaign, where no man could expect better, and might be glad for a cow-byre to lay his head in. To be deposited like baggage on the cold unhealthy stones, stained years-dark with street refuse, was something other; the dragons might at least have been granted use of the open farmland outside the city.

And it was no conscious malice: only the common unthinking assumption by which men treated dragons as inconvenient if elevated livestock, to be managed and herded without consideration for their own sentiments; an assumption so ingrained that Laurence had recognized it as outrageous only when forced to do so by the marked contrast with the conditions he had observed in China, where dragons were received as full members of society.

"Well," Temeraire said reasonably, while Laurence laid out his own bedroll inside the house beside his head, with the windows open so they might continue to speak, "we knew how matters were here, Laurence, so we cannot be very surprised. Besides, I did not come to make myself more comfortable, or I might have stayed in China; we must improve the circumstances of all our friends. Not," he added, "that I would not like my own pavilion; but I would rather have liberty. Dyer, will you pray get that bit of gristle out from between my teeth? I cannot reach forward to put my claw upon it."

Dyer startled up from his half-doze upon Temeraire's back and, fetching a small pick from their baggage, scrambled obediently into Temeraire's opened jaws to scrape away.

"You would have more luck in achieving the latter, if there were more men ready to grant you the former," Laurence said. "I do not mean to counsel you to despair; we must not, indeed. But I had hoped to find on our arrival more respect than when we left, not less; which must have been a material advantage to our cause."

Temeraire waited until Dyer had climbed out again to answer. "I am sure we must be listened to on the merits," he said, a large assumption, which Laurence was not at all sanguine enough to share, "and all the more, when I have seen Maximus and Lily, and they are ranged with me. And perhaps also Excidium, for he has been in so many battles: no one could help but be impressed with him. I am sure *they* will see all the wisdom of my arguments; *they* will not be so stupid as Eroica and the others were," Temeraire added, with shades of resentment. The Prussian dragons had at first rather disdained his attempts at convincing them of the merits of greater liberty and education, being as fond of their tradition of rigorous military order as ever were their handlers, and preferring instead to ridicule as effete the habits of thought which Temeraire had acquired in China.

"I hope you will forgive me for bluntness; but I am afraid even if you had the hearts and minds of every dragon in Britain aligned with your own, it would make very little difference: as a party you have not very much influence in Parliament," Laurence said.

"Perhaps we do not, but I imagine if we were to *go* to Parliament, we would be attended to," Temeraire said, an image most convincing, if not likely to produce the sort of attention which Temeraire desired.

Laurence said as much, and added, "We must find some better means of drawing sympathy to your cause, from those who have the influence to foster political change. I am only sorry I cannot apply to my father for advice, as relations stand between us."

"Well, I am *not* sorry, at all," Temeraire said, putting back his ruff. "I am sure he would not have helped us; and we can do perfectly well without him." Aside from his loyalty, which would have resented coldness to Laurence on any grounds, he not unnaturally viewed Lord Allendale's objections to the Aerial Corps as objections to his own person; and despite their never having met, he felt violently as a matter of course towards anyone whose sentiments would have seen Laurence separated from him.

"My father has been engaged with politics half his

life," Laurence said: with the effort towards abolition in particular, a movement met with as much scorn, at its inception, as Laurence anticipated for Temeraire's own. "I assure you his advice would be of the greatest value; and I do mean to effect a repair, if I can, which would allow our consulting him."

"I would as soon have kept it, myself," Temeraire muttered, meaning the elegant red vase which Laurence had purchased in China as a conciliatory gift. It had since traveled with them five thousand miles and more, and Temeraire had grown inclined to be as possessive of it as any of his own treasures; he now sighed to see it finally sent away, with Laurence's brief and apologetic note.

But Laurence was all too conscious of the difficulties which faced them; and of his own inadequacy to forward so vast and complicated a cause. He had been still a boy when Wilberforce had come to their house, the guest of one of his father's political friends, newly inspired with fervor against the slave trade and beginning the parliamentary campaign to abolish it. Twenty years ago now; and despite the most heroic efforts by men of ability and wealth and power greater than his own, in those twenty years surely a million souls or more had yet been carried away from their native shores into bondage.

Temeraire had been hatched in the year five; for all his intelligence, he could not yet truly grasp the weary slow struggle which should be required to bring men to a political position, however moral and just, however necessary, in any way contrary to their immediate self-interest. Laurence bade him good-night without further disheartening advice; but as he closed the windows, which began to rattle gently from the sleeping dragon's breath, the distance to the covert beyond the castle walls seemed to him less easily bridged than all the long miles which had brought them home from China.

The Edinburgh streets were quiet in the morning, unnaturally so, and deserted but for the dragons sleeping in stretched ranks over the old grey cobbles. Temeraire's great bulk was heaped awkwardly before the smoke-stained cathedral, and his tail running down into an alley-way scarcely wide enough to hold it. The sky was clear and cold and very blue, only a handful of terraced clouds running out to sea, a faint suggestion of pink and orange early light on the stones.

Tharkay was awake, the only soul stirring when Laurence came out; he was sitting, crouched against the cold, in one of the other narrow doorways to an elegant home, the heavy door standing open behind him, looking into the entry hall, tapestried and deserted. He had a cup of tea, steaming in the air. "May I offer you one?" he inquired. "I am sure the owners would not begrudge it."

"No, I must go up," Laurence said; he had been woken by a runner from the castle, summoning him to a meeting at once. Another piece of discourtesy, when they had only arrived so late; and to make matters worse, the boy had been unable to tell him of any provisions made for the feeding of the hungry dragons. What the ferals should say when they awoke, Laurence did not like to think.

"You need not worry; I am sure they will fend for themselves," Tharkay said, not a cheering prospect, and offered Laurence his own cup for consolation; Laurence sighed and drained it, grateful for the strong, hot brew. He gave Tharkay back the cup, and hestitated; the other man was looking across the cathedral square with a peculiar expression—his mouth twisted at one corner.

"Are you well?" Laurence asked; conscious he had thought not enough about his men, in his anxiety over Temeraire; and Tharkay he had less right to take for granted.

"Oh, very; I am quite at home," Tharkay said. "It is some time since I was last in Britain, but I was tolerably familiar with the Court of Session, then," nodding across the square at Parliament House, where the court met: Scotland's highest civil court, and a notorious pit of broken hopes, endless dragging suits, and wrangling over technicalities and estates; presently deserted by all its solicitors, judges, and suitors alike, and only a scattering of harried papers blown up against Temeraire's side like white patches, relics of old settlements. Tharkay's father had been a man of property, Laurence knew; Tharkay had none; the son of a Nepalese woman perhaps would have been at some disadvantage in the British courts, Laurence supposed, and any irregularity in his claims easily exploited.

At least he did not look at all enthusiastic to be home; if home he considered it, and Laurence said, "I hope," tentatively, and tried awkwardly to suggest that Tharkay might consider extending his contract, when they had settled such delicate matters as payment for those services already rendered: Tharkay had been paid for guiding them along the old silk trading routes from China, but since then he had recruited the ferals to their cause, which demanded a bounty beyond Laurence's private means. And his services could by no means be easily dispensed with now, not until the ferals were settled somehow into the Corps, Tharkay being, apart from Temeraire, almost the only one who could manage more than a few words of their odd, inflected language. "I would gladly speak to Admiral Lenton at Dover, if you would not object," Laurence added; he did not at all mean to discuss any such irregular question with whichever notable was commanding here, after the treatment which they had so far received.

Tharkay only shrugged, noncommittal, and said, "Your messenger grows anxious," nodding to where the young runner was fidgeting unhappily at the corner of the square, waiting for Laurence to come along.

The boy took him the short distance up the hill to the castle gates; from there Laurence was escorted to the admiral's office by an officious red-coated Marine, their path winding around to the headquarters building through the medieval stone courtyards, empty and free from hurry in the early-morning dimness. The doors were opened, and he went in stiffly, straight-shouldered; his face had set into disapproving lines, cold and rigid. "Sir," he said, eyes fixed at a point upon the wall; and only then glanced down, and said, surprised, "Admiral Lenton?"

"Laurence; yes. Sit, sit down." Lenton dismissed the guard, and the door closed upon them and the musty, book-lined room; the Admiral's desk was nearly clear, but for a single small map, a handful of papers. Lenton sat for a moment silently. "It is damned good to see you," he said at last. "Very good to see you indeed. Very good."

Laurence was very much shocked at his appearance. In the year since their last meeting, Lenton seemed to have aged ten: hair gone entirely white, and a vague, rheumy look in his eyes; his jowls hung slack. "I hope I find you well, sir," Laurence said, deeply sorry, no longer wondering why Lenton had been transferred north to Edinburgh, the quieter post; he wondered only what illness might have so ravaged him, and who had been made commander at Dover in his place.

"Oh . . ." Lenton waved his hand, fell silent. "I suppose you have not been told anything," he said, after a moment. "No, that is right; we agreed we could not risk word getting out."

"No, sir," Laurence said, anger kindling afresh. "I have heard nothing, and been told nothing; with our allies asking me daily for word of the Corps, until there was no more use in asking."

He had given his own personal assurances to the Prussian commanders; he had sworn that the Aerial Corps would not fail them, that the promised company of dragons, which might have turned the tide against Napoleon, in this last disastrous campaign, would arrive at any moment. He and Temeraire had stayed and fought in their place when the dragons did not arrive, risking their own lives and those of his crew in an increasingly hopeless cause; but the dragons had never come.

Lenton did not immediately answer, but sat nodding to himself, murmuring. "Yes, that is right, of course." He tapped a hand on the desk, looked at some papers without reading them, a portrait of distraction.

Laurence added more sharply, "Sir, I can hardly believe you would have lent yourself to so treacherous a course, and one so terribly shortsighted; Napoleon's victory was by no means assured, if the twenty promised dragons had been sent."

"What?" Lenton looked up. "Oh, Laurence, there was no question of that. No, none at all. I am sorry for the secrecy, but as for not sending the dragons, that called for no decision. There were no dragons to send."

Victoriatus heaved his sides out and in, a gentle, measured pace. His nostrils were wide and red, a thick flaking crust around the rims, and a dried pink foam lingered about the corners of his mouth. His eyes were closed, but after every few breaths they would open a little, dull and unseeing with exhaustion; he gave a rasping, hollow cough that flecked the ground before him with blood; and subsided once again into the half-slumber that was all he could manage. His captain, Richard Clark, was lying on a cot beside him: unshaven, in filthy linen, an arm flung up to cover his eyes and the other hand resting on the dragon's foreleg; he did not move, even when they approached.

After a few moments, Lenton touched Laurence on the arm. "Come, enough; let's away." He turned slowly aside, leaning heavily upon a cane, and took Laurence back up the green hill to the castle. The corridors, as they returned to his offices, seemed no longer peaceful but hushed, sunk in irreparable gloom.

Laurence refused a glass of wine, too numb to think of refreshment. "It is a sort of consumption," Lenton said, looking out the windows that faced onto the covert yard; Victoriatus and twelve other great beasts lay screened from one another by the ancient windbreaks, piled branches and stones grown over with ivy.

"How widespread—?" Laurence asked.

"Everywhere," Lenton said. "Dover, Portsmouth, Middlesbrough. The breeding grounds in Wales and Halifax; Gibraltar; everywhere the couriers went on their rounds; everywhere." He turned away from the windows and took his chair again. "We were inexpressibly stupid; we thought it was only a cold, you see."

"But we had word of that before we had even rounded the Cape of Good Hope, on our journey east," Laurence said, appalled. "Has it lasted so long?"

"In Halifax it started in September of the year five," Lenton said. "The surgeons think now it was the American dragon, that big Indian fellow: he was kept there, and then the first dragons to fall sick here were those who had shared the transport with him to Dover; then it began in Wales when he was sent to the breeding grounds there. *He* is perfectly hearty, not a cough or a sneeze; very nearly the only dragon left in England who is, except for a handful of hatchlings we have tucked away in Ireland."

"You know we have brought you another twenty," Laurence said, taking a brief refuge in making his report.

"Yes, these fellows from where, Turkestan?" Lenton said, willing to follow. "Did I understand your letter correctly; they were brigands?"

"I would rather say jealous of their territory," Laurence said. "They are not very pretty, but there is no malice in them; though what use twenty dragons can be, to cover all England—" He stopped. "Lenton, surely something can be done—must be done," he said.

Lenton only shook his head briefly. "The usual remedies did some good, at the beginning," he said. "Quieted the coughing, and so forth. They could still fly, if they did not have much appetite; and colds are usually such trifling things with them. But it lingered on so long, and after a while the possets seemed to lose their effect— some began to grow worse—"

He stopped, and after a long moment added, with an effort, "Obversaria is dead."

"Good God!" Laurence cried. "Sir, I am shocked to hear it—so deeply grieved." It was a dreadful loss: she had been flying with Lenton some forty years, the flag-dragon at Dover for the last ten, and though relatively young had produced four eggs already; perhaps the finest flyer in all England, with few to even compete with her for the title.

"That was in, let me see; August," Lenton said, as if he had not heard. "After Inlacrimas, but before Minacitus. It takes some of them worse than others. The very young hold up best, and the old ones linger; it is the ones between who have been dying. Dying first, anyway; I suppose they will all go in the end."

Chapter 2

"CAPTAIN," KEYNES SAID, "I am sorry; any gormless imbecile can bandage up a bullet-wound, and a gormless imbecile you are very likely to be assigned in my place. But I cannot stay with the healthiest dragon in Britain when the quarantine-coverts are full of the sick."

"I perfectly understand, Mr. Keynes, and you need say nothing more," Laurence said. "Will you not fly with us as far as Dover?"

"No; Victoriatus will not last the week, and I will wait and attend the dissection with Dr. Harrow," Keynes said, with a brutal sort of practicality that made Laurence flinch. "I have hopes we may learn something of the characteristics of the disease. Some of the couriers are still flying; one will carry me onwards."

"Well," Laurence said, and shook the surgeon's hand. "I hope we shall see you with us again soon."

"I hope you will not," Keynes said, in his usual acerbic manner. "If you do, I will otherwise be lacking for patients, which from the course of this disease will mean they are all dead."

Laurence could hardly say his spirits were lowered; they had already been reduced so far as to make little difference out of the loss. But he was sorry. Dragon-surgeons were not by and large near so incompetent as the naval breed, and despite Keynes's words Laurence did not fear his eventual successor, but to lose a good man, his courage and sense proven and his eccentricities known, was never pleasant; and Temeraire would not like it.

"He is not hurt?" Temeraire pressed. "He is not sick?"

"No, Temeraire; but he is needed elsewhere," Laurence said. "He is a senior surgeon; I am sure you would not deny his attentions to those of your comrades who are suffering from this illness."

"Well, if Maximus or Lily should need him," Temeraire said crabbily, and drew furrows in the ground. "Shall I see them again soon? I am sure they cannot be so very ill. Maximus is the biggest dragon I have ever seen, even though we have been to China; he is sure to recover quickly."

"No, my dear," Laurence said uneasily, and broke the worst of the news—"The sick have none of them recovered, and you must take the very greatest care not to go anywhere near the quarantine-grounds."

"But I do not understand," Temeraire said. "If they do not recover, then—" He paused.

Laurence only looked away. Temeraire had good excuse for not understanding at once. Dragons were hardy creatures, and many breeds might live a century and more; he might have justly expected to know Maximus and Lily for longer than a man's lifetime, if the war had not taken them from him.

At last, sounding almost bewildered, Temeraire said, "But I have so much to tell them—I came for them. So they might learn that dragons may read and write, and have property, and do things other than fight."

"I will write a letter for you, which we can send to them with your greetings, and they will be happier to know you well and safe from contagion than for your company," Laurence said. Temeraire did not answer; he was very still, and his head bowed deeply to his chest. "We will be near-by," Laurence went on, after a moment, "and you may write to them every day, if you wish; when we have finished our work."

"Patrolling, I suppose," Temeraire said, with a very unusual note of bitterness, "and more stupid formation-work; while they are all sick, and we can do nothing."

Laurence looked down, into his lap, where their new orders lay amid the oilcloth packet of all his papers, and had no comfort to offer: brusque instructions for their immediate removal to Dover, where Temeraire's expectations were likely to be answered in every particular.

He was not encouraged, on reporting to the head-quarters at Dover directly they had landed, by being left to cool his heels in the hall outside the new admiral's office for thirty minutes, listening to voices by no means indistinct despite the heavy oaken door. He recognized Jane Roland, shouting; the voices that answered her were unfamiliar; and Laurence rose to his feet abruptly, straightening as the door was flung open. A tall man in a naval coat came rushing out with clothing and expression both disordered, his lower cheeks mottled to a moderate glow under his sideburns; he did not pause, but threw Laurence a furious glare before he left.

"Come in, Laurence; come in," Jane called, and he went in; she was standing with the admiral, an older man dressed rather astonishingly in a black frock coat and knee-breeches with buckled shoes.

"You have not met Dr. Wapping, I think," Jane said. "Sir, this is Captain Laurence, of Temeraire."

"Sir," Laurence said, and made his leg deep to cover his confusion and dismay. He supposed that if all the dragons were in quarantine, to put the covert in the charge of a physician was the sort of thing which might make sense to landsmen, as with the notion advanced to him once, by a family friend seeking his influence on behalf of a less-fortunate relation, to advance a surgeon—not even a naval surgeon—to the command of a hospital ship.

"Captain, I am honored to make your acquaintance," Dr. Wapping said. "Admiral, I will take my leave; I beg your pardon for having been the cause of so unpleasant a scene."

"Nonsense; those rascals at the Victualing Board are a pack of unhanged scoundrels, and I am happy to put them in their place; good day to you. Would you credit, Laurence," Jane said, as Wapping closed the door behind himself, "that those wretches are not content that the poor creatures eat scarcely enough to feed a bird anymore, but they must send us diseased stock and scrawny?

"But this is a way to welcome you home." She caught him by the shoulders and kissed him soundly on both cheeks. "You are a damned sight; whatever has happened to your coat? Will you have a glass of wine?" She poured for them both without waiting his answer; he took it in a sort of appalled blankness. "I have all your letters, so I have a tolerable notion what you have been doing, and you must forgive me my silence, Laurence; I found it easier to write nothing than to leave out the only matter of any importance."

"No; that is, yes, of course," he said, and sat down with her at the fire. Her coat was thrown over the arm of her chair; now that he looked, he saw the admiral's fourth bar on the shoulders, and the front more magnificently frogged with braid. Her face, too, was altered but not for the better; she had lost a stone of weight at least, he thought, and her dark hair, cropped short, was shot with grey.

"Well, I am sorry to be such a ruin," she said ruefully, and laughed away his apologies. "No, we are all of us decaying, Laurence; there is no denying it. You have seen poor Lenton, I suppose. He held up like a hero for three weeks after she died, but then we found him on the floor of his bedroom in an apoplexy; for a week he could not speak without slurring. He came along a good ways afterwards, but still he has been a shade of himself."

"I am sorry for it," Laurence said, "though I drink to your promotion," and by herculean effort he managed it without a stutter.

"I thank you, dear fellow," she said. "I would be et up with pride, I suppose, if matters were otherwise, and if it were not one annoyance after another. We glide along tolerably well when left to our own devices, but I must deal with these idiotish creatures from the admiralty. They are told, before they come, and told again, and still they will simper at me, and coo, as if I had not been a-dragonback before they were out of dresses, and then they stare if I dress them down for behaving like kiss-my-hand squires."

"I suppose they find it a difficult adjustment," Laurence said, with private sympathy. "I wonder the Admiralty should have—" and belatedly he paused, feeling he was treading on obscure and dangerous ground. One could not very well quarrel with pursuing whatever means necessary to reconcile Longwings, perhaps Britain's most deadly breed, to service, and as the beasts would accept none but female handlers, some must be offered them; Laurence was sorry for the necessity that would thrust a gently born woman out of her rightful society and into harm's way, but at least they were raised up to it. And where necessary, they had perforce to act as formation-leaders, transmitting the maneuvers to their wings; but this was a far cry from flag rank, not to say commanding the largest covert in Britain, and perhaps the most critical.

"They certainly did not like to give it to me, but they had precious little choice," Jane said. "Portland would not come from Gibraltar; Laetificat is not up to the sea-voyage anymore. So it was me or Sanderson, and he is making a cake of himself over the business; goes off into corners and weeps like a woman, as though that would help anything: a veteran of nine fleet actions, if you would credit it." Then she ran her hand through her dis-ordered crop and sighed. "Never mind, you are not to listen to me, Laurence; I am impatient, and his Animosia does poorly."

"And Excidium?" Laurence ventured.

"Excidium is a tough old bird, and he knows how to husband his strength: has the sense to eat, even though he has no appetite. He will muddle along a good while yet, and you know, he has close on a century of service; many his age have already shot themselves of the whole business and retired to the breeding grounds." She smiled; it was not whole-hearted. "There; I have been brave. Let us to pleasanter things: you have brought me twenty dragons, and by God do I have a use for them. Let us go and see them."

"She is a handful and a half," Granby admitted lowly, as they considered the coiled serpentine length of Iskierka's body, faint threads of steam issuing from the many needle-like spikes upon her body, "and I haven't ridden herd on her, sir, I am sorry."

Iskierka had already established herself to her own satisfaction, if no one else's, by clawing out a deep pit in the clearing next to Temeraire's where she had been housed, then filling it with ash: this acquired from some two dozen young trees which she had unceremoniously uprooted and burnt up inside her pit. She had then added to the powdery grey mixture a collection of boulders, which she fired to a moderate glow before going to sleep, comfortably, in her heated nest. The bonfire and its lingering smolder were visible for some distance, even to the farmhouses nearest the covert, and a few hours past her arrival had already produced several complaints and a great deal of alarm.

"Oh, you have done enough keeping her harnessed out in the countryside, without a head of cattle to your name," Jane said, giving the drowsing Iskierka's side a pat. "They may bleat to me all they like, for a fire-breather, and you may be sure the Navy will cheer your name when they hear we have our own at last. Well done; well done indeed, and I am happy to confirm you in your rank, Captain Granby. Should you like to do the honors, Laurence?"

Most of Laurence's crew had already been employed in Iskierka's clearing, in beating out the stray embers which flew out of her pit and threatened to ignite all the covert if left unchecked. Ash-dusty and tired as they all were, they had none of them gone away, lingering consciously without the need of any announcement, and now lined up on a muttered word from young Lieutenant Ferris to watch Laurence pin the second pair of gold bars upon Granby's shoulders.

"Gentlemen," Jane said, when Laurence had done, and they gave a cheek-flushed Granby three huzzahs, whole-hearted if a little subdued, and Ferris and Riggs stepped over to shake him by the hand.

"We will see about assigning you a crew, though it is early days yet with her," Jane said, after the ceremony had dispersed, and they proceeded on to make her acquainted with the ferals. "I have no shortage of men now, more's the pity. Feed her twice daily, see if we cannot make up for any growth she may have been shorted, and whenever she is awake I will start you on Longwing maneuvers. I don't know if she can scorch herself, as they can with their own acid, but we needn't find out by trial."

Granby nodded; he seemed not the least nonplussed at answering to her. Neither did Tharkay, who had been persuaded to stay on at least a little longer, as one of the few of them with any influence upon the ferals at all. He rather looked mostly amused, in his secretive way, once past the inquiring glance which he had first cast at Laurence: as Jane had insisted upon being taken to the new-come dragons at once, there had been no chance for Laurence to give Tharkay a private caution in advance of their meeting. He did not reveal any surprise, however, but only made her a polite bow, and performed the introductions quite calmly.

Arkady and his band had made very little less confusion of their own clearings than Iskierka, preferring to knock down all the trees between and cluster together in a great heap. The chill of the December air did not trouble them, used as they were to the vastly colder regions of the Pamirs, but they spoke disapprovingly of the dampness, and on understanding that here before them was the senior officer of the covert, at once demanded from her an accounting of the promised cows, one apiece daily, by which they had been lured into service.

"They make the position that if they do not happen to eat the cows upon a given day, still they are owed the cattle, which they may call in at a future time," Tharkay explained, provoking Jane's deep laugh.

"Tell them they shall have as much as they like to eat

on any occasion, and if they are too suspicious for that to satisfy them, we shall make them a tally: they may each of them take one of these logs they have knocked about over to the feeding pens, and mark it when they take a cow," Jane said, more merry than offended at being met with such negotiations. "Pray ask will they agree to a rate of exchange, two hogs for a cow, or two sheep, should we bring in some variety?"

The ferals put their heads together and muttered and hissed and whistled amongst themselves, in a cacophony made private only by the obscurity of their language, and finally Arkady turned back and professed himself willing to settle on the trade agreement, except that he insisted goats should be three to a cow, they having some contempt for that animal, more easily obtained in their former homeland and likely there to be scrawny.

Jane bowed to him to seal the arrangement, and he bobbed his head back, his expression deeply satisfied, and rendered all the more piratical by the red splash of mongrel color which covered one of his eyes and spilled down his neck. "They are a gang of ruffians and make no mistake," Jane said, as she led them back towards her offices, "but I have no doubt of their flying, at any rate: with that sort of wiry muscle they will go in circles around anything in their weight-class, or over it, and I am happy to stuff their bellies for them."

"No, sir; there'll be no trouble," the steward of the headquarters said, rather low, of finding rooms for Laurence and his officers; even arriving as they had out of nowhere and without notice. Most of the captains and officers were encamped out in the quarantine-grounds with their sick dragons, despite the cold and wet, and the building was queerly deserted: hushed and silent, as it had not been even at the low-ebb of the days before

Trafalgar, when nearly all the formations had gone south to help bring down the French and Spanish fleets.

They all drank Granby's health together, but the party broke up early, and Laurence was not disposed to linger afterwards: a few wretched lieutenants sitting together at a dark table in the corner, not talking; an older captain snoring with his head tipped against the side of his armchair, a bottle of brandy empty by his elbow. Laurence took his dinner alone in his rooms, near the fire; the air was chill, from the rooms to either side being vacant.

He opened the door at a faint tapping, expecting perhaps Jane, or one of his men with some word from Temeraire, and was startled to find instead Tharkay. "Pray come in," Laurence said, and belatedly added, "I hope you will forgive my state." The room was yet disordered, and he had borrowed a dressing-gown from a colleague's neglected wardrobe; it was considerably too large around the waist, and badly crumpled.

"I am come to say good-bye," Tharkay said, and shook his head, when Laurence had made an awkward inquiry. "No, I have nothing to complain of; but I am not of your company. I do not care to stay only to be a translator; it is a rôle which must soon pall."

"I would be happy to speak to Admiral Roland— perhaps a commission—" Laurence said, trailing away; he did not know what might be done, or how such matters were arranged in the Corps, except to imagine them a good deal less formally prescribed than in the Army, or the Navy, but he did not wish to promise what might be wholly infeasible.

"I have already spoken to her," Tharkay said, "and have been given one, if not the sort you mean; I will go back to Turkestan and bring back more ferals, if any can be persuaded into your service on similar terms."

Laurence would have been a good deal happier to have the ferals already in their service remotely manageable; a quality they were not more likely to gain, after Tharkay's departure. But he could not object; it was hard to imagine Tharkay's pride should allow him to remain as a supernumerary, even if restlessness alone did not drive him on. "I will pray for your safe return," Laurence said, and offered him instead a glass of port, and supper.

"What an odd fellow you have found us, Laurence," Jane said in her offices, the next morning. "I ought to give him his weight in gold, if the Admiralty would not squawk: twenty dragons talked out of the trees, like Merlin; or was it Saint Patrick? Anyway, I am sorry to rob you of the help, and pray don't think me ungrateful, if you *are* in your rights to complain; it is enough of a miracle you should have brought us Iskierka and one egg whole, considering the way Bonaparte has been romping about the Continent, much less our amiable band of brigands. But I cannot spare the chance of more, however mean and scrawny they might be; not with matters as they stand."

The map of Europe was laid out topmost on her table, great clots of markers, representing dragons, spread from the western borders of Prussia's former territory all the way to the footsteps of Russia. "From Jena to Warsaw in three weeks," she said, as one of her runners poured out wine for them. "I would not have given a bad ha'penny for the news, if you had not brought it yourself, Laurence; and if we hadn't had it from the Navy, too, I would have sent you to a physician."

Laurence nodded. "And I have a great deal to tell you of Bonaparte's aerial tactics, which are wholly changed from what they were. Formations are of no use against him; at Jena, the Prussians were routed, wholly routed.

We must at once begin devising counters to his new methods."

But she was already shaking her head. "Do you know, Laurence, I have less than forty dragons fit to fly? and unless he is a lunatic, he will not come across with less than a hundred. He shan't need any fine tactics to do for us. For our part, there is no one to learn any new."

The scope of the disaster silenced him: forty dragons, to try and patrol all the coastline of the Channel, and give cover to the ships of the blockade.

"What we want at present is time," Jane continued. "There are a dozen hatchlings in Ireland, preserved from the disease, and twice as many eggs due to hatch in the next six months: we bred a good many of them, early on. If our friend Bonaparte will only be good enough to give us a year, things will look something more like: the rest of these new shore batteries in place, the young dragons brought up, your ferals knocked into shape; not to mention Temeraire and our new fire-breather."

"Will he give us a year?" Laurence said, low, looking at the counters: not very many yet, upon the Channel coastline; but he had seen first-hand how swiftly Napoleon's dragon-borne army could now move.

"Not a minute, if he hears anything of our pitiable state," Jane said. "But that aside— well, we hear he has made a very good friend in Warsaw, a Polish countess they say is a raving beauty; and he would like to marry the Tsar's sister. We will wish him good fortune in his courting, and hope he takes a long leisurely time about it. If he is sensible, he will want a winter night for crossing the Channel, and the days are already growing longer.

"But you may be sure that if he learns how thin we are on the ground, he will come posting back quick as light-ning, and damn the ladies. So our task of the moment is to keep him properly in the dark. A year's time, then we will have something to work with; but until then, for you all it must be—"

"Oh, patrolling," Temeraire said, in tones of despair, when Laurence had brought their orders.

"I am sorry, my dear," Laurence said, "very truly sorry; but if we can serve our friends at all, it will be by taking on those duties which they have had to set aside." Temeraire was silent and brooding, unconsoled; in an attempt to cheer him, Laurence added, "But we need not abandon your cause, not in the least. I will write my mother, and those of my acquaintance who may have the best advice to give, on how we ought to proceed—"

"Whatever sense is there in it," Temeraire said, miserably, "when all our friends are ill, and there is nothing to be done for them? It does not matter if one is not allowed to visit London, if one cannot even fly an hour. And Arkady does not give a fig for liberty, anyway; all he wants are cows. We may as well patrol; or even do formations."

This was the mood in which they went aloft, a dozen of the ferals behind them more occupied in squabbling amongst themselves than in paying any attention to the sky; Temeraire was in no way inclined to make them mind, and with Tharkay gone, the few hapless officers set upon their backs had very little hope of exerting any form of control.

These young men had been chosen—from no shortage of officers, so many men having been grounded by the illness of their assigned beasts—for their skill in language. The ferals were all of them far too old to acquire a new tongue easily; so the officers should have to learn theirs instead. To hear them trying to whistle and cluck out the awkward syllables of the Durzagh language had quickly palled as entertainment and grown a nuisance to the ear, but it had also to be endured; no-one knew the tongue with any fluency aside from Temeraire, and a few of Laurence's younger officers who had acquired a smattering in the course of their journey to Istanbul.

Laurence had indeed lost two of his already-diminished number of officers entirely to the cause: one of the riflemen, Dunne, and Wickley of the bellmen had both of them enough grasp of Durzagh to make the basic signals understood to the ferals, and they were not so young as to make a command absurd. They had been set aboard Arkady in a highly theoretical position of authority; there was none of that natural bond which the first harnessing seemed to produce, of course, and Arkady was far more likely to obey his own whimsical impulse than any orders which they might give. The feral leader had already given it as his opinion that this flying over the ocean was absurd, as a useless territory in which no reasonable dragon would interest itself, and the likelihood he would veer away at any moment in search of better entertainment seemed to Laurence high.

Jane had set them a course along the coastline, for their first excursion; no risk at all of an action, so near to land, but at least the cliffs interested the ferals, and the bustle of shipping around Portsmouth, which they would gladly have investigated further if not called to order by Temeraire. They flew on past Southampton and westward along towards Weymouth, setting a leisurely pace; the ferals resorting to wild acrobatics to entertain themselves, swooping to such heights as must have rendered them dizzy and ill, save for their former habituation among the most lofty mountains of the earth, and plummeting thence into absurd and dangerous diving maneuvers, so close they threw up spray as they skimmed up again from the waves. It was a sad waste of energy, but well-fed as the ferals now were, by comparison to their previous state, of energy they had a surfeit which Laurence was glad enough to see spent in so restrained a manner, if the officers clinging sickly to their harnesses did not agree.

"Perhaps we might try a little fishing," Temeraire suggested, turning his head around, when abruptly Gherni cried out above them, and the world spun and whirled as Temeraire flung himself sidelong; a Pêcheur-Rayé went flying past, and the champagne-popping of rifle-fire spat at them from his back.

"To stations," Ferris was shouting, men scrambling wildly; the bellmen were casting off a handful of bombs down on the recovering French dragon below while Temeraire veered away, climbing. Arkady and the ferals were shrilly calling to one another, wheeling excitedly; they flung themselves with eagerness on the French dragons: a light scouting party of six, as best Laurence could make out among the low-lying clouds, the Pêcheur the largest of the lot and the rest all light-weights or couriers; both outnumbered and outweighed, therefore, and reckless to be coming so close to British shores.

Reckless, or deliberately venturesome; Laurence thought grimly it could not have escaped the notice of the French that their last encounter had brought no answer from the coverts.

"Laurence, I am going after that Pêcheur; Arkady and the others will take the rest," Temeraire said, curving his head around even as he dived.

The ferals were not shy by any means, and gifted skirmishers, from all their play; Laurence thought it safe to leave the smaller dragons entirely to them. "Pray make no sustained attack," he called, through the speaking-trumpet. "Only roust them from the shore, as quickly as you may—" as the hollow *thump-thump* of bombs, exploding below, interrupted.

Without the hope of surprise, the Pêcheur knew himself thoroughly overmatched, Temeraire a more agile flyer and in a wholly different class so far as weight. Having risked and lost a throw of the dice, he and his captain were evidently not inclined to try their luck again; Temeraire had scarcely stooped before the Pêcheur dropped low to the water and beat away quickly over the waves, his riflemen keeping up a steady fusillade to clear his retreat.

Laurence turned his attention above, to the furious howling of the ferals' voices: they could scarcely be seen, having lured the French high aloft, where their greater ease with the thin air could tell to their advantage. "Where the devil is my glass?" he said, and took it from Allen. The ferals were making a sort of taunting game of the business, darting in at the French dragons and away, setting up a raucous caterwauling as they went, without very much actual fighting to be seen. It would have done nicely to frighten away a rival gang in the wild, Laurence supposed, particularly one so outnumbered, but he did not think the French were to be so easily diverted; indeed as he watched, the five enemy dragons, all of them only little Pou-de-Ciels, drew into close formation and promptly bowled through the cloud of ferals.

The ferals, still putting on a show of bravado, scattered too late to evade the rifle-fire, and now some of their shrill cries were for real pain. Temeraire was beating up furiously, his sides belling out like sails as he heaved for the breath to get himself so high aloft, but he could not easily gain their height, and would be at a disadvantage himself against the smaller French when he had. "Give them a gun, quickly, and show the signal for descent," Laurence shouted to Turner, without much

hope; but the ferals came plummeting down in a rush
when Turner put out the flags, none too reluctant to put
themselves around Temeraire.

Arkady was keeping up a low, indignant clamoring
under his breath, nudging anxiously at his second
Wringe, the worst-hit, her dark grey hide marred with
streaks of darker blood. She had taken several balls to
the flesh and one unlucky hit to the right wing, which
had struck her on the bias and scraped a long, ugly fur-
row across the tender webbing and two spines; she was
listing in mid-air awkwardly as she tried to favor it.

"Send her below to shore," Laurence said, scarcely
needing the speaking-trumpet with the dragons crowded
so close that they might have been talking in a clearing,
and not the open sky. "And pray tell them again, they
must keep well-clear of the guns; I am sorry they have
had so hot a lesson. Let us keep together and—" but this
came too late, as the French were coming down in
arrow-head formation, and the ferals followed too
closely on his first instruction and spread themselves out
across the sky.

The French also at once separated; even together they
were not a match for Temeraire, whom they had surely
recognized, and by way of protection engaged themselves closely with the ferals. It must have been an odd
experience for them; Pou-de-Ciels were generally the
lightest of the French combat breeds, and now they were
finding themselves the relative heavy-weights in battle
against the ferals, who even where their wingspan and
length matched were all of them lean and concave-
bellied creatures, a sharp contrast against the deep-
chested muscle of their opponents.

The ferals were now more wary, but also more savage, hot with anger at the injury to their fellow and their
own smaller stinging wounds. They used their darting

lunges to better effect, learning quickly how to feint in and provoke the rifle volleys, then come in again for a real attack. The smallest of them, Gherni and motley-colored Lester, were attacking one Pou-de-Ciel together, with the more wily Hertaz pouncing in every now and again, claws blackened with blood; the others were engaged singly, and more than holding their own, but Laurence quickly perceived the danger, even as Temeraire called, "Arkady! *Bnezh s'li taqom—*" and broke off to say, "Laurence, they are not listening."

"Yes, they will be in the soup in a moment," Laurence agreed; the French dragons, though they seemed on the face of it to be fighting as independently as the ferals, were maneuvering skillfully to put their backs to one another; indeed they were only allowing the ferals to herd them into formation, which should allow them to make another devastating pass. "Can you break them apart, when they have come together?"

"I do not see how I will be able to do it, without hurting our friends; they are so close to one another, and some of them are so little," Temeraire said anxiously, tail lashing as he hovered.

"Sir," Ferris said, and Laurence looked at him. "I beg your pardon, sir, but we are always told, as a rule, to take a bruising before a ball; it don't hurt them long, even if they are knocked properly silly, and we are close enough to give any of them a lift to land, if it should go so badly."

"Very good; thank you, Mr. Ferris," Laurence said, putting strong approval in it; he was still very glad to see Granby matched off with Iskierka, even more so when dragons would now be in such short supply, but he felt the loss keenly, as exposing the weaknesses in his own abbreviated training as an aviator. Ferris had risen to his occasions with near-heroism, but he had been but a third lieutenant on their departure from England, scarcely a year ago, and at nineteen years of age could not be expected to put himself forward to his captain with the assurance of an experienced officer.

Temeraire put his head down and puffed up his chest with a deep breath, then flung himself down amongst the shrinking knot of dragons, and barreled through with much the effect of a cat descending upon an unsuspecting flock of pigeons. Friend and foe alike went tumbling wildly; the ferals flung into higher excitement. They flew around with much disorderly shrilling for a few moments, and as they did, the French righted themselves: the formation leader waved a signal-flag, and the Pou-de-Ciels wheeled together and away, escaping.

Arkady and the ferals did not pursue, but came gleefully romping back over to Temeraire, alternating complaints at his having knocked them about, with boastful prancing over their victory and the rout of the enemy, which Arkady implied was in spite of Temeraire's jealous interference. "That is not true, at all," Temeraire said, outraged, "you would have been perfectly dished without me," and turned his back upon them and flew towards land, his ruff stiffened up with indignation.

They found Wringe sitting and licking at her scarred wing in the middle of a field. A few clumps of blood-stained white wool upon the grass, and a certain atmosphere of carnage in the air, suggested she had quietly found herself some consolation; but Laurence chose to be blind. Arkady immediately set up as a hero for her benefit, and paraded back and forth to re-enact the encounter. So far as Laurence could follow, the battle might have raged a fortnight, and engaged some hundreds of enemy beasts, all of them vanquished by

Arkady's solitary efforts. Temeraire snorted and flicked his tail in disdain, but the other ferals proved perfectly happy to applaud the revisionary account, though they occasionally jumped up to interject stories of their own noble exploits.

Laurence meanwhile had dismounted; his new surgeon Dorset, a rather thin and nervous young man, bespectacled and given to stammering, was going over Wringe's injuries. "Will she be well enough to make the flight back to Dover?" Laurence inquired; the scraped wing looked nasty, what he could see of it; she uneasily kept trying to fold it close and away from the inspection, though fortunately Arkady's theatrics were keeping her distracted enough that Dorset could make some attempt at handling it.

"No," Dorset said, with not the shade of a stammer and a quite casual authority. "She needs lie quiet a day or so under a poultice, and those balls must come out of her shoulder presently, although not now. There is a courier-ground outside Weymouth, which has been taken off the routes and will be free from infection; we must find a way to get her there." He let go the wing and turned back to Laurence blinking his watery eyes.

"Very well," Laurence said, bemused; at the change in his demeanor more than the certainty alone. "Mr. Ferris, have you the maps?"

"Yes, sir; though it is twelve miles straight flying to Weymouth covert across the water, sir, if you please," Ferris said, hesitating over the leather wallet of maps.

Laurence nodded and waved them away. "Temeraire can support her so far, I am sure."

Her weight posed less difficulty than her unease with the proposed arrangement, and, too, Arkady's sudden fit of jealousy, which caused him to propose himself as a substitute: quite ineligible, as Wringe outweighed him by several tons, and they should not have got a yard off the ground.

"Pray do not be so silly," Temeraire said, as she dubiously expressed her reservations at being ferried. "I am not going to drop you unless you bite me. You have only to lie quiet, and it is a very short way."

Chapter 3

$\mathscr{B}$UT THEY REACHED Weymouth covert only a little short of dusk, in much perturbation of spirit, Wringe having expressed the intention, five or six times during the course of their flight, of climbing off mid-air to fly the rest of the way herself. Then she had accidentally scratched Temeraire twice, and thrown a couple of the topmen clean off his back with her uneasy shifting, their lives saved only by their carabiner-locked straps. On landing, they were both handed down bruised and ill from the knocking-about they had taken, and helped away by their fellows to be dosed liberally, with brandy, at the small barracks-house.

Wringe put up a singular fuss to having the bullets extracted, sidling away her hindquarters when Dorset approached knife in hand, insisting she was quite well, but Temeraire was sufficiently exasperated by now to have no patience with her evasions; his low rumbling growl, resonating upon the dry, hard-packed earth, made her meekly flatten to the ground and submit to being picked over with a lantern suspended overhead. "That will do," Dorset said, having pried out the third and final of the balls. "Now some fresh meat, to be sure, and a night's quiet rest. This ground is too hard," he added, with disapproval, as he climbed down from her shoulder with the three balls rattling bloodily in his little basin.

"I do not care if it is the hardest ground in Britain; only pray let me have a cow and I will sleep," Temeraire said wearily, leaning his head so Laurence could stroke his muzzle while his own shallow cuts were poulticed. He ate the cow in three tremendous tearing gulps, hooves-to-horns, tipping his head backwards to let the last bite of the hindquarters go down his throat. The farmer who had been prevailed upon to bring some of his beasts to the covert stood paralyzed in a macabre sort of fascination, his mouth gaping, and his two sons likewise with their eyes starting from their heads. Laurence pressed a few more guineas into the man's unresisting hand and hurried them all off; it would do Temeraire's cause no good to have fresh and lurid tales of draconic savagery spreading.

The ferals disposed of themselves directly around the wounded Wringe, sheltering her from any draft and pillowing themselves one upon the other as comfortably as they could manage, the smaller ones among them crawling upon Temeraire's back directly he had fallen asleep.

It was too cold to sleep out, and they had not brought tents with them on patrol; Laurence meant to leave the barracks, small enough in all conscience without dividing off a captain's partition, to his men, and take himself to a hotel, if one might be had; in any case he would have been glad of a chance to send word back to Dover by the stage, that their absence would not occasion distress. He did not trust any of the ferals to go alone yet, with their few officers so unfamiliar.

Ferris approached as Laurence made inquiry of the few tenants of the covert. "Sir, if you please, my family are here in Weymouth; I am sure my mother would be very happy if you chose to stay the night," he said, adding, with a quick, anxious glance that belied the easy way in which he issued this invitation, "I should only like to send word ahead."

"That is handsome of you, Mr. Ferris; I would be grateful, if I should not be putting her out," Laurence said. He did not miss the anxiety. In courtesy, Ferris likely felt compelled to make the invitation, if his family had so much as an attic corner and a crust of bread to spare. Most of his younger gentlemen, indeed most of the Corps, were drawn from the ranks of what could only be called the shabby-genteel, and Laurence knew they were inclined to think him higher than he did himself: his father kept a grand state, certainly, but Laurence had not spent three months together at home since taking to sea, without much sorrow on either side, except perhaps his mother's, and was better accustomed to a hanging berth than a manor.

Out of sympathy he would have spared Ferris, but for the likely difficulty of finding any other lodgings, and his own weary desire to be settled, even if it *were* only in an attic corner, with a crust of bread. The noise of the day behind them, he was finding it difficult not to yield to a certain lowness of spirit. The ferals had behaved quite as badly as expected, and he could not help but see how impossible it should be, to guard the Channel with such a company. The contrast could not have been greater, to the fine and ordered ranks of British formations, those ranks now decimated; and he felt their absence all the more keenly for it.

The word was accordingly sent, and a carriage summoned; it was waiting outside the covert gates by the time they had gathered their things, and walked to meet it down the long narrow path which led away from the dragon-clearings.

A twenty-minutes' drive brought them to the outskirts of Weymouth. Ferris grew steadily more hunched as they bowled along, and so miserably white that Laurence might have thought him taken ill with the motion, if he had not seen Ferris perfectly settled through thunderstorm aloft and typhoon at sea, and not likely to be distressed by the motion of a comfortable, well-sprung chaise. The carriage turned, then, drawing into a heavily wooded lane, and Laurence realized his mistake as the forest parted, and they drew abreast the house: a vast and sprawling gothic sort of edifice, the blackened stone barely to be seen behind centuries of ivy, the windows all illuminated and throwing a beautiful golden light out onto a small ornamental brook which wound through the open lawn before the house.

"A very fine prospect, Mr. Ferris," Laurence said as they rattled over the bridge. "You must be sorry not to be home more often. Does your family reside here long?"

"Oh, a dog's age," Ferris said blankly, lifting his head. "There was some Crusader or other first built the place, I think, I don't know."

Laurence hesitated and a little reluctantly offered, "My own father and I have disagreed on certain of our occasions, I am sorry to say, so I am not often at home."

"Mine is dead," Ferris said. After a moment, he seemed to realize this was a rather abrupt period to the conversation, and added with an effort, "My brother Albert is a good sort, I suppose; he has ten years on me, so we have never really got to know one another."

"Ah," Laurence said, left no more the wiser as to the cause of Ferris's dismay.

There was certainly nothing lacking in their welcome. Laurence had braced himself for neglect: perhaps they

would be shown directly to their rooms, out of sight of
the rest of the company; he was tired enough to even
hope to be so slighted. But nothing of the sort: a dozen
footmen were out with their lights lining the drive, another two waiting with the step to hand them down, and
a substantial body of the staff coming outside to greet
them despite the cold and what must surely have been a
full house within to manage, a wholly unnecessary os-
tentation.

Ferris blurted desperately, just as the horses were
drawn up, "Sir—I hope you will not take it to heart, if
my mother—she means well—" The footmen opened
the door, and discretion stopped Ferris's mouth.

They were shown directly to the drawing room, to
find all the company assembled to meet them, not very
large, but decidedly elegant: the women all in clothing of
unfamiliar style, the surest mark of the height of fashion
to a man who was often from society a year at a time,
and several of the gentlemen bordering on outright
dandyism. Laurence noted it mechanically; he was himself in trousers and Hessians, and those stained with
dust; but he could not be brought to care, very much,
even when he saw the other gentlemen in the greater formality of knee-breeches. There were a couple of military
men among their number, a colonel of Marines whose
long, seamy, sun-leathered face had a certain vague familiarity that meant they had most likely dined together
on one ship or another, and a tall army captain in his red
coat, lantern-jawed and blue-eyed.

"Henry, my dear!" A tall woman rose from her seat to
come and greet them with both her hands outstretched:
too like Ferris to mistake her, with the same high forehead and reddish-brown hair, and the same trick of
holding her head very straight, which made her neck
look longer. "How happy we are you have come!"

"Mother," Ferris said woodenly, and bent to kiss her presented cheek. "May I present Captain Laurence? Sir, this is Lady Catherine Seymour, my mother."

"Captain Laurence, I am overjoyed to make your acquaintance," she said, offering him her hand.

"My lady," Laurence said, giving her a formal leg. "I am very sorry to intrude upon you; I beg you will forgive our coming in all our dirt."

"Any officer of His Majesty's Aerial Corps is welcome in *this* house, Captain," she declared, "at any moment of day or night, I assure you, and should he come with no introduction at all still he should be welcome."

Laurence did not know what to say to this; he himself would no more have descended upon a strange house without introduction than he would have robbed it. The hour was late, but not uncivilized, and he came with her own son, so in any case these reassurances were not much to the point; he could not have supposed it otherwise, having been invited and welcomed. He settled on a vague, "Very kind."

The company was not similarly effusive. Ferris's eldest brother Albert, the present Lord Seymour, was a little high in the instep, and made a point early on, when Laurence had made a compliment to his house, of conveying the intelligence that the house was Heytham Abbey, in the possession of the family since the reign of Charles II; the head of the family had risen from knight to baronet to baron in steady climb, and there remained.

"I congratulate you," Laurence said, and did not take the opening to puff off his own consequence; he was an aviator, and well knew that one evil outweighed any other considerations in the eyes of the world. He could not help but wonder that they should have sent a son to the Corps; there was no sign of the pressure of an encumbered estate, which might have made one reason: while appearances might be kept up on credit, so extravagant a number of servants could not have been managed.

Shortly dinner was announced, to Laurence's surprise; he had hoped for nothing more than a little cold supper, and thought them arrived late for even this much. "Oh, think nothing of it, we are grown modern, and often keep town hours even when we are in the country," Lady Catherine cried. "We have so much company from London that it would be tiresome for them to be always shifting their dinner-hour early, and sending away dishes half-eaten, to be wished-for later. Now, we will certainly not stand on formality; I must have Henry beside me, for I long to hear all you have been doing, my dear, and Captain Laurence, you shall take in Lady Seymour, of course."

Laurence could only bow politely and offer his arm, although Lord Seymour certainly ought to have preceded him, even if Lady Catherine chose to make a natural exception for her son. Her daughter-in-law looked for a moment as if she liked to balk, Laurence thought, but then she laid her hand on his arm without any further hesitation, and he chose not to notice.

"Henry is my youngest, you know," Lady Catherine said to Laurence over the second course; he was on her right. "Second sons in this house have always gone to the drum, and the third to the Corps, and I hope that may never change." This, Laurence thought, might have been subtly directed at his dinner companion, by the direction of her eyes; but Lady Seymour gave no sign she had heard; she was correctly speaking with the gentleman on her right, the army captain, who was Ferris's brother Richard. "I am very glad, Captain, to meet a gentleman whose family feels as I do on the matter."

Laurence, who had only narrowly escaped being thrown from the house by his irate father on his shift in profession, could not in honesty accept this compliment, and with some awkwardness said, "Ma'am, I beg your pardon, I must confess you do us credit we have not earned: younger sons in my family go to the Church, but I was mad for the sea, and would have no other profession." He had then to explain his wholly accidental acquisition of Temeraire and subsequent transfer to the Aerial Corps.

"I will not withdraw my remarks; it is even more to their credit that you were given good principles enough to do your duty, when it was presented to you," Lady Catherine said firmly. "It is shameful, the disdain that so many of our finest families will profess for the Corps, and *I* certainly will never hold with it in the least."

The dishes were being changed again as she made this ringing and over-loud speech, and Laurence noticed that they were going back nearly untouched after all. The food had been excellent, and he could only conceive, after a moment, that all Lady Catherine's protestations were a humbug: they had already dined earlier. He watched covertly as the next course was dished out, and indeed the ladies in particular picked unenthusiastically at their food, scarcely making pretense of conveying a single morsel to their mouths; of the gentlemen only Colonel Prayle was making any serious inroads. He caught Laurence looking and gave him just the slightest bit of a wink, then went on eating with the steady trencherman rhythm of a professional soldier used to take his food when it was before him.

If they had been a large party, coming late to an empty house, Laurence might have conceived of a gracious host holding back dinner for their convenience, or serving a second meal to the newcomers, but not under such pretense, as though they should have been offended with a simple supper, served to them privately, the rest of the company having dined. He was obliged to sit through several more removes, conscious they were a pleasure to no one else of the company; Ferris himself ate with his head down, and only lightly, though in the ordinary course of events he was as rapacious as any nineteen-year-old boy unpredictably fed of late. When the ladies departed to the drawing room, Lord Seymour began to offer port and cigars, with a determined if false note of heartiness, but Laurence refused all but the smallest glass he could take for politeness' sake, and no one objected to rejoining the ladies quickly, they most of them already beginning to droop by the fire even though not half-an-hour had elapsed.

No-one proposed cards or music; the conversation was low and leaden. "How dull you all are to-night!" Lady Catherine rallied them, with a nervous energy. "You will give Captain Laurence quite a disgust of our society. You cannot often have been in Dorsetshire, Captain, I suppose."

"I have not had that pleasure, ma'am," Laurence said. "My uncle lives near Wimbourne, but I have not visited him in many years."

"Oh! Perhaps you are acquainted with Mrs. Brantham's family."

That lady, who had been nodding off, roused enough to say with sleepy tactlessness, "I am sure not."

"It is not very likely, ma'am; my uncle moves very little outside his political circles," Laurence said, after a pause. "In any event, my service has kept me from the enjoyment of much wider society, particularly these last years."

"But what compensations you must have had!" Lady Catherine said. "I am sure it must be glorious to travel by dragon, without any worry that you shall be sunk in a gale, and so much more quickly."

"Ha ha, unless your ship grows tired of the journey and eats you," Captain Ferris said, nudging his younger brother with an elbow.

"Richard, what nonsense, as if there were any danger of such a thing! I must insist on your withdrawing the remark," Lady Catherine said. "You will offend our guest."

"Not at all, ma'am," Laurence said, discomfited; the vigor of her objection gave an undeserved weight to the joke, which in any case he could more easily have borne than her compliments; he could not help but feel them excessive and insincere.

"You are kind to be so tolerant," she said. "Of course, Richard was only joking, but you would be quite appalled how many people in society will say such things and believe them. I am sure it is very poor-spirited to be afraid of dragons."

"I am afraid it is only the natural consequence," Laurence said, "of the unfortunate situation prevailing in our country, which keeps dragons so isolated in their distant coverts as to make them a point of horror."

"Why, what else is to be done with them?" Lord Seymour said. "Put them in the village square?" He amused himself greatly with this suggestion; he was uncomfortably florid in the face, having performed heroically his host's duties at the second dinner. He even now was doing justice to another glass of port, over which he coughed his laugh.

"In China, they may be seen in the streets of every town and city," Laurence said. "They sleep in pavilions no more separated from residences than one town-house from another, in London."

"Heavens; I should not sleep a wink," Mrs. Brantham said, with a shudder. "How dreadful these foreign customs."

"It seems to me a most peculiar arrangement," Seymour said, his brows drawing together. "Look here, how do the horses stand it? My driver in town must go a mile out of his way when the wind is in the wrong quarter and blowing over the covert, because the beasts get skittish."

Laurence was in honesty forced to admit they did not; horses were not often to be seen in the Chinese cities, except for the trained cavalry beasts. "But I assure you the lack is not felt; aside from mule-carts, they have also dragons employed as a sort of living stagecoach, and citizens of higher estate are conveyed by courier, at what you can imagine must be a much higher rate of speed. Indeed, Bonaparte has already adopted the system, at least within his encampments."

"Oh, Bonaparte," Seymour said. "No; thank goodness we organize things more sensibly here. I have been meaning to congratulate you, rather: ordinarily not a month goes by when my tenants are not complaining of the patrols, going overhead and frightening their cattle to pieces; leaving their—" he waved his hand expressively in concession to the ladies "—everywhere, but this sixmonth not a peep. I suppose you have put in new routes, and none too soon. I had nearly made up my mind to speak on the matter in Parliament."

This remark, thoroughly aware as he was of the circumstances which had reduced the frequency of the patrols, Laurence could not make himself answer civilly; so he did not answer at all, and instead went to fill his glass again.

He took it away and went to stand by the window farthest from the fire, to keep himself refreshed by the cool draught which came in. Lady Seymour had taken a seat beside it, for the same reason; she had put aside her wineglass and was fanning herself. When he had stood there a moment she made a visible effort and engaged him. "So you had to shift from the Navy to the Aerial Corps— It must have been very hard. I suppose you went to sea when you were older?"

"At the age of twelve, ma'am," Laurence said.

"Oh!—but then you came home again, from time to time, surely? And twelve is not seven; no one can say there is no difference. I am sure your mother must never have thought of sending you from home at such an age."

Laurence hesitated, conscious that Lady Catherine and indeed most of the other company, which had not already dozed off, were now listening to their conversation. "I was fortunate to secure a berth more often than not, so I was not much at home myself," he said, as neutrally as he could. "I am sure it must be hard, for a mother, in either case."

"Hard! of course it is hard," Lady Catherine said, interjecting here. "What of it? We ought to have the courage to send our sons, if we expect them to have the courage to go, and not this sort of half-hearted grudging sacrifice, to send them so late they are too old to properly take to the life."

"I suppose," Lady Seymour said, with an angry smile, "that we might also starve our children, to accustom them to privation, and send them to sleep in a pigsty, so they might learn to endure filth and cold—if we cared very little for them."

What little other conversation had gone forward, now was extinguished quite; spots of color stood high in

Lady Catherine's cheeks, and Lord Seymour was snoring prudently by the fire, his eyes shut; poor Lieutenant Ferris had retreated into the opposite corner of the room and was staring fixedly out the window into the pitch-dark grounds, where nothing was to be seen.

Laurence, sorry to have so blundered into an existing quarrel, by way of making peace said, "I hope you will permit me to say, I find the Corps as an occupation has been given a character which it does not deserve, being no more dangerous or distasteful, in daily use, than any other branch; I can at least say from my own experience that our sailors face as much hard duty, and I am sure Captain Ferris and Colonel Prayle will attest to the privations of their own respective services." He raised his glass to those gentlemen.

"Hear, hear," Prayle said, coming to his aid, jovially, "it is not aviators only who have all the hard luck, but we fellows, too, who deserve our fair share of your sympathy; and at least you may be sure they have all the latest news at any moment: you must know better than any of us, Captain Laurence, what is going forward on the Continent now; is Bonaparte setting up for invasion again, now he has packed the Russians off home?"

"Oh, pray do not speak of that monster," Mrs. Brantham spoke up. "I am sure I have never heard anything half so dreadful as what he has done to the poor Queen of Prussia: taken both her sons away to Paris!"

At this, Lady Seymour, still high-colored, burst out, "I am sure she must be in agony. What mother's heart could bear it! Mine would break to pieces, I know."

"I am sorry to hear it," Laurence said, to Mrs. Brantham, into the awkward silence. "They were very brave children."

"Henry tells me you have had the honor to meet them, Captain Laurence, and the Queen, during your service," Lady Catherine said. "I am sure you must agree, that however much her heart should break, *she* would never ask her sons to be cowards, and hide behind her skirts."

He could say nothing, but only gave her a bow; Lady Seymour was looking out the window and fanning herself with short jerking strokes. The conversation limped on a very little longer, until he felt he could in politeness excuse himself, on the grounds of the necessity of an early departure.

He was shown to a handsome room, with signs of having been hastily rearranged, and someone's comb left by the washbasin suggested it had been otherwise occupied until perhaps that evening. Laurence shook his head at this fresh sign of over-solicitousness, and was sorry any of the guests should have been shifted on his account.

Lieutenant Ferris knocked timidly on his door, before a quarter-of-an-hour had passed, and when admitted tried to express his regrets without precisely apologizing, as he could scarcely do. "I only wish she would not feel it so. I did not like to go, at the time, I suppose, and she cannot forget that I wept," he said, fidgeting the curtain uneasily; he was looking out the window to avoid meeting Laurence's eyes. "But that was only being afraid at leaving home, as any child would be; I am not sorry for it now, at all, and I would not give up the Corps for anything."

He soon made his good-nights and escaped again, leaving Laurence to the rueful consideration that the cold and open hostility of his father might yet be preferable to a welcome so anxious and smothering.

One of the footmen tapped at the door to valet Laurence, directly Ferris had gone: but he had nothing to do; Laurence had grown so used to doing for himself, that his coat was already off, and his boots in the corner, although he was glad enough to send those for blacking.

He had been abed scarcely a quarter-of-an-hour before he was roused again, by a great clamor of barking from the kennels and the horses shrilling madly. He went to the window: lights were coming on in the distant stables, and he heard a thin faint whistling somewhere aloft, carrying clear from a distance. "Bring my boots at once, if you please; and tell the household to remain within doors," Laurence told the footman, who came hurrying at his ring.

He went down in some disarray, still tying his neck-cloth, the flare in his hand. "Clear away, there," he called strongly, some number of the servants gathered in the open court before the house. "Clear away: the dragons will need room to land."

This intelligence left the courtyard empty. Ferris was already hurrying out, with his own signal-flare and a candle; he knelt down to set off the blue light, which went hissing up into the air and burst high. The night was clear, and the moon only a thin slice; almost at once the whistling came again, louder: Gherni's high ringing voice, and she came down to them in a rustle of wings.

"Henry, is that your dragon? Where do you all sit?" said Captain Ferris, coming down the stairs cautiously. Gherni, whose head did not come up to the second-story windows, indeed would have been hard-pressed to carry more than four or five men. While no dragon could precisely be called charming, her blue-and-white china complexion was elegant, and the dark softened the edges of her claws and teeth into a less threatening shape. Laurence was heartened that some other few of the party, still dressed more or less, had gathered on the stoop to see her.

She cocked her head at the question and said something inquiringly in the dragon-tongue, quite incomprehensible to them all, then sat up on her hind legs to call out a piercing answer to some cry which only she had heard.

Temeraire's more resonant voice became audible to them all, answering, and he came down into the wide lawn behind her: the lamps gleaming on his obsidian-glossy scales in their thousands, and his shivering wings kicking up a spray of dust and small pebbles, which rattled against the walls like small-shot. He curved down his head from its great serpentine height, well clear of the roof of the house. "Hurry, Laurence, pray," he said. "A courier came and dropped a message to tell us there is a Fleur-de-Nuit bothering the ships off Boulogne. I have sent Arkady and the others to chase him away, but I do not trust them to mind without me there."

"No indeed," Laurence said, and turned only to shake Captain Ferris's hand; but there was no sign of him, or of any living soul but Ferris and Gherni: the doors had been shut up tight, and the windows all were close-shuttered before they lifted away.

"Well, we are in for it, make no mistake," Jane said, having taken his report in Temeraire's clearing: the first skirmish off Weymouth and the nuisance of chasing away the Fleur-de-Nuit, and besides those another alarm which had roused them, after a few more hours of snatched sleep; and quite unnecessarily, for they arrived only in time, at the edge of dawn, to catch sight of a single French courier vanishing off over the horizon, chased by the orange gouts of cannon-fire from the fearsome shore battery which had lately been established at Plymouth.

"These were none of them real attacks," Laurence said. "Even that skirmish, though they provoked it. If they had worsted us, they could not have stayed to take any advantage of it, not such small dragons; not if they wished to get themselves home again before they were forced to collapse on shore."

He had given his men leave to snatch some sleep on the way back, and his own eyes had closed once or twice during the flight, but that was nothing to seeing Temeraire almost grey with fatigue, his wings tucked limply against his back.

"No; they are probing our defenses, and more aggressively than I had looked for," Jane said. "I am afraid they have grown suspicious. They chased you into Scotland without hide nor wing of another dragon to be seen: the French are not fools to overlook something like that, however badly it ended for them. If any one of those beasts gets into the countryside and flies over the quarantine-coverts, the game will be up: they will know they have free rein."

"How have you kept them from growing suspicious before?" Laurence said. "Surely they must have noted the absence of our patrols."

"We have managed to disguise the situation, so far, by sending out the sick for short patrols, on clear days when they can be seen for a good distance," Jane said. "A good many of them can still fly, and even fight for a while, although none of them can stand up to a long journey: they tire too easily, and they feel the cold more than they should; they complain of their bones aching, and the winter has only made matters worse."

"Oh! If they are laying upon the ground, I am not surprised they do not feel well," Temeraire said, rousing, and lifting up his head. "Of course they feel the cold; I feel it myself, when the ground is so hard and frozen, and I am not sick at all."

"Dear fellow," Jane said, "I would make it summer again if I could; but there is nowhere else for them to sleep."

"They must have pavilions," Temeraire said.

"Pavilions?" Jane said, and Laurence went into his small sea-chest and brought out to her the thick packet which had come with them all the way from China, wrapped many times over with oilcloth and twine, the outer layers stained nearly black, the inner still pale, until he came to the thin fine rice paper inside, with the plans for the dragon pavilion laid out upon them.

"Just see if the Admiralty will pay for such a thing," Jane said dryly, but she looked the designs over with a thoughtful more than a critical eye. "It is a clever arrangement, and I dare say it would make them a damned sight more comfortable than lying on damp ground; I do hear the ones at Loch Laggan do better, where they have the heat from the baths underground, and the Longwings who are quartered in the sand-pits have held up better, though they do not like it in the least."

"I am sure that if only they had the pavilions, and some more appetizing food to eat, they would soon get better; I did not like to eat at all, when I had my cold, until the Chinese cooked for me," Temeraire said.

"I will second that," Laurence said. "He scarcely ate at all before; Keynes was of the opinion the strength of spices compensated, to some part, for the inability to smell or taste."

"Well, for that, any rate, I can squeeze out a few guineas here and there and manage a trial; we have certainly not been spending half of what we ordinarily would in powder," Jane said. "It will not do for very long, not if we are to feed two hundred dragons spiced meals, and where I am to get cooks to manage it I have no idea, but if we see some improvement, we may have some better luck in persuading their Lordships to carry the project forward."

Chapter 4

❧

GONG SU WAS ENLISTED in the cause, and all but emptied his spice cabinets, making especially vigorous use of his sharpest peppers; much to the intense disapproval of the herdsmen, who were rousted from a post usually requiring little more than dragging cows from pen to slaughter, and set to stirring pungent cauldrons. The effect was a marked one, the dragons' appetites more startled awake than coaxed, and many of the nearly somnolent beasts began clamoring with fresh hunger. The spices were not easily replaced, however, and Gong Su shook his head with dissatisfaction over what the Dover merchants could provide; the cost even of this astronomical.

"Laurence," Jane said, having called him to her quarters for dinner, "I hope you will forgive me for serving you a shabby trick: I mean to send you to plead our case. I do not like to leave Excidium for long now, and I cannot take him over London sneezing as he does. We can manage a couple of patrols here, while you are gone, and make it a rest for Temeraire: he needs one in any case. What? No, thank Heaven, that fellow Barham who gave you so much difficulty is out. Grenville has the place now; not a bad fellow, so far as I can tell; if he does not understand the least thing about dragons, that hardly makes him unique."

"And I will say, privately, in your ear," she added, later that evening, reaching over for the glass of wine by the bed and settling back against his arm; Laurence lying back thoroughly breathless with his eyes half-closed, the sweat still standing on his shoulders, "that I would not hazard two pins for my chances of persuading him to anything. He yielded to Powys in the end, over my appointment, but he can scarcely bear to address a note to me; and the truth is I have made use of his mortification to squeak through half-a-dozen orders I have not quite the authority for, which I am sure he would have liked to object to, if he could do so without summoning me. Our chances are precious small to begin, and we will do a good deal better with you there."

It did not prove the case, however; because Jane, at least, could scarcely have been refused admittance by one of the secretaries of the Navy: a tall, thin, officious fellow, who said impatiently, "Yes, yes, I have your numbers written in front of me; and in any case you may be sure we have taken note of the higher requisitions of cattle. But have any of them recovered? You say nothing of it. How many can fly now that could not before, and how long?"—as if, Laurence felt resentfully, he were inquiring about the improved performance of a ship, given changes in her cordage or sailcloth.

"The surgeons are of the opinion, that with these measures we can hope to greatly retard the further progress of the illness," Laurence said; he could not claim that any had recovered. "Which alone must be of material benefit, and perhaps with these pavilions also—"

The secretary was shaking his head. "If they will do

no better than now, I cannot give you any encouragement: we must still build these shore batteries all along the coastline, and if you imagine dragons are expensive, you have not seen the cost of guns."

"All the more reason to care for the dragons we have, and spend a little more to safeguard their remaining strength," Laurence said. His frustration added, "And especially so, sir, that it is no more than their just deserts from us, for their service; these are thinking creatures, not cavalry-horses."

"Oh; romantical notions," the secretary said, dismissive. "Very well, Captain; I regret to inform you his Lordship is occupied to-day. We have your report; you may be sure he will reply to it, when he has time. I can give you an appointment next week, perhaps."

Laurence with difficulty restrained himself from replying to this incivility as he felt it deserved; and went out feeling he had been a far worse messenger than Jane herself would have been. His spirits were not to be recovered even by the treat of catching a glimpse of the lately created Duke of Nelson in the courtyard: that gentleman splendid in his dress uniform and his peculiar row of misshapen medals. They had been half-melted to the skin at Trafalgar, when a pass by the Spanish fire-breather there had caught his flagship, and his life nearly despaired of from the dreadful burns. Laurence was glad to see him so recovered: a line of pink scarred skin was visible upon his jaw, running down his throat into the high collar of his coat, but this did not deter him from talking energetically with, or rather to, a small group of attentive officers, his one arm gesturing.

A crowd had collected at a respectful distance to overhear, placed so that Laurence had to push his way out to the street through them, making apologies muttered as softly as he could; he might have stayed to listen, himself, another time. At present he had to make his way through the streets, a thick dark slurry of half-frozen ice and muck chilling his boots, back to the London covert, where Temeraire was waiting anxiously to receive the unhappy news.

"But surely there must be *some* means of reaching him," Temeraire said. "I cannot bear that our friends should all grow worse, when we have so easy a remedy at hand."

"We will have to manage on what we can afford within the current bounds, and stretch that little out," Laurence said. "But some effect may be produced by the searing of the meat alone, or stewing; let us not despair, my dear, but hope that Gong Su's ingenuity may yet find some answer."

"I do not suppose this Grenville eats raw beef every night, with the hide still on, and no salt; and then goes to sleep on the ground," Temeraire said resentfully. "I should like to see him try it a week and then refuse us." His tail was lashing dangerously at the already-denuded tree-tops around the edge of the clearing.

Laurence did not suppose it, either: and it occurred to him that the First Lord might very likely dine from home. He called to Emily for paper, and wrote quickly several notes; the season was not yet begun, but he had a dozen acquaintances likely to be already in town in advance of the opening of Parliament, besides his family. "There is very little chance I will be able to catch him," he warned Temeraire, to forestall raising hopes only to be dashed, "and still less that he will listen to me, if I do."

He could not wish whole-heartedly for success, either; he did not think he could easily sustain his temper, in his present mood, against still more of the casual and un-thinking insult he was likely to meet in his aviator's coat, and any social occasion promised to be rather a punishment than a pleasure. But an hour before dinner, he received a reply from an old shipmate from the gunroom of the *Leander*, long since made post and now a member himself, who expected to meet Grenville that night at Lady Wrightley's ball: that lady being one of his mother's intimates.

There was a sad and absurd crush of carriages outside the great house: a blind obstinacy on the part of two of the coach drivers, neither willing to give way, had locked the narrow lane into an impasse so that no one else could move. Laurence was glad to have resorted to an old-fashioned sedan-chair, even if he had done so for the practical difficulties in getting a horse-drawn carriage anywhere near the covert. He reached the steps unspattered, and if his coat was green, at least it was new, and properly cut; his linen was beyond reproach, and his knee-breeches and stockings crisply white, so he felt he need not blush for his appearance.

He gave in his card and was presented to his hostess, a lady he had met in person only once before, at one of his mother's dinners. "Pray how does your mother; I suppose she has gone to the country?" Lady Wrightley said, perfunctorily giving him her hand. "Lord Wrightley, this is Captain William Laurence, Lord Allendale's son."

A gentleman just lately entered was standing beside Lord Wrightley, still speaking with him; he startled at overhearing the introduction, and turning insisted on being presented to Laurence as a Mr. Broughton, from the Foreign Office.

Broughton at once seized on Laurence's hand with great enthusiasm. "Captain Laurence, you must permit me to congratulate you," he said. "Or Your Highness, as I suppose we must address you now, ha ha!" and Laurence's hurried, "I beg you will not—" went thoroughly ignored as Lady Wrightley, astonished as she might justly be, demanded an explanation. "Why, you have a prince of China at your party, I will have you know, ma'am. The most complete stroke, Captain, the most complete stroke imaginable. We have had it all from Hammond: his letter has been worn to rags in our offices, and we go about wreathed in delight, and tell one another of it only to have the pleasure of saying it over again. How Bonaparte must be gnashing his teeth!"

"It was nothing to do with me, sir, I assure you," Laurence said with despair. "It was all Mr. Hammond's doing—a mere formality—" too late: Broughton was already regaling Lady Wrightley and half-a-dozen other interested parties with a representation both colorful and highly inaccurate of Laurence's adoption by the emperor, which had been nothing more in truth than a means of saving face. The Chinese had required the excuse to give their official imprimatur to Laurence serving as companion to a Celestial dragon, a privilege reserved, among them, solely for the Imperial family, and Laurence was quite sure the Chinese had happily forgotten his existence the moment he had departed: he had not entertained the least notion of trading upon the adoption now he was got home.

As the brangle of carriages outside had stifled the flow of newcomers, there was a lull in the party, still in its early hours, which made everyone very willing to hear the exotic story; if in any case its success would not have been guaranteed by the fairy-tale coloration which it had acquired. Laurence thus found himself the interested subject of much attention, and Lady Wrightley herself was by no means unwilling to claim Laurence's attendance as a coup rather than a favor done an old friend.

He would have liked to go, at once; but Grenville had not yet come, and so he clenched his teeth and bore the embarrassment of being presented around the room. "No, I am by no means in the line of succession," he said, over and over, privately thinking he would like to see the reaction of the Chinese to the suggestion; he had been made to feel an unlettered savage more than once, among them.

He had not expected to dance; society was perennially uncertain whether aviators were entirely respectable, and he did not mean to blight some girl's chances, nor open himself to the unpleasant experience of being fended off by a chaperone. But before the first dance, his hostess presented him deliberately to one of her guests, as an eligible partner; so even though much surprised he of course had to ask. Miss Lucas was perhaps in her second season, or her third; a plump attractive girl, still very ready to be delighted with a ball, and full of easy, cheerful conversation.

"How well you dance!" she said, after they had gone down the line together, with rather more surprise than would have made the remark perfectly complimentary, and asked a great many questions about the Chinese court which he could not answer: the ladies had been kept thoroughly sequestered from their view. He entertained her a little instead with the description of a theatrical performance, but as he had been stabbed at the end of it, his memory was imperfect; and in any case it had been carried on in Chinese.

She in turn told him a great deal of her family in Hertfordshire, and her tribulations with the harp, so he might express the hope of one day hearing her play, and mentioned her next younger sister coming out next season. So she was nineteen, he surmised; and was struck abruptly to realize that Catherine Harcourt at this age had been already Lily's captain, and had flown that year in the battle of Dover. He looked at the smiling muslin-clad girl with a strange hollow feeling of astonishment, as if she were not entirely real; and then looked away. He had written already two letters each to Harcourt and to Berkley, on Temeraire's behalf and his own; but no answer had come. He knew nothing of how they did, or their dragons.

He said something polite afterwards, returning her to her mother, and, having displayed himself in public a satisfactory partner, was forced to submit with rigid good manners to filling out one set after another; until at last near eleven o'clock Grenville came in, with a small party of gentlemen.

"I am expected in Dover tomorrow, sir, or would not trouble you here," Laurence said grimly, having approached him; he loathed the necessity of anything like encroachment, and if he had not been introduced to Grenville at least the once, many years before, did not know he could have steeled himself to it.

"Laurence, yes," Grenville said vaguely, looking as though he would have liked to move away. He was no great politician: his brother was Prime Minister, and he had been made First Lord for loyalty, not for brilliance or ambition. He listened without enthusiasm to the carefully couched proposals, which Laurence was forced to make general for the benefit of the interested audience, who were not to know of the epidemic: there would be no concealing such information from the enemy, once the general public was in possession of it.

"There is provision made," Laurence said, "for the relics of the slain, and for the sick and wounded; not least because that care may preserve them or their offspring for future service, and give encouragement to the healthy. The plan which has been advanced is for nothing more than such practical attentions, sir, which have been proven beneficial by the example of the Chinese, whom all the world acknowledge as first in the world, so far as an understanding of dragonkind."

"Of course, of course," Grenville said. "The comfort and welfare of our brave sailors or aviators, and even our good beasts, is always foremost in the considerations of the admiralty," a meaningless platitude, to one who had ever visited in a hospital; or had, as Laurence, been forced to subsist from time to time upon such provisions as were considered suitable for the consumption of those brave sailors: rotting meat, biscuit-and-weevil, the vinegar-water beverage which passed for wine. He had been applied to for support by veterans of his own crews or their widows, denied their pensions on scurrilous grounds, on too many occasions to find such a claim other than absurd.

"May I hope, then, sir," Laurence said, "that you approve our proceeding in this course?" An open avowal, which could not be easily retracted without embarrassment, was what he hoped for; but Grenville was too slippery, and without openly refusing, evaded any commitment.

"We must consider the particulars of these proposals, Captain, more extensively; before anything can be done," he said. "The opinions of our best medical men must be consulted," and so on and so forth, continuing without a pause in this vein until he was able to turn to another gentleman of his acquaintance, who had come up, and address him on another subject: a clear dismissal, and Laurence knew very well that nothing would be done.

* * *

He limped back into the covert in the early hours of the morning, a faint lightness just beginning to show. Temeraire lay fast asleep and dreaming with his slit-pupiled eyes half-lidded, his tail twitching idly back and forth, while the crew had disposed of themselves in the barracks or tucked against his sides: likely the warmer sleeping place, if less dignified. Laurence went into the small cottage provided for his use and gladly sank upon the bed to work off, wincing, the tight buckled shoes, still new and stiff, which had cut sadly into his feet.

The morning was a silent one; besides the failure of the attempt, which had somehow been communicated generally throughout the covert, although Laurence had told no one directly but Temeraire, he had given a general furlough the previous night. Judging by the evidence of their bloodshot eyes and wan faces, the crew had made good use of their leave. There was a certain degree of clumsiness and fatigue apparent, and Laurence watched anxiously as the large pots of oat-porridge were maneuvered off the fire, to break their fast.

Temeraire meanwhile finished picking his teeth with a large leg bone, the remnant of his own breakfast of tender veal stewed with onions, and set it down. "Laurence, do you still mean to build the one pavilion, even if the Admiralty will give us no funds?"

"I do," Laurence answered. Most aviators acquired only a little prize-money, as the Admiralty paid but little for the capture of a dragon compared to that of a ship, the former being less easily put to use than the latter, and requiring substantial expense in the upkeep, but Laurence had established a handsome capital while still a naval officer, upon which he had little charge, his pay being ordinarily sufficient to his needs. "I must consult with the tradesmen, but I hope that by economizing upon the materials and reducing the pavilion in size, I may afford to construct one for you."

"Then," Temeraire said, with a determined and heroic air, "I have been thinking: pray let us build in the quarantine-grounds instead. I do not much mind my clearing at Dover, and I had rather Maximus and Lily were more comfortable."

Laurence was surprised; generosity was not a trait common amongst dragons, who were rather jealous of anything which they considered their own property, and a mark of status. "If you are quite certain, my dear; it is a noble thought."

Temeraire toyed with the leg-bone and did not look entirely certain, but eventually made his assent final. "And in any case," he added, "once we have built it, perhaps the Admiralty will see the benefit, and then I may have a handsomer one: it would not be very pleasant to have a small poky one, when everyone else has a nicer." This thought cheered him considerably, and he crunched up the bone with satisfaction.

Revived with strong tea and breakfast, the crew began to get Temeraire under harness for the return to Dover, only a little slowly; Ferris taking especial pains to see that the buckles were all secure after Laurence dropped a quiet word in his ear. "Sir," Dyer said, as he and Emily came in from the covert gates with the post for Dover, which they would carry with them, "there are some gentlemen coming," and Temeraire raised his head from the ground as Lord Allendale came into the covert with a small, slight, and plainly dressed gentleman at his side.

Their progress was arrested at once, while they stared up at the great inquisitive head peering back at them, Laurence very glad for the delay in which he could gather his own wits: he would scarcely have been more shocked to receive a visit from the King, and a good deal better pleased. He could imagine only one cause for it: more than one person of his parents' acquaintance had been at the ball, and the news of the foreign adoption must have traveled to his father's ears. Laurence knew very well he had given his father just cause to reproach him by having submitted to the adoption, whatever its political expedience; but he was by no means satisfied to endure those reproaches in front of his officers and his crew, aside from any practical consideration of what Temeraire's reaction might be to seeing him abused.

He handed away his cup to Emily and gave his clothing a surreptitious look, devoutly grateful the morning was cold enough he had not been tempted to forgo coat or neckcloth. "I am honored to see you, sir; will you take tea?" he asked, crossing the clearing to shake his father's hand.

"No, we have breakfasted," Lord Allendale said abruptly, his eyes still fixed on Temeraire, and only with a jerk of effort turned away to present to Laurence his companion, Mr. Wilberforce: one of the great movers of the cause of abolition.

Laurence had only met the gentleman once, long before. Wilberforce's face had settled into graver lines in the intervening decades, and now he looked anxiously up at Temeraire; but there was still something warm and good-humored about the mouth, a gentleness to his eyes, confirming that early generous impression which Laurence had carried away, if indeed his public works had not been testament enough. Twenty years of city air and incessant fighting had ruined his health, but not his character; parliamentary intrigue and the West Indies interests had undermined his work, but he had persevered; and besides his tireless labor against slavery, he had stood a resolute reformer all the while.

There was scarcely a man whose advice Laurence

would more have desired, in furthering Temeraire's cause; and if the circumstances had been other, and he had reached that rapprochement with his father, which he had hoped for, he would certainly have sought an introduction. The reverse, however, he could not understand; there was no reason his father should bring Wilberforce hence, unless perhaps he had some curiosity to encounter a dragon.

But the gentleman's expression, looking on Temeraire, did not seem enthusiastic. "I myself would be very happy for a cup of tea, in quiet, perhaps?" he said, and after a certain hesitation yielded to the further question, "Is the beast quite tame?"

"I am not *tame*," Temeraire said very indignantly, his hearing perfectly adequate to the task of overhearing this unwhispered exchange, "but I am certainly not going to hurt you, if that is what you are asking; you had much better be afraid of being stepped upon by a horse." He knocked his tail against his side in irritation, nearly sweeping off a couple of the topmen engaged in pitching the traveling-tent upon his back, and so gave himself the lie even as he spoke. His audience was sufficiently distracted by his remarks not to notice this nice point, however.

"It is most wonderful," Mr. Wilberforce said, after conversing with him a little longer, "to discover such excellent understanding in a creature so far removed from ourselves; one might call it even miraculous. But I see that you are making ready to depart; so I will beg your pardon," he bowed to Temeraire, "and yours, Captain, for so indelicately moving to the subject which has brought us here, to seek your assistance."

"I hope you will speak as frankly as you like, sir," Laurence said, and begged them to sit down, with many apologies for the situation: Emily and Dyer had dragged chairs out of the cabin for their use, as that building was hardly fit for receiving guests, and arranged them near the embers of the cooking-fire for warmth.

"I wish to be clear," Wilberforce began, "that no-one could be insensible of the service which his Grace has rendered his country, or begrudge him the just rewards of that service, and the respect of the common man—"

"You might better say, the blind adoration of the common man," Lord Allendale put in, with more heavy disapproval. "And some not so common, who have less excuse; it is appalling to see the influence the man has upon the Lords. Every day he is not at sea is a fresh disaster," and Laurence gathered, after a few moments more of confusion, that they were speaking of none other than Lord Nelson himself.

"Forgive me; we have spoken so much of these matters, among ourselves, that we go too quickly." Wilberforce drew a hand over his jaw, rubbing down his jowls. "I believe you know something already," he said, "of the difficulties which we have encountered, in our attempts to abolish the trade."

"I do," Laurence said: twice already, victory had seemed in reach. Early in the struggle, the House of Lords had held up a resolution already past the Commons, with some excuse of examining witnesses. On another attempt, a bill had indeed gone through, but only after amendments had changed abolition to *gradual* abolition: so gradual indeed that there were no signs of it as yet to be seen, fifteen years later. The Terror in France had by that time been making a bloody ruin of the word *liberty*, and putting into the hands of the slave traders the choice name of Jacobin to be leveled against abolitionists; no further progress had been made, for many years.

"But in this last session," Wilberforce said, "we were

on the verge of achieving a vital measure: an act which should have barred all new ships from the slave trade. It ought to have passed; we had the votes in our grasp— then Nelson came from the countryside. He had but lately risen from his sickbed; he chose to address Parliament upon the subject, and by the vigor of his opposition alone caused the measure to fail in the Lords."

"I am sorry to hear it," Laurence said, if not surprised: Nelson's views had been pronounced in public, often enough. Like many a naval officer, he thought slavery, if an evil, also a necessary one, as a nursery for her sailors and a foundation of her trade; the abolitionists a cohort of enthusiasts and quixotics, bent on undermining England's maritime power and threatening her hold upon her colonies, while only that domination allowed her to hold fast against the looming threat of Napoleon.

"Very sorry," Laurence continued, "but I do not know what use I can be to you; I cannot claim any personal acquaintance, which might give me the right to try and persuade him—"

"No, no; we have no such hope," Wilberforce said. "He has expressed himself too decidedly upon the subject; also many of his great friends, and sadly his creditors, are slave-owners or involved with the trade. I am sorry to say such considerations may lead astray even the best and wisest of men."

They sought rather, he explained, while Lord Allendale looked morose and reluctant, to offer the public a rival for their interest and admiration; and Laurence gradually understood through circular approaches that they meant him for this figure, on the foundation of his recent and exotic expedition, and the very adoption which he had expected his father to condemn.

"To the natural interest which the public will have, in

your late adventure," Wilberforce said, "you join the authority of a military officer, who has fought against Napoleon himself in the field; *your* voice can dispute Nelson's assertions, that the end of the trade should be the ruin of the nation."

"Sir," Laurence said, not certain if he was sorrier to be disobliging Mr. Wilberforce, or happier to be forced to refuse such an undertaking, "I hope you will not think me lacking in respect or conviction, but I am in no way fitted for such a role; and could not agree, if I wished to. I am a serving-officer; my time is not my own."

"But here you are in London," Wilberforce pointed out gently, "and surely, while you are stationed at the Channel, can on occasion be spared," a supposition which Laurence could not easily contradict, without betraying the secret of the epidemic, presently confined to the Corps and only the most senior officials of the Admiralty. "I know it cannot be a comfortable proposal, Captain, but we are engaged in God's work; we ought not scruple to use any tool which He has put into our way, in this cause."

"For Heaven's sake, you will have nothing to do but attend a dinner party, perhaps a few more; kindly do not cavil at trifles," Lord Allendale said brusquely, tapping his fingers upon the arm of his chair. "Of course one cannot like this self-puffery, but you have tolerated far worse indignities, and made far greater a spectacle of yourself, than you are asked to do at present: last night, if you like—"

"You needn't speak so to Laurence," Temeraire interrupted coldly, giving the gentlemen both a start: they had already forgotten to look up and see him listening to all their conversation. "We have chased the French off four times this last week, and flown nine patrols; we are very tired, and we have only come to London because our friends are sick: and left to starve, and die in the cold; because the Admiralty will do nothing to make them more comfortable."

He finished stormily, a low threatening resonance building in his throat, the instinctive action of the divine wind operating; it lingered as an echo, when he had already stopped speaking. No one spoke for a moment, and then Wilberforce said thoughtfully, "It seems to me we need not be at cross-purposes; and we may advance *your* cause, Captain, with our own."

They had meant, it seemed, to launch him with some social event, the dinner-party Lord Allendale had mentioned, or perhaps even a ball; which Wilberforce now proposed instead to make a subscription-party, "whose avowed purpose," he explained, "will be to raise funds for sick and wounded dragons, veterans of Trafalgar and Dover—there are such veterans, among the sick?" he asked.

"There are," Laurence said; he did not say, all of them: all but Temeraire himself.

Wilberforce nodded. "Those are yet names to conjure with, in these dark days," he said, "when we see Napoleon's star ascendant over the Continent; and will give still further emphasis, to your being also a hero of the nation, and make your words a better counterweight to Nelson's."

Laurence could scarcely bear to hear himself so described; and in comparison with Nelson, who had led four great fleet actions, destroyed all Napoleon's navy, established Britain's complete primacy at sea; who had justly won a ducal coronet by valor and deeds in honorable battle, not been made a foreign prince through subterfuge and political machination. "Sir," he said, with an effort restraining himself from a truly violent rejection,

"I must beg you not to speak so; there can be no just comparison."

"No, indeed," Temeraire said energetically. "I do not think much of this Nelson, if he has anything to say for slavery: I am sure he cannot be half so nice as Laurence, no matter how many battles he has won. I have never seen anything as dreadful as those poor slaves in Cape Coast; and I am very glad if we can help them, as well as our friends."

"And this, from a dragon," Wilberforce said, with great satisfaction, while Laurence was made mute by dismay. "What man can refuse to feel pity for those wretched souls, when it may be stirred in such a breast? Indeed," he said, turning to Lord Allendale, "we ought to hold the assembly here where we sit. I am certain it will answer all the better, so far as producing a great sensation, and moreover," he added, with a glint of humor in his eye, "I should like to see the gentleman who will refuse to consider an argument made to him by a dragon, with that dragon standing before him."

"Out of doors, at this season?" Lord Allendale said.

"We might organize it like the pavilion-dinners in China: long tables, with coal-pits underneath to make them warm," Temeraire suggested, entering with enthusiasm into the spirit of the thing, while Laurence could only listen with increasing desperation as his fate was sealed. "We will have to knock down some trees to make room, but I can do that very easily, and if we were to hang panels of silk from the remainder, it will seem quite like a pavilion, and keep warm besides."

"An excellent notion," Wilberforce said, leaving his chair to inspect the scratched diagrams which Temeraire was making in the dirt. "It will have an Oriental flavor, exactly what is needed."

"Well, if you think it so; all I can say in its favor, it will certainly be the nine-days' wonder of society, whether more than half-a-dozen curiosity-seekers come or not," Lord Allendale said.

"We can spare you for one night, now and again," Jane said, sinking Laurence's final hopes of escape. "Our intelligence is nothing to brag about, now we have no couriers to risk on spy-missions; but the Navy do a good business with the French fishermen, on the blockade, and they say there has yet been no movement to the coast. They might be lying, of course," she added, "but if there were a marked shift in numbers, the prices of the catch would have risen, with livestock going to dragons."

The maid brought in the tea, and she poured for him. "Do not I beg you repine too much upon it," Jane went on, meaning the Admiralty's refusal to give them more funds. "Perhaps this party of yours will do us some good in that quarter, and Powys has written me to say he has cobbled together something for us already, by subscription among the retired senior officers. It will not do for anything extravagant, but I think we can keep the poor creatures in pepper, at least until then."

In the meanwhile, they set about the experimental pavilion: the promise of so substantial a commission proved enough to tempt a handful of more intrepid tradesmen to the Dover covert. Having met them at the gates, with a party of crewmen, Laurence escorted them the rest of the way to Temeraire, who in an attempt to be unalarming hunched himself down as small as a dragon of some eighteen tons could manage, and nearly flattened his ruff down against his neck. Yet he could not help but insinuate himself into the conversation once the construction of the pavilion was well under discussion, and indeed his offerings were quite necessary, as Laurence had not the faintest notion how to convert the Chinese measurements.

"I want one!" Iskierka said, having overheard too much of the proceedings from her nearby clearing: heedless of Granby's protests, she squirmed herself through the trees into Temeraire's clearing, shaking off a blizzard of ash-flakes, and alarming the poor tradesmen very much with a hiccough of fire which sent steam shooting out her spines to clear them. "I want to sleep in a pavilion, too: I do not like this cold dirt at all."

"Well, you cannot have one," Temeraire said. "This is for our sick friends, and anyway you have no capital."

"Then I shall get some," she declared. "Where does one get capital, and what does it look like?"

Temeraire proudly rubbed his breastplate of platinum and pearl. "This is a piece of capital," he said, "and Laurence gave it me: he got it from taking a ship in a battle."

"Oh! that is very easy," Iskierka said. "Granby, let us go get a ship, and then I may have a pavilion."

"Lord, you cannot have anything of the sort, do not be silly," Granby said, nodding his rueful apologies to Laurence as he came into the clearing, along the trail of smashed branches and crushed hedge which she had left in her wake. "You would burn it up in an instant: the thing is made of wood."

"Can it be made of stone?" she demanded, swinging her head around to one of the wide-eyed tradesmen. She was not grown very large, despite the twelve feet in length she had acquired since settling at Dover with a steady diet, being rather sinuous than bulky, in the Kazilik style, and she yet looked little more than a garden-snake next to Temeraire. But her appearance at close quarters was by no means reassuring, with the hissing-kettle gurgle of whatever internal mechanism produced her fire plainly audible and the vents of hot air issuing from her spines, white and impressive in the cold.

No one answered her, except the elderly architect, a Mr. Royle. "Stone? No, I must advise against it. Brick will be a much more practical construction," he opined; he had not looked up from the papers since being handed them, so badly nearsighted he was inspecting the plans with a jeweler's loupe, an inch from his watery blue eyes, and could most likely not make either dragon out in the least. "Silly oriental stuff, this roof, do you insist on having it so?"

"It is not silly oriental stuff at all," Temeraire said, "it is very elegant: that design is my mother's own pavilion, and it is in the best fashion."

"You will need linkboys on it all winter long to brush the snow clear, and I will not give a brass farthing for the gutters after two seasons," Royle said. "A good slate roof, that is the thing, do you not agree with me, Mr. Cutter?"

Mr. Cutter had not the least opinion to offer, as he was backed to the trees and looked ready to bolt, if Laurence had not prudently stationed his ground crew around the border of the clearing to forestall just such panicked flight.

"I am very willing to be advised by you, sir, as to the best plan of construction, and the most reasonable," Laurence said, while Royle blinked around himself looking for a response. "Temeraire, our climate here is a good deal wetter, and we must cut our cloth to suit our station."

"Very well, I suppose," Temeraire said, with a wistful eye for the upturned roof-corners and the brightly painted wood.

Iskierka meanwhile took inspiration, and began to plot the acquisition of capital. "If I burn up a ship, is that good enough, or must I bring it back?" she demanded, and began her piratical career by presenting Granby with a small fishing-boat, the next morning, which she had picked up from Dover harbor during the night. "Well, you did not say it must be a *French* ship," she said crossly, to their recriminations, and curled up to sulk. Gherni was hastily recruited to replace it under cover of darkness, the following night, undoubtedly to the great puzzlement of its temporarily bereft owner.

"Laurence, *do* you suppose that we should be able to get more capital, by taking French ships," Temeraire asked, with a thoughtfulness very alarming to Laurence, who had just returned from dealing with this pretty piece of confusion.

"The French ships-of-the-line are penned in their harbors by the Channel blockade, thank Heaven, and we are not privateers, to go plying the lanes for their shipping," Laurence said. "Your life is too valuable to be risked in such a selfish endeavor; in any case, once you began to behave in such an undisciplined manner, you may be sure Arkady and his lot would follow your example at once, and leave all Britain undefended, not to mention the encouragement Iskierka would take."

"Whatever am I to do with her?" Granby said, wearily taking a glass of wine with Laurence and Jane that evening, in the officers' common room at the covert headquarters. "I suppose it is being dragged hither and yon in the shell, and all the fuss and excitement she has had; but that is no excuse forever. I must manage her somehow, and I am at a standstill. I would not be amazed to find the entire harbor set alight one morning, because she took it into her head that we would not have to sit about defending the city if it were all burnt up; I cannot even make her sit still long enough to get her under full harness."

"Never mind; I will come by tomorrow, and see what I can do," Jane said, pushing the bottle over to him again. "She is a little young for work, by all the authorities, but I think her energy had better be put to use than go in all this fretting. Have you chosen your lieutenants, Granby?"

"I will have Lithgow, for my first, if you've no objection, and Harper for a second, to act as captain of the riflemen also," he said. "I don't like to take too many men, when we don't know what her growth will be like."

"You do not like to turn them off later, you mean, when they like as not cannot get another post," Jane said gently, "and I know it will be hard if it comes to that; but we cannot shortchange her, not with her so wild. Take Row also, as captain of the bellmen. He is old enough to retire if he must be turned off, and a good steady campaigner, who will not blink at her starts."

Granby nodded a little, his head bowed, and the next morning Jane came to Iskierka's clearing in great state, with all her medals and even her great plumed hat, which aviators scarcely wore, a gold-plated saber and pistols on her belt. Granby had assembled all his new crew, and they saluted her with a great noise of arms, Iskierka nearly coiling herself into knots with excitement, and the ferals and even Temeraire peering over the trees to watch with interest.

"Well, Iskierka: your captain tells me that you are ready for service," Jane said, putting her hat under her arm to look sternly at the little Kazilik, "but what are these reports I hear of you, that you will not mind orders? We cannot send you into battle if you cannot follow orders."

"Oh! it is not true!" Iskierka said. "I can follow orders as well as anyone, it is only no one will give me any *good* ones, and I am only told to sit, and not to fight, and to eat three times a day; I do not want any more stupid cows!" she added smolderingly; the ferals, hearing this translated for them by their own handful of officers, set up a low squabbling murmur of disbelief.

"It is not only the pleasant orders we must follow, but the tiresome ones as well," Jane said, when the noise had died down. "Do you suppose Captain Granby likes to be forever sitting in this clearing, waiting for you to grow more settled? Perhaps he would rather go back to service with Temeraire, and have some fighting himself."

Iskierka's eyes went platter-wide, and she hissed from all her spikes like a furnace; in an instant she had thrown a pair of jealous coils around Granby, which bid fair to boil him like a lobster in steam. "He would not! You would not, at all, would you?" she appealed to him. "I will fight just as well as Temeraire, I promise; and I will even obey the stupidest orders; at least, if I may have some pleasant ones also," she qualified hastily.

"I am sure she will mind better in future, sir," Granby managed himself, coughing, his hair already plastered down soaking against his forehead and neck. "Pray don't fret; I would never leave you, only I am getting wet," he added plaintively, to her.

"Hm," Jane said, with an air of frowning consideration. "Since Granby speaks for you, I suppose we will give you your chance," she said, at last, "and here you may have your first orders, Captain, if she will let you come for them and, to be sure, stand still for her harness."

Iskierka immediately let him loose and stretched herself out for the ground crew, only craning her neck a little to see the red-sealed and yellow-tasseled packet, a formality often dispensed with in the Corps, which directed them in very ornate and important language to do nothing more than run a quick hour's patrol down to Guernsey and back. "And you may take her by that old heap of rubble left at Castle Cornet, where the gunpowder blew up the tower, and tell her it is a French outpost, so she may flame it from aloft," Jane added to Granby, in an undertone not meant for Iskierka's ears.

Iskierka's harness was indeed a great deal of trouble to arrange, as the spines were placed quite randomly, and the frequent issuing of steam made her hide slick: an improvised collection of short straps and many buckles, wretchedly easy to tangle, and she could not entirely be blamed for growing tired of the process. But the promise of coming action and the observing crowd made her more patient; at length she was properly rigged out, and Granby with relief said, "There, it is quite secure; now try and see if you can shake any of it loose, dear one."

She writhed and beat her wings quite satisfactorily, twisting herself this way and that to inspect the harness. "You are supposed to say, All lies well, if you are comfortable," Temeraire whispered loudly to her, after she had been engaged in this sport for several minutes.

"Oh, I see," she said, and settling again announced, "All lies well; now we shall go."

In this way she was at least a little reformed; no one would have called her temper obliging, certainly, and she invariably stretched her patrols farther afield than Granby would have them, in hopes of meeting some enemy more challenging than an abandoned old fortification, or a couple of birds. "But at least she will take a little training, and eats properly, which I call a victory, for now," Granby said. "And after all, as much a fright she gives us, she'll give the Frogs a worse; Laurence, do you know, we talked to the fellows at Castle Cornet, and they set up a bit of sail for her: she can set it alight from eighty yards. Twice the range of a Flamme-de-Gloire, and she can go at it for five minutes straight; I don't understand how she gets her breath while she is at it."

They had indeed some trouble in keeping her out of direct combat, for meanwhile the French were continuing their harassment and scouting of the coast, with ever-increasing aggression. Jane used the sick dragons more heavily for patrol, to spare Temeraire and the ferals: they, instead, sat most of the day waiting on the cliffs for one warning flare or another to go up, or listening with pricked ears for the report of a signal-gun, before they dashed frantically to meet another incursion. In the space of two weeks, Temeraire skirmished four times more with small groups, and once Arkady and a few of his band, sent experimentally on patrol by themselves while Temeraire snatched a few more hours of sleep, just barely turned back a Pou-de-Ciel who had daringly tried to slip past the shore batteries at Dover, less than a mile from a clear view of the quarantine-grounds.

The ferals came back from their narrow but solitary victory delighted with themselves, and Jane with quick cleverness took the occasion to present Arkady ceremonially with a long length of chain: almost worthless, being made only of brass, with a large dinner-platter inscribed with his name for a medal, but polished to a fine golden shine and rendering Arkady for once speechless with amazement as it was fastened about his neck. For only a moment: then he burst forth in floods of caroling joy, and insisted on having every single one of his fellows inspect his prize; nor did Temeraire escape this fate. He indeed grew a little bristling, and withdrew in dignity to his own clearing to polish his breastplate more vigorously than usual.

"You cannot compare the two," Laurence said cautiously, "it is only a trinket, to make him complacent, and encourage them in their efforts."

"Oh, certainly," Temeraire said, very haughty, "mine is much nicer; I do not in the least want anything so common as brass." After a moment he added, muttering, "But his is very large."

"Cheap at the price," Jane said the next day, when Laurence came to report on a morning for once uneventful: the ferals more zealous than ever, and rather disappointed not to find more enemies than the reverse. "They come along handsomely: just as we had hoped." But she spoke tiredly; looking into her face, Laurence poured her a small glass of brandy and brought it to her at the window, where she was standing to look out at the ferals, presently cavorting in mid-air over their clearing after their dinner. "Thank you, I will." She took the glass, but did not drink at once. "Conterrenis has gone," she said abruptly, "the first Longwing we have lost; it was a bloody business."

She sat down all together, very heavily, and put her head forward. "He took a bad chill and suffered a haemorrhage in the lungs, the surgeons tell me. At any rate, he could not stop coughing, and so his acid came and came; it began at last to build up on the spurs, and sear his own skin. It laid his jaw bare to the bone." She paused. "Gardenley shot him this morning."

Laurence took the chair beside her, feeling wholly inadequate to the task of offering any comfort. After a little while she drank the brandy and set down her glass, and turned back to the maps to discuss the next day's patrolling.

He went away from her ashamed of his dread of the party, now only a few days' hence, and determined to put himself forward with no regard for his own mortification; if for the least chance of improving the conditions of the sick.

. . . and I hope you will permit me to suggest [Wilberforce wrote] that any oriental touch to your wardrobe, only a little one, which might at a glance set you apart, would be most useful. I am happy to report that we have engaged some Chinese as servants for the evening, by offering a good sum in the ports, where occasionally a few of them may be found having taken service on an East Indiaman. They are not properly trained, of course, but they will only be carrying dishes to and from the Kitchens, and we have instructed them most severely to show no alarm at being in the presence of the dragon, which I hope they have understood. However, I do have some Anxiety as to their comprehension of what faces them, and should you have enough liberty to come early, that we may try their Fortitude, it would be just as well.

Laurence did not indulge in sighs; he folded the letter, sent his Chinese coat to his tailors for refurbishment, and asked Jane her permission to go some hours earlier. In the event, the Chinese servants did set up a great commotion on their arrival, but only by leaving all their work and running to prostrate themselves before Temeraire, nearly throwing themselves beneath his feet in their efforts to make the show of respect generally considered due a Celestial, as symbolic of the Imperial family. The British workmen engaged in the final decoration of the covert were not nearly so complaisant, and vanished one and all, leaving the great panels of embroidered silk, surely made at vast expense, hanging half askew from the tree branches and dragging upon the earth.

Wilberforce exclaimed in dismay as he came to greet Laurence; but Temeraire issued instructions to the Chinese servants, who set to work with great energy, and with the assistance of the crew the covert was a handsome if astonishing sight in time to receive the guests, with brass lamps tied makeshift onto branches to stand in place of Chinese paper lanterns, and small coal-stoves placed at intervals along the tables.

"We may bring the business off, if only it will not come on to snow," Lord Allendale said pessimistically, arriving early to inspect the arrangements. "It is a pity your mother could not be here," he added, "but the child has not yet come, and she does not like to leave Elizabeth in her confinement," referring to the wife of Laurence's eldest brother, soon to present him with his fifth.

The night stayed clear, if cold, and the guests began to arrive in cautious dribs and drabs, keeping well away from Temeraire, who was ensconced in his clearing at the far end of the long tables, and peering at him not very surreptitiously through opera glasses. Laurence's officers were all meanwhile standing by him, stiff and equally terrified in their best coats and trousers: all new, fortunately, Laurence having taken the trouble to direct his officers to the better tailors in Dover, and funding himself the necessary repairs which all their wardrobes had required after their long sojourn abroad.

Emily was the only one of them pleased, as she had acquired her first silk gown for the occasion, and if she tripped upon the hem a little she did not seem to mind, rather exultant in her kid gloves and a string of pearls, which Jane had bestowed upon her. "It is late enough in conscience for her to be learning how to manage skirts,"

Jane said. "Do not fret, Laurence; I promise you no one will be suspicious. I have made a cake of myself in public a dozen times, and no one ever thought me an aviator for it. But if it gives you any comfort, you may tell them she is your niece."

"I may do no such thing; my father will be there, and I assure you he is thoroughly aware of all his grandchildren," Laurence said. He did not tell her that his father would immediately conclude Emily to be his own natural-born child, should he make such a false claim, but only privately decided he should keep Emily close by Temeraire's side, where she would be little seen; he had been in no doubt that his guests would keep a very good distance, whatever persuasion Mr. Wilberforce intended to apply.

That persuasion, however, took the most undesirable form, Mr. Wilberforce saying, "Come; behold this young girl here who thinks nothing of standing in reach of the dragon. If you can permit yourself, madam, to be outdone by trained aviators, I hope you will not allow a child to outstrip you," while Laurence with sinking heart observed his father turning to cast an astonished eye on Emily which confirmed all his worst fears.

Lord Allendale did not scruple, either, to approach and interrogate her; Emily, perfectly innocent of malice, answered in her clear girlish voice, "Oh, I have lessons every day, sir, from the captain, although it is Temeraire who gives me my mathematics, now, as Captain Laurence does not like the calculus. But I had rather practice fencing," she added candidly, and looked a little uncertain when she found herself laughed over, and pronounced a dear, by the pair of society ladies who had been persuaded to venture close to the great table, by her example.

"A masterful stroke, Captain," Wilberforce murmured softly; "wherever did you find her?" and did not wait for an answer before he accosted a few gentlemen who had risked coming near, and worked upon them in the same fashion, adding to his persuasions that if Lady So-and-So had approached Temeraire, surely *they* could not show themselves hesitant.

Temeraire was very interested in all the guests, particularly admiring the more bejeweled of the ladies, and managed by accident to please the Marchioness of Carstoke, a lady of advanced years and receded neckline whose bosom was concealed only by a vulgar set of emeralds-in-gold, by informing her she looked a good deal more the part, in his estimation, than the Queen of Prussia, whom he had only seen in traveling-clothes. Several gentlemen challenged him to perform simple sums; he blinked a little, and having given them the answers inquired whether this was a sort of game performed at parties, and whether he ought to offer them a mathematical problem in return.

"Dyer, pray bring me my sand-table," he said, and when this was arranged, he sketched out with his claw a small diagram for purposes of setting them a question on the Pythagorean theorem, sufficient to baffle most of the attending gentlemen, whose own mathematical skills did not extend past the card-tables.

"But it is a very simple exercise," Temeraire said in some confusion, wondering aloud to Laurence if he had missed some sort of joke, until at last a gentleman, a member of the Royal Society on a quest to observe for himself certain aspects of Celestial anatomy, was able to solve the puzzle.

When Temeraire had audibly spoken to the servants in Chinese, and conversed in fluent French with several of the guests, and had failed to eat or crush anyone, increasing fascination began at last to trump fear and draw more of the company towards him. Laurence shortly found himself quite neglected as of considerably less interest: a circumstance which would have delighted him, if only it had not left him subject to awkward conversation with his father, who inquired stiltedly about Emily's mother: questions whose evasion would only have made Laurence seem the more guilty, and yet whose perfectly truthful answers, that Emily was the natural-born daughter of a Jane Roland, a gentlewoman living in Dover, and whose education he had taken as his charge, left entirely the wrong impression, which Laurence could no more correct than his father would outright ask.

"She is a pretty-behaved girl, for her station in life, and I hope she does not want for anything," Lord Allendale said, in a sort of sidling way. "I am sure if there was any difficulty in finding her a respectable situation, when she is grown, your mother and I would be glad to be of assistance."

Laurence did his best to make it clear that this handsome offer was unnecessary, in some desperation turning to a lie of omission, saying, "She has friends, sir, as must prevent her ever being in real distress; I believe there is already some arrangement made for her future." He gave no details, and his father, his sense of propriety satisfied, did not inquire further; fortunate, as that arrangement, military service in the Corps, would hardly have recommended itself to Lord Allendale. The bleak notion came to Laurence only afterwards, that if Excidium were to die, Emily should have no dragon to inherit, and thus no assured post: though a handful of Longwing eggs were presently being tended at Loch Laggan, there were more women serving in the Corps than would be needed to satisfy these new hatchlings.

He made his escape, saying he saw Wilberforce beckoning him over; that gentleman indeed welcomed his company, if he had not immediately been soliciting it, and took hold of Laurence's arm to guide him through the crowd, and introduce him to all his prodigious acquaintance, amongst the curiously mingled attendance. Many had come merely to be entertained, and for the sensation of seeing a dragon; or more honestly for the right to say they had done so: a substantial number of these being gentlemen of fashion, come already from heavy drinking, whose conversation would have made the noise impenetrable in a smaller space. Those ladies and gentlemen active in the abolition movement, or evangelical causes, were easily distinguished by their markedly more sober appearance, both in dress and mien; the tracts which they were giving out were ending largely upon the ground, and being trodden into the dirt.

There were also a great many patriots, whether from real feeling or the desire to attach their names to a subscription-list with the word *Trafalgar* upon it, as Wilberforce had arranged it should be published in the newspapers, and not inclined to be quibbling over whether those veterans were men or dragons. The political range was thoroughly represented, therefore, and more than one heated discussion had broken out, with the lubrications of liquor and enthusiasm. One stout and red-faced gentleman, identified by Wilberforce as a member from Bristol, was declaring to a pale and fervent young lady trying to give him a tract that "it is all nonsense; the passage is perfectly healthy, for it is in the interest of the traders to preserve their goods. It is as good a thing as ever will happen to a black, to be taken to a Christian land, where he may lose his heathen religion and be converted."

"That is excellent grounds, sir, for importing the

Gospel to Africa; it does less well to excuse the behavior of Christian men, in tearing away the Africans from their homes, for profit," he was answered, not by the lady, but by a black gentleman, who had been standing a little behind her, and assisting her in giving out the pamphlets. A narrow, raised scar, the thickness of a leather strap, ran down the side of his face, and the edges of ridged bands of scar tissue protruded past the ends of his sleeves, paler pink against his very dark skin.

The gentleman from Bristol perhaps had not quite that brazen character which would have permitted him to defend the trade in the face of one of its victims. He chose rather to retreat behind an expression of offended hauteur at having been addressed without introduction, and would have turned aside without reply; but Wilberforce leaned forward and said with gentle malice, "Pray, Mr. Bathurst, allow me to present you the Reverend Josiah Erasmus, lately of Jamaica." Erasmus bowed; Bathurst gave a short jerking nod, and cravenly quitted the field, with an excuse too muttered to be intelligible.

Erasmus was an evangelical minister, "And I hope a missionary, soon," he added, shaking Laurence's hand, "back to my native continent," whence he had been taken, a boy of six years of age, to suffer through that aforementioned healthy passage, chained ankles and wrists to his neighbors, in a space scarcely large enough to lie down in.

"It was not at all pleasant to be chained," Temeraire said, very low, when Erasmus had been presented him, "and I knew at least they would be taken off, when the storm had finished; anyway, I am sure I could have broken them." Those chains of which he spoke, indeed, had been for his own protection, to keep him secured to the deck through a three-days' typhoon; but the occasion had come close on the heels of his witnessing the brutal treatment of a party of slaves, at the port of Cape Coast, and had left an indelible impression.

Erasmus said simply, "So did some of our number; the fetters were not well made. But they had nowhere to go but to throw themselves on the mercy of the sharks: we had not wings to fly."

He spoke without the rancor for which he might have been pardoned, and when Temeraire had expressed, darkly, the wish that the slavers might have been thrown overboard instead, Erasmus shook his head. "Evil should not be returned for evil," he said. "Their judgment belongs to the Lord: my answer to their crimes will be to return to my fellows with the word of God. And I hope that the practice cannot long continue when we are all brothers in Christ, so that the slaver and his prey will both be saved."

Temeraire was dubious of this most Christian speech, and after Erasmus had left them muttered, "I would not give a fig for the slavers, myself; and God ought to judge them more quickly," a blasphemous remark which made Laurence blanch, lest Wilberforce should have overheard; but his attention was fortunately elsewhere at present, on a growing noise at the far end of the long clearing, where a crowd was gathering.

"I wonder he should have come," Wilberforce said: it was Nelson himself, who had entered the clearing in the company of several friends, some of them naval officers of Laurence's acquaintance, and was presently paying his respects to Lord Allendale. "Of course we did not omit an invitation, but I had no real expectation; perhaps because it was sent in your name. Forgive me, I will take myself off awhile; I am happy enough to have him come and lend his reflected glow to our party, but he has said too much in public for me to converse easily with him."

Laurence was better pleased, for his own part, to find Nelson not offended in the least at whatever whispers and comparisons had been put about between them; that gentleman was rather as amiable as anyone could wish, offering his good hand. "William Laurence; you have gone a long way since we last met. I think we were at dinner together on the *Vanguard* in ninety-eight, before Aboukir Bay: how very long ago, and how short a time it seems!"

"Indeed, sir; and I am honored your Grace should remember," Laurence said, and at his request rather anxiously took him back to be presented to Temeraire, adding, when Temeraire's ruff ominously unfurled at the name, "I hope you will make his Grace most welcome, my dear; it is very kind of him to come and be our guest."

Temeraire, never very tactful, was unfortunately not to be warned by so subtle a hint, and rather coldly asked, "What has happened to your medals? They are all quite misshapen."

This, he certainly meant as a species of insult; however Nelson, who famously preferred only to win more glory, than to speak of what he already had gained, could not have been better pleased at the excuse to discuss the battle, told over so thoroughly by the public before ever he had risen from his injuries, with an audience for once innocent of the details. "Why, a rascal of a Spanish fire-breather gave us a little trouble, at Trafalgar, and they were caught in the flame," he said, taking one of the ample number of vacant chairs at the table nearby, and arranging bread rolls for the ships.

Temeraire, growing interested despite himself, leaned in closely to observe their maneuvers on the cloth. Nelson did not flinch back in the least, though the onlookers who had gathered to observe took nearly all of them several steps back. He described the Spanish dragon's passes with a fork and much lurid detail, and further rescued his character, in Temeraire's eyes, by concluding, "And very sorry I am that we did not have you there: I am sure you should have had no trouble in running the creature off."

"Well, I am sure, too," Temeraire said candidly, and peered at the medals again with more admiration. "But would the Admiralty not give you fresh ones? That is not very handsome of them."

"Why, I consider these a better badge of honor, dear creature, and I have not applied for replacement," Nelson said. "Now, Laurence, do I recall correctly; can I possibly have read a report in the *Gazette* that this very dragon of yours lately sank a French ship, called the *Valérie*, I believe, and in a single pass?"

"Yes, sir; I believe Captain Riley of the *Allegiance* sent in his report, last year," Laurence said uneasily; that report had rather understated the incident, and while he was proud of Temeraire's ability, it was not the sort of thing he thought civilian guests would find reassuring; still less so should any of them learn that the French, too, now had their own Celestial, and that the same dreadful power might be turned against their own shipping.

"Astonishing; quite prodigious," Nelson said. "What was she, a sloop-of-war?"

"A frigate, sir," Laurence answered, even more reluctantly. "—forty-eight guns."

There was a pause. "I cannot be sorry, although it was hard on the poor sailors," Temeraire said, into the silence, "but it was not very noble of them, stealing upon us during the night, when their dragon could see in the dark and I could not."

"Certainly," Nelson said, over a certain murmur from

the assembled company; he, having recovered from his surprise, had rather a quick martial gleam in his eye, "certainly; I congratulate you. I think I must have some conversation with the Admiralty, Captain, on your present station; you are on coastline duty at present, am I not correct? A waste; an unconscionable waste; you may be sure they will hear from me on the subject. Do you suppose he could manage as much on a ship-of-the-line?"

Laurence could not explain the impossibility of a change in their assignment without revealing the secret; so he answered a little vaguely, with gratitude for his Grace's interest.

"Very clever," Lord Allendale said grimly, in conference with them and Wilberforce, when Nelson had gone away again, nodding his farewells in the most affable manner to all who sought his attention. "I suppose we must consider it a badge of success that he should prefer to send you away."

"Sir, I believe you are mistaken; I cannot allow his motives on this matter to be other than sincere, in wishing the best use made of Temeraire's abilities," Laurence said stiffly.

"It *is* very boring, always going up and down the coast," Temeraire put in, "and I should much rather have some more interesting work, like fighting fire-breathers, if we were not needed where we are; but I suppose we must do our duty," he finished, not a trifle wistfully, and turned his attention back to the other guests, who were all the more eager to speak with him now in imitation of Nelson's example: the party most assuredly a success.

"Laurence, may we fly over the quarantine-grounds, as we go, and see how comes the pavilion?" Temeraire asked, the next morning, as they made ready for the flight back to Dover.

"It will not be very far advanced," Laurence said; Temeraire's ulterior motive, to look into the quarantine-grounds to see Maximus and Lily, was tolerably transparent: there had been no reply to the letters which Laurence had sent, either to them or to their captains, and Temeraire had begun to inquire after them with increasing impatience. Laurence feared Temeraire's likely reaction to seeing them so reduced by illness as he supposed them to be, but could think of no very good reason with which to divert him.

"But I should like to see it in all its stages," Temeraire said, "and if they have made any mistakes, we ought to correct it early, surely," he finished triumphantly, with the air of having hit upon an unanswerable justification.

"Is there any reason to fear infection in the air?" Laurence asked Dorset quietly, aside. "Will there be a danger to flying over the grounds?"

"No, so long as he keeps a good distance from any of the sick beasts. It is certainly the phlegmatic humors which carry the infection. So long as he does not put himself directly in the way of a sneeze or a cough, I cannot think the danger substantial, not aloft," Dorset said absently, without much consideration to the question, which did not fill Laurence with great confidence.

But he settled for extracting a promise that Temeraire should stay well aloft, where perhaps he might not see the worst of the ravages which had been inflicted on his friends, nor approach any dragon in the air.

"Of course I promise," Temeraire said, adding, unconvincingly, "I only want to see the pavilion, after all; it is nothing to me if we see any other dragons."

"You must be sure, my dear, or Mr. Dorset will not countenance our visit; we must not disturb the sick dragons, who require their rest," Laurence said, resorting to stratagem, which at last won Temeraire's sighs and agreement.

Laurence did not truly expect to see any dragons aloft; the ill beasts only rarely left the ground anymore, for the brief showy patrols which Jane continued to use to keep up their illusion of strength for the French. The day was cloudy and drear, and as they flew towards the coast, they met a thin misting of rain blowing in from the Channel; the exertion surely would not be asked of the sick dragons.

The quarantine-grounds were inland of Dover itself, the borders marked off by smoking torches and large red flags, planted into the ground: low deserted rolling meadows, the dragons scattered about with little cover even from the wind, which snapped all the flags out crisply and made them all huddle down small to escape. But as Temeraire drew near the proscribed territory, Laurence saw three specks, increasing rapidly into three dragons: aloft, and flying energetically, two on the heels of a much smaller third.

Temeraire said, "Laurence, that is Auctoritas and Caelifera, from Dover, I am sure of it, but I do not know that other little dragon at all; I have never seen one of that kind."

"Oh, Hell, that is a Plein-Vite," Ferris said, after a single borrowed look through Laurence's glass. The three dragons were directly over the quarantine-grounds, and the great miserable hulks of other sick beasts were plainly visible for the French dragon to see, even through the mist, in all their bloodstained dirt. And already the two dragons who had attempted to halt her were falling off the pace and drooping earthwards, exhausted, as the tiny French dragon darted and looped and evaded, beating her wings mightily, and flung herself past the borders of the grounds, heading towards the Channel as quick as ever she could go.

"After her, Temeraire," Laurence said, and they leapt into pursuit, Temeraire's enormous wings beating once to every five of hers, but eating up the yards with every stroke.

"They haven't much endurance, they're close-couriers only, for all they're fast as bloody lightning; they must have brought her nearly up to the coast by boat, at night, to save her strength for the flight back," Ferris said, shouting over the knife-cut wind. Laurence only nodded, to save his voice: Bonaparte had likely been hoping to slip so small a messenger-beast through where the larger had not been able to manage.

He raised the speaking-trumpet and bellowed, *"Rendez-vous,"* to no effect. The flare they fired off for emphasis, launched ahead of the little dragon's nose, was a signal less easily missed or misinterpreted, but there was no slackening in the furious pace. The Plein-Vite had only a small pilot, a young boy scarcely much older than Roland or Dyer, whose pale and frightened face Laurence could plainly see in his glass as the boy looked back to see the vast black-winged pursuit ready to engulf him. He turned back to speak encouragement to his beast, casting off bits of harness and buckle as she flew: the boy even kicked off his shoes, and threw overboard his belt with its sword and pistol, flashing briefly against the murk as they turned end-over-end, surely prized treasures; and heartened by her rider's example, with an effort the little dragon began to speed her strokes and pull away, her advantage in speed and small breadth before the wind telling.

"We must bring her down," Laurence said grimly, lowering his glass; he had seen what effect the divine wind had on enemy dragons of fighting-weight, and on soldiers under arms: what damage it might wreak, upon so small and helpless a target, he neither liked to think nor wished to witness, but their duty was plain. "Temeraire, you must stop them; we cannot let them slip away."

"Laurence, she is so very little," Temeraire objected unhappily, turning his head only just enough to be heard; he was still pressing on after her, with all the will in the world, but she would not be caught.

"We cannot try to board her," Laurence answered, "she is too small and too quick; it would be a death-sentence to make any man attempt that leap. If she will not surrender, she must be brought down. She is pulling away; it must be now."

Temeraire shuddered, then with decision drew breath and roared out: but over the French dragon, not directly at her. She gave a startled shrill cry of alarum, backwinging as if she was trying to reverse her course, her pace dropping off to nothing for a moment. With a convulsive gathered lunge, Temeraire was above her and folding his wings, bearing her bodily down towards the earth below: soft pale yellow sand, heaped in rolling dunes, and the little French dragon went tumbling pell-mell as they plowed into the dirt behind her, oceanic waves of dust billowing up in a cloud around them.

They slid across the ground some hundred yards, Laurence blind and trying to shield his mouth from the flying sand, hearing Temeraire hissing in displeasure and the French dragon squalling. Then "Hah!" Temeraire said triumphantly, "*je vous ai attrapé; il ne faut pas pleurer*; oh, I beg your pardon, I am very sorry," and Laurence wiped the grit from his face and nostrils, coughing violently, and clearing his stinging vision found himself looking almost directly into the alarming fiery orange of a Longwing's slit-pupiled eye.

Excidium turned his head to sneeze, acid droplets spraying involuntarily with the gesture, smoking briefly as the sand absorbed them. Laurence gazed in horror as the great head swung wearily back and Excidium said, in a harsh and rasping voice, "What have you done? You ought not have come here," while the sand-cloud settled to show him one among a half-a-dozen Longwings, Lily raising her head out of her shielding wing beside him, all of them huddled close in the sand-pit that was their place of quarantine.

Chapter 5

❧

HEY HAD NO companion in their isolated quarantine-meadow but little Sauvignon, the French courier-beast, who had not even the solace of her captain's presence. He, poor child, had been marched away in irons against her good behavior, while she made piteous cries under the restraint of Temeraire's reluctant but irresistible hold upon her back, his great claw nearly pinning her to the ground entirely.

She huddled upon herself after he was gone, and was only gradually persuaded by Temeraire to eat a little, and then to talk. *"Voici un joli cochon,"* Temeraire said, nudging over one of the spit-roasted hogs which Gong Su had prepared for him, lacquered in dark orange sauce. *"Votre capitaine s'inquiétera s'il apprend que vous ne mangez pas, vraiment."*

She took a few bites, shortly proceeding to greater enthusiasm once Temeraire had explained to her that the recipe was *à la Chinois:* her naïve remark that she was eating *"comme la Reine Blanche"* and a little more conversation confirmed to Laurence that Lung Tien Lien, their bitter enemy, was now securely established in Paris, and deep in Napoleon's councils. The little courier, full of hero-worship for the other Celestial, was not to be led into exposing any secret plans, if she knew of any, but Laurence needed no revelations to tell him that Lien's voice was sure to be loud for invasion, if Napoleon required any additional persuasion, and that she would strive to keep his attention firmly fixed upon Britain and no other part of the world.

"She says Napoleon is having the streets widened, so Lien may walk through all the city," Temeraire said, disgruntled, "and he has already built her a pavilion beside his palace. It does not seem fair that we have such difficulties here, when she has everything her own way."

Laurence answered only dully; he cared very little anymore for such larger affairs, when he was to watch Temeraire die as Victoriatus had died, reduced to that hideous bloody wreckage; a devastation far more complete than any Lien might have engineered from the deepest wells of malice. "You were with them only a few moments; let us hope," Jane had said, but no more than that, and in her lack of encouragement Laurence saw Temeraire's death-warrant signed and sealed. All the sand-pit was surely thick with the contagion; the Longwings had been penned up there for the better part of a year, the effluvia buried in the sand along with their poisonous acid.

He understood, belatedly, why he had seen none of his former colleagues, why Berkley and Harcourt had not answered his letters. Granby came to visit him, once: they could neither of them manage more than half-a-dozen words, painfully stilted; Granby consciously avoiding the subject of his own healthy Iskierka, and Laurence not wishing in the least to speak of Temeraire's chances, especially not where Temeraire himself might hear, and learn to share his own despair. At present Temeraire had no concern for himself, secure in the confidence of his own strength, a comfort which Laurence had no desire to take from him before the inevitable course of the disease should manage the job.

"*Je ne me sens pas bien,*" Sauvignon said, on the morning of the fourth day, waking herself and them with a violent burst of sneezing; she was taken away to join the other sick beasts, leaving them to wait alone for the first herald of disease.

Jane had come to see him daily, with encouraging words as long as he wished to hear them, and brandy for when he could no longer; but she reluctantly said, coming to see him on the unhappy day, "I am damned sorry to speak of this so bluntly, Laurence, but you must forgive me. Would Temeraire have begun to think of breeding yet, do you know?"

"Breeding," Laurence said bitterly, and looked away; it was natural, of course, that they should wish to preserve the bloodline of the rarest of all breeds, acquired with such difficulty, and now also in the possession of their enemy; yet to him it could be only a desire to replace what should be irreplaceable.

"I know," she said gently, "but we must expect it to come on him any day now, and mostly they are disinclined once they get sick; and who can blame them."

Her courage reproached him; she suffered as much herself with no outward show, and he could not yield to his own feelings before her. In any case there was no shading of the truth to be had; he could not lie, and was forced to confess that Temeraire had "grown very fond of a female Imperial, in the retinue of the Emperor, while we were in Peking."

"Well, I am glad to hear it: I must ask if he would oblige us with a mating, to begin as soon as tonight, now he has been without question exposed," Jane said. "Felicita is not very poorly, and informed her captain two days ago that she thinks she has another egg in her;

she has already given us two, good creature, before she fell sick. She is only a Yellow Reaper, a middle-weight; it is not the sort of cross any breeder of sense would choose to make, but I think any Celestial blood must be better than none, and we have few enough who are in any state to bear."

"But I have never seen her in my life," Temeraire said puzzledly, when the question was put to him. "Why should I wish to mate with her?"

"It is akin to an arranged marriage of state, I suppose," Laurence said, uncertain how to answer; it seemed to him belatedly a coarse sort of proposal, as though Temeraire were a prize stallion to be set on to a mare, neither of their preferences consulted, and not even a prior meeting. "You need do nothing you do not like," he added abruptly; he would not see this forced on Temeraire, in the least, any more than he should have lent himself to such an enterprise.

"Well, it is not as though I expect I would *mind*," Temeraire said, "if she would like it so very much, and I am rather bored only sitting about all day," he added, with rather less modesty than candor, "only I do not understand at all why she should."

Jane laughed, when Laurence had brought her this answer, and went out to the clearing and explained, "She would like to have an egg from you, Temeraire."

"*Oh.*" Temeraire immediately puffed out his chest deeply in gratification, his ruff coming up, and with a gracious air bowed his head. "Then certainly I will oblige her," he declared, and as soon as Jane had gone demanded that he be washed and his Chinese talon-sheaths, stored away as impractical for regular use, be brought out and put on him.

"She is so damned happy to be of use, I could weep," said Felicita's captain Brodin, a dark-haired Welshman not many years older than Laurence, with a craggy face which looked made for the grim and brooding lines into which it had presently settled. They had left the two dragons outside in Felicita's clearing to arrange the matter to their own liking, which by the sound they were doing with great enthusiasm, despite the difficulties which ought to have been inherent in managing relations between two dragons of such disparate size. "And I know I have nothing to complain of," he added bitterly, "she does better than nine-tenths of the Corps, and the surgeons think she will last ten years, at this rate of progress."

He poured out an ample measure of wine, and left the bottle on the table between them, with a second and third waiting. They did not speak much, but sat drinking together into the night, drooping gradually lower over their cups until the dragons fell quiet, and the shuddering aspen trees went still. Laurence was not quite sleeping, but he could not think of moving or even to lift his head, weighted with a thick smothering stupor like a blanket; all the world and time dulled away.

Brodin stirred him awake in his chair in the small hours of the morning. "We will see you again tonight?" he asked tiredly, as Laurence stood and bent back his shoulders to crack the angry muscles loose.

"Best so, as I understand it," Laurence said, looking at his hands in vague surprise: they trembled.

He went out to collect Temeraire, whose profoundly smug and indecorous satisfaction might have put him to the blush, were he disposed to be in any way critical of what pleasures Temeraire might enjoy under the present circumstances. "She has already had *two*, Laurence," Temeraire said, laying himself back down to sleep in his own clearing, drowsy but jubilant, "and she is quite sure she will have another; she said she could not tell at all that it was the first time I had sired."

"But is it?" Laurence asked, feeling slow and stupid, "Did not you and Mei . . . ?" Belatedly the nature of the question stopped him.

"That had nothing to do with *eggs,*" Temeraire said dismissively, "it is quite different," and coiling his tail neatly around himself went to sleep, leaving Laurence all the more confused, as he could not dream of prying further.

They repeated the visit the following evening. Laurence looked at the bottle and did not take it up again, but with an effort engaged Brodin upon other things: the customs of the Chinese and the Turks, and their sea-journey to China; the campaign in Prussia and the great battle of Jena, which he could re-create in considerable detail, having observed the whole cataclysm from Temeraire's back.

This was not, perhaps, the best means for relieving anxiety; when he had laid out all that whirling offensive, and the solid massed ranks of the Prussian army, in the form of walnut shells, were swept clean from the table, he and Brodin sat back and looked at one another, and then Brodin stood restlessly up and paced his small cabin. "I would as soon he came across while some of us still can fight, if only I could give more than ninepence for our chances if he did."

It was a dreadful thing to hope for an invasion, with unspoken the suggestion of a desire to be killed in one: perilously close, Laurence felt uneasily, to mortal sin, an extreme of selfishness even if it did not mean that England would be laid bare after, and he was troubled to find a sympathetic instinct in himself. "We must not speak so. They do not fear their own deaths, and God forbid that we should teach them to do so, or show less courage than they themselves do."

"Do you think they do not learn fear by the end?" Brodin laughed unpleasantly and short. "Obversaria scarcely knew Lenton, by the end, and he took her out of the shell with his own hands. She could only cry for water, and for rest, and he could give her none. You may think me a heathen dog if you like: I would thank God or Bonaparte or the black Devil himself for giving her a clean death in battle."

He poured the bottle, and when he was finished Laurence reached for it across the table.

"The breeders prefer two weeks," Jane said, "but we will be glad for as long as he feels himself up to the task," so Laurence dragged himself from his bed the next day, his sleep gone all to pieces, taken half in wine at Brodin's table and half during the early hours of the morning, and crept through his day, supervising the useless harness-work and lessons for Emily and Dyer, until it was time to go again. They repeated the engagement twice more, and then on the fifth day, while he sat lumpen and considering the chessboard dully, Brodin raised his head and said to Laurence abruptly, "Has he not yet begun to cough?"

"Perhaps my throat is a little sore," Temeraire said judiciously. Laurence was sitting, his head bent nearly to his knees, scarcely able to support the weight of hope resting so unexpectedly upon his shoulders, while Keynes and Dorset clambered over Temeraire like monkeys: they had listened to his lungs with a great paper cone placed against the chest, to which they put their ears, and stuck their heads in his jaws to examine his tongue, which remained a healthy and unspotted red.

"We must cup him, I think," Keynes said at last, turning to his medical satchel.

"But I am perfectly well," Temeraire objected, sidling away from the approach of the wicked curved blade of the catling. "It does not seem to me that one ought to be forced to take medicine when one is not sick; anyone would think you had no other work to do," he said, aggrieved, and the operation was only achieved by persuading him of the noble service which it should be, to the sick dragons.

It yet required a dozen attempts: he kept withdrawing his leg at the last moment, until Laurence convinced him not to look, but to keep his eyes turned in quite the opposite direction until the ready basin held by Dorset was filled, and Keynes said, "There," and clapped the cautery, waiting ready in the fire, to the nick at once.

They would have carried the steaming bowlful of dark blood away without another word, if Laurence had not chased after them to demand their verdict: "No, of course he is not sick, and does not mean to be, so far as I can tell," Keynes said. "I will say no more at present; we have work to do," and went away, leaving Laurence almost ill himself with reaction; he felt a man who had stepped out of the shadow of the gallows, two weeks of anxious dread giving way quite suddenly to this almost shattering relief. It was very difficult not to yield to the force of his emotions, with Temeraire saying, "It is not very nice to be cut open, and I do not see what good it will do at all," nosing experimentally at the tiny seared-shut wound, and then nudging him in alarm. "Laurence? Laurence, pray do not worry; it does not hurt so much, and look, it has already stopped bleeding."

* * *

Jane was writing papers before Keynes had half made her his report, her face lit with energy and purpose, the grey shroud of sorrow and weariness fully visible only now with its removal.

"Let us not have any rioting, if you please," Keynes said almost angrily. His hands were still gory with blood crusted under the fingernails; he had come straight from his work, in making comparisons of the samples of blood beneath his microscope. "There is no justification for it. It may very well be merely a difference in physiognomy, or an individual trait. I have said only there is the merest possibility, worthy of a trial—worthy of a small trial, with no expectations—" His protests were useless: she did not pause for a moment. He looked as though he would have liked to snatch away her pen.

"Nonsense; a little riot is just what we need," Jane said, without even looking up, "and you will write the most damned encouraging report ever seen, if you please; you will give no excuses to the Admiralty."

"I am not speaking to the Admiralty at present," Keynes said, "and I do not care to give unfounded hopes. In all likelihood, he has never had the disease—it is some natural resistance, unique to his breed; and the cold which he suffered last year merely coincidence."

The hope was indeed a very tenuous one. Temeraire had been ill en route to China, briefly, the sickness settling itself out of hand after little more than a week in Capetown, and so dismissed at the time and afterwards as a mere trifling cold. Only his present resistance to the disease had given Keynes the suspicion that the illnesses might perhaps have been one and the same. But even if he were not mistaken, there might be no cure; if there were a cure, it might not be easily found; if it were found, still it might not be brought back in time to save many of the sick.

"And it is by no means the least likely possibility," Keynes added peevishly, "that there may be no curative agent whatsoever; many a consumptive has found a temporary relief in warmer climes."

"Whether the climate or the waters or the food, I do not care two pins; if I must ship every dragon in England to Africa by boat to take the cure, you may be sure I will do it," Jane said. "I am almost as glad to find some cause to lift our spirits again as for the chance of a cure, and you will do nothing to depress them again," Little hope riches enough to those who until lately had none, and worth pursuing with every means at hand. "Laurence, you and Temeraire must go, though I hate to give you up again," she added, handing him his orders, hastily written and scarcely legible, "but we must rely on him to remember best whatever might have suited his taste, and be the foundation of the cure. The ferals come along as well as could be hoped, thank Heavens, and with this latest spy captured, perhaps we will be lucky, and Bonaparte will not be in such a hurry to send good dragons after bad.

"And I am sending along all your formation," she continued. "They are in urgent need, having been among the first to take sick; if you bring them back well, which God willing, you can hold the Channel while we treat the others."

"Then I *may* see Maximus and Lily again, now," Temeraire said jubilantly, and would not wait, but insisted that they go at once: they had scarcely set down outside the barren clearing where Maximus slept, before Berkley came striding out to them and seizing Laurence by the arms nearly shook him, saying ferociously, "For God's sake, say it is true, and not some damned fairytale," and he turned aside and covered his face when Laurence gave his assent.

Laurence pretended not to see. "Temeraire, I believe your harness is loose, there over the left flank, will you look at it?" he said firmly, when Temeraire would have kept peering at Berkley's bowed shoulders.

"But Mr. Fellowes was working on it only last week," Temeraire said, diverted, nosing over it experimentally. He delicately took up a bit of the harness between his teeth and tugged on it. "No, it lies perfectly well; it does not feel the least bit loose at all."

"Here, let's have a look at you," Berkley interrupted brusquely, having mastered himself. "A good twelve feet more since you sailed away to China, no? And you look well, Laurence; I expected to see you ragged as a tinker."

"You would certainly have found me so, when we had first returned," Laurence answered, gripping his hand. He could not return any compliment; Berkley had put off some six stone of weight, at first glance, and it did not suit him; his jowls hung loose from his cheeks.

Maximus looked still more dreadfully altered, the great scaly red-and-gold hide sagging in folds around the base of the neck, and forward of his chest with the massive fretwork of his spine and shoulders holding it up like tent-poles, and what Laurence supposed to be the air-sacs swollen and bulging from his wasted sides. His eyes were slitted nearly shut, and a thin raspy noise of breathing issued from his cracked-open jaws, a trail of drool puddling beneath them; the nostrils were caked over with dried flaking effluvia.

"He will wake up in a bit, and be glad to see you both," Berkley said gruffly, "but I don't like to wake him when he can get any rest. The blasted cold will not let him sleep properly, and he don't eat a quarter of what he should."

Temeraire, having followed them into the clearing, made no sound, but crouched himself down, his neck curved back upon itself like a wary snake, and sat there utterly still, his wide unblinking gaze fixed on Maximus, who slept on, rasping, rasping. Laurence and Berkley conversed in low voices, discussing the sea-voyage. "Less than three months to the Cape," Laurence said, "to judge by our last voyage; and we had some fighting off the Channel to see us off, which did not speed matters."

"However long, better on a ship to some purpose than lying about like this, if we all drown at it," Berkley said. "We will be packed by morning, and the lummox will eat properly for once if I have to march the cows down his gullet."

"Are we going somewhere?" Maximus said sleepily, in a voice much thickened, and turned his head aside to cough low and deep, several times, and spit into a small leaf-covered pit dug for the purpose. He rubbed each of his eyes against his foreleg, in turn, to clear away the mucus, and then seeing Temeraire slowly brightened, his head rising. "You are back; was China very interesting?" he asked.

"It was, oh, it was, but," Temeraire burst out, "I am sorry I was not at home, while all of you were sick; I am so very sorry," and hung his head, miserably.

"Why it is only a cold," Maximus said, only to be interrupted by another bout of coughing, after which he added regardless, "I will be perfectly hearty soon, I am sure; only I am tired." He closed his eyes almost directly he had said this, and fell again into a light stupor.

"They have the worst of it," Berkley said heavily, seeing Laurence away; Temeraire had crept very quietly out of the clearing again, so they might go aloft without disturbing Maximus. "All the Regal Coppers. It is the damned weight; they do not eat, so they cannot keep up their muscle, and then one day they cannot breathe.

Four lost already, and Laetificat will not see summer, unless we find your cure." He did not say that Maximus would follow soon after, if not precede her; he did not need to.

"We shall find it," Temeraire said fiercely, "we shall, we shall, we shall."

"I hope to find you well, and your charge, when we return," Laurence said, shaking Granby's hand; behind him a great bustle and commotion were under way as the crew made their final preparations: they would depart tomorrow on the evening tide, the wind permitting, and needed to be well aboard by morning, with so many dragons and their crews to be stowed. Emily and Dyer were busily folding his clothing into his battered old sea-chest, which had only just survived their most recent voyage, and Ferris was saying sharply, "Don't think I do not see you with that bottle, Mr. Allen; you may pour it out directly, do you hear?"

He had a great many new men aboard, replacements for the unhappy number of his crew who had been lost in their year's absence. Jane had sent them all on trial, for his approval, but in the torment and anxiety of the past two weeks, and the heavy work of those before, he had grown only indifferently acquainted with them; now suddenly there was no more time, and he must make do with whomever had been given him. He was not a little sorry to be making his farewells to a man whose character he knew and understood, and upon whom he would have been happy to rely.

"I expect you will find us all to pieces," Granby said, "with half of England on fire, and Arkady and his lot celebrating in the ruins, roasting cows; it will be wonderful otherwise."

"Tell Arkady from me that they are all to mind properly," Temeraire said, craning his head over carefully, so as not to dislodge the harness-men scurrying upon his back, "and that we will certainly be back very soon, so he need not think he has everything all to himself, even if he does have a medal now," he finished, still disgruntled.

They were prolonging their conversation over a cup of tea when a young ensign came for Laurence. "Begging your pardon, sir, but there is a gentleman to see you, at the headquarters," the boy said, and added, in tones of amazement, "a *black* gentleman," so a very puzzled Laurence had to say his last farewells more abruptly and go.

He came into the officers' common room; there was no difficulty in picking out his guest, although Laurence struggled for a moment before recalling his name: Reverend Erasmus, the missionary whom Wilberforce had presented to him, at the party two weeks before—had it been so short a time? "You are very welcome, sir; but I am afraid you find me at sixes and sevens," Laurence said, beckoning to the servants, who had not yet brought him any refreshment. "We are leaving port tomorrow—a glass of wine?"

"Only a cup of tea, I thank you," Erasmus said. "Captain, I knew as much; I hope you will forgive me for descending on you at such a time, without notice. I was with Mr. Wilberforce this morning, when your letter of apology arrived, informing him you were bound for Africa: and I have come to beg you for passage."

Laurence was silent. He had every right, as a point of etiquette, to invite some number of guests; this being the prerogative of dragon captains aboard a transport as much as that of the captain of the ship herself. But the situation was not a simple one, for they would travel on the *Allegiance,* under a captain, who though one of Laurence's dearest friends, and indeed his former first officer, owed no small portion of his fortune to his family's substantial plantations in the West Indies, manned by slaves. Erasmus himself, Laurence realized with a sinking feeling, might even once have toiled in their very fields: he believed some of Riley's father's holdings were in Jamaica.

Aside from all the discomfort which any strong difference of politics among shipmates might ordinarily engender, in the close quarters of a journey, Laurence had on previous occasions failed to conceal his sentiments towards the practice, and some ill-feeling had unhappily resulted. To now inflict upon Riley a passenger whose very presence would seem a silent and unanswerable continuation of their argument, had the look of a calculated insult.

"Sir," Laurence said slowly, "I believe you said you had been taken from Louanda? We are bound for Capetown, far to the south. It will not be your own nation."

"Beggars cannot be choosers, Captain," Erasmus said simply, "and I have only been praying for passage to Africa. If God has opened a path for me that leads to Capetown, I will not refuse it."

He made no further appeal, but only sat expectantly, his dark eyes leveled steadily across the table. "Then I am at your service, Reverend," Laurence said, as of course he had to, "if you can only manage to be ready in time; we cannot miss the tide."

"Thank you, Captain." Erasmus rose and shook his hand vigorously. "Have no fear: in hopes of your consent, my wife has already been making our arrangements, and by now will already herself be on the road with all our worldly substance; there is not much of it," he added.

"Then I will hope to see you tomorrow morning," Laurence said, "in Dover harbor."

The *Allegiance* stood waiting for them in the cold sunny morning, looking oddly squat with her masts stubby and bare, the topmasts and yards laid out upon the deck, and the enormous chains of her best bower and kedge anchors stretching out from the water, groaning softly as she rocked on the swell. She had come into harbor some four weeks earlier, Laurence and Temeraire having reached England, in the end, scarcely any sooner than their ocean passage would have brought them, if they had sailed home with the *Allegiance* after all.

"You may not complain of your delays; I am too happy to find you alive and well and not skeletons in some Himalayan pass," Riley said, shaking his hand eagerly in welcome, nearly before Laurence had stepped off Temeraire's back. "And you brought us home a firebreather, after all. Yes, I could scarcely help but hear of her; the Navy is bursting with the news, and I believe the ships on blockade take it in turn to go past Guernsey and watch her flaming away at that old rock heap through their glasses.

"But I am very happy we shall make shipmates again now," he continued, "and though you will be more crowded, I hope we will make shift to see you all comfortable; you are a party of seven this time?"

He spoke with so much earnest friendliness and concern that Laurence was stricken with a sense of dishonesty and said abruptly, "Yes, we are a full complement; and Captain, I must tell you, I have brought a passenger along, with his family. He is a missionary, bound for the Cape, and applied to me only yesterday afternoon—he is a freedman."

He regretted his words as soon as he had spoken; he

had meant to make the introduction more gently, and was conscious that he had let guilt make him clumsy and indelicate. Riley was silent. "I am sorry I could not give you more warning," Laurence added, in an attempt to make apology.

"I see," Riley said only, "—of course you may invite anyone whom you wish," very shortly, and touching his hat went away without further conversation.

He made no pretense of courtesy to Reverend Erasmus when that gentleman came aboard a little later that morning, neglecting even a greeting, which would have offended Laurence on the part of any guest, much less a man of the cloth; but when he saw the minister's wife left sitting in the small and poky boat which had been sent for them, with her two small children, and no offer made to rig a bosun's chair over the side to bring them aboard, he had had enough.

"Ma'am," he said, leaning over the side, "pray be easy, and only keep hold of the children; we will have you aboard in a moment. I beg you will not be alarmed," and straightening said, "Temeraire, will you lift that boat up, if you please, so the lady may come aboard."

"Oh, certainly, and I will be very careful," Temeraire said, and leaning over the side of the ship—well-balanced, to her other side, by Maximus, still prodigious in weight despite his reduced state—he seized the boat carefully in one enormous forehand, and plucked it dripping from the water. The boat's crew were loud in their protestations of alarm, while the two little girls clung to their stoic-faced mother, who did not permit herself to look at all anxious; the entire operation scarcely covered the space of a moment, and then Temeraire was setting the boat upon the dragondeck.

Laurence offered his hand to Mrs. Erasmus: she

silently accepted, and having climbed down, reached in herself to lift out the children, one after another, and then her own portmanteau and satchel. She was a tall, stern-faced woman, more substantial in build and considerably darker of skin than her husband, with her hair pinned severely down under a plain white kerchief. Her two small daughters, in perfectly white pinafores, having been admonished briefly to stay quiet and out of the way, clutched each other's hands tightly.

"Roland, perhaps you will see our guests to their cabin," Laurence said to Emily quietly, hoping her presence might comfort them. To his regret, it was time to give over any attempt to conceal her sex. The progression of a year and more having its natural consequences upon her figure, which bid fair to take after her mother's, it would soon be quite impossible anyone should be deceived, and he must henceforth simply brazen out any challenge, hoping for the best; thankfully, in the present case, it could not signify what the Erasmuses should think of her, or the Corps, as they were to be left securely behind in Africa.

"There is nothing to be afraid of," Emily informed the girls blithely as she led them away, seeing their stares, "at least, not the dragons; although we had some terrific storms on our last sea-voyage," which left them as easy in their minds as they had been; they looked very meek as they followed her below to their quarters.

Laurence turned back to Lieutenant Franks, commanding the boat's crew, who had gone silent, having been set down amidst seven dragons, even if these were mostly sleeping. "I am sure Temeraire would be happy to put the boat back in her traces," he said, but when that young man only stammered miserably, a pang of guilt made him add, "but perhaps you have another return to make," and on Franks's relieved assent, had Temeraire set the boat back down into the water.

He then went himself below, to his cabin, much reduced from the previous voyage, as the space was now divided with six other captains; but he had been given a forward room, with a share of the bow windows, and it was better than many a cabin he had endured in the Navy. He did not have to wait long; Riley came and knocked—unnecessarily, as the door was standing open—and begged the favor of a word.

"That will do, Mr. Dyer," Laurence said, to the young runner presently ordering his things, "pray go see if Temeraire needs anything, then you may attend to your lessons," as he wanted no audience.

The door was shut; Riley began stiffly, "I hope you are settled to your satisfaction."

"—I am." Laurence did not mean to begin the quarrel; if Riley wished to stand upon the point, he might do so.

"Then I am sorry to say," Riley said, not looking very sorry, only pale with anger, "I am very sorry to say, that I have received a report, which I could scarcely credit, if I had not seen with my own eyes—"

He was not speaking loudly, yet; the door swung open in the middle of his sentence, and Catherine Harcourt looked in. "Pray forgive me," she said, "but I have been trying to find you these twenty minutes, Captain Riley; this ship is too damned large. Not that I mean to complain of her in the least, of course: we are very obliged to you indeed for our passage."

Riley stammered a vague polite reply, staring very fixedly at the top of her head. He had not known her for a woman at the time of their first meeting, which had encompassed little more than a day, and that the day after a battle. Catherine was of a slimmer stature than Jane, and with her hair pulled back snugly in her customary plait, her wide pleasant face with its snub nose freckled and brown with sun and wind, she might more easily be mistaken by the unsuspecting. But the general secret had slipped out during their previous voyage to China, and Riley had been very much shocked and disapproving at the intelligence.

"And I hope you are comfortably— that your cabin—" he said now, at a loss for the form of address.

"Oh, my bags are stowed; I suppose I will find them sometime," Harcourt said briskly, either unconscious or deliberately blind to Riley's awkward constraint. "That makes no nevermind; it is these tubs of oiled sand, for Lily to rest her head upon. I am very sorry to have to trouble you, but we are quite at a loss where·they are to be stowed: we must have them near the dragondeck, in case she should have a fit of sneezing and we must change them out quick."

As the acid of a Longwing was perfectly capable, unchecked, of eating through an entire ship straight down to the hull and sinking her, this topic naturally engaged all the interest which could be imagined, of the ship's captain, and Riley answered her with energy, his discomfort forgotten in the practical concern. They settled it that the tubs should be stored in the galley, directly below the dragondeck, and this decided, Catherine nodded and thanked him, adding, "Will you dine with us to-night?"—an inconvenient friendliness, but of course her prerogative: to make a technical point of the matter, she was Laurence's superior officer, as formally their assignment remained to form a part of Lily's formation, although Temeraire had operated under independent orders now for so long that Laurence himself scarcely remembered the fact.

But it was delivered informally, at least, so it did not

seem offensive when Riley said, "I thank you, but I must be on deck to-night, I am afraid," a polite excuse, which she accepted on its face, and nodding her farewells left him alone with Laurence once again.

It was awkward to resume, with the first natural impulse of anger thus blunted, but with a will they rose to the occasion, and after only a few more moderate exchanges, Riley's "And I hope, sir, that I need never again see the ship's crew or her boats subjected to, I am sorry to call it so, outright interference, under not only the permission but the encouragement—" progressed very neatly to Laurence's reply,

"And for *my* part, Captain Riley, I would be glad to never again be witness to such a positive disdain not only for all the generally understood requirements of courtesy, but for the very safety of her passengers, from the crew of one of His Majesty's vessels—I will not say deliberate insult—"

They were soon in such fine form as might be expected from two men both in the habit of command, and of full voice, whose former acquaintance made it no difficulty to touch upon such subjects as might provoke the most dramatic reaction. "You cannot claim," Riley said, "not to have a proper understanding of precedence in these matters; you can make no such excuse. You know your duty perfectly well. You set your beast deliberately onto the ship's crew, without permission. You might have asked for a chair, if you wished one slung—"

"If I had imagined that such a request *needed* to be made, upon what I had supposed to be a well-run ship, when a lady was to come aboard—" Laurence said.

"I suppose we must mean a little something different by the term," Riley retorted, sarcastic and quick.

He at once looked heartily embarrassed, when the remark had escaped him; but Laurence was in no way inclined to wait for him to withdraw, and said angrily, "It would grieve me indeed to be forced to impute any ungentlemanlike motive—any selfish consideration, which might prompt a gentleman to make remarks so nearly intolerable upon the character and respectability of a clergyman's wife, and a mother, wholly unknown to him and therefore offering no grounds whatsoever to merit his scorn—save perhaps as an alternative, preferable to the examination of his own conscience—"

The door flung open without a knock; Berkley thrust his head into the cabin. They stopped at once, united in appalled indignation at this perfect disregard for privacy and all shipboard etiquette. Berkley paid no attention to their stares. He was unshaven and gaunt; Maximus had passed an uncomfortable night after his short flight aboard, and Berkley had slept no more than his dragon. He said bluntly, "We can hear every damned word on deck; in a moment Temeraire will pull up the planking and stick his nose in. For God's sake go knock each other down somewhere quietly and have done."

This outrageous advice, more suitable for a pair of schoolboys than grown men, was not heeded, but the quarrel was necessarily ended by the open reproof; Riley begged to be excused, and went at once away.

"I must ask you to go-between for us, with Captain Riley, I am afraid, henceforth," Laurence said to Catherine, some time afterwards, when his temper had been as much relieved as could be managed by the violent pacing of the narrow length of his cabin. "I know we agreed I should manage it, but matters have arisen so that—"

"Of course, Laurence, you need say nothing more," she interrupted, in practical tones, leaving him in some despair of the discretion of all his fellow aviators; it was such a settled part of his understanding of shipboard life, that one should *pretend* not to have heard, even what of necessity had been perfectly audible, that he hardly knew how to answer their frankness, "and I will give him a private dinner, instead of making it a common one with all of us, so there will be no difficulty. But I am sure you will make up the matter in a trice. What is there worth arguing about, when we have three months of sailing together ahead of us?—unless you mean to entertain us all with the gossip of the thing."

Laurence did not in the least like to form the subject of whispers, but he drearily knew her optimistic hopes to be ill-founded. No unforgivable remarks had been made but many unforgettable ones, a good number by himself, he was sorry to recall, and if they did not need for honor's sake to avoid one another entirely, he felt they could hardly be on such terms of camaraderie as they had formerly known, ever again. He wondered if he was to blame, perhaps for continuing, too much, to think of Riley as his subordinate; if he had presumed too far on their relationship.

He went to sit with Temeraire as the ship made ready to weigh anchor: the familiar old shouts and exhortations strangely distant from him, and he felt a disconnect from the life of the ship such as he had never expected to know; almost as though he had never been a sailor at all.

"Look there, Laurence," Temeraire said; south of the harbor, a small ragged knot of dragons could be seen winging away from the covert: towards Cherbourg, Laurence guessed, by their line of flight. His glass was not to hand, and they were little larger than a flock of birds at the distance, too far to make out their individual markings, but as they flew, one among them briefly fired out a small exuberant tongue of flame, yellow-orange-hot against the blue sky: Iskierka set out with a handful of the ferals, for the first time on a real patrol; the measure of the desperate circumstances which they left behind.

"Are we not leaving soon, Laurence?" Temeraire asked; he was painfully impatient to be under way. "If we would make better speed, I would be very happy to pull, at any time," and he turned to look at Dulcia, presently lying in an uneasy sleep upon his back, coughing miserably every so often without even opening her eyes.

She and Lily, who lay with her head half-buried up to the bone spurs in a great wooden tub full of sand, were yet in much better state than the rest of the formation; poor Maximus had made the flight to the ship in easy short stages, and even so with much difficulty. He had been given all the far side of the dragondeck and was sleeping there already, heedless of the furious bustle around him as the last of the preparations to launch them commenced. Nitidus lay sprawled in exhaustion tucked against Maximus's side, where once the Pascal's Blue would have lain comfortably on his back, and Immortalis and Messoria, huddled to either side of Lily in the middle of the deck, were grown a sort of pale lemon yellow like milk custard.

"I could drag up the anchors in a trice, I am sure, much quicker," Temeraire added. The topmasts had been sent up, and the yards, and they were warping up to the kedge: fully four hundred men or more could heave on the massive quadruple-capstan at once, and all of them would be needed to bring up the massive weight of the best bower. The sailors on deck were most of them already stripped to the waist, despite the cold morning, to get about it; Temeraire certainly could have provided material aid, but Laurence was under no illusion how such an offer would presently be received.

"We would only be in the way," he said; "they will manage quicker without us." He laid his hand on Temeraire's side, looking away from the labor in which they could have no part, to the open ocean ahead.

II

Chapter 6

OH," TEMERAIRE SAID, in a very strange tone, and he pitched forward and vomited tremendously all over the open ground before him, heaving up an acrid stinking mess in which the traces of banana leaves, goat horns, cocoanut shells, and long green ropes of braided seaweed might be distinguished among the generalized yellowish mulch, scattered through with unrecognizable scraps of cracked bones and shreds of hide.

"Keynes!" Laurence bellowed, having leapt out of the way just in time, and to the two hapless medicine-men who had offered the latest remedy, savagely said, "Get you gone, and take that worthless draught with you."

"No, let us have it, if you please, and the receipt," Keynes said, approaching a little gingerly, and bending to sniff at the pot which they had presented. "A purgative may be of some use on future occasions, if this is not simply a case of excess; were you feeling ill before?" Keynes demanded of Temeraire, who only moaned a little and closed his eyes; he was lying limp and wretched, having crept a little way off from the former contents of his stomach, which steamed unpleasantly even in the overheated late-summer air. Laurence covered his mouth and nostrils with a handkerchief and beckoned to the deeply reluctant groundsmen to bring the midden-shovels, and bury the refuse at once.

"I wonder if it is not the effects of the protea," Dorset said absently, poking through the pot with a stick and fishing out the remnants of the spiny blossom. "I do not believe we have seen it used as an ingredient before: the Cape vegetation has quite a unique construction, among the plant kingdom. I must send the children for some specimens."

"As glad as we must be to have delivered you a curiosity, it is certainly nothing which he ever ate before; perhaps you might consider how we are to proceed, instead, without making him ill again," Laurence snapped, and went to Temeraire's side before he could make a further display of his ill-temper and frustration. He laid a hand on the slowly heaving muzzle, and Temeraire twitched his ruff in an attempt at bravery.

"Roland, go you and Dyer and fetch some sea-water, from beneath the dock," Laurence said, and taking a cloth used the cool water to wipe down Temeraire's muzzle and his jaws.

They had been in Capetown now two days, experimenting lavishly: Temeraire perfectly willing to sniff or swallow anything which anyone should give him, if only it might by some chance be a cure, and exercise his memory; so far without any notable success, and Laurence was prepared to consider this latest episode a notable failure, whatever the surgeons might say. He did not know how to refuse them; but it seemed to him they were trying a great deal of local quackery, without any real grounds for hope, and making a reckless trial of Temeraire's health.

"I already feel a good deal better," Temeraire said, but his eyes were closing in exhaustion as he said it, and he did not want to eat anything the next day; but said wistfully, "I would be glad of some tea, if it would not be much trouble," so Gong Su made a great kettle of it, using a week's supply, and then to his disgust they put in an entire brick of sugar. Temeraire drank it with great pleasure when it had cooled, and afterwards stoutly declared himself perfectly recovered; but he still looked rather dismally when Emily and Dyer came huffing back from the markets, hung all over with the day's new acquisitions in net-bags and parcels, and stinking from ten-yards' distance.

"Well, let us see," Keynes said, and went poking through the materials with Gong Su: a great many local vegetables, including a long pendulous fruit like an oversized yam, which Gong Su dubiously picked up and thumped against the ground: not even the skin so much as split, until he at last took it into the castle, to the smith, and had it smashed open upon the forge.

"That is from a sausage-tree," Emily said. "Maybe it is not quite ripe, though; and also we did find some of the hua jiao today, from a Malay stall-keeper," she added, showing Laurence a small basket of the red peppery seeds, for which Temeraire had acquired a great liking.

"Not the mushroom?" Laurence asked: this being a hideously pungent specimen they all recalled vividly from their first visit, which in its cooking had rendered the entire castle nearly uninhabitable from its noxious fumes. Laurence had his share of the seaman's instinctive faith in unpleasant medicine, and secretly the best part of his own hopes lay on the thing. But it was surely a wild growth, uncultivated: no person in their senses would ever deliberately eat the thing, and so far it was not to be found, for any price.

"We found a boy who had a little English and told him that we would pay gold for it, if they would bring some," Dyer piped up; a group of native children had brought them the first example mostly as a curiosity.

"Perhaps the seed husks in combination with another of the native fruits," Dorset suggested, examining the hua jiao and stirring them with a finger. "They might have been used on any number of dishes."

Keynes snorted, and, dusting his hands as he straightened from the survey, he shook his head at Gong Su. "No, let his innards have another day's rest, and leave off all this unwholesome stuff. I am increasingly of the opinion that the climate alone must cook it out of them, if there is to be any benefit to this enterprise at all."

He prodded the ground with the stick he had been using to turn over the vegetables: dry and hard several inches down, with only the stubborn frizz of short yellow grass to hold it together, the roots long and thin and spidery. A few days into March, they were deep in the local summer, and the steady hot weather made the hard-packed bare ground a baking stone, which fairly shimmered with heat during the peak of the day.

Temeraire cracked an eye from his restorative drowse. "It is pleasant, but it is not so much warmer than the courtyard at Loch Laggan," he said doubtfully, and in any case the suggestion was not a very satisfying one, as this cure could not be tried until the other dragons arrived.

And for the moment they were alone, although the *Allegiance* was expected now daily. As soon as the ship had come in flying distance of the Cape, Laurence had packed the surgeons and the barest handful of men and supplies aboard Temeraire's back, and taken them on ahead, that they might begin this desperate business of attempting to find the cure.

It had not been merely an excuse: their orders unequivocally stated *without the loss of a moment,* and

Maximus's ragged, gurgling cough was a constant spur to their sides. But in all honesty, neither had Laurence been sorry in the least to go. The quarrel had *not* been made up, at all.

Laurence had made attempts: once, three weeks into the journey, he paused, belowdecks, as they passed one another by chance, and removed his hat; but Riley only just touched his own brim and shouldered by, a quick surge of red color mounting in his cheeks. This had stiffened Laurence another week, long enough to make him refuse an offer of a share in one of the ship's milch goats, when the one which he had provided himself ran dry and was sacrificed instead to the dragons.

Then regret won out again, and he said to Catherine, "Perhaps we ought to invite the captain and the ship's officers to dinner?" on deck and perfectly audible to anyone who might be curious, so when the invitation was sent it could not be mistaken as anything but a peace offering. But though Riley came, and his officers, he was utterly withdrawn all the meal, scarcely answering except when Catherine spoke to him and never lifting his head from his plate. His officers, of course, would not speak without he or another captain addressing them, so it was a strange and silent affair with even the younger aviators stifled by the uneasy sense that their manners did not suit the formality of the occasion.

With such a standing quarrel among the officers, the men, who at no time made any great secret of their dislike of the dragons and their aviators, now made still less of one. Their hostility was leashed tightly by their fear, of course, even among those who had sailed with Laurence and Temeraire on the previous voyage to China. Seven dragons made a great difference from one, and the sudden violent fits of coughing or sneezing which wracked the poor creatures and ate at their strength only made them all the more fearsomely unpredictable to the common sailors, who could scarcely be made to ascend the foremast for its being too close to the beasts.

What was worse, their officers corrected them none too sharply for their hesitation, with predictable results: off the coast of the Horn she missed stays, and had to be hurriedly box-hauled, because the men were slow moving on the dragondeck to shift over the jib and foretopmast staysail sheets. The maneuver jarred the dragons sadly about, setting them to coughing, and then nuisance in a moment nearly became tragedy: Nitidus went tumbling off Temeraire's back and knocked Lily's head askew.

Her greasy tub of oiled sand slid with ponderous majesty over the edge of the dragondeck, and plunged immediately into the ocean. "Over the side, dearest, put your head over the side," Catherine cried, her crew all of them to a man rushing to fetch one of the other replacements from the galley below. Lily had with a tremendous effort lunged forward and now was clutching precariously at the edge of the ship, her head thrust out over the water and her shoulders curled up into great knots as she tried to hold from coughing; drops spilled from her bone spurs and smoked thin black hissing streams from the tarry sides of the ship: the *Allegiance* was coming up through the wind, which blew them back against the wood.

"Shall I try and carry you away from the ship?" Temeraire asked anxiously, wings half-spread. "Will you climb on my back?"—a dangerous maneuver at the best of times, with a dragon not dripping poisonous acid from her jaws, if Lily could even have managed to get upon him.

"Temeraire," Laurence called instead, "will you see if you can break up the deck, here," and Temeraire turned his head. Laurence had only meant him to try and wrench the planks up, but instead Temeraire opened his jaws experimentally over the place and gave a queer, throttled version of his usual roar: four planks cracked, one opening up along the ring-pattern of the wood and dropping a knot straight down onto the startled heads of the galley cooks, crouched and covering themselves in terror.

The space was nearly wide enough: with a few frantic moments of work they had it enlarged, and Temeraire could reach down and heave up the tub directly. Lily pressed her jaw down into the sand and coughed and coughed, miserably and long, the fit worsened by her having repressed it at first. The oily sand hissed and smoked and stank with the fumes of the acid, and the deck gaped with the splintered hole, jagged edges threatening the dragons' bellies and letting the steam out of the galley which kept them warm.

"A damned disgrace; we might as well be sailing on a Frenchman," Laurence said, angrily and not low; it had already been in his mind that tacking into the wind was incautious for so large and ponderous a vessel, better suited to old-fashioned wearing about, particularly when weighted down as she was with so many dragons.

Riley had appeared on the quarterdeck, and across the ship faintly drifted the sound of his furious voice, calling Owens, the deck officer, to account, and the men to fresh order. But Laurence's voice carried, too; there was a momentary pause in Riley's tirade, and then it finished more abruptly.

Riley made his stiff and formal apologies for the incident only to Catherine, catching her as she came off the dragondeck to go below, at the end of the day, in what Laurence could only imagine a design to avoid going up to speak to all of the aviators together. Her hair had come loose from its plait, her face was smudged with smoke and charred soot, and she had taken off her coat to pad under Lily's jaw, where the bare edge of the tub had chafed. When he stopped her, she straightened and put her hand through her hair, loosening it entirely about her face, and his speech, undoubtedly prepared with care, quite fell apart. He only said, "I beg your pardon—deeply regret—" incoherently, and looked all confusion, until she interrupted tiredly, "Yes, of course, only pray not again, and do let us have the carpenters make the repairs at once tomorrow. Good-night," and brushed past him and went below.

She meant nothing by it but that she was tired, and wished to go to sleep; but it looked cutting to one who did not know her well enough to know her not in the least likely to resort to social stratagem to express offense; and perhaps Riley was ashamed. In any case, by morning all the ship's carpenters were at work on the dragondeck before even the aviators arose, with not a word of grumbling or fear even if a great deal of sweating, particularly when the dragons roused and began watching with close interest. By the end of the day they had not only repaired the injury, but also put in a smooth hatch, which could be opened up into the galley if the operation required repeating.

"Well, I call that handsome," Catherine said, though Laurence felt it small amends for the earlier neglect; and when she added, "we ought to thank him for it," glancing at him, he said nothing and made no shifts to take her place. When she did go and ask Riley to dine again, this time Laurence was careful to absent himself for the meal.

It was an end to any hope of resolution. The rest of the journey passed in a cold distance between them, barely an exchange of greetings and only the briefest gesture when passing on deck or below: made rarer still, as the Navy officers were quartered to the stern. There could be nothing comfortable in traveling aboard a ship while at unconcealed and bitter odds with her captain; the officers likewise cold, if they were men who had never served with Laurence himself, or stiff with discomfort otherwise. These constant chafing indignities of cold treatment from the ship's complement daily refreshed not only of the pain of the quarrel but his resentment of Riley's anger.

There was one saving grace; thus isolated from the life of the ship, and naturally brought into the closest contact with his fellow captains of the Corps and their habits, Laurence had sailed this time not merely in theory but in practice as an aviator: a very different experience, and he startled himself by preferring it. They had little practical work to do; by noon the daily slaughter was over, the dragondeck had been holystoned as best as could be managed without shifting the dragons too much, the younger officers examined on their schoolwork, and they were all at liberty: as much liberty as could be had within the space of a fully occupied dragondeck, and their half-a-dozen small cabins below.

"Do you mind if we knock down the bulkhead, Laurence?" Chenery had said, putting in his head scarcely three days into the journey, as Laurence was writing letters in his cabin: a habit he had much neglected on shore of late. "We want to set up a card-table, but it is too wretchedly cramped," an odd request, but he gave his assent; it was pleasant to have the larger space restored, and to write his letters with the companionable noise of their game and conversation. It became so settled a practice among them that the crewmen would have the bulkheads down without asking, no sooner had they finished dressing; and restored only for sleeping.

They took their meals almost always thus in common: a convivial and noisy atmosphere, with Catherine presiding and all talking across the table heedless of etiquette, the junior officers squeezed in at the lower half in order of their promptness in arrival rather than their rank; and afterwards they gave the loyal toast standing on deck, followed with coffee and cigars in the company of their dragons, who were dosed with a posset against coughing, for what little relief it gave them, in the cooler hours of the evening. And after supper, he would read to Temeraire, occasionally from the Latin or the French, with Temeraire translating for the other dragons.

Laurence assumed Temeraire particularly unusual, among dragons, for his scholarship; to better suit the rest, he kept, at first, to their small store of literature, and only then gave way to those mathematical and scientific treatises which Temeraire doted upon and he himself found hard going. Many of these interested the company as little as Laurence had expected, but he was surprised in reading a sadly wearing treatise upon geometry to be interrupted by Messoria, who said sleepily, "Pray skip ahead a little; we do not need it *proven*, anyone can tell it is perfectly correct," referring to great circles. They had no difficulty at all with the notion that a curved course rather than a straight was the shortest distance for sailing, which had confused Laurence himself for a good week when he had been obliged to learn it for the lieutenant's examination, in the Navy. The next evening he was further interrupted in his reading by Nitidus and Dulcia taking up an argument with Temeraire about Euclid's postulates, one of which, referring to the principle of parallel lines, they felt quite unreasonable.

"I am not saying it is correct," Temeraire protested, "but you must accept it and go on: everything else in the science is built upon it."

"But what use is it, then!" Nitidus said, getting agitated enough to flutter his wings and bat his tail against Maximus's side; Maximus murmured a small reproof without quite waking. "Everything must be quite wrong if he begins so."

"It is not that it is *wrong*," Temeraire said, "only it is not so plain as the others—"

"It *is* wrong, it is perfectly wrong," Nitidus cried decidedly, while Dulcia pointed out more calmly, "Only consider a moment: if you should begin in Dover, and I a little south of London, on the same latitude, and we should then both fly straight northward, we should certainly meet at the Pole if we did not mistake our course, so what on earth is the sense of arguing that straight lines will never meet?"

"Well," Temeraire said, scratching at his forehead, "that is certainly true, but I promise you the postulate makes good sense when you consider all the useful calculations and mathematics which may be arrived at, starting with the assumption. Why, all of the ship's design, which we are upon, is at base worked out from it, I imagine," a piece of intelligence which made nervous Nitidus give the *Allegiance* a very doubtful eye.

"But I suppose," Temeraire continued, "that we might try beginning without the assumption, or the contrary one—" and they put their heads together over Temeraire's sand-table, and began to work out their own geometry, discarding those principles which seemed to them incorrect, and made a game of developing the theory; which entertained them a good deal more than most amusements Laurence had ever seen dragons engage in, with those listening applauding particularly inventive notions as if they were performances.

Shortly it became quite an all-encompassing project, engaging the attention of the officers as well as the dragons; the scant handful of aviators with good penmanship Laurence was soon forced to press into service, for the dragons began to expand upon their cherished theory quicker than he alone could take their dictation, partly out of an intellectual curiosity, and partly because they very much liked the physical representation of their work, which they insisted on having separately copied out one for each of them, and treated in much the same way that Temeraire treated his much-beloved jewels.

"I will make you a handsome edition of it, bound up like that nice book which you see Laurence reads from," Laurence found Catherine saying to Lily, shortly, "if only you will eat something more every day: here, a few more bites of this tunny," a bribery which succeeded where almost all else had failed.

"Well, perhaps a little more," Lily said, with a heroic air, adding, "and may it have gold hinges, too, like that one?"

All this society Laurence might have enjoyed, though a little ashamed to find himself preferring what he could not in justice call anything but a very ramshackle way of going on. But for all their courage and good humor, improved by the interest of the sea-voyage, the dragons still coughed their lungs away little by little. What would have otherwise seemed a pleasure-cruise carried on under a ceaseless pall, where each morning the aviators came on the deck and put their crews to work washing away the bloodstained relics of the night's misery, and each night lay in their cabins trying to sleep to the rattling wet accompaniment of the slow, weary hacking above. All their noise and gaiety had a forced and hectic edge, defiance of fear as much as real pleasure: fiddling as Rome burned.

The sentiment was not confined to the aviators, either. Riley might have had other excuses besides the political for preferring not to have Reverend Erasmus aboard, for the ship was already loaded besides him with a large number of passengers, most of them forced upon Riley by influence with the Admiralty, and well-found in the article of luggage. Some number departed at Madeira, to take other ship for the West Indies or Halifax from there, but others were bound for the Cape as settlers, and still others going on to India: an uneasy migration driven, Laurence was forced to suspect, little though he liked to think so ill of perfect strangers, by a dread of invasion.

He had some evidence for his suspicion; the passengers, when he chanced to overhear them speaking as they took the air on the windward side of the quarterdeck, spoke wistfully amongst themselves of the airy chances of peace, and pronounced Bonaparte's name with fear. There was little direct communication, separated as the dragondeck was, nor did the passengers make much effort to become friendly, but on a few occasions, Reverend Erasmus joined Laurence for dinner. Erasmus did not carry tales, of course, but asked, "Captain, is it your opinion that invasion is a settled certainty?" with a curiosity which to Laurence spoke of its being a topic much discussed among the passengers with whom they ordinarily dined.

"I must call it settled that Bonaparte would like to *try*," Laurence said, "and being a tyrant he may do as he likes with his own army. But if he is so outrageously bold as to make a second attempt where the first failed so thoroughly, I have every confidence he will be pushed off once again," a patriotic exaggeration; but he had no notion of disparaging their chances publicly.

"I am glad to hear you say so," Erasmus said, and added after a moment thoughtfully, "It must be a confirmation of the doctrine of original sin, I think, that all the noble promise of liberty and brotherhood which the revolution in France first brought up to light should have so quickly been drowned by blood and treasure. Man begins in corruption, and cannot achieve grace striving only for victory over the injustices of the world, without striving also for God, and obeying His commandments."

Laurence a little awkwardly offered Erasmus the dish of stewed plums, in lieu of an agreement which should have felt dishonest; he was uneasily aware that he had not heard services for the better part of a year; barring the Sunday services on board, where Mr. Britten, the ship's official chaplain, droned through his sermon with a notable lack of either inspiration or sobriety: and for those, Laurence had often to sit beside Temeraire, to keep him from interrupting.

"Do you suppose, sir," Laurence ventured instead to ask, "that dragons are subject to original sin?" This question had from time to time preyed upon him; he had quite failed to interest Temeraire in the Bible. Scripture rather induced the dragon to pursue such thoroughly blasphemous lines of questioning that Laurence had very soon given it up entirely, from a superstitious feeling that this would only invite greater disaster.

Erasmus considered, and gave it as his opinion that

they were not, "For surely the Bible would mention it, if any had eaten of the fruit besides Adam and Eve; and though resembling the serpent in some particulars, the Lord said unto the serpent that upon its belly it should go, whereas dragons are as creatures of the air, and cannot be considered under the same interdiction," he added convincingly, so it was with a heart lightened that Laurence could return to the deck that evening, to once again try and persuade Temeraire to take a little more to eat.

Though Temeraire had not taken sick, he grew limp and faded in sympathy with the other dragons' illness, and, ashamed of his appetite when his companions could not share in it, began to disdain his food. Laurence coaxed and cajoled with little effect, until Gong Su came up to him on deck and in flowery Chinese of which Laurence understood one word in six, but Temeraire certainly followed entire, offered his resignation in shame that his cooking was no longer acceptable. He dwelt at elaborate length upon the stain on his honor and that of his teacher and his family, which he would never be able to repair, and declared his intentions to somehow return home at the nearest opportunity, so that he might remove himself from the scene of failure.

"But it is very good, I promise, only I am not hungry just now," Temeraire protested, which Gong Su refused to credit as anything but a polite excuse, and added, "Good cooking ought to make you hungry, even if you are not!"

"But I *am*, only—" Temeraire finally admitted, and looked sadly at his sleeping companions, and sighed when Laurence gently said, "My dear, you do them no good by starving yourself, and indeed some harm; you must be at your full strength and healthy when we reach the Cape."

"Yes, but it feels quite wrong, to be eating and eating when everyone else has stopped and gone to sleep; it feels as though I am sneaking food, behind their backs, which they do not know about," Temeraire said, a perplexing way of viewing the situation, as he had never shown the least compunction about out-eating his companions while they were awake, or jealously guarding his own meals from the attention of other dragons. But after this admission, they gave him his food in smaller portions throughout the day, while the other dragons were wakeful; and Temeraire exhibited no more very extreme reluctance, even though the others still refused any more food themselves.

But he was not happy with their situation, any more than was Laurence; and grew still less so as they traveled southward, Riley's caution keeping them near the shore. They did not put in at Cape Coast, or at Louanda or Benguela; and from a distance these ports looked gaily enough, full of white sails clustering together. But there was reminder enough at hand of their grim commerce, the ocean being full of sharks that came eagerly leaping to the ship's wake, trained like dogs by the common passage of slave-ships to and from those harbors.

"What city is that?" Mrs. Erasmus asked him abruptly. She had come to take the air with her daughters, who were parading themselves decorously back and forth under a shared parasol, for once unattended by their mother.

"Benguela," Laurence said, surprised to be addressed; in nearly two months of sailing she had never spoken to him direct before. She was never forward on any occasion, but rather in the habit of keeping her head bowed and her voice low; her English still heavily accented with Portuguese when she used it at all. He knew from Erasmus that she had gained her manumission only a little while before her marriage; not through the indulgence of her master but by his ill-fortune. That gentleman, a landowner from Brazil, had gone on business to France, passenger on a merchant ship taken in the Atlantic; she and his other slaves had been made free, when the prize had been brought in to Portsmouth.

She was drawn up very tall and straight, both her hands gripping the rail, though she had excellent sea-legs and scarcely needed the support; and she stood a long time looking there, even after the little girls had grown tired of their promenade and abandoned both parasol and decorum to go scrambling over the ropes with Emily and Dyer.

A great many slave-ships went to Brazil from Benguela, Laurence recalled; he did not ask her, but offered her instead his arm to go below again, when at last she turned away, and some refreshment. She refused both, with only a shake of her head, and called her children back to order with a quick low word; they left off their game, abashed, and she took them down below.

Past Benguela there were no more slave ports, at least; both from the hostility of the natives to the trade, and the inhospitable coastline, but the oppressive atmosphere on board was no less. Together Laurence and Temeraire often went aloft to escape, flying in closer to shore than Riley would risk the *Allegiance* and pacing her from there, so they might watch the African coastline wear away: here impenetrably forested, here spilling yellow rock and yellow sand into the ocean, here the shore crammed with lazy seals; then the long stretch of endless orange desert, bound regularly in thick banks of fog, which made the sailors wary. Almost hourly the officer of the watch called for them to take soundings of the ocean floor, voices muffled and oddly far-away in the mist. Very occasionally a few black men might be glimpsed on shore, observing them in turn with wary attention; but for the most part there was only silence, watchful silence, except for the shrieking of birds.

"Laurence, surely we can reach Capetown from here, quicker than the ship can go," Temeraire said at last, grown weary of the oppressive atmosphere. They were still nearly a month's sailing from that port, however, and the country too dangerous to risk a long overland passage. The interior of the continent was notoriously impenetrable and savage, and had without a trace swallowed whole parties of men; more than one courier-dragon tempted off the coastal route had likewise vanished. But the suggestion appealed, with its prospects of quitting sooner the unhappy conditions of the voyage, and advancing more quickly the crucial research which was their purpose.

Laurence persuaded himself that he should not be derelict in going on early, once they should be near enough to make the flight one which might be accomplished in a day, if a strenuous one. With this incentive, Temeraire was easily induced to eat properly and go for long and uninteresting circular flights around the ship, to build up his strength; and no one else raised objection to their departure. "If you are quite sure you will reach in safety," Catherine said, with only the most obligatory reluctance; none of the aviators could help but share the urgent desire to have the work begun, now they were so close.

"You shall of course do as you please," Riley said, when officially informed, without looking Laurence in the face; and bent his head down again over his maps to pretend to be making calculations: a pretense which succeeded not at all, Laurence being perfectly aware that Riley could not do so much as a sum in his head without scratching it out on paper.

"I will not take all the crew," Laurence told Ferris, who looked dismal, but even he did not protest overmuch. Keynes and Dorset would come, of course, and Gong Su: the cooks in the employ of Prince Yongxing, on their previous visit, had experimented with great enthusiasm on the local produce, which thus formed one of the surgeons' foremost hopes of reproducing the cure.

"Do you suppose you can prepare these ingredients in the same way as they might have used?" Laurence asked Gong Su.

"I am not an Imperial chef!" Gong Su protested, and to Laurence's dismay explained that the style of cooking in the south of China, whence he hailed, was entirely different. "I will try my poor best, but it is not to be compared; although northern cooking is not very good usually," he added, in a burst of parochialism.

Roland and Dyer came to be assistants to him, and run and fetch in the markets, their slight weight a negligible burden; for the rest, Laurence packed aboard a chest of gold, and took little more baggage than his sword and pistols and a pair of clean shirts and stockings. "I do not feel the weight at all; I am sure I could fly for days," Temeraire said, grown still more urgent: Laurence had forced himself to let caution keep them back a full week, so they were now less than two hundred miles distant: still a desperately long single day's flight, but not an impossible one.

"If the weather holds until morning," Laurence said.

One final invitation he made, which he did not think would be accepted, to Reverend Erasmus. "Captain Berkley begs me inform you he would be happy if you continued aboard as his guests," Laurence said, rather more elegantly than Berkley's, "Yes, of course. Damned formal nonsense; we are not going to put them overboard, are we?" could be said to have deserved. "But of course you are my personal guests, and welcome to join me, if you would prefer it."

"Hannah, perhaps you would rather not?" Erasmus said, looking to his wife.

She lifted her head from her small text on the native language, whose phrases she was forming silently with her mouth. "I do not mind," she said; and indeed climbed up to Temeraire's back without any sign of alarm, settling the girls around her and chiding them firmly for their own anxiety.

"We will see you in Capetown," Laurence told Ferris, and saluted Harcourt; with one grateful leap they were gone, flying and flying over clean ocean, with a good fresh wind at their heels.

A day and a night of flying had seen them coming in over the bay at dawn: the flat-topped fortress wall of Table Mount standing dusty and golden behind the city, light spilling onto the striated rock face and the smaller jagged sentinel peaks to either side. The bustling town crammed full the crescent slice of level ground at the base of the slope, with the Castle of Good Hope at its heart upon the shore, its outer walls forming a star-shape from above with the butter-yellow pentagon of the fort nested within, gleaming in the early morning as her cannon fired the welcoming salute to leeward.

The parade grounds where Temeraire was lodged were beside the castle, only a few dragon-lengths from where the ocean came grumbling onto the sandy beach: a distance inconvenient when the wind was blowing too strongly at high tide, but which otherwise made a pleasant relief against the summer heat. Although the courtyard enclosed within the fort itself was large enough to house a few dragons in times of emergency, it would not have made a comfortable situation, either for the soldiers stationed in the castle barracks, or for Temeraire; and happily, the grounds had been much improved since their last visit breaking their journey to China. While the couriers no longer flew routes this far south, too remote for their failing strength, a fast frigate had been sent on ahead of the *Allegiance* with dispatches to warn the acting-governor, Lieutenant-General Grey, both of their arrival and, secretly, of their urgent purpose. He had widened the grounds to house all the formation, and put up a low fence around.

"I am not afraid you will be pestered; but it may keep away prying eyes, and stifle some of this damned noise," he said to Laurence, referring to the protests of the colonists at their arrival. "It is just as well that you have come on ahead: it will give them some time to get over the notion, before we have seven dragons all in a lump. The way they wail, you would think they had never heard of a formation at all."

Grey had himself reached the Cape only in January; he was the lieutenant-governor, and would soon be superceded by the arrival of the Earl of Caledon, so that his position, with all the awkwardness of a temporary situation, lacked a certain degree of authority; and he was much beset by cares not a little increased by their arrival. The townspeople disliked the British occupation, and the settlers, who had established their farms and estates farther out into the countryside and down the coast, despised it and indeed anything in the shape of government that would have interfered with their independence, which they considered dearly and sufficiently paid for by the risk which they ran, in pressing the frontier into the wild interior of the continent.

The advent of a formation of dragons was viewed by them all with the deepest suspicion, especially as they were not to be permitted to know the real purpose. Thanks to much slave labor cheaply acquired, in the earlier years of the colony, the settlers had come to disdain manual labor for themselves and their families; and their farms and vineyards and herds had expanded to take advantage of the many hands which they could forcibly put to the work. Slaves were not exported from the Cape; they wanted rather more slaves than they could get: Malay by preference, or purchased from West Africa, but not disdaining, either, the unhappy servitude of the native Khoi tribesmen, who if they were not precisely *slaves* were very little less constrained, and their wages unworthy of the term.

Having thus arranged to be outnumbered, the colonists now exerted themselves to maintain the serenity of their establishments by harsh restrictions and an absolutely free hand with punishment. A resentment yet lingered that under the previous British government, the torture of slaves had been forbidden; on the further outskirts of the town might yet be observed the barbaric custom of leaving the corpse of a hanged slave upon his gibbet, as an illustrative example to his fellows of the cost of disobedience. The colonists were well informed, also, of the campaign against the trade, which they viewed with indignation as likely to cut them off from additional supply; and Lord Allendale's name was not unknown to them as a mover of the cause.

"And if that were not enough," Grey said tiredly, when they had been in residence a few days, "you brought this damned missionary with you. Now half the town thinks the slave trade has been abolished, the other half that their slaves are all to be set free at once and given license to murder them in their beds; and all are certain you are here to enforce it. I must ask you to present me to the fellow; he must be warned to keep more quiet. It is a miracle he has not been already stabbed in the street."

Erasmus and his wife had taken over a small establishment of the London Missionary Society, lately abandoned by the death of its previous tenant, a victim of malarial fevers, and in far from an ordered state. There was neither a school nor a church building, yet, only a mortally plain little house, graced by a few depressed and straggling trees, and a bare plot of land around it meant for a vegetable-garden, where Mrs. Erasmus was presently laboring in the company of her daughters and several of the young native women, who were being shown how to stake tomato plants.

She stood up when Laurence and Grey came into view, and with a quiet word left the girls at work while she led the two of them inside the house: built in the Dutch style, the walls made of thick clay, with broad wooden beams exposed above supporting the thatched roof. The windows and door all stood open to let air the smell of fresh whitewash; inside the house was only a single long room, divided into three, and Erasmus was seated in the midst of a dozen native boys scattered around on the floor, showing them the letters of the alphabet upon a slate.

He rose to greet them and sent the boys outside to play, an eruption of gleeful yelling drifting in directly they had gone spilling out into the street, and Mrs. Erasmus disappeared into the kitchen, with a clatter of kettle and pot.

"You are very advanced, sir, for three-days' residence," Grey said, looking after the horde of boys in some dismay.

"There is a great thirst for learning, and for the Gospel, too," Erasmus said, with pardonable satisfaction. "Their parents come at night, after they have finished working in the fields, and we have already had our first service."

He invited them to sit: but as there were only two chairs, it would have made an awkward division, and they remained standing. "I will come at once to the point," Grey said. "There have been, I am afraid, certain complaints made." He paused, and repeated, "Certain complaints" uneasily, though Erasmus had said nothing. "You understand, sir, we have but lately taken the colony, and the settlers here are a difficult lot. They have made their own farms, and estates, and with some justice consider themselves entitled to be masters of their own fate. There is some sentiment—in short," he said abruptly, "you would do very well to moderate your activity. You need not perhaps have so many students— take three or four, most promising; let the rest return to work. I am informed the labor of the students is by no means easily spared," he added weakly.

Erasmus listened, saying nothing, until Grey had done; then he said, "Sir, I appreciate your position: it is a difficult one. I am very sorry I cannot oblige you."

Grey waited, but Erasmus said nothing more whatsoever, offering no ground for negotiation. Grey looked at Laurence, a little helplessly, then turning back said, "Sir, I will be frank; I am by no means confident of your continued safety, if you persist. I cannot assure it."

"I did not come to be safe, but to bring the word of God," Erasmus said, smiling and immovable, and his wife brought in the tea-tray.

"Madam," Grey said to her, as she poured the cups at the table, "I entreat you to use your influence; I beg you to consider the safety of your children." She raised her head abruptly; the kerchief which she had been wearing outside to work had slipped, and by pulling her hair back away from her face revealed a dull scarred brand upon her forehead, the initials of a former owner blurred but legible still, and superimposed on an older tattooed marking, of abstract pattern.

She looked at her husband; he said gently, "We will trust in God, Hannah, and in His will." She nodded and made Grey no direct answer, but went silently back outside to the garden.

There was of course nothing more to be said; Grey sighed, when they had taken their leave, and said dismally, "I suppose I must put a guard upon the house."

A heavy moist wind was blowing from the south-east, draping the Table Mount in a blanket of clouds; but it abated that evening, and the *Allegiance* was sighted the next afternoon by the castle lookout, heralded by the fire of the signal-guns. The atmosphere of suspicion and hostility was a settled thing by then, throughout the town; although sentiments less bitter would have sufficed to make her arrival unsettling for the inhabitants.

Laurence watched her come in, by Grey's invitation, from a pleasant cool antechamber set atop the castle, and seeing her from this unfamiliar and reversed direction was struck by the overwhelming impression of terrible force: not only the sheer vastness of her size, but the hollow eyes of her brute armament of thirty-two-pounders, glaring angrily out of portholes, and what seemed at this distance a veritable horde of dragons coiled upon her deck, uncountable for their lying so intertwined that their heads and tails could not quite be separated one from another.

She advanced slowly into harbor, dwarfing all the shipping in the port into insignificance, and a kind of grim silence descended upon the town as she fired her salute to the fort: a rolling thunder of guns that echoed back from the face of the mountain, and settled gently upon the town like a fog. Laurence could taste the powder-smoke at the back of his mouth. The women and children had vanished from the streets by the time her anchors were let plunging down.

It was dreadful to see how little they had truly to fear, when Laurence went down to the shore and had himself rowed across to aid with the maneuvers under way to get the dragons transferred off the deck. The long cramped journey had stiffened them all badly, and though the *Allegiance* had made good time, still every day of the two months and more had eaten steadily away at their strength. The castle was established only steps from the sandy beach, the parade grounds beside it, but even this short flight wearied them now.

Nitidus and Dulcia, the smallest, came across first, to give the others more room; they drew deep breaths and lunged valiantly off the deck, their short wings beating sluggish and slow, and giving them very little lift, so that their bellies nearly scraped the top of the low fence around the parade grounds; they landed heavily and sank down into a heap on the warm ground without even folding their wings back. Messoria and Immortalis then dragged themselves up so wearily to their feet that Temeraire, who was watching anxiously from the grounds, called out, "Pray wait, and I will come and carry you in," and ferried them one after another upon his back, heedless of the small scrapes and scratches which he took from their claws, as they clutched at him for balance.

Lily nosed Maximus gently, on the deck. "Yes, go on, I will be there in a moment," he said sleepily, without opening his eyes; she gave a dissatisfied rumble of concern.

"We will get him across, never fear," Harcourt said coaxingly; and at last Lily was persuaded to submit to their precautionary arrangements for her own transfer: a muzzle had to be fitted over her head, from which a large metal platter was suspended beneath her jaws, and this covered with more of the oiled sand.

Riley had come to see them off; Harcourt turned to him and held out her hand, saying, "Thank you, Tom; I hope we will be coming back across soon, and you will visit us on land." He took her hand in an awkward sideways grip and bowed over it, somewhere between saluting her and shaking her hand, and backed away stiffly; he still avoided looking at Laurence at all.

Harcourt put her boot on the railing and jumped up to Lily's back; she took hold of the harness to steady it, and Lily unfurled her great wings, the feature from which the breed took its name: rippled along the edges in narrow bands of black and white with the dark blue of her body shading across their length to a brilliant deep orange the color of old marmalade; they shone iridescent in the sun. Fully extended, they made double the length of her entire body, and once she had fairly launched herself aloft, she scarcely needed to beat them, but glided stately along without great exertion.

They managed the flight across without spilling too much of the sand, or dripping acid upon the castle battlements or the dock; and then there was only Maximus left upon the deck. Berkley spoke to him quietly, and with a great heaving sigh the enormous Regal Copper pushed himself up to his feet, the *Allegiance* herself rocking a little in the water. He took two slow gouty steps to the edge of the dragondeck and sighed again; his shoulder-muscles creaked as he tried his wings, and then let them sink against his back again; his head drooped.

"I could try," Temeraire offered, calling from shore; quite impractically: Maximus still made almost two of him by weight.

"I am sure I can manage it," Maximus said hoarsely, then bent his head and coughed a while, and spat more greenish phlegm out over the side. He did not move.

Temeraire's tail was lashing at the air, and then with an air of decision he plunged into the surf and came swimming out to them instead. He reared up with his forelegs on the edge of the ship and thrust his head up over the railing to say, "It is not very far: pray come in the water. I am sure together we can swim to the shore."

Berkley looked at Keynes, who said, "A little sea-bathing can do no harm, I expect; and perhaps even some good. It is warm enough in all conscience, and we will have sun another four hours at this time of year, to dry him off."

"Well, then, into the water with you," Berkley said, gruffly, patting Maximus's side, and stepping back. Crouching down awkwardly, Maximus plunged forequarters-first into the ocean; the massive anchor-cables complained with deep voices as the *Allegiance* recoiled from the force of his leap, and ten-foot ripples swelled up and went shuddering away from him to nearly overturn some of the unsuspecting slighter vessels riding at anchor in the bay.

Maximus shook water from his head, bobbing up and down, and paddled a few strokes along before stopping, sagging in the water; the buoyancy of the air-sacs kept him afloat, but he listed alarmingly.

"Lean against me, and we shall go together," Temeraire said, swimming up to his side to brace him up; and little by little they progressed towards the shore until the ocean floor came up abruptly to meet them, clouds of white sand stirring up like smoke, and Maximus could stop to rest, half-submerged yet, with the waves lapping against his sides.

"It is pleasant in the water," he said, despite another fit of coughing. "I do not feel so tired here," but he had still to be got out and onto the shore: no little task, and he managed it only in slow easy stages, with all the assistance which Temeraire and the oncoming tide could offer, crawling the final dozen yards nearly on his belly.

Here they let him rest, and brought him the choicest cuts from the dinner which Gong Su had spent the day preparing to tempt the dragons' appetites after their exertion: local cattle, fat and tender, spit-roasted with a crust of pepper and salt pressed into their flesh, as a flavoring strong enough to overcome the dulling effect of the illness on the dragons' senses, and stuffed with their own stewed tripes.

Maximus ate a little, drank a few swallows of the water which they carried out to him in a large tub, and afterwards fell back into sluggish torpor, coughing, and slept the night through on shore, with the ocean still coming in and his tail riding up on the waves like a tethered boat. Only in the cool early hours of the morning did they get him the rest of the way to the parade grounds, and there settled him in the best place at its edge beneath the young stand of camphor trees, where he might have a little shade as well as sun, and very near the well which had been sunk to easily bring them water.

Berkley saw him established, and then took off his hat and went to the water trough, to duck his head and bring a couple of cupped handfuls to his mouth to drink, and wipe his red and sweating face. "It is a good place," he said, his head bent, "a good place; he will be comfortable here—" and ending abruptly went inside the castle, where they breakfasted together in silence. They did not discuss the matter, but no discussion was required; they all knew Maximus would not leave again, without a cure, and they had brought him otherwise to his grave.

Chapter 7

❧

ABOARD, THEY HAD counted every day; they had hurried, they had fretted; now they were arrived and could only sit and wait, while the surgeons went through their fastidious experiments, and refused to give any opinion whatsoever. More outrageous local supplies were brought to them in succession, presented to Temeraire, occasionally tried on one of the sick dragons, and discarded again. This proceeded without any sign of useful effect, and on one unfortunate occasion again distressed Temeraire's digestive system, so that the shared dragon-midden took on a very unpleasant quality, and had at once to be filled in and a new one dug. The old one promptly sprang up a thick carpet of grass and a bright pink weedy flower, which to their great exasperation could not be rooted out, and attracted a species of wasps viciously jealous of their territory.

Laurence did not say so, but it was his private opinion that all this experimentation was only half-hearted, and meant to occupy their attention while Keynes waited for the climate to do its work; though Dorset made careful notes of each trial in his regular hand, going from one dragon to the next in rounds thrice daily, and inquiring with heartless indifference how much the patient had coughed since the last inquiry, what pains he suffered, how he ate; this last was never much.

At the close of the first week, Dorset finished his latest interrogation of Captain Warren, on the condition of Nitidus, and shut his book and went and spoke quietly with Keynes and the other surgeons. "I suppose they are all prodigious clever, but if they keep on with these secret councils, and telling us nothing, I will begin to want to push their noses in for them," Warren said, coming to join the rest of them at the card-table, which had been set up under a pavilion in the middle of the grounds. The game was mostly a polite fiction to occupy the days: they did not have much attention to the cards at any time, and now had none, all of them instead watching the surgeons as they huddled together in deep discussion.

Keynes evaded them skillfully for two more days, and finally cornered into giving some report said crabbily, "It is too soon to tell," but admitted that they had seen some improvement, so far as they could determine merely from the climate: the dragons had shown some resurrection of appetite and energy, and they coughed less.

"It will be no joke, ferrying all the Corps down here," Little said quietly, after their first early jubilation. "How many transports have we, in all?"

"Seven, I think, if the *Lyonesse* is out of dry-dock," Laurence said.

There was a pause; then he added strongly, "But consider, we scarcely need a ship of a hundred guns only to move dragons; transports are meant foremost to deliver them to the front," this being not entirely a misrepresentation, but only because there was little cause other than war to go to the difficulty and expense of shifting dragons about. "We can put them on barges at Gibraltar instead, and send them along the coast, with an escort of frigates to keep the French off them."

It sounded well enough, but they all knew that even if not inherently impractical, still such an operation was wholly unlikely to be carried out on the scale of the entire Corps. They might return with the dragons of their own formation preserved, but such a cure was likely to be denied half their comrades or more. "It is better than nothing," Chenery said a little defiantly, "and more than we had; there is not a man of the Corps who would not have taken such odds, if offered him," but the odds would be unequal ones.

Longwings and Regal Coppers, heavy-combat dragons and the rarer breeds, no expense or difficulty would be spared to preserve; but for the rest—common Yellow Reapers or quick-breeding Winchesters; older dragons likely to be difficult when their captains died; the weaker or less-skilled flyers; these, a brutal political calculus would not count worth the saving, and leave to die in neglect and misery, isolated undoubtedly in the most distant quarantines which could be arranged. Their cautious satisfaction was dimmed by this shadow, and Sutton and Little took it worst; their dragons were both Yellow Reapers, and Messoria was forty. But even guilt could not extinguish all their eager hope; they slept very little that night, counting coughs instead, tallies to go into Dorset's book; and in the morning, with only a little coaxing, Nitidus was persuaded to try his wings. Laurence and Temeraire went with him and Warren, for company and in case the little Pascal's Blue should exhaust his strength; Nitidus was panting hoarsely from his mouth and coughing, now and again, as they flew.

They did not go far. The local hunger for grazing land and timber had scraped the fields and hillsides down to scrubby low grass, all the way to the base of Table

Mountain and its satellite peaks, where the slopes grew prohibitive: loose conglomerations of grey and yellow rock in stepped terraces like old rotting stone walls held together by grass and green moss, and clayey dirt for mortar. They halted there and rested on the loose scrubby ground in the shadow of the sheer cliff wall. An extensive scurrying went on in the underbrush as the small game fled from their presence, small furry creatures like brown badgers.

"It is a very strange sort of mountain," Temeraire observed, craning his head to look back and forth along the long ridge of the peak above them, sheared smooth and flat as if by a leveling knife.

"Yes; oh, very; and how hot it is," Nitidus said, meaninglessly and half-asleep, and tucked his head beneath his wing to nap. They let him sleep in the sun, and Temeraire yawned, too, and followed his example; Laurence and Warren stood together looking back down into the deep bowl of the harbor where it ran down into the ocean, the *Allegiance* a toy ship among ants at this distance. The neat geometric pentagon of the castle was drawn in yellow upon the dark earth, with the dragons small, still lumps upon the parade grounds beside it.

Warren took off his glove and rubbed the back of his hand across his brow to wipe the sweat off; he left a careless smudge. "I suppose you would go back to the Navy, if it were you?" he asked.

"If they would have me," Laurence said.

"A fellow might buy a cavalry commission, I suppose," Warren said. "There will be no shortage of soldiers needed if Bonaparte continues to have things his way; but it could hardly compare."

They were silent a while, considering the unpleasant options which would be the portion of so many men cast effectively on shore, by the death of the dragons on which they served.

"Laurence," Warren went on, after a moment, "this fellow Riley, what sort of a man is he? Ordinarily, I mean; I know you were lately both standing on your honor."

Laurence was astonished to be appealed to in such a way, but answered, "A gentleman and one of the finest officers of my acquaintance; I cannot say a word against him, personally."

He wondered very much what should have spurred the inquiry. With the *Allegiance* confined by her orders to harbor, until the dragons should once again be ready to depart, Riley had of course come to the castle and dined with General Grey on more than one occasion. Laurence had absented himself, but Catherine and the other captains had gone more often than not. Perhaps some quarrel had taken place to give rise to such a question, and Laurence hoped that perhaps Warren would elaborate. But he only nodded, and changed the subject to the likelihood that the wind would change, before their return, so Laurence's curiosity remained unsatisfied, and the question had only the effect of making him sorry afresh for the quarrel, which he now supposed should never be made up, and the termination of their friendship.

"Nitidus does seem better, does he not?" Temeraire murmured to Laurence, in confidential tones audible only to anyone within twenty feet, while they made ready to return; Laurence could answer wholeheartedly that he thought so as well, and when they returned to the parade grounds, the light-weight ate almost to his healthy standard, putting a period to two goats before he again fell asleep.

On the morrow Nitidus did not want to repeat the ex-

ercise, and Dulcia would only go half so far before dropping down to rest. "But she did for a whole one of those
oxen, a yearling calf," Chenery said, doing for a substantial glass of whiskey and water himself, "and a
damned good sign I call it; she has not eaten so much in
a sixmonth."

The next day neither of them would go, but sat down
again, almost as soon as they had been persuaded to get
up on their feet, and begged to be excused. "It is too
hot," Nitidus complained, and asked for more water;
Dulcia said more plaintively, "I would rather sleep some
more, if you please."

Keynes put a cup to her chest to listen, and straightening up shook his head. None of the others could be
stirred much beyond their sleeping places. When the tallies over which the aviators had labored were examined
closely together, the dragons did indeed cough less, but
it was not *much* less; and this benefit had been exchanged, their anxious observers soon perceived, for
listlessness and lethargy. The intense heat made the
dragons sleepy and disinclined to move, the interest of
their new surroundings having now palled, and the brief
resurgence in their appetites had evidently been spurred
only by the better eating available on shore, as compared to the late stages of the sea-journey.

"I would not have regretted it, not at all," Sutton
muttered, hunched over the table and speaking to himself, but so violently that it could not but be overheard.
"How could there be any regret, in such circumstances;
there could be none," in anguish as great as though his
guilt over the prospect of a cure for his own Messoria,
when so many others might be left to die, had been the
very cause of failure; and Little was so white and
stricken that Chenery took him into his tent, and plied
him with rum until he slept.

"The rate of progress of the disease has been slowed," Keynes said, at the close of their second week. "It is not an inconsequential benefit," he added, little consolation for their better hopes.

Laurence took Temeraire away flying, and kept him on the shore all the night, to spare his fellow captains at least briefly the contrast between Temeraire's health and that of their own dragons. He felt keenly his own portion of guilt and shame, the confused mirror of Sutton's unhappiness and Little's: he would not have contemplated trading Temeraire's health for all the rest, and though he knew his fellow-captains would understand perfectly and feel each of them the same for their own partner, in as irrational a way he felt the failure a punishment for this private selfishness.

In the morning, new sails stood in the harbor: the *Fiona,* a quick-sailing frigate, had come in during the night, with dispatches. Catherine opened them slowly, at the breakfast-table, and read off the names: Auctoritas, Prolixus, Laudabilis, Repugnatis; gone since the new year.

Laurence, too, had a letter, from his mother:

All is desolation; we are done, for at least another year, and likely more, if the Government should fall again. The Motion was carried in the Commons; the Lords again defeated it, despite everything which could be done, and a most extraordinary Speech, by Mr. Wilberforce, which should have moved the Possessor of any Soul deserving of the name. The Newspapers at least are with us, and speak with all the Outrage merited by so disgusting an Event: the *Times* writes, "Those Nay-sayers who give no Thought to the Future may sleep easy this Night; the others must try if they can to find Rest, in the sure Knowledge that they have laid up a Store of Misery and Sorrow, which they shall be asked to repay, if not in this World, then in that To Come," only a just Reproach . . .

He folded it and put it aside in his coat pocket; he had no heart to read further, and they left the dining room a silent party.

The castle barracks were large enough to house a larger party than they made, but with the disease marching implacable along, the captains by silent agreement preferred to stay closer by their sick beasts. The other officers and men not wishing to be outdone, a small battalion of tents and pavilions sprang up about the grounds, where they most of them spent their days and nights, barring the infrequent rain. All the better to discourage the occasional invasion of the local children, who remembered Temeraire's last visit of a year ago enough to have lost some of their fear; they had now formed the game of working one another up, until one, challenged past the point of endurance, would make a mad flurrying dash through the parade grounds among the sleeping dragons, before fleeing back out again to receive the congratulations of his peers.

These escalating adventures Sutton quelled for good one afternoon, when a boy dashing in slapped his hand against Messoria's side, and startled her out of a rare sound sleep. She reared up her head into snorting wakefulness, and the guilty culprit fell over into the dust, scuttling crab-like backwards on hands and feet and rump in his alarm, much greater than hers.

Sutton rose from the card-table and went over to take the boy by the arm, heaving him up to his feet. "Bring me a switch, Alden," he said to his runner, and leading the intruder stumbling out of the grounds, applied himself with vigor, while the other children scattered and ran a little distance away, peeking out from behind the bushes. At length the unlucky boy's howls faded to whimpering sobs, and Sutton returned to the table. "I beg your pardon, gentlemen," he said, and they resumed their desultory play; there were no more incursions that day.

But Laurence woke shortly after dawn, the subsequent morning, and went out of his own tent to find a loud squabbling at their gates, two knots of older children wrestling and kicking at each other with a polyglot confusion of yelling: a handful of Malay and scruffy Dutch boys together, and against them a smaller band of the black natives of the Cape, the Khoi, although previously the two groups had all been equal offenders together. Unhappily their quarrel had roused the dragons, who thus began an hour early their morning bouts of coughing; Maximus, who had suffered badly during the night, gave a heavy sighing groan. Sutton came rushing out of his tent in a mottled rage, and Berkley would have set among the lot of them with the flat of his sword, if Lieutenant Ferris had not thrown himself in the way, his arms outspread, as Emily and Dyer scrambled out from the dusty melee.

"We did not mean to", she said, muffled by the hand with which she tried to stanch her bloodied nose, "only they both brought some"; by some evil genius, the two parties had at the same time after weeks of searching finally uncovered some of the mushroom. Now the rival bands were squabbling over their claim to be the first to present the enormous mushroom caps, two feet and more across, and stinking even in their natural state to high Heaven.

"Lieutenant Ferris, let us have a little order, if you please," Laurence said, raising his voice, "and let them know they will all of them be paid: there is not the least need for this fuss."

Despite attempts to convey this reassurance, it took some time to drag apart the angry combatants, who if they did not speak one another's language certainly understood the salient phrases which were being exchanged, at least well enough to keep their tempers fired up, and who kicked and swung their arms at each other even when hauled apart by main force. They stopped abruptly, however: Temeraire, having woken up also, put his head over the low fence to snuffle with appreciation at the caps, left abandoned by both sides in the grass while they attempted to settle their quarrel by might at arms.

"Ah, mm," said Temeraire, and licked his chops; in spite of their earlier bravado, the boys did not quite dare to run at him and snatch them away from his jaws, but they all joined into a general cry of protest, seeing themselves on the verge of being robbed, and as a consequence were at last convinced to settle down and accept their payment, counted out in gold coins with precisely equal amounts on both sides.

The Dutch-and-Malay contingent were inclined to grumble, as theirs had been the larger specimen, with three separate caps arranged upon a single stem, as compared to the two upon the mushroom brought by the Khoi, but a speaking glare from Sutton silenced them all. "Bring us some more, and you shall be paid again," Laurence said, but this produced discouraged looks rather than hope, and they looked at his closed-up purse a little resentfully before they scattered away, to quarrel now amongst themselves over the division of spoils.

"They cannot be edible?" Catherine said doubtfully, in a stifled voice, her handkerchief pressed over her mouth as she examined the things: growths more than proper mushrooms, lopsided and bulging oddly, a pallid fish-belly white irregularly spotted with brown.

But Temeraire said, "Certainly I remember these; they were very tasty," and only regretfully let Gong Su carry the mushrooms away, which he did by holding them at arm's-length, gingerly, with two very long sticks.

Having learnt from their earlier experience, they set up the cauldron out of doors instead of within the castle kitchens, Gong Su directing the crews to lay a substantial bonfire underneath the big iron pot, suspended from stakes, with a ladder beside it so he might stir from afar with a long-handled wooden ladle. "Perhaps the red pepper-corns," Temeraire offered, "or maybe the green; I do not quite remember," he said apologetically, as Gong Su consulted his spice-box at length in attempts to reproduce the former recipe.

Keynes shrugged and said, "Stew the thing and have done; if we must rely on your reproducing some trick of spicing invented a year ago by five cooks, we may as well go back to England now."

They stewed it all the morning, Temeraire bending over the pot, sniffing at the bouquet as critically as any drinker of wine and making further suggestions: until at last he licked up a taste from the rim of the cauldron and pronounced it a success, "Or at least, it seems to me familiar; and it is very good," he added, to an audience of none: they had all been driven away to the edge of the clearing, choking, and barely heard him. Poor Catherine had been taken violently ill, and was still retching behind a bush.

They covered their noses and carried Maximus the posset, which he seemed to enjoy, even stirring himself so far as to put a talon inside the cauldron to tip it over, so he might lick out the last scrapings. After an initial somnolence, it put him in a thoroughly good mood, so that he roused up and even ate all of the tender young kid which Berkley had acquired for his dinner more in hope than in expectation, and asked for more; though he fell asleep again before this could be arranged.

Berkley would have woken him to feed him another goat, and his own surgeon Gaiters agreed; but Dorset took the strongest exception and would have denied him even the first, on the grounds that the digestive processes might interfere with the effect of the posset. This shortly devolved into an argument, as violent as hissing whispers could make it, until, Keynes said finally, "Let him sleep," overruling both, "but henceforth we will feed him as much as he can eat, after each dose; the importance of restoring his weight cannot be overstated, to the cause of his general preservation. Dulcia is better-fleshed: we will try her on the posset tomorrow as well, without food."

"I ate it with some oxen; or perhaps some antelope," Temeraire said reminiscently, nosing a little sadly at the empty pot. "There was some very nice fat, I remember that particularly, the fat with the mushroom sauce; so perhaps it was the oxen after all," the local breed possessing a queer fatty shoulder-hump over the forequarters.

This single meal had been all Temeraire's prior experience, but Keynes had divided their meager sample, and beginning with the following morning, Maximus and Dulcia were fed upon it three days in succession, until all the supply was gone. As Laurence remembered it, the concoction had made Temeraire mostly drowsy, and so Maximus became, but on the third day Dulcia alarmed them all by turning unexpectedly manic with excitement on the repeated dose, and nearly insisting on going for a long hectic flight, quite likely beyond her strength, and at the least sure not to be beneficial to her health.

"I can, I am well, I am well!" she cried, her wings fanning at the air; and she went hopping about the parade grounds evasively on her back legs with the surgeons chasing after in attempts to calm her. Chenery was of no use: he had spent the intervening days since the failure of their first hopes keeping himself and Captain Little half-drunk at all times, and in defiance of all the pessimism which Keynes could inflict would happily have thrown himself aboard and gone.

Dulcia was finally persuaded not to go flying off, with the temptation of a couple of lambs dressed hastily by Gong Su with some of the peppery local seed-pods which Temeraire liked; no one suggested she should not be allowed to eat, this time, and she devoured them so readily as to spray bits of meat around the feeding grounds, though ordinarily a rather delicate eater.

Temeraire watched her enviously; not only was he not allowed more than a taste of the posset itself, which he so enjoyed, but his belly was still inclined to be delicate after his excessive adventuring; so that Keynes had placed him on a strict and uninteresting diet of plain-roasted meat which his palate now disdained. "Well, at least we have found the cure, then, surely?"

Dulcia, having finished her repast, fell down asleep and began at once snoring loudly, with a thin wheezing whine on the exhale: nevertheless an improvement, as she had only lately been perfectly unable to breathe save through her mouth. Keynes came over and sat down heavily on the log beside Laurence, mopping his sweating red face with a kerchief, and said disgruntled, "Enough, enough of this casting ourselves into alt; have none of you learnt your lesson? The lungs are by no means clear."

A heavy bank of clouds blew in during the night, so they all woke to a steady dripping grey rain and clammy wet ground, the air still unpleasantly hot and clinging damply to the skin like sweat. Dulcia was worse again, drooping and tired after her previous day's cavorting, and the dragons were all of them more inclined to sneeze than ever; even Temeraire sighed and shivered, trying to get more of the rain off his hide and out of the hollows of bone and muscle where it collected. "I do miss China," he said, picking unhappily at his wet dinner; Gong Su had been unable to sear the antelope carcass properly.

"It must be something else; we will find it, Laurence," Catherine said, giving him his coffee-cup at the breakfast table inside the castle. Laurence accepted it mechanically and sat down among the rest of them; they ate silently, only the clatter of forks and plates; no one even offered around the salt-cellar, or asked for it. Chenery, ordinarily their life and gaiety, had bruised hollows under his eyes as if he had been beaten about the face, and Berkley had not come in to breakfast at all.

Keynes came in stamping his feet clear of mud, his coat sodden with rain and traces of whitish mucus, and said heavily, "Very well: we must have more of the thing." They looked at him, made uncomprehending by his tone, and he glared back ferociously before he admitted with reluctance, "Maximus can breathe again," and sent them all running for the door.

Keynes disliked greatly giving them even this much hope, and resisted all their demands for more; but they could stand by Maximus's head and hear for themselves the slow wheeze of air through his nostrils, and the same for Dulcia also. The two of them yet coughed and coughed and coughed, but the aviators all agreed amongst themselves that the tenor of the sound was entirely altered: a salutary and productive cough, and not the wet terrible lung-rattle which did not end; or so they contrived to persuade one another.

Dorset still made his daily implacable notations, however, and the surgeons continued with the other experiments: a sort of custard made out of green bananas and cocoanut meat was offered to Lily, who tasted one swallow and refused any more point-blank. Messoria was persuaded to lie curled on one side and a battery of candles were melted onto her skin, lit and cupped, to attempt and heat the lungs, with no apparent effect except to leave great streaks of wax upon her hide. A tiny white-haired Khoi matron appeared at their gates dragging behind her a laundry tub nearly her own size, packed to the brim with a preparation made of monkey livers; with only her broken bits of pidgin Dutch she managed to convey the impression she had brought them a sovereign remedy for any illness whatsoever. When tried on Immortalis, he ate one unenthusiastic bite and left the rest; but they had still to pay, as the remainder was quickly raided by Dulcia, who cleaned out the tub and looked for more.

Her appetite increased by leaps and bounds as the sensation of taste returned, and she coughed less daily; by the end of the fifth day almost not at all, except for an occasional hacking. Maximus coughed a while longer, but in the middle of the night towards the end of the week, they were all woken by a terrible squealing, distant shrieks of terror and fire; in a panic they burst out from the tents to discover Maximus attempting guiltily to sneak unnoticed back into the parade grounds, with as much success as was to be expected in this endeavor, and carrying in his already-bloodied jaws a spare ox. This he hurriedly swallowed down almost entire, on finding himself observed, and then pretended not to know what they were talking about, insisting he had only got up to stretch his legs and settle himself more comfortably. The track of his dragging tail, followed through dust spotted liberally with blood, led them to a nearby stable now half-collapsed, the paddock circled by the wreckage of a fence, and the owners apoplectic with rage and terror at the loss of their valuable team of oxen.

"It is just that the wind turned, and they smelled so very good," Maximus confessed finally, when confronted with the evidence, "and it has been so long since I have had a nice fresh cow, with no cooking or spices."

"Why you ridiculous lummox, as though we would not feed you whatever you liked," Berkley said, without any heat whatsoever, petting him extravagantly. "You will have two of them tomorrow."

"And let us have no more damned excuses out of you for not eating, during the day, when you will go wandering about at night like a rampaging lion to stuff your belly," Keynes added more peevishly, scruffy with his night's growth of beard and disgruntled; he had for once sought his bed at a reasonable hour, after having sat up nearly every night the week observing the dragons. "Why you did not think to tell anyone, I can scarcely understand."

"I did not like to wake Berkley: he has not been eating properly," Maximus said earnestly, at which accusation Berkley, who had indeed shed another two stone of weight since their arrival, nearly spluttered himself into a fit.

Afterwards they fed Maximus on the ordinary British diet of fresh-slaughtered cattle, occasionally sprinkled with a little salt, and he began to eat through the local herds—and their own purses—at a truly remarkable rate, until Temeraire was recruited to hunt for him northward of the Cape among the vast herds of wild buffalo; although these were not as tasty in Maximus's mournful opinion.

By then even Keynes had ceased to affect displeasure, and they were wholly engaged on a fresh, a desperate, search, for more of the wretched fungus. The local children had given up the hunt as too unlikely of return: despite every promise which Laurence and his fellow captains could make of their open and waiting purses, none seemed inclined to hazard their time on the pursuit.

"We can do it ourselves, I suppose," Catherine said doubtfully, and in the morning Laurence and Chenery took a party of men out to seek hunting grounds less picked-over, Dorset along to confirm the identity of the mushroom; the other captains would not willingly leave their sick dragons, and Berkley was plainly not up to a long traipse through wilderness, although he offered to go.

"No need, old fellow," Chenery said cheerfully, very cheerfully: since Dulcia's recovery he was little short of getting on a table to sing for joy, given the least encouragement. "We will manage all right, and you had better stay here and eat with your dragon; he is right, you need fattening up again."

He proceeded to put himself together in the most outlandish manner imaginable, leaving off his coat and tying his neckcloth around his forehead to keep sweat off his face, and arming himself with a heavy old cavalry saber from the castle armory. The resulting appearance would not have shamed a disreputable pirate, but emerging into the clearing, Chenery looked at Laurence, who was waiting for him in coat and neckcloth and hat, with an expression as dubious as the one which Laurence himself, with more tact, was repressing.

The dragons struck out north, over the bay with Table

Mountain at their backs, the *Allegiance* flashing by below; crossed the glass-green shallows and scalloped curve of pale gold-sand beach at the farther shore, and curved their course north-east and inland, towards a long solitary ridge, the Kasteelberg, which jutted out alone from the rich heartland, an outlier of the mountain ranges farther inland.

Chenery and Dulcia took the lead, signal-flags exuberantly waving, and carried them past the settlements and over a swath of thickening wilderness, setting a brisk and challenging pace that stretched Temeraire's wings and kept her ahead and out of hailing-distance until very nearly the dinner-hour; only reluctantly did she finally set down, upon a riverbank some ten miles beyond the mountain where they had meant to stop.

Laurence did not have the heart to say anything; he doubted the wisdom of going so far afield, when the mushrooms were perhaps native to the Cape, and they knew nothing of the territory into which they were flying, but Dulcia was stretching her wings out to the sun, drinking deep from the running river, great gulps traveling down her throat visibly. She cast her neck back in an ecstatic spray, and Chenery laughed like a boy and pressed his cheek against her foreleg.

"Are those lions?" Temeraire asked with interest as he folded his wings, his head cocked to listen: there was a deal of angry roaring off in the bush, not the drum-and-bassoon thunder-roll of dragons, but a deep huffed breathy noise, perhaps in protest at the invasion of their territory. "I have never seen a lion," Temeraire added, nor was likely to, so long as the lions had anything to do with the matter: however annoyed they might be, they would surely not venture anywhere in range.

"Are they very large?" Dulcia said anxiously; neither she nor Temeraire were very enthusiastic about letting the crew continue on foot into the ground cover, despite the party of riflemen which had been brought for their protection. "Perhaps you ought to stay with us."

"Pray, how are we to see any mushrooms from mid-air?" Chenery said. "You shall have a nice rest, and maybe eat something, and we will be back in a trice. We will manage quite well if we meet any lions; we have six guns with us, my dear."

"But what if there are *seven* lions," Dulcia said.

"Then we shall have to use our pistols," Chenery said to her cheerfully, showing her his own as he reloaded them fresh to give her comfort.

"I promise you, no lion will come to us to be shot," Laurence said to Temeraire. "They will run as soon as they hear the first gun, and we will fire away a flare if we need you."

"Well; so long as you are careful," Temeraire said, and settled his head on his forelegs, disconsolate.

Chenery's old saber served well to hack their way into the forest, where Dorset thought the mushroom most likely to be found in the cool and damp soil, and all the game they saw, slim antelope and birds, was at a distance and bounding away quickly: frightened away by the noise of their passage, which was incredible. The undergrowth was ferociously impenetrable, full of immense silver thornbushes, their teeth nearly three inches long and sharp as needles at the tip, treacherously buried in a wealth of green leaves. They were at all times beating down clinging vines and tearing branches, except occasionally where they broke across the trail where some large animals had trampled a path, leaving behind them trees scraped free of bark with red weeping sores like blood. But these offered only brief respite; Dorset would not let them follow the paths for long, from anxiety at meeting their creators, most likely elephants; he was in any case doubtful that they would find any of the mushroom in the open.

They were very hot and tired indeed by dinner-time, no man of them having escaped bloody scratches, and would have been wholly lost but for their compasses, when at last Dyer, who had suffered less, being still a small boy and thin, gave a cry of triumph. Throwing himself flat on his belly, he wriggled beneath another thornbush and emerged again backwards holding a specimen which had been growing against the base of a dead tree.

It was small and clotted with dirt, with two caps only, but this success at once renewed all their energy, and after giving Dyer a huzzah and sharing a glass of grog, they threw themselves again into the task and into the brush.

"How long," Chenery said, panting as he hacked away, "do you suppose it would take, for every dragon in England; if we must find them all like this—"

There was a low crackling of brush like water droplets sizzling in a skillet of hot fat, and a low coughing sound, dyspeptic, came from the other side of the choked-off shrub. "Be cautious—cautious," Dorset said, repeating the stammered word as Riggs went closer. Chenery's first lieutenant Libbley held out his hand, and Chenery gave him the sword. "There may be—"

He stopped. Libbley had worked the sword into the brush to cut away the entangling moss, and Riggs had with his hands pulled apart the branches; a massive head was regarding them thoughtfully through the empty space. It was a pebbled leathery grey, with two enormous horns in a line at the end of its snout and piggishly small black eyes, hard and shiny, its odd hatchet-shaped lip moving ruminatively as it chewed. It was not large compared to a dragon; compared to an ox or even the local buffalo it was very, and so massively built and armored that it took on an inexorable quality.

"Is it an elephant?" Riggs asked in a hushed voice, turning his head, and abruptly the thing snorted and came at them: smashing all the thicket into splinters, astonishing fast for so heavy a creature, with its head bowed forward so the horns thrust out before it as it came. There was a confused ringing clamor of yells and shouts, and Laurence had barely the presence of mind to take hold of Dyer's and Emily's collars and pull them back against the trees; groping only afterwards for his pistol, his sword. Too late: the thing had already gone crashing away madly on its set course, and not one of them had got off a shot.

"A rhinoceros," Dorset was saying calmly. "They are near-sighted, and prone to ill-temper, or so I understand from my reading. Captain Laurence, will you give me your neckcloth?"—and Laurence looked up to see Dorset working busily on Chenery's leg, a copious flow of blood pumping freely from the thigh where a thick jagged branch jutted out.

Dorset sliced open the breeches with a large catling, intended for use on the delicate layered membranes of dragon wings, maneuvering the tip deftly, and performed a skillful ligature of the pumping vein; afterwards he wrapped the neckcloth several times around the thigh. Meanwhile Laurence had directed the others in making a litter of tree-branches and their coats. "It is only the merest scratch," Chenery said vaguely, "pray do not disturb the dragons," but at the quick negative shake of Dorset's head, Laurence paid Chenery's protests no attention and fired away the blue gun, sending up the flare.

"Only lie easy," he said to Chenery, "they will come

in a moment, I am sure," and almost instantly the great shadow of dragon wings came spilling over them, Temeraire's backlit form solidly black against the sun, the outline too bright to look at him directly. The trees and branches crackled and shattered under his weight, and then he thrust his head in close among them, sniffing, a great reddish head with ten curving ivory tusks set in its upper lip: it was not Temeraire at all.

"Christ preserve us," Laurence said involuntarily, reaching for his pistol. The beast was not very much smaller than Temeraire, larger than he had imagined ever seeing a feral dragon, built heavy in the shoulders with a double ridge of spikes, the color of red-brown mud, patterned liberally with yellow and grey. "Another gun, Riggs, another gun—"

Riggs fired away, and the feral dragon hissed in irritation, batting, too late, at the streaking flare that burst blue light overhead. His head snaked back towards them, the pupils of his virulent yellow-green eyes narrowing, and he bared his jaws; then Dulcia came darting through the canopy of the trees, crying, "Chenery, Chenery," and flung herself clawing madly at the much larger feral's head.

Taken aback by the ferocity of her reckless attack, the red-brown dragon recoiled at first, but snapped back at her with astonishing speed, caught the leading edge of her wing in his mouth, and shook her up and down by it. She shrilled in pain, but when he let her go, apparently satisfied that she had learnt her lesson, she dived back at him again, her teeth bared, despite blood spiderwebbing blackly over the membrane of her wing.

He backed away a few paces as best as he could in the close press of the forest, crushing over a few more trees with his rump, with rather a bewildered air, and hissed at her again. She had put herself between them and the feral, and, spreading her wings wide and sheltering, reared up as large as she could make herself, foreclaws raised. Still she looked rather toy-like next to his massive bulk, and instead of attacking, he sat back on his haunches and scratched his nose against his foreleg, in an attitude almost of embarrassed confusion. Laurence had seen Temeraire often express a certain reluctance at fighting a smaller beast, conscious of the difference in their weight-class; but in turn, smaller dragons would not offer battle to one so much larger, ordinarily, without supporting allies to make the contest a more equal one; only the incentive of her captain's safety was inducing Dulcia to do so now.

Temeraire's shadow fell over them, and the feral jerked his head up, shoulders bristling, and launched himself aloft to meet the new threat, more his match. Laurence could not see very well what was going forward, though he craned desperately: they had Dulcia to contend with, who in her anxiety to see Chenery and gauge his injuries was bending close and interfering. "Enough, let us get him aboard," Dorset said, rapping her smartly upon the breast until she backed away. "In the belly-rigging; he must be strapped down properly," and they hurriedly secured the makeshift litter to the harness.

Meanwhile above the feral darted back and forth about Temeraire in short half-arcs, hissing and clicking at him like a kettle on the boil. Temeraire paused in mid-air, his wings beating the hovering stroke which only Chinese dragons could manage, and his ruff came up and spread wide as his chest expanded deeply. The feral promptly beat away a few more wing-spans, widening the distance between them, and kept his position until Temeraire gave his terrible thundering roar: the trees shaking with the force of it so that a hail of old leaves and twigs, trapped in the canopy, came shedding down upon them, and also some of the ugly lumpen sausage-shaped fruits, whose impact thumped deep aggressive dents in the ground around them; Chenery's midwing-man Hyatt uttered a startled oath as one glanced off his shoulder. Laurence rubbed dust and pollen from his face, squinting up: the feral looked rather impressed, as well he might be, and after a moment's more hesitation peeled away and flew out of their sight.

Chenery was got aboard with no less haste, and they flew at once back to Capetown, Dulcia constantly cran-ing her head down towards her own belly to see how he did. They unloaded him sadly in the courtyard, and he was carried into the castle, already become feverish and excited, to be examined by the governor's physician, while Laurence took in the one poor sample that was all the day's work had won them.

Keynes regarded it somberly, and finally said, "Ni-tidus. If we must worry about ferals in the forests, even so near, you must have a small dragon to carry you into the woods; and Dulcia will not go away when Chenery is so ill."

"The thing grows hidden, under bushes," Laurence said. "We cannot be hunting from dragon-back."

"You cannot be getting yourselves knocked about by rhinoceri and eaten by ferals, either," Keynes snapped. "We are not served, Captain, by a cure which consists in losing more dragons than are made healthy, in the process of acquiring it," and turning, stamped away with the sample to Gong Su, to have it prepared.

Warren swallowed when he heard Keynes's decision, and said in a voice which did not rise very high, "Lily ought to have it," but Catherine said strongly, "We will not quarrel with the surgeons, Micah; Mr. Keynes must make all such determinations."

"When we have enough," Keynes said quietly, "we may experiment to see how far the dose may be stretched: at present we must have some strength in dragons to get more, and I am by no means confident that this quantity would do for Lily's size. Maximus will be in no condition to do more than a little easy flying for weeks yet."

"I understand perfectly, Mr. Keynes, let us say not another word on the subject," she said, so Nitidus was fed upon the posset, and Lily continued to cough miserably; Catherine sat by her head all the night, stroking her muzzle, heedless of the real danger to herself from the spatters of acid.

Chapter 8

"WHOLLY UNLIKELY—WHOLLY unlikely," Dorset said severely, when Catherine in despair suggested, two weeks later, that they had already acquired all the specimens which there were in the world.

Nitidus had suffered less than most of the dragons, although complained somewhat more, and he recovered with greater speed even than Dulcia, despite a nervous inclination to cough even after the physical necessity had gone. "I am sure I feel a little thickness in my head again this morning," he said fretfully, or his throat was a little sensitive, or his shoulders ached.

"It is only to be expected," Keynes said of the last, scarcely a week since he had been dosed, "when you have been lying about for months with no proper exercise. You had better take him out tomorrow, and enough of this caterwauling," he added to Warren, and stamped away.

With this encouraging permission, they had promptly renewed the search which had been curtailed by Chenery's injury, confining the sphere a little closer to the immediate environs of the Cape; but after two more weeks had gone by, they had met with no more feral dragons and also with no more success. They had brought back in desperation several other varieties of mushroom, not entirely dissimilar in appearance, two of which proved instantly poisonous to the furry local rodents which Dorset made their first recipients.

Keynes prodded the small curled dead bodies and shook his head. "It is not to be risked. You are damned fortunate not to have poisoned Temeraire with the thing in the first place."

"What the devil are we to do, then?" Catherine demanded. "If there is no more to be had—"

"There will be more," Dorset said with assurance, and for his part, he continued to perform daily rounds of the marketplace, forcing the merchants and stall-keepers there to look at his detailed sketch of the mushroom, rendered in pencil and ink. His steady perseverance was rewarded by the merchants growing so exasperated that one of the Khoi, whose Dutch and English encompassed only the numbers one through ten, all he ordinarily required to sell his wares, finally appeared at their gates with Reverend Erasmus in tow, having sought his assistance to put a stop to the constant harassment.

"He wishes you to know that the mushroom does not grow here in the Cape, if I have understood correctly," Erasmus explained, "but that the Xhosa—" He was here interrupted by the Khoi merchant, who impatiently repeated the name quite differently, incorporating an odd sort of clicking noise at the beginning which reminded Laurence of nothing more than some sounds of the Durzagh language, difficult for a human tongue to render.

"In any case," Erasmus said, after another unsuccessful attempt to repeat the name properly, "he means a tribe which lives farther along the coast and, having more dealings inland, may know where more is to be found."

Pursuing this intelligence, however, Laurence soon discovered that to make any contact would be difficult in the extreme: the tribesmen who dwelt nearest the Cape had withdrawn farther and farther from the Dutch settlements, after their last wave of assaults—not unprovoked—had been flung back, some eight years before. They were now settled into an uneasy and often-broken truce with the colonists, and only at the very frontiers was any intercourse still to be had with them.

"And that," Mr. Rietz informed Laurence, the two of them communicating by means of equally halting German on both sides, "the pleasure of having our cattle stolen: twice a month we lose a cow or more, for all they have signed one truce after another."

He was one of the chief men of Swellendam, one of the oldest villages of the Cape, and still nearly as far inland as any of the settlers had successfully established themselves: nestled at the foot of a sheltering ridge of mountains, which deterred incursions by the ferals. The vineyards and farmland were close-huddled around the neat and compact white-washed homes, only a handful of heavily fortified farmhouses more widely flung. The settlers were wary of the feral dragons who often came raiding from over the mountains, against whom they had built a small central fort bolstered with two six-pounders, and resentful of their black neighbors, of whom Rietz further added, "The kaffirs are all rascals, whatever heathenish name you like to call them; and I advise you against any dealings with them. They are savages to a man, and more likely will murder you while you sleep than be of any use."

Having said so much mostly under the unspoken but no less potent duress of Temeraire's presence on the outskirts of his village, he considered this final and was by no means willing to be of further assistance, but sat mutely until Laurence gave it up and let him go back to his accounts.

"Those certainly are very handsome cows," Temeraire said, with a healthy admiration of his own, when Laurence rejoined him. "You cannot blame the ferals for taking them, when they do not know any better, and the cows are just sitting there in the pen, doing no-one any good. But how are we to find any of these Xhosa, if the settlers will not help? I suppose we might fly about looking for them?"—a suggestion which would certainly ensure they did not catch the least sight of a people who surely had to be deeply wary of dragons, as likely as the settlers to be victims of the feral beasts.

General Grey snorted, when Laurence had returned to Capetown seeking an alternative, and reported Rietz's reaction. "Yes; and I imagine if you find one of the Xhosa, he will make you the very same complaint in reverse. They are all forever stealing cattle from one another, and the only thing they would agree on, I suppose, is to complain of the ferals worse. It is a bad business," he added, "these settlers want more grazing land, badly, and they cannot get it; so they have nothing to do but quarrel with the tribesmen over what land the ferals do not mind leaving to them."

"Can the ferals not be deterred?" Laurence asked. He did not know how ferals were managed, precisely; in Britain he knew they were largely induced to confine themselves to the breeding grounds, by the regular provision of easy meals.

"No; there must be too much wild game," Grey said. "They are not tempted enough, at any rate, to leave the settlements alone, and there have been trials made enough to prove it. Every year a few young hotheads make a push inland; for what good it does them, which is none." He shrugged. "Most of our adventurers are not heard from again, and of course the inaction of the government is blamed. But they will not understand the expense and difficulty involved. I tell you I should not undertake to carve out any more sizable territory here without at the least a six-dragon formation, and two companies of field artillery."

Laurence nodded; there was certainly no likelihood of the Admiralty sending such assistance at present, or for that matter in the foreseeable future; even apart from the disease, which had so wracked their aerial strength, any significant force would naturally be committed to the war against France.

"We will just have to make shift as best we can," Catherine said, when he had grimly reported his lack of success that night. "Surely Reverend Erasmus can help us; he can speak with the natives, and perhaps that merchant will know where we can find them."

Laurence and Berkley went to apply to him the next morning at the mission, already much altered since the last visit which Laurence had made: the plot of land was now a handsome vegetable-garden, full of tomato and pepper plants; a few Khoi girls in modest black shifts were tending the rows, tying up the tomato plants to stakes, and another group beneath a broad mimosa tree were sewing diligently, while Mrs. Erasmus and another missionary lady, a white woman, took it in turn to read to them out of a Bible translated into their tongue.

Inside, the house was almost wholly given over to students scratching laboriously away at writing on scraps of slate, paper too valuable to be used for such an exercise. Erasmus came walking outside with them, for lack of room to talk, and said, "I have not forgotten to be grateful to you for our passage here, Captain, and I would gladly be of service to you. But there is likely as much kinship between the Khoi tongue and that of the

Xhosa as there is between French and German, and I am
by no means yet fluent even in the first. Hannah does
better, and we do remember a little of our own native
tongues; but those will be of even less use: we were both
taken from tribes much farther north."

"You still have a damned better chance to jaw with
them than any of us do," Berkley said bluntly. "It cannot be that bloody difficult to make them understand:
we have a scrap of the thing left, and we can wave it in
their faces to show them what we want."

"Surely having lived neighbor to the Khoi themselves," Laurence said, "there may be those among them
who speak a little of that tongue, which would allow
you to open some communication? We can ask only," he
added, "that you try: a failure would leave us no worse
than we stand."

Erasmus stopped before the garden gate, watching
where his wife was reading to the girls, then said low
and thoughtfully, "I have not heard of it, if anyone has
brought the Gospel to the Xhosa yet."

Though barred from much expansion inland, the settlers had been creeping steadily out along the coast east-
ward from Capetown. The Tsitsikamma River, some
two long days' flight away, was now a theoretical sort of
border between the Dutch and the Xhosa territories:
there were no settlements nearer than Plettenberg Bay,
and if the Xhosa were lurking in the brush five steps beyond the boundaries of the outermost villages, as many
of the settlers imagined they were, no-one would have
been any the wiser. But they had been pushed across the
river in the last fighting, it was a convenient line upon a
map, and so it had been named in the treaties.

Temeraire kept to the coastline in their flight: a
strange and beautiful series of low curved cliffsides,

thickly crusted with green vegetation and in some places lichen of bright red, cream and brown rocks spilling from their feet; and beaches of golden sand, some littered with squat penguins too small to be alarmed by their passage overhead: they were not prey for dragons. Late in their second day of flying they passed the lagoon of Knysna sheltered behind its narrow mouth to the ocean, and arrived late in the evening on the banks of the Tsitsikamma, the river driving its way inland, deep in its green-lined channel.

In the morning, before crossing the river, they tied onto two stakes large white sheets, as flags of parley, to avoid giving provocation; and set these streaming out to either side of Temeraire's wings. They flew cautiously onwards into Xhosa territory, until they came to an open clearing, large enough to permit them to settle Temeraire some distance back, and divided by a narrow, swift-running stream: no obstacle, but perhaps enough of a boundary to provide comfort to someone standing on the other side.

Laurence had brought with him, besides a small but substantial heap of gold guineas, a wide assortment of those things which were commonly used in the local barter, in hopes of tempting out the natives: foremost among them several great chains of cowrie shells, strung on silk thread; in some parts of the continent these were used as currency, and the sense of value persisted more widely; locally they were highly prized as jewellery. Temeraire was for once unimpressed: the shells were not brightly colored enough nor glittery nor iridescent, and did not awaken his magpie nature; he eyed the narrow chain of pearls which Catherine had contributed to the cause with much more interest.

The whole collection the crew laid out upon a large blanket, near enough the edge of the stream to be visible plainly to an observer on the other bank, and with these hoped to coax out some response. Temeraire crouched down as best he could, and then they waited. They had made enough noise, to be sure, but the region was vast: they had flown two days to reach the river, and Laurence was not sanguine.

They slept that night on the bank with no response; and the second day also passed without event, except that Temeraire went hunting and brought back four antelope, which they roasted on a spit for dinner. Not very successfully: Gong Su had remained back at the camp, to feed the other dragons who yet continued ill, and young Allen, detailed to turn the spit, grew distracted and forgot, so that they were scorched black on one side and unappetizingly raw on the other. Temeraire put back his ruff in disapproval; he was, Laurence sadly noted, becoming excessive nice in his tastes, an unfortunate habit in a soldier.

The third day crept onward, hot and clinging from the first, and the men wilted gradually into silence; Emily and Dyer scratched unenthusiastically at their slates, and Laurence forced himself to rise at intervals to pace back and forth, that he would not fall asleep. Temeraire gave a tremendous yawn and put down his head to snore. At an hour past noon they had their dinner: only bread and butter and a little grog, but no one wanted more in the heat, even after the debacle of the previous evening's meal. The sun dipped only reluctantly back towards the horizon; the day stretched.

"Are you comfortable, ma'am?" Laurence asked, bringing Mrs. Erasmus another cup of grog; they had set her up a little pavilion with the traveling-tents, so she might keep in the shade: the little girls had been left back at the castle, in the charge of a maid. She inclined her head and accepted the cup, seeming as always quite careless of her own comfort. A necessary quality, to be sure, for a missionary's wife being dragged the length of the globe, yet it felt uncivilized to be subjecting her to the violence of the day's heat for so little evident use; she did not complain, but she could not have enjoyed being packed aboard a dragon, however well she concealed her fears, and she wore a high-necked gown with sleeves to the wrist, of dark fabric, while the sun beat so ferociously that it glowed even through the leather of the tent.

"I am sorry we have imposed upon you," he said. "If we hear nothing tomorrow, I think we must consider our attempt a failure."

"I will pray for a happier outcome," she said, in her deep steady voice, briefly, and kept her head bowed down.

Mosquitoes sang happily as dusk drew on, though they did not come very close to Temeraire; the flies were less judicious. The shapes of the trees were growing vague when Temeraire woke with a start and said, "Laurence, there is someone coming, there," and the grass rustled on the opposite bank.

A very slight man emerged in the half-light on the far bank: bare-headed, and naked but for a small blanket which was draped rather too casually around his body to preserve modesty. He was carrying a long, slim-hafted assegai, the blade narrow and spade-shaped, and over his other shoulder was slung a rather skinny antelope. He did not come across the stream, keeping a wary eye on Temeraire; he craned his neck a little to look over their blanket of goods, but plainly he would come no farther.

"Reverend, perhaps if you would accompany me," Laurence said softly and set out, Ferris following along doggedly behind them without having been asked. Laurence paused at the blanket and lifted up the most elaborate of the cowrie chains, a neck-collar in six or seven bands of alternating dark and light shells, interspersed with gold beads.

They forded the river, shallow here and not coming over the tops of their boots; Laurence surreptitiously touched the butt of his pistol, looking at the javelin: they would be vulnerable, coming up the bank. But the hunter only backed away towards the woods as they emerged from the water, so in the dim light he was very nearly invisible against the underbrush, and could easily have dived back into the obscurity which this afforded: Laurence supposed he had more right than they to be alarmed, alone to their large party, with Temeraire behind them sitting cat-like on his haunches and regarding the situation with anxiety.

"Sir, pray let me," Ferris said, so plaintively Laurence surrendered the neck-chain to him. He edged cautiously out across the distance, the necklace offered across his palms. The hunter hesitated, very obviously tempted, and then he tentatively held out the antelope towards them, with a slightly abashed air, as if he did not think it a very fair exchange.

Ferris shook his head, and then he stiffened: the bushes behind the hunter had rustled. But it was only a small boy, no more than six or seven, his hands parting the leaves so he could peek out at them with large, curious eyes. The hunter turned and said something to him sharply, in a voice which lost some of its severity by cracking halfway through the reprimand. He was not stunted at all, but only a boy himself, Laurence realized; only a handful of years between him and the one hiding.

The small boy vanished again instantly, the branches closing over his head, and the older one turned back to Ferris with a defiant wary look; his hand was clenched sufficiently on the assegai to show pale pink at the knuckles.

"Pray tell him, if you can, that we mean them no harm," Laurence said quietly to Erasmus. He did not wonder very much what might have lured them here to take a risk perhaps others of his clan had preferred not to run; the hunter was painfully thin, and the younger boy's face had none of the soft-cheeked look of childhood.

Erasmus nodded, and approaching tried his few words of dialect, without success. Retreating to more simplistic communication, he tapped his chest and said his name. The boy gave his as Demane; this exchange at least served to make him grow a little easier: he did not seem quite so ready to bolt, and he suffered Ferris to approach him closer, to show him the small sample of the mushroom.

Demane exclaimed, and recoiled in disgust; with no little cause: its confinement in the leather bag during the day's heat had not improved its aroma. He laughed at his own reaction, though, and came back; but though they pointed to the mushroom, and the string of shells in turn, he continued to look perfectly blank; although he kept reaching out to touch the cowries with rather a wistful expression, rubbing them between thumb and forefinger.

"I suppose he cannot conceive anyone should want to trade for it," Ferris said, not very much under his breath, his face averted as much as he could.

"Hannah," Erasmus said, startling Laurence: he had not noticed Mrs. Erasmus come to join them, her skirts dripping over her bare feet. Demane stood a little straighter and dropped his hand from the shells, very like he had been caught at something by a schoolteacher, and edged back from her. She spoke to him a little while in her low voice, slowly and clearly; taking the mushroom from Ferris, she held it out, imperiously gesturing when Demane made a face. Once he had gingerly taken it from her, she grasped him by the wrist and showed him holding it out to Ferris. Ferris held out the shells in return, miming the transfer, and comprehension finally dawned.

A small voice piped up from the bushes; Demane answered it quellingly, then began to talk volubly at Mrs. Erasmus, a speech full of the odd clicking, which Laurence could not imagine how he produced, at such speed; she listened, frowning intently as she tried to follow. He took the mushroom and knelt down to put it on the ground, next to the base of a tree, then mimed pulling it up and throwing it on the ground. "No, no!" Ferris sprang only just in time to rescue the precious sample from being stamped upon by his bare heel.

Demane observed his behavior with a baffled expression. "He says it makes cows sick," Mrs. Erasmus said, and the gesture was plain enough: the thing was considered a nuisance, and torn up where it was found; which might explain its scarcity. It was no wonder, the local tribesmen being cattle-herders by livelihood, but Laurence was dismayed, and wondered where they should look for the enormous quantities necessary to their cause if it had been the settled practice of generations, perhaps, to eradicate what to them was nothing more than an unpleasant weed.

Mrs. Erasmus continued to speak to the boy, taking the mushroom, and miming a gesture of stroking it, gently, to show him they valued it. "Captain, will you have the crew bring me a pot?" she asked, and when she had put the mushroom into it, and made stirring motions, Demane looked at Laurence and Ferris with a very dubious expression, but then shrugged expressively and pointed upwards, drawing his hand from horizon to horizon in a sweeping arc. "Tomorrow," she translated, and the boy pointed at the ground where they stood.

"Does he think he can find us some?" Laurence asked intently, but either the question or the response she was unable to convey, and only shook her head after a moment. "Well, we must hope for the best; tell him if you can that we will return," and the next day, at the same hour near dusk, the boys came out of the brush again, the younger now trotting at Demane's heels, perfectly naked, and with them a small raggedy dog, its mongrel fur mottled yellow and brown.

It planted itself on the bank and yapped piercingly and continuously at Temeraire while the older boy attempted to negotiate for its services over the noise. Laurence eyed it dubiously; but Demane took the mushroom piece again and held it out to the dog's nose, then kneeling down covered the dog's eyes with his hands. The younger boy ran and hid the mushroom deep in the grass, and came back again; then Demane let the dog go again, with a sharp word of command. It promptly returned to barking madly at Temeraire, ignoring all his instructions, until, looking painfully embarrassed, Demane snatched up a stick and hit it on the rump, hissing at it, and made it smell the leather satchel where the mushroom had been kept. At last reluctantly it left off and went bounding across the field, came trotting back with the mushroom held in its mouth, and dropped it at Laurence's feet, wagging its tail with enthusiasm.

Having decided, very likely, that they were fools, or at least very rich, Demane now turned up his nose at the cowries, wishing rather to be paid in cattle, evidently the main source of wealth among the Xhosa: he opened the negotiations at a dozen head. "Tell him we will give them one cow, for a week of service," Laurence said. "If he leads us to a good supply of the mushroom, we will consider extending the bargain, otherwise we will return the two of them here with their payment." Demane inclined his head and accepted the diminished offer with a tolerable attempt at calm gravity; but the wide eyes of the younger boy, whose name was Sipho, and his rather excited tugging at Demane's hand, made Laurence suspect he had even so made a poor bargain by local standards.

Temeraire put his ruff back when the dog was carried squirming towards him. "It is very noisy," he said disapprovingly, to which the dog barked an answer equally impolite, by the tone of it, and tried to jump out of its master's arms and run away; Demane was no less anxious. Mrs. Erasmus sought to coax him a little closer, and reached out to pat Temeraire's forehand to show there was no danger: perhaps not the best encouragement, since it drew his attention to the very substantial talons: Demane pushed a more interested than alarmed Sipho behind him, the wriggling dog clutched against him with his other arm, and shaking his head vocally refused to come nearer.

Temeraire cocked his head. "That is a very interesting sound," he said, and repeated one of the words, mimicking the clicking noise with more success than any of them but still not quite correctly. Sipho laughed from behind Demane's shoulder and said the word to him again; after a few repetitions Temeraire said, "Oh, I have it," although the clicking issued a little oddly, from somewhere deeper in his throat than the boys produced it; and they were gradually reconciled by the exchange to being loaded aboard.

Laurence had learnt the art of carrying livestock

aboard a dragon from Tharkay, in the East, by drugging the beasts with opium before they were loaded on, but they had none of the drug with them at present, so with a dubious spirit of experimentation they put the whining dog aboard by main force instead, and strapped it down. It was inclined to squirm and struggle against the makeshift harness, making several abortive attempts to leap off into the air, until Temeraire lifted away; then after a few yelps of excitement, it sat down on its haunches with its mouth open and tongue lolling out, thrashing its tail furiously with delight, better pleased than its unhappy master, who clung anxiously to the harness and to Sipho, although they were both well hooked on with carabiners.

"Proper circus you make," Berkley said, with a snort of laughter Laurence considered unnecessary, when they landed in the clearing and set the dog down; it promptly went tearing around the parade grounds, yelling at the dragons. For their part they were only interested and curious until the dog bit a too-inquisitive Dulcia on the tender tip of her muzzle, at which she hissed in anger; the dog yelped and fled back to the dubious shelter of Temeraire's side; he looked down at it in irritation, and tried unsuccessfully to nudge it away.

"Pray be careful of the creature; I have no idea how we should get or train another," Laurence said, and Temeraire at last grumbling allowed it to curl up beside him.

Chenery limped out to eat with them that evening in the parade grounds to reassure Dulcia of his improvement, professing himself too tired for any more bed-rest, so they made a merry meal of optimism and roast beef, and passed around the bottle freely; perhaps too freely, for shortly after the cigars were passed, Catherine said, "Oh, damnation," and getting up went to the side of the clearing to vomit.

It was not the first time she had been ill lately, but the bout was an enthusiastic one. They politely averted their faces, and in a little while she rejoined them at the fire, with a dismal expression. Warren offered her a little more wine, but she shook her head and only rinsed her mouth with water and spat on the ground, and then looking around them all said heavily, "Well, gentlemen, I am sorry to be indelicate, but if I am going to be sickly like this all the way through, you had better know now. I am afraid I have made a mull of it. —I am increasing."

Laurence only gradually realized that he was staring, with an intolerably rude gaping expression. He closed his mouth at once and held himself rigidly still, fighting the inclination to look at his fellow captains, the five of them sitting around the fire, and study them in the light of candidates.

Berkley and Sutton, both senior to him by ten years, he thought stood more in the relation of uncle to Catherine than anything else. Warren also was older, and had been matched to his rather nervous beast Nitidus for the very steadiness of his nature, which made it difficult to easily imagine him in the light of a lover, under their present circumstances. Chenery was a younger man of high and cheerful spirits, thoroughly innocent of any sense of decorum, and made more handsome by his smiles and a rough careless charm than his looks deserved, being a little thin in the chest and face, with an unfortunately sallow complexion and hair generally blown straight as straw. He was perhaps in personality the most likely, although Immortalis's captain Little, of a similar age, was the better-looking despite a nose which was inclined to be beaky, with china-blue eyes and wavy dark hair kept a little long in a poetic style; but this, Laurence suspected, was due more to a lack of attention than any deliberate vanity, and Little was rather abstemious in his habits than luxurious.

There was of course Catherine's first lieutenant, Hobbes, an intense young man only a year her junior, but Laurence could scarcely believe she would engage herself with a subordinate, and risk all the resentment and difficulties which he had known similar practices, albeit of a more illegal nature, to produce aboard ship. No; it must be one of them; and Laurence could not help but see, from the corner of his eye, that Sutton and Little at least bore expressions more or less of surprise, and that he was being looked at with the same spirit of speculation he himself had been unable to repress, exhibited more openly.

Laurence was unhappily conscious that he could not object. He had committed an equal indiscretion, without ever considering what he should say, or do, if he and Jane were to similarly be taken aback. He could hardly imagine his father's reaction and even his mother's, on being presented with such a match: a woman some years his senior, with a natural-born child, of no particular family wholly aside from her complete sacrifice of respectability to her duty. But marriage it would have to be; anything else should be as good as offering insult, to one who deserved from him the confusion of respect of a gentlewoman and a comrade-in-arms, and exposing her and the child to the censure of all society.

Therefore to just such a dreadful situation he had willingly hazarded himself, and he could hardly complain if he were now to suffer a share of that pain on another party's behalf. Only the one who knew himself guilty could know the truth, of course; and so long as he remained unconfessed, Laurence and his fellow captains should all jointly have to endure the curiosity of the world, however unpleasant, without remedy.

"Well, it is damned bad luck," Berkley said, setting down his fork. "Whose is it?"

Harcourt said easily, "Oh, it is Tom's, I mean Captain Riley; thank you, Tooke," and held out her hand for the cup of tea which her young runner had brought her, while Laurence blushed for all of them.

He passed an uncomfortable and wakeful night, suffering the incessant shrill barking of the dog outside, and, within, all the confusion which could be imagined: whether to speak to Riley, and on what grounds, Laurence scarcely knew.

He felt a certain responsibility for Catherine's honor and the child's; irrational under the circumstances, perhaps, when she herself seemed wholly unconcerned. But though *she* might not care for the good opinion of society or feel herself dishonored, nor her fellow aviators, Laurence was well aware that *Riley* could claim no such disdain for the eyes of the world. All Riley's odd constraint, towards the end of the voyage, now bespoke a guilty conscience; certainly he had not approved the notion of women officers, and Laurence did not for a moment imagine that his opinion had altered in consequence of this affair. Riley had only taken personal advantage where it became available to him, and with full knowledge had entered into what for him must be seen as the ruin of a gentlewoman, an act selfish if not vicious, and deserving of the strongest reproof. But Laurence had no standing whatsoever in the world to pursue it; any attempt would only make a thorough scandal of the whole, and as an aviator he was forbidden to enter into personal challenges in any case.

To complicate matters still further, he had a wholly separate motive for speaking, and that to give Riley intelligence of the child's existence, of which he might well be ignorant. Jane Roland, at least, thought nothing of her daughter Emily's illegitimacy; by her own admission she had not so much as seen the father since the event of conception, nor seemed to think he had anything to do with the child in the least. This perfect lack of sensibility Catherine evidently shared. Laurence had not dwelt long on this pragmatic ruthlessness before the event; but now he put himself in Riley's place, and felt that Riley at once deserved all the difficulties of the situation, and the opportunity of rising to meet them.

Laurence rose undecided and unrested, and without much enthusiasm entered into their first attempt to take out the dog. Seeing them make ready, the cur did not wait to be carried aboard, but leapt onto Temeraire's back and settled itself in pride of place at the base of his neck, just where Laurence ordinarily sat, and barked officiously to hurry the rest of their preparations. "Cannot it ride with Nitidus?" Temeraire said, disgruntled, craning his neck to give it a repressive hiss. Familiarity had already bred contempt; the dog only wagged its tail back at him.

"No, no; I do not want it," Nitidus said, mantling his wings in resistance. "You are bigger, it does not weigh on you at all." Temeraire flattened his ruff against his neck and muttered.

They crossed over the mountains again and settled themselves just past the leading edge where the settlements petered out, on a slope lately somewhat bared by a rockslide, which offered the dragons the best opportunity to land deep in the undergrowth. Nitidus managed to wedge himself into a gap left among the trees, where a larger had fallen, but Temeraire was forced to try and make himself a landing place by trampling down the smaller but more stubborn shrubs which had invaded the space. The acacia thorns were long and slender enough to probe between his scales, and catch the flesh beneath, so he flinched to one side or another several times before at last he had something like sure footing and could let them clamber down off his back, to hack themselves out some room and pitch the tents once again.

The dog made itself a nuisance while they made camp, inclined to frolic and startle up the fat brown-and-white pheasants, which ran away from it unhappily, their heads bobbing; until all at once it went very quiet, and its lean rangy body stiffened with excitement. Lieutenant Riggs raised his rifle to his ear, and they all froze, remembering the rhinoceros; but in a moment a troop of baboons came out from among the trees. The largest, a grizzled fellow with a long sour face and a shining rump of bright scarlet protruding from his fur, impossible to ignore, sat back on his haunches and gave them a jaundiced eye; then the band ambled off, the smallest clinging to their mothers' fur and turning their heads around to stare with curiosity as they were carried away.

There were few large trees; the thickness was made rather of yellow grass everywhere, higher than a man's head, which filled in every gap the green thornbrake allowed. Above, the thin trees threw up little cloud-like clusters of branches, which gave no relief from the sun. The air was close and hot and full of dust, crumbled grass and dried leaves, and clouds of small birds twitting each other in the brush. The dog led them on an aimless straggling path through the ferocious underbrush; it more easily than they could work through the tangled shrubs and deadwood.

Demane gave the dog occasional encouragement by

lectures and yelling, but for the most part gave the cur its head. He and his brother followed on its heels closely and quicker than the rest of them could manage, occasionally disappearing up ahead. Their young clear voices came calling back impatiently to guide them, now and then, and at last, in the mid-afternoon, Laurence came stumbling out of the brush and caught them up to find Sipho proudly holding out one of the mushrooms for their inspection.

"Better by far, but we will still need a week at this rate to get enough for the rest of the formation alone," Warren said that evening, offering Laurence a glass of port in front of his small tent, with an old stump and a smooth rock serving them as formal seating. The dog had found three more mushrooms on the way back to camp, all of them small ones which would have escaped attention otherwise. They were of course happily collected; but they would not make much of the posset, or the draught.

"Yes, at least," Laurence said tiredly; his legs ached from their unaccustomed labor. He unfolded them with an effort towards the heat of the small twiggy fire, smoky from the green wood but pleasantly hypnotic.

Temeraire and Nitidus had made good use of their idleness to improve upon the camp, trampling down the earth of the slope to make it more level and tearing up several trees and bushes to clear more ground. Temeraire had rather vengefully hurled the bristling acacia far down the slope, where it could now be seen, incongruously, sitting caught upon two tree-tops with a great clump of dirt around its roots in mid-air.

They had provided also a couple of antelope for the party's dinner, or had meant to; but the hours had dragged, and with nothing better to do they had eventually eaten most of the kill themselves, and were found licking their chops and empty-handed at the end of the day. "I am sorry, but you were so very long," Temeraire said apologetically. Happily, Demane showed them the trick of catching the plentiful local pheasants, by driving them towards a waiting collaborator with a net, and these, roasted quickly on a spit and rounded out with ship's biscuit, made the company a dinner pleasant enough: the birds not the least gamy, having fed evidently only on the local grass-seeds and berries.

Now the dragons had curled around the borders of their camp; protection enough to ward off any nightly dangers; the crews had arranged themselves for sleep on beds of crumpled brush, coats used haphazardly for pillows, or were playing at dice and cards in distant corners, murmuring their wagers and occasionally a cry of victory or despair. The boys, who had been eating like wolves, and already looked rather better fleshed, were stretched upon the ground at Mrs. Erasmus's feet. She had persuaded them to put on some loose duck trousers, sewn by girls from the mission; her husband was methodically laying out for them on the ground, one at a time, stiff picture-cards showing objects to be identified in their language, and rewarding them with doled-out sweetmeats while she noted down the answers in her log-book.

Warren prodded the fire with a long branch, idly, and Laurence felt at last that they were near enough alone to satisfy discretion; that he might speak, however awkwardly.

"No; I did not know about the child," Warren said, with not the least discomfiture at the inquiry, but gloomily. "It is a bad business: God forbid she should come to a bad pass here; that little runner of yours is the only girl we have, and she is no wise ready to make a captain, even if Lily would have her. And what the devil we should do for Excidium if she did, I would like to know; the admiral cannot be running about having another child now, with Bonaparte on the other side of the Channel, ready to toss his glove across at any minute.

"I damned well hope *you* have been taking precautions? But I am sure Roland knows her business," Warren added, without waiting for reply; just as well, as Laurence had never been asked a question he would have less liked to answer; all the more as it had abruptly and appallingly illuminated certain curious habits of Jane's, which he had never brought himself to inquire into, and her regular consultations of the calendar.

"Oh, pray don't take me wrong," Warren said, misunderstanding Laurence's fixed expression. "I don't mean to carp in the least; accidents will happen, and Harcourt has had every excuse for distraction. Bad enough for us, these last months, but what the devil was ever to become of her? Half-pay would keep body and soul together, but money don't make a woman respectable. That is why I asked you, before, about the fellow; I thought, if Lily died, they might make a match of it."

"She has no family?" Laurence asked.

"None left, none to speak of. She is old Jack Harcourt's daughter—he was a lieutenant on Fluitare. He cut straps in the year two, damned shame; but at least he knew she'd been tapped for Lily, by then," Warren said. "Her mother was a girl down Plymouth way, near the covert there. She went off in a fever when Catherine was scarce old enough to crawl, and no relations to take her in: that is how she was thrown on the Corps."

Laurence said, "Then, under the present circumstances—I know it is damned officious, but if she has no one else, ought one not speak to him? Of the child, I mean," he added awkwardly.

"Why, what is there for him to do?" Warren said. "If it is a girl, God willing, the Corps needs her with both hands; and if it is a boy, he could go to sea instead, I suppose; but whatever for? It can only hurt him there, to be a by-blow, and meanwhile a captain's son in the Corps is pretty sure to get a dragon, if he has any merit of his own."

"But that is what I mean," Laurence said, puzzled to find himself so misunderstood. "There is no reason the child must be illegitimate; they might easily be married at once."

"Oh, oh," Warren said, dawning wonder, confusion. "Why, Laurence, no; there's no sense in it, you must see that. If she had been grounded, it might have answered; but thank God, no need to think of that anymore, or anything like," and he jerked his chin gladly at the tightly lidded box which held the fruits of their day's labors, to be carried back to Capetown in the morning: Lily would certainly be the next recipient. "A comfortable wife she would make him, with orders to follow and a dragon to look after; I dare say they would not see one another one year in six, him posted to one side of the world and she to the other, ha!"

Laurence was little satisfied to find his sentiments so unaffectedly laughed at, but more so for the uncomfortable sensation that there was some rational cause for so dismissive an answer; and he was forced to go to sleep with his resolution yet unformed.

Chapter 9

~~~

"MR. KEYNES," CATHERINE said, cutting through the raised voices, "perhaps you will be so good as to explain to us what alternative you prefer, to Mr. Dorset's suggestion."

Experience had improved on their rate of return, a little, and Nitidus had carried their spoils back to Cape-town daily; so they returned, after a tired and dusty week, to find Lily dosed, Messoria and Immortalis also, and a small and putrid heap of mushrooms yet remaining. Of these, two had been preserved in oil, two in spirits of wine, two only wrapped in paper and oilcloth, and the lot boxed neatly up with the receipt for the cure. They would be sent back to England by the *Fiona*, which had been held back this long for their report: she would go with the tide.

But there was no sentiment of triumph at their dinner back, only muted satisfaction; at best the results of all their hunting would not do for more than three dragons; six if the surgeons back in Dover took the risk of halving the dose, or used it on smaller beasts, and that only if all three methods preserved whatever virtue the mushrooms held; Dorset would have liked to dry some, also, but there were not enough of them for this final experiment.

"Well, we are not going to do any better, not unless we hire an army of men and hounds; and where to get them, you may tell me and much obliged," Warren said, holding the bottle in one hand as he drained his glass in the other, so he might refill the tumbler straight away. "Nemachaen is a clever little beast," meaning the dog, who had acquired this grandiose name after the lion, courtesy of some of the younger ensigns presently being subjected to a haphazard education in the classics, "but there is only so much blasted forest we can hack through in a day, to find one mushroom or two at a time when we need scores of the things."

"We must have more hunters," Laurence said, but they were rather in danger of losing those they had; the agreed-on week having passed, Demane gave signs of wishing for himself and Sipho to be returned to their home village with their reward. Laurence with many un-pleasant pangs of conscience had refused to immediately understand his signs, and instead had taken him to see the pen near the castle, where the cow had been set aside: a large, handsome milch cow, placid, with her six-months' calf browsing the grass beside her; the boy ducked through the fence slats and slipped in to touch her soft brown side with cautious, almost wary delight. He looked at the calf, and back at Laurence, a question in his face; Laurence nodded to say they would give him the other, too. Demane came out, protests silenced by this species of bribery, and Laurence went away feeling that he had behaved himself like a desperate scrub; he hoped very much the boys did not have family to be made anxious for them, although he had rather gained the impression they were orphaned, and at the very least neglected.

"Too slow," Dorset said, very decidedly despite his stammer. "Too slow, by half. All the searching in the world—we will only help to stamp it out. It has been the target of systematic eradication; we cannot hope to find much nearby. Who knows how long, how many years, the herdsmen have been digging it up. We must go away, farther away, where it may yet grow in quantity—"

"Perfect speculation," Keynes snapped, "on which to recommend the pursuit of wild chances. How much distance will satisfy you? I dare say all the continent has been used for herding, at some time or another. To risk the formation, dragons scarcely risen from their sickbeds, and go deep into feral territory, on such a hope? The height of folly—"

The argument rose, grew warm, surged across the table; Dorset's stammer grew more violent so he was scarcely comprehensible, and Gaiters and Waley, Maximus's and Lily's surgeons, were ranged with Keynes against him; until at last Catherine had silenced all of them, standing up to make her demand with her hands planted on the cloth.

"I do not quarrel with your concern," she added, more quietly, "but we did not come here to find a cure only for ourselves. You have heard the latest dispatches; nine more dead since March, and by now more gone, when we could not spare any of them in the least." She looked at Keynes steadily. "Is there any hope?"

He was silent, displeased, and only with a surly lowering look allowed there to be some chance of a better harvest, farther away; she nodded and said, "Then we will endure the risk, and be glad that our own dragons are well enough to do so."

There was no question, yet, of sending Maximus, who had only lately begun to try at flying again: with a deal of flapping and kicking up dust, often ending only in an exhausted collapse; he could not quite manage the launching spring, which was necessary to get him aloft, although once in the air could remain for some time. Keynes shook his head and felt at his paunchy sides.

"The weight is coming back unevenly. You are doing your exercises?" he demanded; Maximus protested that he was. "Well, if we cannot get you in the air, we must find you room to walk," Keynes said, and so Maximus had been set to making a circuit of the town, back and forth several times daily: the only stretch of cleared ground large enough for him, as he could not go far up the mountain-slopes without pulling them down in small avalanches.

No-one was very happy with this solution: ridiculous to have a dragon the size of a frigate ambling about like a lap-dog on an airing, and Maximus complained of the hard ground, and the pebbles which introduced themselves into his talons. "I do not notice them at first," he said unhappily, while Berkley's runners struggled with hoof-picks and knives and tongs to pry them out from under the hard, callused hide around the base of the claws, "not until they are quite far down, and then I cannot easily say how very unpleasant it becomes."

"Why do you not swim, instead?" Temeraire said. "The water is very pleasant here, and perhaps you might catch a whale," which suggestion brightened Maximus remarkably, and infuriated the fishermen, particularly the owners of the larger boats; they came in a body to protest.

"I am damned sorry to put you out," Berkley said to them. "You may come with me, and tell him yourselves you do not like it."

Maximus continued his outings, in peace, and might be seen daily paddling about the harbor. Sadly the whales and dolphins and seals, too clever by half, stayed well-clear of him, much to his disappointment: he did not much like tunny or sharks, the latter of which occasionally beat themselves against his limbs in confused fits perhaps provoked by some traces of blood or flesh from his latest repast: on one occasion he brought back one of these to show, a monster some nineteen feet in length, weighing close on two tons, with its angry snoutish face full of teeth. He had lifted the shark straight out of the water whole, and when he laid it down on the parade grounds before them, it abruptly went into a paroxysm of thrashing: knocking over Dyer, two ensigns, and one of the Marines, snapping and gnashing furiously at the air, before Dulcia managed to pin it to the ground with her foretalons.

Messoria and Immortalis, both older beasts, were perfectly happy to lie in the parade grounds and sleep in the sun, after their short daily flights for exercise; but Lily, having stopped coughing, shortly displayed that same restless energy which had overcome Dulcia, and began to insist on activity. But if she were to go flying anywhere, she must go far abroad, where a stray lingering sneeze or cough would not spray anyone below; Keynes, quite ignoring the covert gestures, the attempts at signaling, of nearly every senior officer, examined her and declared that she was perfectly fit to fly, "had better fly, I should say; this agitation is unnatural, and must be worked off."

"But perhaps," Laurence said, voicing the reluctance which the captains all privately shared, and they as a body began to suggest flights out over the ocean, along the scenic and settled coastline and back; gentle exercise.

"I hope," Catherine said, going pink clear up to her forehead in a wave of color, "I hope that no-one is going to fuss; I would dislike fuss extremely," and insisted on joining the hunting party, with Dulcia and Chenery, who likewise declared himself perfectly well, although Dulcia would only agree if he was bundled aboard in a heavy cloak, with a warming brick at his feet.

"After all, it cannot hurt to have more of us: we can make several parties and cover more ground; we do not need the dog so badly if the notion is we are looking for larger patches of the stuff," Chenery said. "Just as well to have more of the dragons in hailing-distance, if any of us should run into a larger band of ferals, and your natives can keep us out of trouble with the animals."

Laurence applied to Erasmus and his wife for their persuasive assistance, and pressed the cowrie necklace on Demane to open the conversation, as a preliminary bit of bribery. He objected vehemently nonetheless, his voice rising in high complaint, and Mrs. Erasmus said, "He does not like to go so far, Captain: he says that country belongs to the dragons, who will come and eat us."

"Pray tell him there is no reason why the feral dragons should be angry with us; we will only stay a very little while, to get more of the mushrooms, and our own will protect us if there is any difficulty," Laurence said, waving at the fine display the dragons made now. Since their recovery, even the older beasts who had not acquired the habit of bathing had been stripped of their harnesses and scrubbed in the warm ocean until their scales shone, and all the leather worked and polished until it, too, gleamed, warm and supple, the buckles glittering bright in the sun.

The parade grounds themselves had been plowed clean, and the refuse-pits filled in, now there was only occasional coughing to manage; the whole fit to welcome an admiral for inspection, aside from the wreckage of a couple of goats, whose bones Dulcia and Nitidus were presently meditatively gnawing. Maximus alone still had a fragile air, but he was bobbing in the ocean a little way off, his hollow sides buoyed up by the water and the somewhat faded orange and red of his hide refreshed by the lingering sunset pouring in over the wide ripples of the water. The rest of the dragons were rather bright-eyed and tigerish, having been worn lean over the course of the sickness; their reawakened appetites were savage.

"And that is another reason it will be just as well for us all to go," Chenery said, when Demane had at last been brought around to reluctant agreement, or at least worn out from trying to convey his objections through translation. "Grey is a good fellow, and he has not said as much outright, yet; but the townsfolk are kicking up a real dust. It is not just having the dragons about; we are eating them out of hearth and home. The game is getting shy; as for cattle, no one can afford to eat beef anymore at all, and the prices are only getting higher. We had much better get out into wild country and shift for ourselves, where we needn't annoy anyone."

It was settled: Maximus would stay to continue his recovery, and Messoria and Immortalis, to sleep and hunt for him; Temeraire and Lily would go abroad as far as a strong day's flight could take them, with little Nitidus and Dulcia to ferry back their acquisitions, perhaps every other day, and bring back messages.

They were packed and gone with the sun, in the morning, in the usual pell-mell way of aviators; the *Fiona* in the harbor rising up and falling with the swell, a great deal of activity on her deck in preparation for the morrow. The *Allegiance* was riding farther out to sea; the watch would be changing in a moment, but for now all was quiet aboard her. Riley had not come ashore; Laurence had not written. He turned his face away from the ship and towards the mountains, dismissing the matter for the present with a vague sense of leaving the question up to fate: by the time they returned with mushrooms in any quantity, perhaps there would be no need to *speak;* they would have to go home by way of the *Allegiance,* and it could not be hidden forever; he wondered if Catherine did not already look a little plumper.

Lily set a fine, fast pace; the wind poured over Temeraire's back as Table Bay rolled away behind them. Barring a few banks of clouds, penned up against the slopes, the weather held clear and not windy, good flying, and there was an extraordinary relief in being once again in company: Lily on point, with Temeraire bringing up the rear and Nitidus and Dulcia flying in wing positions, so their shadows falling on the ground below made the points of a diamond, skimming over the vineyard rows below in neat perforated lines of red and brown, past their first autumnal splendor.

Thirty miles on the wing north-west from the bay took them past the swelling outcroppings of grey granite at Paarl, the last settlement in this direction; they did not stop, but continued on into the rising mountains. A few isolated and intrepid farmsteads could be glimpsed as they wound through the passes, clinging to sheltered folds of the mountain-slopes: the fields browning, the houses nearly impossible to see without a glass, buried as they were in stands of trees and their roofs disguised with brown and green paint.

They stopped to water after mid-day, having come to another valley between the mountain lines, and to discuss their course; they had not seen a cultivated field for some half-an-hour now.

"Let us go on another hour or two, and then we shall stop at the first likely place to make a search," Harcourt said. "I do not suppose that there is any chance of the dog scenting them from aloft? The smell of the things is so very strong."

"The best-trained foxhound in the world cannot pick up a vixen's trail from horseback, much less from mid-air," Laurence said, but they had been aloft again only a turn of the glass when the dog began barking in furious excitement, and trying to wriggle free of its harness in the most heedless way. Fellowes had gradually taken the handling of the dog into his own hands, disapproving of Demane's haphazard discipline; his father had been a master of hounds, in Scotland. He had been giving the thin creature a gobbet of fresh meat every time it discovered them a mushroom; by now it would tear away after the least trail of scent with the greatest enthusiasm.

Temeraire had scarcely landed when it escaped its straps and went skidding down his side and abruptly vanished into the high grasses at a place where the slope rose up sharply. They had come into a wide valley, very warm, cupped in a bowl of mountains and still richly green despite the advancing season: fruit-trees every-where in curiously even rows.

"Oh; I can smell it, too," Temeraire said, unexpect-edly, and when Laurence had slid down from his shoul-der, he was no longer surprised at the dog's frenzy: the smell was pronounced, hanging like a miasma in the air.

"Sir," Ferris said, calling: the dog was still invisible, but its barking was coming to them with a hollow echo-ing ring, and Ferris was bending down to the slope; Lau-rence came up to him and saw half-hidden by a thicket there was an opening, a fissure in the dirt and limestone rock. The dog went silent; in another moment it came scrambling out of the hole and back up to them, an enormous, an absurdly enormous mushroom in its mouth, so large its third cap was dragging upon the ground between the dog's legs and making it stumble.

It flung the mushroom down, wagging. The opening was near five feet high, and a gentle slope led downwards. The stench was astonishing. Laurence pushed up the clot of vines and moss which hung over the fissure like a curtain, and stepped inside and down, eyes watering from the smoky torch which Ferris had improvised out of rags and a tree-branch. There was surely a draught somewhere at the far end of the cavern; it drew like a chimney. Ferris was looking at him with a half-disbelieving, half-joyful expression, and as his eyes adjusted to the dimness, Laurence made out the strange hillocky appearance of the cavern floor, and knelt to touch: the floor was covered, covered in mushrooms.

"There is not a moment to lose," Laurence said. "If you hurry, the *Fiona* may not yet have gone; if she has, you must go and recall her—she will not have gone far; she will not have rounded Paternoster Bay."

All the crews were busy, breathless; the grass of the field had been trampled flat, and Temeraire's belly-netting and Lily's was spread out on the ground, every bag and chest emptied out to be filled with mushrooms, heaps and heaps. A small pale cream-colored breed shared the cavern with the great double- and triple-capped monsters, and also a large black fungus which grew in slabs, but the harvesters were making no attempt to discriminate: sorting could wait. Nitidus and Dulcia were already vanishing into the distance, sacks and sacks slung across their backs giving them a curiously lumpy appearance in silhouette against the sky.

Laurence had the map of the coastline dug out of Temeraire's bags, and was showing him the likely course the *Fiona* would have followed. "Go as quickly as you can, and bring back more men. Messoria and Immortalis, too, if they can manage the flight; and tell Sutton to ask the governor for everyone who can be spared from the castle, all the soldiers, and no damned noise about flying, either."

"He can always get them drunk if need be," Chenery said, without lifting his head; he was sitting by the netting and keeping a tally as the mushrooms were thrown in, his lips moving in the count along with his fingers. "So long as they can stumble back and forth by the time you have got them here, they may be soused to their skulls."

"Oh, and barrels, also," Harcourt added, looking up from the stump where she was sitting, with a cool cloth soaked in water upon her forehead: she had attempted to help with the harvest, but the stink had overwhelmed her, and after a second round of vomiting, painful to all of them to hear, Laurence had at last persuaded her to go and sit outside instead. "That is, if Keynes thinks the mushrooms had better be preserved here; and oil and spirits."

"But I do not like our all leaving you here," Temeraire said a little mulishly. "What if that big feral should come back again, or another one? Or lions: I am sure I hear lions, not very far away." There was not the least sound of anything but monkeys, howling in the tree-tops at a fair distance, and birds clamoring.

"We will be perfectly safe: from dragons, or lions, too," Laurence said. "We have a dozen guns and more, and we need only step into the cave to hold them off forever: that mouth would not let in an elephant, much less a dragon, and they will not be able to fetch us out."

"But Laurence," Temeraire said quietly, putting his head down to speak confidentially; at least, as he fancied. "Lily tells me that Harcourt is carrying an egg; surely at least *she* ought to come, and I am sure she will not, if you refuse."

"Why, damn you for a back-alley lawyer; I suppose you have cooked this up between the two of you," Laurence said, outraged at the deliberate calculation of this appeal, and Temeraire had the grace to look ashamed of himself, but only a little. Lily did not even do as much, but abandoning subterfuge only said to Harcourt, wheedling, "Pray, pray, do come."

"For Heaven's sake, enough cosseting," Catherine said. "In any case, I will do much better sitting here in the cool shade than tearing back and forth, weighing you down to no purpose when you might be carrying another pair of hands instead. No, not a man will you take; only make all the speed in the world, and the sooner you have gone, the sooner you will come back again," she added.

The belly-netting was as full as it could be without cramming, and Temeraire and Lily were got off at last, still making wistful complaints. "Near enough five hundred, already," Chenery said triumphantly, looking up from his tally, "and most of them fat, handsome things; enough to dose half the Corps, if only they will last the journey."

"We will give them their damned herd of cows," Laurence said to Ferris, meaning Demane and Sipho, who were now taking their ease stretched out upon the ground before the cavern mouth, making grass whistle and refusing to pay much attention to Reverend Erasmus's attempts to read them an instructive tract for children, his first attempt at translation into their tongue; his wife was helping with the harvest.

Ferris blotted his forehead against his sleeve and said, in stifled, choked tones, "Yes, sir."

"We will need larger quantities than required of the fresh," Dorset said, joining them. "Should some potency be lost in the journey, a concentrated dose will compensate for the preservation. Pray stop the harvesting for now: at this rate no one will be left to carry." The frantic pace had already slackened, with the wearing away of the first flush of excitement and the urgency of getting the dragons loaded, and many of the men looked sick and wan; several were being noisily sick into the grass.

The tents had all gone to make sacks of mushrooms, and there would certainly be no sleeping in the cavern, so they cleared instead the ground before it, chopping through the thornbushes with swords and axes. The remnants they used to build a low encircling break about the edge of the clearing, thorny and obdurate enough to give pause to smaller beasts, and a few parties were set to collecting dry wood for a fire. "Mr. Ferris, let us establish a watch," Laurence said, "and now that we have all been rested, we will go to work in shifts: I should like to see a more efficient job of it."

A quarter-of-an-hour seemed long enough, inside that damp, dark space beneath, with only the narrow crack of white light at one end. Besides the mushrooms themselves, there was a grassy stink very like damp manure throughout, and the sour smell of fresh vomit which they had themselves added to the atmosphere. Where they had already cleared the mushrooms, the earth was strangely springy underfoot, almost matted, not like dirt at all.

Laurence staggered out again into the fresh air, gratefully, with his arms full. "Captain," Dorset said, following him out: he was not carrying a mushroom, and when Laurence had deposited his armload before the newly organized sorters, Dorset showed him a torn-edged square of matted grass and muck, the flooring of the cave. Laurence gazed at it uncomprehendingly. "It is elephant dung," Dorset said, breaking apart the chunk, "and dragon also."

"Wing, two points west of north." Emily Roland's treble voice rang out high and sharp, before Laurence had fully understood; at once all was a confused hurrying into the shelter of the cave. He looked for Reverend Erasmus, and the children; but before he could be herded inside the cave, Demane with one quick look at the oncoming dragon snatched his brother up bodily from the ground, and ran instead away into the underbrush, the dog dashing off after them; its barking came back twice, at increasing distances, and then cut off into a muzzled whine.

"Leave the mushrooms, take the guns," Laurence cupped his hands over his mouth to roar over the commotion; he snatched up his own sword and pistols, put aside to help with the carrying, and gave Mrs. Erasmus his hand to descend into the cavern, past the riflemen already crouched down by the door; shortly the rest of them were crammed in also, all of them jostling involuntarily to keep as near the entrance and its fresh air as they could, until the dragon landed with an earth-trembling heavy thud, and thrust his muzzle directly up against the opening.

It was the self-same feral: dark red-brown, with the queer ivory tusks in his muzzle. The hot queasy kerosene smell of dragon-breath came in upon them as he roared furiously, and the faint undertaste of rot from old meals. "Hold fast, men," Riggs was yelling, by the entrance, "hold fast, wait for it—" until the dragon shifted his position, his open jaws before them, and the volley went off into the soft flesh of its mouth.

The dragon squalled in fury and jerked back. His talons came scrabbling in at the edges of the hole, too large to come all the way inside, and began to pull and claw at the rock. Small pebbles and stones worked loose; dirt rained down upon them from the ceiling.

Laurence looked around for Mrs. Erasmus: she was silent, and only bracing herself against the wall of the cavern for steadiness, her shoulders rigid. The riflemen were coughing as they reloaded urgently; but the dragon had already learnt, and did not present them another target. Its claws came curling in on both sides of the fissure, and then it began to throw its weight back, until all the chamber trembled and groaned.

Laurence drew his sword and leaped forward to hack at the talons, then to stab, the hard scaly flesh resisting the edge but not the point; Warren was beside him, and Ferris, in the dark. The dragon roared again outside and flexed its talons, blindly knocking them down as easily as gnats might be swatted. The hard polished bony curve of one claw slid across Laurence's coat in a line over the belly, thrusting him hard against the matted cavern floor, and the tip caught and pulled a long green thread from the seam as the talons withdrew again from the fissure.

Warren caught Laurence by the arm and together they staggered back from the entry. The gunpowder smoke was bitter and acrid, overlaid on the rotting-sweet stink of the mushrooms; already Laurence could scarcely breathe for the slaughterhouse thickness of the place, and he heard to all sides men heaving, like the lower decks of a ship in a roaring gale.

The feral did not immediately renew the attack. They cautiously crept forward again to peer out: he had settled himself in the clearing outside; by bad luck, far back enough to be out of firing-range of their rifles, and his pale yellow-green eyes were fixed malevolently upon the fissure. He was licking at his hacked-about talons, and making grimaces with his mouth, pulling his lips back from his serrated teeth and forward again, spitting occasionally a little bit of blood upon the ground, but plainly he had taken no great harm. As they watched, he raised his head up and roared again thunderously in anger.

"Sir, we might put gunpowder in a bottle," his gunner Calloway said, crawling over to Laurence, "or the flash-powder, maybe, would give him a start; I have the sack here—"

"We are not going to frighten that beauty away with a little flash and bang, not for long," Chenery said, craning his head back and forth to study their enemy. "My God. Fifteen tons at least, or I miss my guess: fifteen tons in a feral!"

"I would call it closer to twenty, and damned unfortunate, too," Warren said.

"We had better save what you have, Mr. Calloway," Laurence said to the gunner. "It will do us no good only to startle him away briefly; we must wait until the dragons return, and reserve our fire to give them support."

"Oh, Christ; if Nitidus or Dulcia are the first back," Warren said, and did not need to continue: the little dragons would certainly be frantic, and wholly over-matched.

"No; they will all be loaded down, remember?" Harcourt said. "The weight will tell on the light-weights more, and keep them back; but however are they to fight when they get here—"

"Lord, let us not be borrowing trouble, if you please," Chenery interrupted. "That big fellow is no trained flyer; a nice thing if four dragons of the Corps couldn't black his eye in a trice, even if Messoria and Immortalis don't come along. We have only to keep quiet in here until they come."

"Captain," Dorset said, stumbling back towards them, "I am—I beg to recall your attention—the floor of the cavern—"

"Yes," Laurence said, recalling the earlier sample

which Dorset had shown him, of the dung upon the floor of the cave, elephant and dragon, where neither animal could have managed entry. "Do you mean there is another way into this cavern somewhere, where it could come in upon us?"

"No, no," Dorset said. "The dung has been spread. Deliberately," he added, seeing their confusion. "These are cultivated."

"What, do you mean men, farming the things?" Chenery said. "What the devil would a person want with the nasty stuff?"

"Did you say there was dragon dung?" Laurence said, and a shadow falling over the mouth of the cave drew their attention outside: two more dragons landing, smaller creatures but sleek, wearing harness made of ropes, and a dozen men armed with assegai, leaping down off their sides.

The new arrivals all stayed well out of rifle-range, conferring. After a little while, one of them came towards the entry cautiously and shouted something in at them. Laurence looked at Erasmus, who shook his head uncomprehending and turned to his wife; she was staring out the door. She had her handkerchief pressed over her mouth and nostrils to hold out the smell, but she lowered it and edging a little closer called back, haltingly. "They say to come out, I think."

"Oh, certainly." Chenery was rubbing his face against his sleeve; some grit had entered his eyes. "I am sure they would like it of all things; you may tell them to—"

"Gentlemen," Laurence said, breaking in hastily, since Chenery had evidently forgotten his audience, "these are no ferals after all, plainly, but under harness; and if we have trespassed upon the cultivated grounds of these men, we are in the wrong: we ought make amends if we can."

"What a wretched mischance," Harcourt said, agreeing. "We should have been perfectly happy to pay for the damned things, after all. Ma'am, will you come out and speak to them with us? We should of course understand if you do not wish it," she added, to Mrs. Erasmus.

"A moment," Warren said, low and cautiously, catching at Harcourt's sleeve. "Let us remember that we have never heard of anyone coming through the interior; couriers have been lost, and expeditions, and how many settlements have we heard tell of, destroyed, in just this region north of the Cape? If the dragons are not feral, then these men have been responsible, viciously responsible; we are not to rely on their character."

Mrs. Erasmus looked at her husband. He said, "If we do not conciliate them, there will surely be battle when your dragons come back, for they will attack in fear for your safety. It is our Christian duty to make peace, if it can be done," and she nodded and said softly, "I will go."

"I believe I am senior, gentlemen," Warren said, "as our dragons are not here," a specious claim, as precedence in the Corps went by dragon-rank regardless, with no such qualifier involved, outside flag-rank. Coming from the Navy, with its rigid adherence to seniority, Laurence had often found the system confusing if not outright maddening, but it was a pragmatic concession to reality: dragons had their own native hierarchies, and in nature the twenty-year-old handler of a Regal Copper had more authority, on the battlefield, over the instinctive obedience of other dragons, than did a thirty-year veteran on the back of a Winchester.

"Pray let us have no nonsense—" Harcourt began

impatiently, when her first lieutenant Hobbes broke in to say, "It is all a hum; you shan't go at all, none of you, and you ought know better," a little reproachfully. "Myself and Lieutenant Ferris shall escort the parson and his lady, with their permission, and if all goes well, we will try and bring one of the fellows back here, to speak with you."

Laurence could not like the arrangement in the least, but for its keeping Catherine out of harm's way, but the other captains looked guilty and did not argue. They cleared back from the entrance, the riflemen covering the open ground from either side. Mrs. Erasmus cupped her hands over her mouth and called a warning, then Hobbes and Ferris stepped out, one after another, cautiously, each with a pistol held muzzle-down and ready, swords loosened on their belts.

The strangers had stood back again, spears held lightly, the tips pointing towards the ground, but gripped ready to pull back and let fly. They were tall men, all of them, with close-cropped heads and very dark coloring, skin so deep black it had almost a bluish cast in the sunlight. They were dressed very scantily, in loincloths of a remarkable deep purple, decorated in a running fringe with what looked like gold beads, and wore thin laced leather sandals which left the tops of their feet bare, and rose to mid-thigh.

They did not move to attack, and when Hobbes turned and beckoned, Reverend Erasmus climbed out of the cave, and gave his wife his hand to assist her. They joined the lieutenants, and Mrs. Erasmus began speaking, slowly and clearly: she had taken a mushroom from the cave, and held it out to them to show. The red-brown dragon stooped suddenly, its head bending towards her, and spoke; she looked directly up at him, startled but not visibly afraid, and it jerked its head back with an ugly, squawking cry: not a roar or a growl, wholly unlike any sound Laurence had ever heard from a dragon's throat.

One of the men reached out and catching her by the arm drew her towards him. His other hand pressed her forehead backwards, bending her neck in an awkward exposed curve, and his hand pushed her hair away from her face, where the scar and the tattoo marred her forehead.

Erasmus sprang forward, and Hobbes on his other side, to pull her free. The man let her go, without resistance, and took a step towards Erasmus, speaking low and rapidly, pointing at her. Ferris caught her in his arms as she fell back shaking, supporting her.

Erasmus spread his hands, placating, continuing to speak even while he carefully sought to interpose himself before her. He was plainly not understood; he shook his head and tried again, in the Khoi language. This was not understood, either; at last he tried another, haltingly, and tapping his own chest said, "Lunda." The dragon snarled, and with no other warning, the man took up his spear and drove it directly through Erasmus's body, in one unbroken and terrible motion.

Hobbes fired; the man fell; Erasmus also went toppling to his knees. He had an expression of only mild surprise on his face; his hand was on the spear-haft, protruding from just above his breastbone. Mrs. Erasmus gave a single hoarse cry of horror; he turned his head a little in her direction, tried to lift his hand towards her; it fell, limply, and he dropped to the ground.

Ferris half-carried, half-dragged Mrs. Erasmus back towards the cave, the red-brown dragon lunging after them; Hobbes went down in spraying blood under that raking claw. Then Ferris was pushing Mrs. Erasmus into the cavern, backing her into their waiting arms just as the dragon flung itself at the entrance again: roaring at a wild, shrieking pitch, its talons scrabbling madly at the opening and shaking all the hollow hill.

Laurence caught Ferris by the arm as he fell stumbling backwards from the impact, blood in a thin streak crossing his shirt and face. Harcourt and Warren had Mrs. Erasmus. "Mr. Riggs," Laurence shouted, over the rattling din outside, "a little fire; and Mr. Calloway, let us have those flares, if you please."

They gave the dragon another volley and a blue light, straight into the face, which at least made it recoil momentarily; the two smaller dragons leapt into the breach and made an effort to herd the larger one back from the cavern, speaking to it in shrill voices, and at last it drew away again, its sides heaving, and dropped back into its crouch at the far end of the clearing.

"Mr. Turner, do you have the time?" Laurence asked his signal-officer, coughing: the clouds from the flare were not dying away.

"I'm sorry, sir, I forgot to turn the glass for a while," the ensign said unhappily "but it is past four in the afternoon watch."

Temeraire and Lily had not left until past one: a four-hours' flight in either direction, and a great deal of labor and packing to be done in Capetown, before they would even begin the return journey. "We must try and get a little sleep by watches," Laurence said quietly to Harcourt and Warren; Dorset had taken charge of Mrs. Erasmus and guided her deeper into the cave. "We can hold them at the fissure, I think, but we must stay vigilant—"

"Sir," Emily Roland said, "beg pardon, sir, but Mr. Dorset says to tell you, there is smoke coming into the cave, from the back."

A narrow vent, at the back, higher up than they could

reach: propped up on Mr. Pratt's broad shoulder, Laurence could see, through the thin stream of black smoke, the orange glow of the fire which the men had set to smoke them out. He dropped back to his own feet and cleared out of the way: Fellowes and Larring, Harcourt's ground-crew master, were trying together with their men to block the vent with scraps of harness and leather, using their own coats and shirts besides. They were having little success, and time worked against them; already the cavern was nearly unbreathable, and the rising heat only worsened the natural stench.

"We cannot last long this way," Catherine said, hoarse but steady, when Laurence had come back to the front of the cave. "I think we had better make a dash for it, while we still can, and try and lose them in the forest."

Outside the entrance, the thorny brush which they had torn up to make their camp was now being heaped up closer by the dragons, forming stacks higher than a man's head all around the cavern-mouth, and the dragons had arranged themselves carefully behind this barrier: screened from rifle-fire, and blocking their avenues of escape. There would be precious little hope of breaking through; but no better alternative would offer itself.

"My crew is the largest," Laurence said, "and we have eight rifles. I hope you will all agree we should make the first attempt, and the rest of you come upon our heels: Mr. Dorset, perhaps you will be so kind as to wait with Mrs. Erasmus until we have cleared a little way, and I am sure Mr. Pratt will assist you," he added.

The order of emergence was settled upon, in haste; they agreed upon a rendezvous point in the woods, consulting their compasses. Laurence felt his neckcloth, to be sure it was tied, and shrugged back into his coat in the dark, adjusting the gold bars upon his shoulders; his hat was gone. "Warren, Chenery; your servant, Harcourt," he said, shaking their hands. Ferris and Riggs were crouched by the opening, ready; his own pistols were loaded. "Gentlemen," he said, and drawing his sword went through the cavern exit, a roar of God and King George behind him.

Chapter 10

⊱❈⊰

LAURENCE STUMBLED AS the rough hands dragged him up; his legs would not answer, and when he was flung forward they crumpled at once, casting him full-length on the ground, beside the other prisoners. They were being flung roughly into a rig much like their own belly-netting, but of coarser rope and designed less for passengers than for baggage. In a few sharp jerks, they were hauled up and slung below the red-brown dragon's belly, their arms and legs left to dangle through the large haphazardly knotted gaps, and their bodies crammed in one atop another. The netting was loose, and swung in great sickening curves with every shift in the wind or direction, every sudden diving movement.

There was no guard set to watch them, nor any personal restraint, but they were thoroughly immobilized regardless, and had no opportunity to shift their positions or converse. He was low in the netting, with his face pressed directly into the raw cords, which scraped him now and again; but he was grateful for the air despite the thin ribbons of blood which came dripping past him, and the wider arc of swinging. Dyer was pushed up against his side; Laurence had his arm around the boy, to keep him in: the netting was uneven, and the cords moving might have easily let him slip through to plunge to his death.

The wounded had been thrown in with the whole. A young midwingman from Chenery's crew, badly clawed, lay with his jaw pressed against Laurence's arm, blood seeping slowly from the corner of his mouth and soaking through the cloth. Some time during the night he died, and his corpse stiffened slowly as they flew on. Laurence could distinguish no-one else around him, only the anonymous pressure of a boot in the small of his back, a knee jammed up against his own, so that his leg was bent back upon itself.

He had glimpsed Mrs. Erasmus only briefly, in the dreadful confusion of their taking, as the nets were flung down upon them from the trees; she had certainly been dragged away alive. He did not wish to think on it; he could do little else, and Catherine's fate weighed on him heavily.

They did not stop. He slept, or at least passed into a state more distant from the world than wakefulness, the wind passing over his face in gusts, the rocking of the netting not wholly unlike the querulous motion of a ship riding at anchor in a choppy cross-sea. A little while after dawn, the dragon brought up sharp, cupping the wind in its wings as it descended, bird-like, and came to the ground jarringly, skipping a few steps along the earth before dropping onto its forelegs.

The netting was cut loose, roughly, and they were picked over quickly and efficiently, the men prodding them with the butt ends of their spears and heaving away the corpses. Laurence could not have risen to his legs with all the liberty in the world to do so, his knee afire with returning blood, but he raised his head, and saw Catherine lying a little way distant: flat upon her back, pale and her eyes shut, with blood on the side of her face. There were two bloody rents in her coat also, near the arm, but she had kept it, and buttoned; her hair was still tightly plaited, and there was no sign she had been distinguished.

No time for anything more: a little water was splashed in their faces, and the netting folded back over their heads; the dragon stepped over them and they were hoisted back up with quick, jerking pulls. Away again. The motion was worse in daylight, and they were a lighter load now, swaying more easily with the wind and every slight change of direction; the Corps was a service that hardened the stomach, but even so filth trickled down now through the press of bodies, the sour smell of bile. Laurence breathed through his mouth so far as he could, and turned his face to the ropes when he himself had to vomit.

There was no more sleep, until at last with the sun they descended again, and this time at last they were taken out from the netting one and two at a time, weak and ill, and lashed together at wrists, upper arms, and ankles, into a human chain. They were fixed to a pair of trees at either end, and their captors came around with water in dripping leather bags, fresh and delicious, the spout dragged too soon away from their seeking mouths; Laurence held the last swallow on his parched tongue as long as he could.

He leaned forward and glanced down the line: he did not see Warren at all, but Harcourt looked up at him, a quick nod; Ferris and Riggs looked as well as could be expected, and Roland was tied on at the very end, her head drooping against the tree to which she was fastened. Chenery was tied the other side of Dyer from him; his head was tipped awkwardly onto his own shoulder, his mouth hung open in exhaustion; he had a great purpling bruise all across his face, and he had his hand clenched upon his thigh, as though the older wound pained him.

They were near the banks of a river, Laurence gradually became aware, hearing the slow soft gurgling of the water behind him though he could not turn about to look, a torment when they were all still thirsty. They were in a matted grassy clearing; sending his eyes to the side he could see a border of large stones encircling the flattened grounds, and a fire-pit blackened with use: a hunting camp, perhaps, used regularly; the men were walking around the boundary, tearing up the greenery which had sent encroaching tendrils into the clearing.

The great red-brown beast settled itself at the far side of the fire-pit, and closing its eyes down to slits went to sleep; the other two took wing again: a mottled green, and a dark brown creature, both with pale grey underbellies gilded with a kind of iridescence, which quickly made them melt into the deepening sky above on their leap.

A long-legged plover wandered through the clearing, picking at the ground for seeds and chirping, a high metallic sound like a small bell struck with a hammer. In a little while the smaller dragons returned, carrying the limp bodies of several antelope; two of these were respectfully deposited before the red-brown dragon, who tore into them with appetite; another they shared amongst themselves; and the last was given to the men, butchered quickly, and put into a large cauldron already steaming.

Their captors were quiet over their dinner, clustering to one side of the fire and eating from bowls with their fingers; when one of them rose to go to the boiling-pot again, and the flames leapt with the sizzle of water, Laurence glimpsed briefly Mrs. Erasmus on the other side of the fire beside the dragon, sitting bent over a bowl in her hands and eating, steadily and calmly. Her hair had come loose from its ruthless restraints, and curved out around her face in a stiff bell-shape; she had no expression at all, and her dress was torn.

After their own meal, the men came over and in a handful of bowls fed them all off the remnants, a kind of grain-porridge cooked in meat broth. There was not a great deal for any of them, and humiliating to have to eat with their faces bent forward into the bowl held for them, like rooting in a trough, the remnants left dripping from their chins. Laurence closed his eyes and ate, and when Dyer would have left some broth in the bowl said, "You will oblige me by eating everything you can; there is no telling when they will feed us again."

"Yes, sir," Dyer said, "only they will put us back aboard, and I am sure I will have it all up again."

"Even so," Laurence said, and thankfully it seemed that their captors did not mean to set out again immediately. They instead spread out woven blankets upon the ground, and carried out a long bundle from among their things; they set it down upon the blankets and undid the wrappings, and Laurence recognized the corpse: the man whom Hobbes had shot, the one who had murdered Erasmus. They laid him out with ceremony, and washed him down with water carried from the spring, then wrapped him again in the skins of the antelope lately caught. The bloody spear they set beside him, as a trophy perhaps. One of them brought out a drum; others took up dry sticks from the ground, or began simply clapping or stamping their feet, and with their hands and voices made a chant like a single unending cry, one taking up the thread when another paused for breath.

It was grown wholly dark; they were still singing. Chenery opened his eyes and looked over at Laurence. "How far do you suppose we have come?"

"A night and day, flying straight, at a good pace; making steadily north by north-east, I think," Laurence said, low. "I cannot tell more; what speed do you think he would make, the big one?"

Chenery studied the red-brown dragon and shook his head. "Wingspan equal to his length, not too thickset; thirteen knots at a guess, if he didn't want to throw the light-weights off his pace. Call it fourteen."

"More than three hundred miles, then," Laurence said, his heart sinking; three hundred miles, and not a track left behind them to show the way. If Temeraire and the others could have caught them, he would have had no fear, not of this small rag-tag band; but in the vastness of the continent, they could disappear as easily as if they had all been killed and buried, and waste the rest of their lives imprisoned.

Already they had scarcely any hope of making their way back to the Cape overland, even setting aside the great likelihood of pursuit. If they made directly westward for the coast, avoiding all native perils and managing to find food and water enough to sustain them over a more reasonable month's march, they might at last reach the ocean; then what? A raft, perhaps, might be contrived; or a pirogue of a sort; Laurence did not set himself up as a Cook or a Bligh, but he supposed he could navigate them to a port, if they escaped gale and dangerous currents, and bring back aid for the survivors. A great many *ifs*, all of them unlikely in the extreme, and sure to only grow more so the farther they were carried; and meanwhile Temeraire would certainly have come into the interior after them, searching in a panic, and exposing himself to the worst sort of danger.

Laurence twisted his wrists against the ropes: they were good stuff, strong and tightly woven, and there was little yield. "Sir," Dyer said, "I think I have my pocket-knife."

Their captors were winding down their ceremony; the two small dragons were digging a hole, for the burial. The pocket-knife was not very sharp, and the ropes were tough; Laurence had to saw for a long time to free one arm, the thin wooden hilt slippery in his sweating hand, and his fingers cramping around it as he tried to bend the knife against the bindings around his wrist. At last he succeeded, and passed it along to Chenery; with one arm free he could work on the knots between him and Dyer.

"Quietly, Mr. Allen," Laurence said, on his other side; the ensign was tugging clumsily at the knots holding him to one of Catherine's midwingmen.

The mound was raised, and their captors were asleep, before they had more than half disentangled themselves. There was a noisy groaning of hippopotami in the darkness; it sounded very near-by at times, and occasionally one of the dragons would raise a sleepy head, listening, and make a quelling growl, which silenced all the night around them.

They worked more urgently now, and those of them already freed risked creeping from their places to help the others; Laurence worked with Catherine, whose slim fingers made quick work of the worst knots, and then he whispered softly, when they had loosed her man Peck, the last, "Pray take the others into the woods and do not wait for me; I must try and free Mrs. Erasmus."

She nodded, and pressed the pocket-knife on him: dulled to uselessness, but at least a moral support; and then they quietly one by one crept into the forest, away from the camp, except for Ferris, who crawled over to Laurence's side. "The guns?" he asked softly.

Laurence shook his head: the rifles had unhappily

been bundled away, by their captors, into the rest of their baggage, which lay tucked beside the head of one of the snoring dragons: there was no way to get at them. It was dreadful enough to have to creep past the sleeping men, lying exhausted and sprawled upon the ground after the catharsis of their wake: every ordinary snuffled noise of sleep magnified a hundredfold, and the occasional low crackles of the fire, burning down, like thunderclaps. His knees were inclined to be weak, and some of his steps sagged, involuntarily, almost so they brushed the ground; he had to steady himself with a hand against the dirt.

Mrs. Erasmus was lying apart from the men, to one side of the fire, very near the head of the great redbrown dragon; his forelegs were curled shallowly to either side of her. She was huddled very small, with her hands tucked beneath her head; but Laurence was glad to see she did not seem to have been injured. She jerked almost loose when Laurence's hand came over her mouth, the whites of her eyes showing all around, but her trembling quieted at once when she saw him; she nodded, and he lifted his hand away again, to help her to her feet.

They crept as softly away, and slowly, around the great taloned claw, the black horny edges serrated and gleaming with the red firelight, the dragon's breath coming deep and evenly; his nostrils flared in their regular pace, showing a little pink within. They were ten paces away, eleven; the dark eyelid cracked, and the yellow eye slid open upon them.

He was up and roaring at once. "Go!" Laurence shouted, pushing Mrs. Erasmus onward with Ferris; his own legs would not answer quickly, and one of the men waking leapt upon him, taking him by the knees and to the ground. They fell wrestling in the dust and dirt, near the fire; Laurence grimly hoping for nothing more, now, than to cover the escape. It was a clumsy, drunken struggle, like the last rounds of a mill with both parties weaving and bloodied; both of them exhausted, and Laurence's weakness matched by his opponent's confusion of having been woken from sound sleep. Rolling upon his back, Laurence managed to lock an arm around the man's throat, and pulled with all his might upon his own wrist to hold it; he lashed out with his booted foot to trip another who was snatching for his spear.

Ferris had pushed Mrs. Erasmus towards the forest; a dozen of the aviators were running out, to come to her aid, and to Laurence. "Lethabo!" the dragon cried—whatever the threat or meaning, it brought her to a distracted halt, looking around; the dragon was lunging for Ferris.

She called out in protest herself and, running back where Ferris had dived to the ground to evade in desperation, threw herself between, holding up a hand; the claw, descending, stopped, and the dragon put it down again before her.

This time the men set a watch, learning from their mistake, and tied them up closer by the fire: there would be no second attempt. The two small dragons had herded them back to the camp with contemptuous ease, and an air of practice; if in the process they had also stampeded a small herd of antelope, they did not mind that, and made a late supper to console themselves for the effort. They missed only Kettering, one of Harcourt's riflemen, and Peck and Bailes, both harness-men; but the latter two stumbled demoralized back into camp and surrendered, early in the morning, with the intelligence that Kettering had been killed, trying to ford the river, by a hippo; their pale and nauseated expressions precluded any wish of knowing more.

"It was my name," Mrs. Erasmus said, her hands tight around her cup of dark red tea. "Lethabo. It was my name when I was a girl."

She had not been permitted to come and speak to them, but at her pleading they had at length consented to bring Laurence over, hobbled at the ankles with his wrists tied together before him, and one of the spearmen standing watch lest he try to reach towards her. The red-brown dragon himself was bent over their conversation alertly, with a malevolent eye on Laurence at every moment.

"Are these men of your native tribe, then?" he asked.

"The men, no. They are of a tribe, I think, cousins to my own, or allied. I am not very sure, but they can understand me when I speak. But—" She paused, and said, "I do not understand it properly myself, but Kefentse," she nodded towards the great hovering beast, "says he is my great-grandfather."

Laurence was baffled, and supposed she had misunderstood; or translated wrong. "No," she said, "no; there are many words I do not remember well, but I was taken with many others, and some of us were sold together also. We called all the older men Grandfather, for respect. I am sure that is all it means."

"Have you enough of the tongue to explain to him we meant no harm?" Laurence asked. "That we only sought the mushrooms—"

She made the halting attempt, but the dragon snorted in a disdainful manner before she had even finished. He at once insinuated his great taloned forehand between them, glaring as if Laurence had offered her an insult, and spoke to the men: they at once pulled Laurence to his feet and dragged him back to the line of prisoners.

"Well," Chenery said, when Laurence had been tied up with them again, "it sounds a little promising: I dare say when she has had a chance to talk to him, she will be able to bring him round. And in the meantime, at least they do not mean to kill us, or I expect they would have done so already and saved themselves the trouble of our keep."

For what motive they *had* been preserved, however, was quite unclear; there was no attempt made to question them, and Laurence was growing bewildered as their journey extended further and further, past what could ever have been the reasonable extent of the territory of a small tribe, even one in the possession of dragons. He might have thought they were circling about, to lose pursuit, but the sun during the day and the Southern Cross at night gave it the lie: their course was steady and purposeful, always north by north-east, veering only to bring them to a more comfortable situation for the night, or to running water.

Early the next day they stopped by a wide river, looking almost orange from its muddy bottom, and populated by more of the noisy hippopotami, which darted away through the water with surprising speed from the pouncing dragons, submerging through wide ripples to evade. At last one of them was served out, by the two small dragons cornering it from both sides, and laid down to be butchered in the clearing. Their captors had grown confident enough to untie a few of them to assist with the tedious labor, Dyer and Catherine's young runner Tooke set to carrying water back and forth in a bowl, fetching it uneasily from the water's edge: there was a substantial crocodile sleeping on the farther bank, whose green eye was wide open and fixed upon them; its flesh was evidently not a temptation to the dragons, for it showed not the least sign of fear.

The dragons lay drowsing in the sun, their tails flicking idly at the enormous clouds of flies which gathered round them, their heads pillowed on their forelegs. Mrs. Erasmus was speaking into Kefentse's ear; mid-sentence, he reared abruptly up and began to make questions of her, demandingly; she flinched back, and only shook her head, refusing. At last he left off, and cast his eyes southward, sitting up on his haunches like a coat of arms: a dragon sejant erect, gules; then slowly he settled himself back down; he spoke to her once more, and pointedly shut his eyes.

"Well, I don't suppose we need ask what he thinks of letting you go," Chenery said, when she had crept around to them.

"No," she said, speaking low to keep from rousing the dragons up again, "and matters are only worse: I spoke of my daughters, and now Kefentse wants nothing more than to go back for them also."

Laurence was ashamed to feel an eager leap of hope, at a situation which naturally could cause her only the greatest anxiety; but such an attempt would at least reveal to the rest of the formation the identity of their captors. "And I assure you, ma'am," he said, "that any such demand would be received with the utmost scorn: I am confident that our fellow officers and General Grey will consider your children their own charge."

"Captain, you do not understand," she said. "I think he would be ready to attack all the colony to get at them. He thinks there may be more of their stolen kindred there, too, among the slaves."

"I am sure I wish them much luck, if they like to try it," Chenery said. "Pray don't be worried for the girls: even if these fellows have another few beauties like this grandfather of yours at home, it would take a little more than that to crack a nut like the castle. There are twenty-four-pounders there; not to speak of pepper guns, and a full formation. I don't suppose he would like to come back with us, instead; to England, I mean?" he added, with a flash of cheerful optimism. "If he has taken to you so strong, you ought to be able to persuade him."

But it was very soon clear that Kefentse, whatever else he meant by calling himself her great-grandfather, certainly considered himself in the light of her elder; even though she thought now, that she vaguely recalled his hatching. "Not well, but I am almost sure of it," she said. "I was very young, but there were many days of feasting, and presents; and I remember him often in the village, after," which Laurence supposed answered for her lack of fear of dragons; she had been taken as a girl of some nine-years' age, old enough to have lost the instinctive terror.

Remembering her only as a child, Kefentse, far from being inclined to obey, had instead concluded from her efforts to secure their freedom that she was their dupe, either frightened or tricked into lying for their sake, and he was grown all the angrier for it. "I beg you do not risk any further attempts at persuasion," Laurence said. "We must be grateful for his protection of you; I would have you make no more fruitless attempts, which might cause him to reconsider his sentiments."

"He would do nothing to hurt me," she said, a strange certainty; perhaps the restoration of some childhood confidence.

Having breakfasted on roasted hippo, they flew on some hours more and landed again only a little while before dark, beside what seemed to be a small farming village. The clearing where they descended was full of children at play, who shrieked with delight at their arrival, and ran eagerly around the dragons, chattering away at them without the slightest evidence of fear; although they peered very nervously at the prisoners. A broad spreading mimosa tree stood at the far end of the clearing, giving pleasant shade, and beneath it stood an odd little shed with no front, raised several feet from the ground and housing within it a dragon egg of substantial size. Around it a circle of women sat with mortar and pestle, pounding grain; they put aside their tools and patted the dragon egg, as if speaking to it, and rose to greet the visitors as they leapt down from the smaller dragons' backs, and to stare with curiosity.

Several men came in from the village, to clasp arms with the handlers and greet the dragons. An elaborately carved elephant's tooth hung from a tree, the narrow end cut open to make a horn, and one of the villagers took this down and blew on it, several long hollow ringing blasts. Shortly another dragon landed in the clearing, a middle-weight of perhaps ten tons, a delicate dusty shade of green with yellow markings and sprays of red spots upon his breast and shoulders, and two sets of long foreteeth which protruded over his jaw above and below. The children were even less shy of this newcomer, clustering close about his forelegs, even climbing upon his tail and pulling on his wings, a treatment which he bore with perfect patience while he talked with the visiting dragons.

The four of them settled around the enshrined dragon egg, in company with their handlers and the men of the village; and one older woman also sat with them, her dress marking her apart: a skirt of animal-skins and strings of long beads like reed-joints, and many heaped necklaces of animal claws and colored beads also. The rest of the women brought a large steaming pot of porridge, the grain boiled up in milk rather than broth, for their dinner; with fresh greens cooked with garlic, and dried meat preserved in salt: a little tough, but flavorful, vinegary and spiced.

Bowls were brought for the prisoners, and their hands were untied to allow them to eat for themselves for once, their captors less wary with so large a company around them; and in the celebratory bustle, Mrs. Erasmus was able to slip away from Kefentse to join them once again: he had been given pride of place beside the dragon egg, and presented a large cow to eat; and they seemed to hold the evening's entertainment until he had finished. At least when the remnants of the carcass on which he feasted had been carried away, and fresh dirt scattered over the ground before him to soak up the blood, only then did the old woman stand up, the one oddly dressed, and coming to stand before the dragon egg began to sing and clap.

The audience took up the rhythm, with clapping and with drums, and their voices joined with her on the refrains; each verse was different, without rhyme or pattern that Laurence could see. "She is saying, she is telling the egg," Mrs. Erasmus said, staring at the ground, unseeing; intent upon following the words. "She is telling him of his life. She is saying, he was a founder of the village; he brought them to a good safe country, past the desert, where the kidnappers do not come. He was a great hunter, and killed the lion with his own hands, when it would have raided among the cattle; they miss his wisdom, in the council, and he must hurry up and come back to them: it is his duty—"

Laurence stared, entirely baffled. The old priestess had finished her own verses, and began to lead one after another some of the men of the village to stand in front of the egg and recite, with a little prompting assistance from her. "They say they are his sons," Mrs. Erasmus said, "telling him they long to hear his voice again; that is his grandson, born since his death," when one of them carried an infant in swaddling to the egg, to pat its small hand against the shell. "It is only some heathen superstition, of course," Mrs. Erasmus added, but uneasily.

The dragons joined their own voices to the ceremony: the local beast addressing the egg as his old friend, whose return was eagerly awaited; the smaller dragons of the distant border spoke of the general pleasures of the hunt, of taking wing, of seeing their descendants prosper. Kefentse was silent, until the priestess chided him, and coaxed; then at last in his deep voice he gave warning rather than encouragement, and spoke of grief at failing in his duty: of coming back to the deserted village, the smoke of dying fires, all the houses empty; his children lying in the dust, still and not answering his calls, and the hyena slinking through the herds. "He searched, and searched, until he came to the shore, and at the ocean he knew—he knew he would not find us," Mrs. Erasmus said, and Kefentse put his head down and moaned, very low; abruptly she rose and crossed the clearing to him, and put her hands upon his lowered muzzle.

There was a certain sluggishness to the next morning's preparations for departure, the dragons and men both having indulged in some brewed liquor, late in the evening's festivities, which now rendered them all dragging; the small green dragon yawned and yawned, as if he would unhinge his jaw.

Woven baskets were being brought out to the clearing, so large they required two men each to carry, and full of foodstuffs: small pale yellow kidney beans spotted black, hard and dried; red-brown grains of sorghum; small onions of yellow and purple-red; more strips of the pungent dried meat. The men of their party nodded over the tribute, and the baskets were covered with woven lids, tied securely on with strips of tough thin rope braided of bark. The baskets in pairs were slung over the necks of the smaller dragons, who bent their heads to receive them.

There was at all times a watchful guard upon them, however; and also upon the perimeters of the village: younger boys, with a large cow-bell sort of contraption, which they could have rung out in an instant. It was a shameful consequence of the rapacity of the slave trade, that having exhausted the natural supply of prisoners of war among the kingdoms of the coast, the native suppliers of the trade had turned to kidnapping and raiding, without even the thin excuse of a quarrel over territory, solely to acquire more human chattel. These efforts were extending further into the interior with every year, and had evidently made the villagers begin to be wary.

It was not a condition of long standing, for the village was not designed upon defensible lines, being only a collection of handsome but small, low houses made of clay and stones and roofed in straw. These were circular, with nearly a quarter of the circumference open to the elements to let the smoke of their cooking-fires out, and would have offered little shelter against a marauding band intent on capture or slaughter. Indeed there was no great wealth here, which they should have studied to protect: only a small herd of cattle and goats, browsing idly beyond the village boundaries under the attention of a few older children; respectable fields, adequate for subsistence and a little more; a few of the women and older men wore handsome trinkets of ivory and gold and brightly woven cloth. But nothing which would have tempted the rapacity of an ordinary robber, save the inhabitants themselves, for their being peaceful, healthy, and well-fleshed; and the caution sat new and uneasily upon their shoulders.

"They have had no-one stolen here, yet," Mrs. Erasmus said. "But three children were snatched from a village a day's flight from here. One was hiding near-by, and slipped away to give the warning; so the ancestors— the dragons—caught them." She paused and said, oddly calm, "That is why the slave-takers killed all my family, I think; the ones too old or too young to sell. So they could not tell Kefentse where we had gone."

She stood up and went to go stand watching the village, while the packing went forward: the smallest children at play before their grandmothers, the other women working together, pounding flour out of sorghum, and singing. Her dark, high-collared dress was dusty and torn, incongruous among their bright if immodest garments; and Kefentse lifted his head to watch her with anxious, jealous attention.

"He must have gone half-mad," Chenery said to Laurence in an undertone, "as though his captain and all his crew were gone in an instant." He shook his head. "This is a kettle and no mistake: he will never let her go."

"Perhaps she may find an opportunity to slip away," Laurence said grimly; he reproached himself bitterly that they had ever involved her and Erasmus at all.

For another day and night they did not stop again, except very briefly for water, and Laurence's heart sank at the vast expanse of hard, dry desert which rolled away below them, a succession of red-brown sands and arid scrubland, and great white salt pans barren of all life. Their course continued north-east, bearing them still farther inland and away from the coast; their thin hopes of escape or rescue wasting away entirely.

At last they left behind the wastelands, and the desert

yielded to milder scenery of green trees and yellow ground overgrown with thick grasses; late in the morning, the belly of the dragon rumbled loud above them with his roar of greeting: answered momentarily with several voices from up ahead, and they came abruptly into view of an astonishing prospect: a vast moving herd of elephants, creeping slowly across the savannah as they tore at the shrubs and low-hanging branches in their path, and enduring with perfect docility the supervision of two dragons and some thirty men, who ambled along comfortably behind, only a few lengths short of the rear of the herd.

The herdsmen carried long sticks with dangling rattles, by which means they kept the herd from turning back; a little farther along, perhaps a quarter-of-a-mile into the wreckage the herd had left behind, women worked busily, spreading great bushels of red-stained manure and planting young shrubs: they sang as they worked, rhythmically.

The prisoners were let down. Laurence almost was distracted from the water-bag for staring at the fat, sluggish creatures, larger than any he had ever heard bragged of. He had visited India twice, as a naval officer, and once seen an impressive old creature carrying a native potentate and his retinue upon its head, some six tons in weight. The most impressive here would have he guessed outweighed that one by half again, and rivaled Nitidus or Dulcia in size, with great ivory tusks jutting out like spears some three feet beyond its head. Another of the behemoths put its head down against a young tree, of no mean size, and with a groaning implacable push brought it crashing to the ground; pleased with its success, the elephant ambled lazily down its length, to devour at leisure the tender shoots from the crown.

After some little conversation with their captors, the

herd-dragons went aloft and chivvied away a few of the beasts from the main body of the herd: older animals, by the length of their tusks, without young. These having been coaxed downwind and behind the line of herdsmen, Kefentse and the two other dragons fell upon them skillfully: a single piercing of talons slew the creatures, before they could make any outcry which might have distressed the rest. The dragons made their repast greedily, murmuring with satisfaction, as might a contented gentleman over his pleasing dinner; when they were done, the hyenas crept out of the grass to deal with the bloody remains, and cackled all through the night.

Throughout the next two days, they were scarcely an hour aloft without sight of some other dragons, calling greetings from afar; more villages flashed past beneath them, and occasionally some small fortification with walls of clay and rock, until in the distance they glimpsed a tremendous plume of smoke rising, like a great grass-fire, and a thin silvery line winding away over the earth.

"Mosi oa Tunya," Mrs. Erasmus had told them, was the name of their destination, meaning *smoke that thunders;* and a low and continuous roaring built higher around them as Kefentse angled directly towards the plume.

The narrow shining line upon the earth resolved itself swiftly into a river of great immensity: slow and very broad, fractured into many smaller streams, all winding together past rocks and small grassy islets towards a narrow crack in the earth like an eggshell broken down the middle, where the river suddenly boiled up and plunged into the thunder of a waterfall more vast than anything Laurence might have conceived, the gorges of its descent so full of white-plumed spray that its base could not be seen.

Into these narrow gorges, which seemed barely wide enough for him to go abreast, Kefentse dived at speed, pocket rainbows gleaming in puddles collected upon his hide through the first clouds of steam. Pressed hard up against the netting, Laurence wiped water from his face and one-week's beard, and palmed it away from the hollows of his eyes, squinting as they broke through into a widening canyon.

The lower slopes were thickly forested, a jewel-green tangle of tropical growth reaching some halfway up the walls, where abruptly the vegetation ended and the cliff faces rose sheer and smooth to the plain above, gleaming like polished marble and pockmarked only by the gaping holes of caverns. And then Laurence realized he was not looking at caverns, but at great carved archways, mouths for vaulted halls which penetrated deep within the mountain-side. The cliff walls did not gleam like polished marble; they *were* polished marble, or as good as: a smooth speckled stone, with quantities of ivory and gold inlaid directly into the rock in fantastical pattern.

Façades were carved and sculpted around the openings, ornamented gorgeously in vivid color and odd abstract patterns, and towering more vast than Westminster or St. Paul's, the only and inadequate measures of comparison which Laurence possessed. Narrow stairs, their railings carved of stone and smoothed by the water-spray, climbed between the archways to give the perspective: five ordinary town-houses, laid foundation-to-roof atop one another, might have approximated the heights of the largest.

Kefentse was going at a lazy speed now, the better to avoid collision: the gorge was full of dragons. Dragons flew back and forth busily among the halls, some carrying baskets or bundles, some carrying men on their backs; dragons lay sleeping upon the carved ledges, tails drooping downward from the mouths. Upon the stairways and in the halls, men and women stood talking or at labor, dressed in animal-skins or wrapped cloth garments of dazzling-bright colors, indigo and red and yellow ochre against their dark brown skin, many with elaborate chains of gold; and softly running above the sounds of all their mingled speech came the unending voice of the water.

Chapter 11

KEFENTSE DEPOSITED THEM rudely within one of the smaller caverns dug into the face of the rock: he could not fit inside himself, but only balanced upon the lip of the cave while the netting was undone. They were shaken out onto the floor in a heap, still tied up, and he flew at once away, taking poor Mrs. Erasmus with him, and abandoning them to work themselves loose. There was no sharp edge to help them; the cavern walls were smoothed. Dyer and Roland and Tooke managed eventually to squirm their smaller hands out of their bindings, and began to help untie the others.

Thirty of them left all together, from four crews. They were not crowded, nor could their circumstances be called cruel; the floor was strewn liberally with dry straw to soften the hard rock, and despite the lingering day's heat outside, the chamber remained cool and pleasant. A necessary-pit was carved out of the stone at the back of the chamber; it must surely have connected with a drainage channel somewhere beneath, but the opening was small, and drilled through solid rock: there was no way to get to it. There was a small pool also, in the back, refreshed continuously from a trickling channel and waist-deep on a man, large enough to swim across a few strokes: they would by no means die of thirst.

It was a strange prison, with neither guard nor bars upon the door, but as impregnable as any fortress; there were none of the carved steps leading to their cavern, and nothing but the yawning gorge beneath. The scale of the whole, the carved and gothic ceiling vaulting overhead, would have made a comfortable stall for a small dragon; it ought to have seemed an airy and spacious environment, but had the effect of making them feel rather Lilliputian than comfortable, children wandering in a giant's house, with their numbers so painfully small and dwindled.

Dorset was alive, with a terrible bruising down along the side of his face, and he pressed his hand now and again to his side, as if his ribs or his breathing pained him. "Mr. Pratt is dead, Captain," he said. "I am very sorry to be sure: he tried to stand before Mrs. Erasmus, and the beast carved him to the hip," a grievous loss, the smith's quiet capability no less than his immense strength.

There was no way to be certain of the full extent of their losses: Hobbes killed before their eyes, and Laurence had seen Chenery's midwingman Hyatt dead; Chenery's lieutenant Libbley remembered the surgeon Waley fallen also; but another dozen at least had been heaved out after that first night, the rest of them too sick and dazed to recognize in dim lighting, and more had been left dead upon the field; others still, they hoped, had slipped away in the general confusion, to leave at least some faint direction behind. There was no-one who had seen Warren.

"But I hope to God that Sutton will have the sense to turn back straightaway for the Cape," Harcourt said. "No-one could ever conceive we had been brought so far; they will wear themselves to rags with fretting, and never find a trace: we must find some way to get them word, at least. Those men knew something about guns, did you notice? There must be some trade, some merchants must be tempted to come: more ivory than they know what to do with, when they build their walls out of the stuff."

They ventured cautiously to the edge of the cavern-mouth to look out again into the gorges. The first impression of immensity and splendor was not to be undone, but the degree perhaps fell off a little here, farther from the falls and near the end of the inhabited portion of the gorges; the façade of their own prison was plain rock, although the native cliff wall had been polished to a smoothness that would have defied a monkey to climb.

Chenery bent down over the ledge and rubbed his hand over the wall, as far down as he could reach, and came up discouraged. "Not a finger-hold to be had: we are not going anywhere, until we manage to sprout wings of our own."

"Then we had better rest, while we may," Harcourt said, in practical tones, "and if you gentlemen will be so good as to give me your backs, I am going to bathe."

They were roused up early not by any attentions paid to them, for there were none, but by a dreadful noise which could most easily be compared to a swarm of horse-flies in continuous agitation. The sun had not yet penetrated into the twisting canyons, though the sky above was the thorough-going blue of mid-morning, and a faint glaze of mist yet clung to the smooth rock near the cavern mouth.

Across the gorge, a pair of dragons were engaged in a peculiar exercise, flying back and forth hauling alternately upon what looked to be a thick grey hawser coiled about and passed through the end of a tremendous iron shaft, spinning it steadily. The other end of the shaft was plunged into the depths of a cavern only partially hollowed-out, and from here issued the malevolent buzzing. Dust and chalky powder blew out in great gusts, speckling the dragons' hides so they were coated thickly ochre; occasionally one or the other would turn his head and sneeze powerfully, without ever losing the rhythm.

A great cracking noise heralded a leap forward: loose pebbles and great stones came spilling from the mouth of the hall into a large sack stretched out upon a frame to catch them. The dragons paused in their labor, and withdrew the enormous drill; one clung on to the rough, unpolished cliff, holding the mechanism suspended, while the other perched upon the ledge and scraped out the boulders and loose rock which had shattered. A third dragon, smaller, came winging down the gorge when the operation was complete; he carried away the laden sack, to let the pair resume.

While this work proceeded, almost directly above them another cavern, already sunk deep within the hillside, crawled with human masons finishing the rough work, the distant musical *plink-plink* of tapping hammers on the rock drifting across the divide; each man bringing his own discards to the cave-mouth as they smoothed down the walls.

They were very industrious all the morning; then midday arriving they quitted their work. Their tools were heaped inside the cavern, the vast drill also; and the dragons flying up collected the men, who without any harness leapt with casual fearlessness onto the dragon's backs, wings, limbs, and clapped on to the handful of woven straps, or merely clung, and were borne away along the gorge, back to the more settled area.

Still no-one had come. They had among their pockets some biscuit, a little dried fruit, which would not have made a meal for even one man; it was pressed on Catherine, who at first disdained it scornfully, until Dorset insisted upon it as a medical matter.

The workmen did not return, but several dragons appeared in a party upon the plain on the far side of the gorge, each carrying a goodly sized bundle of wood, and laid down a large bonfire; then one among them bent its head and breathed out a flame, igniting the whole. It was not perhaps a great stream of fire; but then none was called for by the circumstances. "Oh, that is a pity," Chenery said, rather low; understating the case.

They grew only sorrier when another pair arrived, carrying what looked to be the component parts of three or four elephants among them, butchered and neatly skewered on long iron stakes, to roast over the bonfire. The wind was in their quarter, carrying towards the caves. Laurence had to wipe his mouth with his handkerchief, twice; even the very back of the cavern offered no shelter from the torment of the delicious smell. It was very disheartening to observe the dragons cast away the scorched and cracked bones, when they had done, into the massive thicket of jungle which lined the floor of the gorge below; still more regrettable were the satisfied growls and yelping which presently rose up in reply, lions, perhaps, or wild dogs: a fresh obstacle to any escape.

Two hours more passed, or nearly, by the cracked glass which Turner had managed to salvage from the wreck of their capture; it began to grow dark. Dragons came flying to many of the plain cave-mouths near-by, carrying netting full of men, whom they let down inside the caves just as the aviators had been deposited: the dragons had a sort of trick of setting their hind legs upon the lip of each cavern, and setting their foreclaws into some ridges carved above the mouth, while their riders unhooked the netting, so they did not have to squeeze into some of these smaller caverns. It bore some resemblance to the passenger-dragons, which Laurence had seen in China, save for the perfect disregard for the comfort of the passengers in the nets.

When these deliveries had finished, a small dragon flew down the gorge towards them, with many baskets slung over its shoulders. It halted in sequence at the cave-mouths, leaving behind a few of the bundles every time, until at last it reached their own. There was a single man upon its back, who looked their number over with a critical eye, then untied some three of the baskets before taking wing again.

Each held a cold and thickened mass of sorghum-porridge cooked in milk: filling if not savory, and the portions not quite so large as desirable. "One basket for every ten men," Harcourt said, counting cave-mouths, "so as many as fifty men, in that large one: they must have near a thousand prisoners here, spread out."

"A regular Newgate," Chenery said, "but less damp, for which be thanked; do you suppose they mean to sell us? A charming solution, if we could get ourselves shipped to Cape Coast and not a French port; and if they were not unpleasant about it."

"Maybe they will eat us," Dyer said thoughtfully, his piping voice quite clear; all the other men were engaged deeply with their dinners.

There was a general pause. "A thoroughly morbid suggestion, Mr. Dyer; let me hear no more of this sort of speculation," Laurence said, taken aback.

"Oh, yes, sir," Dyer said, surprised, and went directly

back to his dinner, with no particular sign of dismay; some of the younger ensigns looked greenly, and it required perhaps a full minute before hunger once again overcame their temporary qualms.

The line of sunlight crept up the far wall and slid away over the edge; dusk came early into the narrow gorge. For lack of anything else to do, they slept, while the sky above was still a daylit blue, and the next morning roused from an uneasy night into darkness, with the dreadful buzzing of the drill suddenly muffled; Dyer's breathless, "Sir, sir—" in Laurence's ear.

Kefentse was there; he had thrust as much of his head as would fit into the opening of their cavern, blocking both light and noise from outside. Mrs. Erasmus was with him, difficult to recognize in the native dress which she had been given, and weighted down as if she were in danger of floating away: earrings, armbands like coiled snakes on upper arms and lower, a great neck-collar of gold pieces strung on wire, interspersed with pieces of ivory, dark green jade, and ruby, certainly worth fifty thousand pounds at least, and a great emerald like an egg, set in gold, pinning a turban of silk upon her head.

Most of the native women which they had seen, from their vantage point, had been carrying water, or hanging washing to dry upon the steps, and wore only a kind of leather skirt, reaching to the knees but leaving their breasts quite bare: much to the covert interest of the younger officers. Perhaps formal garments were of different style, or she had prevailed upon them to give her others; she wore instead a long skirt of plain white cotton, and over it another length of cotton cloth woven of bright colors, wrapped and folded elaborately about her shoulders.

She required the assistance of a hand on her elbow to

climb down from Kefentse's back. "They would have me wear more if it would not make it impossible for me to walk: it is the tribal property," she said. It was evasion; her expression was uneasy, and after a moment's pause she said, low, "I am sorry: Kefentse is here to take our leader, to go and speak with the king."

Harcourt was pale but composed. "I am senior, ma'am; he may take me."

"He may sooner go to the Devil," Chenery said. "Laurence, shall we have lots for it?" Taking up a small twig from the rushes he snapped it in two and held them out with the top ends even, the lower concealed.

It was at least a good deal more comfortable to be carried in Kefentse's talons, than in the former netting; and Laurence did not feel his appearance wholly disgraceful: the idleness and heat of the day had left them nothing but time, and thanks to the convenience of the waterpool, he had sponged his coat as best he could, and thoroughly washed his breeches and his linen. He had not shaved, but that could not be helped.

The roar of the falls increased steadily, and the tangle of jungle below, until they were brought at last to a curve of the gorge very near the falls; here a great hall stood open, three times the width of the other archways, the entryway pillared for support. Kefentse dived low and swiftly within, and coming to a stop rolled him unceremoniously out of his talons onto the damp floor, before more carefully setting Mrs. Erasmus onto her feet.

Laurence had already come to expect these indignities, and picked himself up without more than irritation, an emotion promptly vanquished in favor of concern. A makeshift workshop had been established recently, it seemed, along the right side of the chamber, and besides the rifles which the aviators themselves had lost, some sixty or seventy muskets more were laid out upon the floor on woven mats, in various states of disassembly and repair; and worse, far worse: a six-pound gun, its housing cracked but not gone, and a barrel of gunpowder besides. A small group of men were working upon the collection, taking apart a musket and pressing low harsh questions on a man sitting dejectedly on a stool before them; his back, turned to Laurence, was marked with half-a-dozen bloody weals, and flies crawled upon it.

A young man was overseeing their work with great attention; he left off, as Kefentse landed, and came over towards them: tall, with a long face infused with a certain quality of sorrow, not by emotion but only the angle of his cheekbones, like a hound; the nose sculpted and a narrow black beard around the full mouth. He had a small escort of warriors, all of them bare-chested and armed with short spears, leather-skirted; he was distinguished from the rest of them by a thick neck-collar of gold with a fringe of what looked to be the claws of some great cat, and a leopard-skin cape draped over the shoulders: physically powerful, and his eyes were shrewd.

Laurence bowed; the young man ignored him, looking to the other side of the great hall, and from a chamber within came a great creature of golden-bronze hide, the underside of her wings lined in purple like royalty. She was in battle-array formidable as a Crusader, great heavy plates of iron slung across the vulnerable expanse of her breast, with a fine mesh of chain beneath to protect the belly, and the spikes bristling down her spine were sheathed in caps of iron, as were her talons, and these were yet discolored a little with blood; Mrs. Erasmus gave him to understand that this was the king, Mokhachane, and his eldest son Moshueshue.

She—or he?—Laurence was at a loss; he was standing

scarcely half-a-length away, and the king was quite certainly, quite visibly a female dragon—seated herself sphinx-like on the floor, her tail curling along her flanks, and regarded Laurence with a cold and amber eye. The young man, Moshueshue, seated himself on a wooden throne, which was brought to him and set by her side, and several older women trailing after settled themselves on wooden stools behind him: these identified as the king's wives.

Kefentse lowered his head respectfully, and began to speak, evidently giving his account of their capture and journey, which Mrs. Erasmus with great courage dared to dispute, at several points, on their behalf; while trying to help Laurence understand the accusations which had been made. That they had stolen medicines, cultivated for the use of the king's own subjects, was only the least offense; the foremost, that they had offered a territorial challenge, by invading in the company of their own ancestors, as Kefentse considered the dragons of the formation to be; and in league with enemy tribes had been stealing their children, for which he offered as one portion of evidence that they had been traveling with a man of the Lunda, notorious kidnappers—

Mrs. Erasmus paused and said unevenly, "—he means my husband."

She did not continue her translation at once, but pressed a fold of her gown briefly to her face, while Kefentse bent low and anxiously over her, crooning, and snapping at Laurence with a hiss, when he would have offered his arm for her support.

"The medicine we took only for necessity, because our own dragons were ill; and without knowing the mushroom cultivated," Laurence said, but he did not know how else to defend himself. He could not very well deny they had brought dragons; they had, and in any case, this seemed rather to stand in for making a territorial claim, which he could certainly not as a serving-officer deny. The British and the Dutch would alike have been surprised to know their colony had been thought unworthy of notice, and casually to be violated, until the arrival of the formation.

And he was in no fair way armed to justify the practice of slavery, or to deny that it was carried on at the behest of white men, if he might refute some few of the particulars which were leveled against them— "No, good God, of course we do not eat them," he said, but beyond this could make very little more argument. The dreadful incident of the *Zong,* where more than a hundred slaves had been deliberately flung overboard, for the sake of insurance-money, chose the moment to come uncomfortably to his mind, with a blush for the guilt and shame of his nation; made him look a liar, if they had not already thought him so.

He could only repeat, that he was not himself a slaver, and was not surprised to find this excuse hold no water with them, nor even when Mrs. Erasmus had explained to them her husband's perfect innocence; the objection plainly was wider than such personal acts. There was no sympathy offered, for the illness which had driven them to seek the medicine; Laurence rather received the impression that they thought it little more than just deserts, drawing as they did no particular distinction between the British and their dragons, and their temper grew rather more fixed, than less, for all Laurence's attempts to explain.

The king turned, and, in response to a beckoning flick of her tail, Laurence was led farther back into the chamber, where stood a low table of enormous size, no higher than his knee but some twelve feet long and across. The women folded away the wooden covers, and a hollow space perhaps a foot deep was revealed, like a sort of display-case; inside lay a strange sculpture in the shape of the African continent. It was a map, an enormous map in thick relief to show elevation, gold-dust for sand and mountains of bronze, jewel-chip forests and rivers of silver; and with great dismay Laurence perceived the puff of white featherdown used to stand for the falls. It stood almost halfway between the tip of the continent, where Capetown lay, and the sharp jutting prominence of the African Horn: in his worst fears, he had not thought they had been brought so far into the interior.

They did not let him look at it long; instead they drew him to the other end, where the table had been lately extended: the wood was darker, and the sections of the map laid down only in soft painted wax. He did not at first know what to make of it, until by relative position he understood the blue oval stretch of water at the top of the continent must be the Mediterranean, and realized it was meant to figure as Europe: the outlines of Spain and Portugal and Italy misshapen and the whole continent shrunk; Britain itself nothing but a scattering of small whitish lumps in the upper corner. The Alps and the Pyrenees stood in pinched-up relief, approximately correct, but the Rhine and Volga were strangely meandering, and smaller than he was used to see them marked.

"They wish you to draw it properly," Mrs. Erasmus said, and one of the prince's men handed him a stylus; Laurence gave it back. The man repeated the instructions in his own tongue, exaggeratedly, as if Laurence were a slow child; and attempted to press the stylus on him once more.

"I beg your pardon; I will not," Laurence said, shaking off his hand; the man spoke loudly and struck him abruptly across the face. Laurence pressed his lips together and said nothing, his heart pounding in a furious temper. Mrs. Erasmus had turned to speak urgently to Kefentse; the dragon was shaking his head.

"Having been taken prisoner, in what I must consider an act of war, I must refuse under these conditions to answer any questions whatsoever," Laurence said.

Moshueshue shook his head, while the dragon-king lowered her head and fixed him with a glittering and furious eye, her head so close that he could see that what he had taken for tusks in Kefentse were a kind of jewelry: ivory rings banded with gold, set in the flesh of her upper lip like ear-rings. She snorted hot breath across his face, and bared serrated teeth; but he had too much use of being so close to Temeraire to be frightened thus, and her eyes slitted down angrily as she drew her head back.

The king said coldly, "You were taken as a thief, and a kidnapper, in our country; you will answer, or—" and Mrs. Erasmus paused and said, "Captain, you will be flogged."

"Brutality and further ill-usage will in no wise alter my determination," Laurence said, "and I beg your pardon, ma'am, if you are forced to witness it."

His answer provoked her only further; Moshueshue laying a hand on the king's foreleg spoke in low tones, but she shivered her skin impatiently, and threw him off. She spoke in a low angry continuous rumble, which Mrs. Erasmus could only manage piecemeal to convey: "*You* speak of ill-usage to us, kidnapper, invader—you will answer—we will hunt you all, we will break your ancestors' eggs."

She finished and violently cracked her tail above her back, issuing orders. Kefentse held his forehand out to Mrs. Erasmus; she threw Laurence one look of deep concern before she was carried briskly away, which he would have been glad to think unmerited, and then his arms were seized, on either side; his coat cut away down the middle of the back, also his shirt, and he was forced to his knees with the rags still hanging from his shoulders.

He fixed his gaze out through the archway, which opened upon the loveliest prospect he had ever beheld: the sun still low in the sky beyond the falls, newly risen, and glowing small and molten through the gusting clouds of mist. The torrents of water churned to pure white were roaring steadily over the verge, the tangled branches of trees yearning out towards the water, from the canyon-walls where they had taken root; the gauzy insubstantial suggestion of a rainbow, which refused to be seen head-on, but clung to the edge of his vision. His shoulders ached as they drew him taut.

He had seen men take a dozen lashes without a sound; foremast hands, under his very own orders, he reminded himself after every stroke: by the tenth, however, the argument lost its potency, and he was only trying raggedly to endure, in an animal sort of way, the pain which no longer ceased between the strokes but only ebbed and flowed. The whip struck awry once; the man holding his right arm cursed, the edge of his hand having been caught by the lash, by the sound of it, and yelled a complaint at the flogger, good-natured. The whip did not cut the skin, but the weals broke, after some time; blood ran down over his ribs.

Laurence was not precisely insensible when another dragon returned him to the cave, only very far away, his throat raw and stretched to ruin. He was grateful for it, or would have been; otherwise he would have screamed again when they put hands on him, to lift him face-downwards onto the ground, even though they did not touch his torn back: every nerve had been woken to pain. Sleep did not come, only a kind of murky absence of thought, which darkened by degrees into unconsciousness.

Water was put to his lips. With sharp authority Dorset ordered him to drink; the habit of obedience carried Laurence through the effort. He faded again, and for a long time a grey heat stifled him. He thought perhaps he drank a little more, and another time dreamt his mouth was welling up with salty blood, and choking half-woke to Dorset squeezing cold broth into his mouth from a rag, before again he slept and wandered in fever-dreams.

"Laurence, Laurence," Temeraire said, through the haze, in a strange hollow voice, and Ferris was hissing in his ear, saying, "Captain, you *must* wake up, you *must,* he thinks you're dead—" His voice was full of so much fear that Laurence tried to speak to comfort him, although his mouth would not quite form words properly, then the dream fell away again into a terrible roaring; he felt as though the earth shook; then all gone, into a comfortable darkness.

Chapter 12

❦

$\mathcal{T}$HE NEXT HE knew of the world was a cup of clean water held for him by Emily Roland. Dorset was kneeling on the floor beside him, and bracing him up by the waist. Laurence managed to put a hand around the cup and guide it to his mouth, spilling a little; he was palsied as an old man and trembling. He was lying on his stomach on a thin pallet of gathered straw covered with shirts, bare to the chest himself; and he was desperately hungry.

"A little at a time," Dorset said, giving him small round balls of cooled porridge, one after another. They had eased him onto his side to eat.

"Temeraire?" Laurence said, around an involuntary and desperate gluttony, wondering if he had only dreamed. He could not move his arms freely: his back had scabbed over, but if he reached too far forward the edges split, fresh blood trickling down the skin.

Dorset did not at once answer. "Was he here?" Laurence said sharply.

"Laurence," Harcourt said, kneeling down by him, "Laurence, pray do not get distressed; you have been ill a week. He was here, but I am afraid they ran him off; I am sure he is quite well."

"Enough; you must sleep," Dorset said, and for all

the will in the world, Laurence could not resist the command; he was already fading again.

When he woke it was daylight outside, and the cavern nearly empty, except for Roland and Dyer and Tooke. "They take the others to work, sir, in the fields," she said. They gave him a little water, and reluctantly at his insistence the support of their shoulders, so he might stagger to the edge of the cave and look outside.

The cliff face, opposite, was cracked, and the dark stains of dragon blood looked deep burnt orange-red on the striated walls. "It is not his, sir, or not much," Emily said anxiously, looking up at him.

She could tell him nothing more: not how Temeraire had found them, nor if he had been quite alone, nor his condition; there had been no time for conversation. With the number of dragons flying at all hours through the gorges, Temeraire had passed for a few moments as one in the throng, but he was too large and remarkably colored to escape notice, and when he had put his head into the cave to see them, he had at once raised an alarm.

Temeraire had penetrated so far only because their captors evidently did not anticipate an incursion of dragons, so deep into their stronghold; but there was a guard now, newly stationed above their cell: Laurence could see its tail, hanging down from the top of the cliff, if he painfully turned his neck, as far as he could, to look directly upwards. "And I expect that means he got clear away from them," Chenery said comfortingly, when the others had been returned, late in the afternoon. "He can fly rings around half the Corps, Laurence; I am sure he gave them the slip."

Laurence would have liked to believe it, more than he did; three days had gone by since that delirious state had broken, and if Temeraire had been able, Laurence knew very well he would have made another attempt in the teeth of any opposition; perhaps *had,* and out of their sight had been injured again, or worse.

Laurence was not taken, the next morning, with the others: they had been set along with the other prisoners of war to working in the elephant-fields, spreading the manure, much to the satisfaction of the young women to whom the work ordinarily fell. "Nonsense; I would be perfectly ashamed if I could not manage it," Catherine said, "when all those girls do: a good many of them are further along than I am, and it is not as though I have not been brought up to work. Besides, I am perfectly stout; indeed I am much better than I was. But you have been very sick, Laurence, and you are to listen to Dr. Dorset and stay lying down, when they come."

She was very firm, and Dorset also; but they had been gone a little more than an hour when another dragon came for Laurence: the rider issuing peremptory commands, and beckoning. Roland and Dyer were ready to back him into the depths of the cave, but the dragon was a smallish creature, not much bigger than a courier, and could easily have put himself inside. Laurence struggled to his feet, and for decency's sake took one of the sweat-and blood-stained shirts which had helped make up his pallet to cover himself, if he was not truly fit to be seen.

He was carried back to the great hall: the king was not there, but the iron-works were in full swing under the supervision of Prince Moshueshue; the smiths were engaged in pouring bullets, with the help of another dragon, who nursed their forge regularly with narrow breathed tongues of flame, rousing the coals within to a fever-pitch of heat. They had somehow acquired several bullet-molds, and there were still more muskets stacked upon the floor, if marked here and there with bloody fingerprints. The room was sweltering, even with a couple of smaller dragons fanning away vigorously to make the air move; but the prince looked satisfied.

He took Laurence back towards the map again; it had been already a little improved, and an entirely new addition made to the west: a vague distance allowed for the Atlantic, and then the approximate shapes of the American continents drawn out: the great harbor of Rio most prominently marked, and the islands of the West Indies placed a little tentatively somewhere to the north. There was none of the exactness needed to make it of practical use for navigation, Laurence was glad to see; he was far from that earlier complacency, during their abduction, which had dismissed their captors as a threat against the colony itself: there were too many dragons here.

Mrs. Erasmus had also been brought, and Laurence braced himself for a further interrogation, to which he would not allow himself to feel unequal, but Moshueshue did not repeat the king's demands or his violence; his servants instead gave Laurence a drink, oddly sweet, of pressed fruits and water and cocoanut milk, and his questions were of generalities and trade, wide-ranging. He had a bolt of cloth to show Laurence, calico-patterned and certainly from the mills of England; some bottles of whiskey, unpleasantly harsh and cheap by the smell, also of foreign manufacture. "You sell these things to the Lunda," Moshueshue said, "and those also?" indicating the muskets.

"They have lately fought a war against them," Mrs. Erasmus said, quickly adding her own explanation, at the tail of the translation: there had been a battle won, two-days' flight from the falls. "North-west, I think," she said, and asked Moshueshue permission to show him the territory, on the great map of the continent: north-west, and still deep inland, but in a few days' striking-distance of the ports of Louanda and Benguela.

"Sir," Laurence said, "I have never heard of the Lunda before two weeks ago; I believe they must have these goods from perhaps the Portuguese traders, upon the coast."

"And do you only want captives, or will you take other things in trade? The medicines you stole, or—" and one of the women carried over at Moshueshue's beckoning a box of jewels, absurdly magnificent, which would have made the Nizam stare: polished emeralds tumbled like marbles with diamonds, and the box itself of gold and silver. Another carried over carefully a tall curious vase, made of woven wire strung occasionally with beads, in an elaborate pattern without figures, and another an enormous mask, nearly tall as she herself was, carved of dark wood inlaid with ivory and jewels.

Laurence wondered a little if this were meant for another sort of inducement. "A trader would oblige you, sir, I am sure. I am not a merchant myself. We would be glad—would have been glad—to pay you for the medicines, in what barter you desired."

Moshueshue nodded, and the treasure was taken away. "And the—cannon?" He used the English word, himself, with tolerable pronunciation. "Or your boats which cross the ocean?"

There were enough jewels in the box to have tolerably purchased and outfitted a fleet of merchantmen, Laurence would have guessed, but he did not think the Government would be very pleased to see such a project go forward; he answered cautiously, "These are dearer, sir, for the difficulty in their construction; and would do you very little good without the men who understand their operation. But some men might be found, willing to take service with you, and such an arrangement made possible; if there were peace between our countries."

Laurence thought this was not further than he could

in justice go, and as much attempt at diplomacy as he knew how to make; he hoped as a hint, it would not be badly received. Moshueshue's intentions were not disguised; it was not wonderful that he, more than the king, should have taken to heart the advantages of modern weaponry, more easily grasped at musket-scale by men than by dragons, and should have cared to establish access to them.

Moshueshue put his hand on the map-table and gazed thoughtfully down upon it. At last he said, "You are not engaged in this trade, you say, but others of your tribe are. Can you tell me who they are, and where they may be found?"

"Sir, I am sorry to say, that there are too many engaged in the trade for me to know their names, or particulars," Laurence said awkwardly, and wished bitterly that he might have been able to say with honesty it had been lately banned. Instead he could only add, that he believed it soon would be; which was received with as much satisfaction as he had expected.

"We will ban it ourselves," the prince said, the more ominously for the lack of any deliberately threatening tone. "But that will not satisfy our ancestors." He paused. "You are Kefentse's captives. He wants to trade you for more of his tribe. Can you arrange such an exchange? Lethabo says you cannot."

"I have told them that most of the others cannot be found," Mrs. Erasmus added quietly. "—it was nearly twenty years ago."

"Perhaps some investigation could locate the survivors," Laurence said to her doubtfully. "There would be bills of sale, and I suppose some of them must yet be on the same estates, where they first were sold—you do not think it so?"

She said after a moment, "I was taken into the house

when I was sold. Those in the fields did not live long, most of them. A few years; maybe ten. There were not many old slaves."

Laurence did not quarrel with her finality, and he thought she did not translate her own words, either; likely to shield him from the rage which they could provoke. She said enough to convince Moshueshue of the impossibility, however, and he shook his head. "However," Laurence said, trying, "we would be glad to ransom ourselves, if you would arrange a communication with our fellows at the Cape, and to carry an envoy with us, to England, to establish peaceful relations. I would give my own word, to do whatever could be done to restore his kin—"

"No," Moshueshue said. "There is nothing I can do with this, not now. The ancestors are too roused up; it is not Kefentse only who has been bereft, and even those who have not lost children of their own are angry. My father's temper was not long when he was a man, and it is shorter since his change of life. Perhaps after." He did not say, after what, but issued orders to the attending dragons: without a chance to speak, Laurence was snatched up, and carried out at once.

The dragon did not turn back for the prison-cave, however, but turned instead for the falls, rising up out of the gorge and to the level of the plateau across which the great river flowed. Laurence clung to the basketing talons as they flew along its banks and over another of the great elephant-herds, too quickly for him to recognize if any of his compatriots were among the followers tending the ground; and to a distance at which the sound of the falls was muted, although the fine cloud of smoke yet remained visible, hovering perpetual in place to mark their location. There were no roads below at all, but at regular intervals Laurence began to notice cairns of stones, in circles of cleared ground, which might have served as signposts; and they had flown ten minutes when there came rearing up before them a vast amphitheater.

It was near to nothing, in his own experience, but the Colosseum in Rome; built entirely of blocks of stone fitted so snugly that no mortar, visibly, held them together, the outer enclosure was built in an oval shape, with no entrances but a few, at the base, formed with great overlapping slabs of stone laid one against another like the old stone circles in England. It stood in the middle of a grassy field, undisturbed, as he would have expected from some ancient unused ruin; only a few faintly worn tracks showed where men had come into the entries on foot, mostly from the river, where stakes had been driven in the ground, and a few simple boats were tied up.

But they flew in directly over the walls, and there were no signs of disuse within. The same drymortar method of construction had raised a series of terraces, topped and leveled out with more stone slabs, laid flat, and irregularly arranged; instead of even tiers, narrow stairways divided the theater into sections, each a haphazard arrangement of boxes intended for human use and filled with wooden benches and stools, some beautifully carved, and large stalls surrounding them for dragons. The higher levels simplified further, into wide-open stands with sections marked off only with rope; at the center of it all, a large grassy oval stood bare, broken up with three large stone platforms, and on the last of these, a prisoner with drooping head, was Temeraire.

Laurence was set down a few lengths away, with the usual carelessness, jarring his back sorely; at his repressed gasp, Temeraire growled, a deep and queerly stifled noise. He had been muzzled, with a piece of dreadful iron basketry, secured upon his head with many thick leather straps, which allowed his jaws a scant range of motion: not enough to roar. A thick iron collar around his throat, at the top of his neck, was leashed with three of the massive grey hawsers, which Laurence could now see were made of braided wire, rather than rope; these were fixed to iron rings set in the ground, equidistant from one another, so if Temeraire sought to gain slack in any one of them, the others choked him.

"Laurence, Laurence," Temeraire said, straining his head towards him with all the inches the cables would yield; Laurence would have gone to him at once, but the dragon which had brought him set its foreleg down between them: he was not permitted.

"Pray do not hurt yourself, my dear; I am perfectly well," Laurence called, forcing himself to straighten; he was anxious lest Temeraire should have done himself some mischief, flinging himself against the collar: it looked to be digging into the flesh. "You are not very uncomfortable, I hope?"

"Oh, it is nothing," Temeraire said, panting with a distress which belied his words, "nothing, now I see you again; only I could not move very much, and no-one comes to talk to me, so I did not know anything: if you were well or hurt; and you were so strange, when I saw you last."

He backed slowly and cautiously one pace and let himself down again, still breathing heavily, and gave his head a little shake, as much as the chains would allow, so they rang around him; like a horse in traces. "And it makes eating a little difficult," he added bravely, "and water taste of rust, but it does not signify: are you sure you are well? You do not look well."

"I am, and very glad to see you," Laurence said, business-like, though in truth he was at some pains to keep his feet, "if beyond words with surprise; we were mortally certain we should never be found."

"Sutton said we would never find you, by roaming wild about the continent," Temeraire said, low and angry, "and that we ought to go back to Capetown. But I told him that was a very great piece of nonsense, for however unlikely we should find you looking in the interior, it was very much less likely we should find you back at the Cape. So we asked directions—"

"Directions?" Laurence said, baffled.

He had consulted with some of the local dragons, who, living farther to the south, had not been subject yet to the slave-raiding, and were not so disposed to be hostile. "At least, not once we had made them a few presents of some particularly nice cows—which, I am sorry, Laurence, we took quite without permission, from some of the settlers, so I suppose we must pay them when we have got back to Capetown," Temeraire added, as confidently as if nothing stood in the way of their return. "It was a little difficult to make them understand what we wanted, at first, but some of them understood the Xhosa language, which I had got a little of from Demane and Sipho, and I have learnt a little of theirs as we came closer: it is not very difficult, and there are many bits which are like Durzagh."

"But, forgive me; I do not mean to be ungrateful," Laurence said, "—the mushrooms? What of the cure? Were there any left?"

"We had already given all those we collected to the *Fiona*," Temeraire said, "and if those were not enough, then Messoria and Immortalis could do very well taking back the rest, without us," he finished defiantly, "so Sutton had no right to complain, if we liked to go; and hang orders anyway."

Laurence did not argue with him; he had no wish of

giving any further distress, and in any case, Temeraire's insubordination having been answered by a success so improbable, he would certainly not be inclined to listen to any criticism on the subject: the sort of break-neck reckless venture crowned inevitably, Laurence supposed, by either triumph or disaster; speed and impudence having their own virtue. "Where are Lily and Dulcia, then?"

"They are hiding, out upon the plains," Temeraire said. "We agreed that first I should try, as I am big enough to carry you all; and then if anything should go wrong, they would still be loose." He switched his tail with something halfway between irritation and unease. "It made very good sense at the time, but I did not quite realize, that anything *would* go wrong, and then I would not be able to help them plan," he added plaintively, "and now I do not know what they mean to do; although I am sure they will think of something"—but he sounded a little dubious.

As well he might; while they had been speaking, dragons had been coming in a steady stream, carrying in large woven baskets or upon their backs men and women and even children, and settling all down within the stands: a vast company, larger than Laurence had yet suspected. The people arranged themselves in a hierarchy of wealth, those sitting on the lowest levels dressed in the most elaborate finery, panoply of furs and jewellery in a splendid vulgar display. There was a great variety among the beasts, in size and shape, and no sign of recognizable breeds, save perhaps a tendency towards similar coloring, in those who sat near-by one another, or in their pattern of markings. There was one constant, or nearly, however: the hostile looks which were bent upon Laurence and Temeraire, from all sides. Temeraire flared his ruff, as best he could with the constricting straps, and muttered, "They needn't all stare so; and I think they are great cowards for keeping me chained."

Soldiers were being brought in, now, by dragons more armored than ornamented, and many of them in blood-stained gear: no mark of slovenly habits but deliberate, worn proudly; many of the stains were fresh as though they had come straight from the recent battle which Mrs. Erasmus had mentioned. These took up places around the floor of the great stadium, in even ranks, while servants began to cover the large central stage with furs, lion-skins and leopard, and similarly draped a wooden throne; drums had been carried in, and Laurence was thankful when they set up a great thunder, and drew all eyes away: the king and the prince had arrived.

The soldiers beat their short-hafted spears against the shields, and the dragons roaring their own salute set up a wave of rattling noise, on and on, while the royalty seated themselves upon the central dais. When they were settled, a small dragon, wearing an odd sort of necklace of fur tails around his neck, leapt up on his haunches, beside the dais, and clearing his throat hushed the crowd with startling speed; his next deep breath was audible in the sudden silence. And then he launched himself into something between story and song: chanted, and without rhyme, to the beat of only one soft drum which kept time for him.

Temeraire tilted his head, to try and make it out; but when he looked at Laurence, and would have spoken, the dragon guarding them gave him a shocked glare even before a word had issued, which quelled him in embarrassment; until with sunset, the chant finished, and the raucous applause burst out again as torches were lit all around the dais. It had evidently been, from what Temeraire could gather, a kind of history of the deeds of the king and his ancestors, and more generally of the many assembled tribes, delivered entirely from memory, and covering some seven generations.

Laurence could not help but feel the liveliest anxiety for the purpose of the convocation; the opening ceremonies thus completed, it proceeded swiftly to angry speeches, greeted with roaring approval and again that thunder of spears against shields. "That is not true at all," Temeraire said indignantly, during one of these, having picked out a few of the words. One highly decorated dragon, a grey-black fellow of middle-weight size, wearing a thick neck-collar of tiger furs banded with gold, had come and ranged himself opposite Temeraire, and was gesturing at him pointedly. "I would not want your crew anyway; I have my own." He and Laurence were evidently figuring, in most of these exhortations, as material evidence, to prove the existence of the threat and of its magnitude.

Another dragon, very old, whose wing-spurs dragged upon the ground, and whose eyes were milky with cataracts, was led out into the field by a small escort of hard-faced men whose box, upon the lowest level, was left empty by their departure: they had no family with them. No-one spoke as the dragon crept to the dais, and heaved himself upon it; he raised his trembling head, his speech a thin and fragile lament which silenced all the crowd, and made the women draw to them their children, the dragons curl anxious tails around the clustered knots of their nearest tribesmen; one of the escort wept silently, with his hand over his face, his fellows giving him the courtesy of pretending they did not see.

When he had done, and returned slowly to his place, several of the soldiers began to stand forward to make their remarks: one general, a heavy barrel-chested gentleman, discarded his leopard-skin drape impatiently as he paced, with so much energy his skin gleamed in the torchlight with sweat, arguing vehemently in a voice projected to reach the highest tiers, gesturing at them at regular intervals, striking his fist into his hand, and pointing occasionally at Temeraire. His speech roused them all not only to cheering, but to agreement, grim nodding; he was warning them, that many more such dragons would come, if they did not take action now.

The night dragged on, grim and long; when the children had all fallen into exhausted sleep, some of the dragons and the women carried them away; those left kept speaking, climbing lower down in the stands as room opened, and voices grew more hoarse. Fatigue at last freed Laurence from dread; they had not been stoned yet, nor offered any other violence but words, and his back throbbed and itched and burned, sapping the energy even to be afraid. It was still not easy to stand and be pilloried, even if Laurence thankfully could escape the understanding of the better part of the accusations leveled against them; he solaced himself by keeping as straight as he could make himself, and fixing his gaze beyond the top ranks of the audience. But he was looking *not* to see, unfocused, so he did not immediately notice, until a vigorous waving made him realize, with a start, that Dulcia was perched on the top rank of seats, now empty.

She was small enough, and her green-and-mottled coloring sufficiently common, to pass for one of the company, whose attention was in any case fixed upon the speakers; when she saw she had Laurence's eyes, she sat up and held up in her forehands a ragged grey sheet. Laurence had no notion what it was, at first; and then realized it was an elephant-hide, with three holes painstakingly sawed out of it, in the shape of signal-flags: *tomorrow,* was all the message, and when he had seen it, and nodded to her, she as quickly vanished away again into the dark.

"Oh; I hope they will come and let me loose, first," Temeraire murmured, fretful at the prospect of a rescue in which he had no say. "There are so many dragons; I hope they will not do anything rash."

"Oh! I do too," Harcourt said anxiously, when Laurence had been returned to them, well-roasted and spat-upon, after the conclusion of the ceremonies; she went to the mouth of the cave at once to peer up at their sentinel. The dragon was slumped rather unhappily upon his ledge, with his head drooping down; in the distance the drums were still going, in a celebration which bid fair to continue deep into the night.

They could not prepare, save in the most general way, by drinking as much as they could hold, and washing up; but they all applied themselves to these tasks with more energy than they deserved. "Bother; it is moving again," Harcourt said, as she squeezed out her wet hair, and she put her hand to the small of her back and rubbed. Inconveniently she had just begun to show; her breeches were now obliged to be left open, and the sides held together over her middle with a bit of bark-string left from their bindings; her shirt was loose, to cover the arrangement. "Oh, if only it is a girl! I will never, never be so careless again."

By grace they slept well: the masons did not return to their work, perhaps given holiday, and so for once they were not woken with the dawn. No dragon came to carry any of them to the fields; although for an unpleasant balance, no dragon came to bring them any porridge, either, so they would have to make their attempt empty-stomached. There were still a good many dragons flying back and forth through the gorges, all day, but as evening fell their activity reduced, and the women went back early to their cavern-halls, singing, with the baskets full of washing balanced upon their heads.

Of course they had all expected the rescue to be made at night, rationally; but without certain knowledge, the day was full of tension and constant anxiety, and the urge to be always looking out of the cavern-mouth, in a way which could only have roused suspicion. Sunset roused them all to feverish attention; no-one spoke, all of them straining, until a little while after dark the heavy sailcloth-flapping of Lily's enormous wings could be heard, distantly, on the quiet air.

They all waited for the sound to approach more closely, to see her head in the cavern-entrance; but it did not come. There was only a sneeze, and then another, and a third; concluded shortly with a sort of grumbling cough, and then the retreat of her wings. Laurence looked at Catherine, perplexed, but she was edging towards the cave-mouth, beckoning him and Chenery over; a faint sizzling noise, like bacon on a too-hot frying-pan, a pinched sharp vinegared stink: there were a few pockmarks bubbling on the floor near the cavern-mouth.

"Look," Catherine said softly, "she has made us handholds," and she pointed where thin smoky trails rose, barely visible, from the cliff face.

"Well, I dare say we can manage the climb, but what do we do when we are down?" Chenery said, with more optimism than Laurence felt. He had been made to go rock-climbing at Loch Laggan, by the training master Celeritas, some twenty years past the time most aviators began the habit, and had learned thereby to manage upon a dragon's back without too much discredit to himself; but he remembered the experience, cramped beetle-like creeping one hand or foot at a time, without anything like pleasure, and there he had been wearing carabiners.

"If we walk along the line of the gorge, away from the falls, we are sure to get past the borders of their territory," Catherine said. "The dragons will have to find us, from there, I suppose."

The waiting now graduated into sheer agony: they could not begin to climb down, until the acid had eaten itself away into the rock. The salvaged quarter-glass alone kept them on any real sense of time, and the wheeling Southern Cross in the sky above. Twice Laurence looked, to be sure Turner had not missed the glass running out, only to find it nearly full; then by an exercise of will he forced himself not to watch, but rather to close his eyes, and press his hands against his sides, beneath his arms, for warmth. It was the first week of June, and the night was grown sharply and unexpectedly chill.

"Sir, that's nine," Turner said softly, at last, and the hissing of the acid had faded. They poked a twig into one of the pitted depressions by the entrance: a good two inches deep, and the stick came out unmarked, except for the very end, which smoked a little.

"And his tail hasn't moved, sir," Dyer reported in a whisper, meaning the guard-dragon, up above, after he had put his head out to peer quickly.

"Well, I think it may do," Catherine said, when she had cautiously felt around with a rag. "Mr. Ferris, you may begin. Gentlemen: no more conversation; no calls, no whispers."

Ferris had tied his boots together by their laces and slung them backwards around his neck, to keep them out of his way. He tucked a few twists of straw from the floor of the cavern into his waist, then put his head over the side, first, and reached down to feel cautiously around. He looked up and nodded, then swung his leg over; in a moment he vanished, and when Laurence risked a quick look over the edge, he was already only a darker blot on the surface of the wall, fifteen feet down, moving with the limber quickness of youth.

There was no waving, no calling from below; but their ears were stretched, and Turner had the glass still before him: fifteen minutes went, then twenty, and no sound of disaster. Chenery's first, Libbley, went to the edge and let himself over, in similar array; and after him the ensigns and midwingmen began to go, quicker: two and three at a time; Lily had sprayed the wall thoroughly, and there were hand-holds broadly scattered.

Chenery went, and a little after him, Catherine with her midwingman Drew. Most of the younger aviators had already gone. "I'll go below you, sir, and guide your feet," Martin said very softly, his yellow hair darkened with rubbed-in dirt and water. "Let me have your boots." Laurence nodded silently, and handed them over, and Martin tied them up with his own.

Martin's hand on his ankle guided his foot to one of the narrow holds: a rough shallow scrape in the face of the rock, which just admitted the grip of his toes; another, to the right. Laurence eased himself over the edge, groping for hand-holds beneath the lip; he could not see the face of the cliff beneath him, his own body blocking what little glimmer the stars gave, and could only rely on the sense of touch: the stone cold, beneath his cheek, and his breathing very loud in his own ears, with the strange amplified quality of being underwater; blind, deaf, he pressed his body flat as he could against the rock.

There was a dreadful moment when Martin touched his ankle again, and waited for him to lift it from the cliff; Laurence thought he would not be able to make himself yield the support. He willed the movement; nothing happened, then he took another breath and at last his foot moved; Martin drawing him gently downward, toes brushing lightly over the rock, to another hold.

The second foot, then one hand, then the next, mindlessly. It was easier to continue, once he had gone into motion, so long as he did not again allow himself to settle into a fixed position. A slow deep bruising ache began between his shoulders, and in his thighs. The tips of his fingers burned a little, as he went; he did not wonder if it was some trace of the acidic fluids left, or tried not to; he did not trust his grip well enough to wipe them against the rag hanging uselessly from his waistband.

Bailes, Dulcia's harness-man, was near beside him, a little way farther down; a heavy-set man, going cautiously; ground crewmen did not ordinarily go into combat, and had less practice of climbing. He gave suddenly a queer, deep grunt, and jerked his hand; Laurence looked down and saw his face pressed open-mouthed into the rock, making a horrible, low, stifled sound, his hand clawing madly at the stone: clawing, and coming to shreds, there was white bone gleaming at the fingertips, and abruptly Bailes flung out his arm and fell away, his bared teeth clenched and visible, for a brief moment.

Branches cracked, below. Martin's hand was on his ankle, but not moving, a faint tremor. Laurence did not try to look up, only held to the rock face and breathed, softly, softly; if they were lost, there was nothing to be done: one sweep of a dragon's foreleg would scrape them off the wall.

At last they resumed. Down again; and to the side, Laurence caught the gleam of translucent rock at the surface: a vein of quartz, perhaps, on which the venom might have pooled, unabsorbed.

Some time later, some ages later, a dragon flew by, going quickly through the night. It was well overhead: Laurence felt its passing only as wind and the sound of wings. His hands were numb with cold and raw. There were pockets of grass beneath his seeking fingers; in a few more steps a slope, scarcely less than vertical; then a tree-root beneath his heel, and they were nearly down: their feet were in dirt, and the bushes were catching at them. Martin tapped his ankle, and they turned and slithered down on their rumps, until they could stand up to put back on their boots. The water could be heard somewhere below, rushing; the jungle a tangle of palm leaves and tough-skinned vines hanging across their path. A clean, damp smell of moving water, fresh earth, and dew trembling and thick upon the leaves; their shirts were soon wet through and chill against their skin. A different world entirely than the dusty brown and ochre of the cliffs above.

They had all agreed none should wait for long, but go on ahead in small parties, hoping if they were discovered at this stage, at least some might yet escape. Winston, one of his harness-men, was waiting a little way on, squatting and rising to stretch out his legs; also young Allen, nervous and gnawing on the side of his thumb, and his fellow ensign Harley. The five of them went on together, following the course of the cliff wall: the earth was soft, and the vegetation full of juice, compliant; easier by far to work through than the dry underbrush, if the vines reached up to trip them from time to time. Allen stumbling almost continuously, his latest growth making him gangly and awkward, all long coltish limbs. They could not avoid some degree of noise; they could not cut their way through, but from time to time were forced to haul upon the vines to make enough slack to get through them, with corresponding groans of protest from the branches on which they hung.

"Oh," Harley breathed out very softly, frozen; they looked, and eyes looked back: cat-pupiled, bright green. They regarded the leopard; it regarded them; no one moved. Then it turned its head and melted away, solitary and unconcerned.

They went on a little faster, still following the channel of the gorge, until at last the jungle thinned out and dredged up to a point where the river's course had divided, and two channels followed separate paths: and he could see through the last stretch of jungle Lily and Temeraire waiting there anxiously, astride the narrow banks, and squabbling a little.

"But what if you had missed?" Temeraire was muttering, a little disconsolate and critical, while he stretched his neck to try and peer into the jungle. "You might have hit the cave-mouth, or some of our crew."

Lily mantled at this suggestion, her eyes very orange. "I hope I do not need to be near-by to hit a *wall*," she replied quellingly, and then leaned eagerly forward, as Harcourt came stumbling down the wet slope towards her. "Catherine, Catherine; oh, are you well? Is the egg all right?"

"Hang the egg," Catherine said, putting her head against Lily's muzzle. "No, there, dearest; it has only been a nuisance, but I am so very glad to see you. How clever you were!"

"Yes," Lily said complacently, "and indeed it was much easier than I thought it would be; there was no-one about to pay any mind, except that fellow on the hill, and he was asleep."

Temeraire nuzzled Laurence gratefully, too, all his quibbling silenced: he still wore the thick iron collar, much to his disgust, and a few clubbed lengths of cable dangling off it, blackened and brittle at the ends where Lily's acid had weakened the metal enough for the two of them to break it. "But we cannot leave without Mrs. Erasmus," Laurence said to him, low; but Dulcia was landing among them, and Mrs. Erasmus was clutching to the harness on her back.

They fled cautiously but quickly homeward, the rich husbanded countryside providing: Temeraire savage and quick, cutting out elephants from a herd, while the smaller herd-dragons yelled angry imprecations but did not dare give pursuit when he had roared them down; Lily doubling back sharp on herself, when a heavy-weight roused up in a village on their course and bellowed challenge, to spit with unerring precision at a branch of the great sprawling bao-bab tree beside him. Her acid sent it crashing down upon his shoulders: he jumped and thought better of giving chase; looking back he might be seen gingerly nosing the thick branch, large as an entire tree, away from the clearing.

The aviators wove grasses into makeshift cords, to tie themselves on with, and pinned their limbs under straps of harness so that whenever they paused for water, they all went down in staggering heaps, pounding on their thighs to drown out the prickling of returning blood. The desert they flew across almost without a pause, pale rock and yellow dust, the curious heads of small animals popping up from holes in the ground in hopes of rain as the dragon-shadows passed by like racing clouds. Temeraire had taken all of Dulcia's crew but Chenery himself; and also some of Lily's; the three of them made all the haste which could be imagined, and they broke over the mountains into the narrow coastal province of the settlements in the hour before dawn on the sixth day of flight, and saw the tongues of flame, where the cannon at the Cape were speaking.

Narrow pillars of smoke were lying back against the face of Table Mountain as they came across the bay driving into the city, drifting before a hard wind blowing into the bay, and fires all through the city: ships beating desperately out of the harbor into the wind, close-hauled as they could go. The cannon of the castle were speaking without cease, thunder-roll of broadsides from the *Allegiance* in the harbor also, her deck swathed deeply in grey powder-gusts spilling down her sides and rolling away on the water.

Maximus was fighting in mid-air, above the ship: his sides still gaunt, but the enemy dragons gave him still a wide and respectful berth, and fled from his charges; Messoria and Immortalis flanked him, and Nitidus was darting beneath their cover to harry the enemy in their retreat. So far they had preserved the ship, but the position was untenable; they were only trying to hold long enough to carry away those who could be saved: the harbor full of boats, crammed and wallowing boats, trying to get to her shelter.

Berkley signaled, from Maximus's back, as they came on: *holding well, retrieve company*; so they flashed on past and towards the shore, where the castle lay under full siege: a vast body of spearmen, crouched beneath great shields of oxhide and iron. Many of their fellows lay dead in the fields just before the walls, cut dreadfully apart by canister shot, and musketry; other corpses floated in the moat. They had failed to carry the walls by climbing, but the survivors had withdrawn past the substantial rubble that had been made of the nearby houses by the cannon-fire, and now sheltered there from the guns, waiting with terrible patience for a breach in the walls.

Another corpse lay dreadfully stretched, upon the parade grounds: a yellow-and-brown dragon, its eyes cloudy and its body half-burst upon the ground by impact, a gaping hole torn into its side by the round-shot which had brought it down; scraps of bloody hide stood on the grass even a hundred yards distant. Some thirty dragons more were in the air, now making their passes from very high, dropping not bombs but sacks of narrow iron blades, flat and triangular and sharpened along every edge, which drove even into stone: as Temeraire dropped into the courtyard, Laurence could see them bristling from the earth as if it had been sowed with teeth; there were many dead soldiers upon the heights.

King Mokhachane was standing on the lower slopes of Table Mountain clear of cannon-shot, observing grimly, and occasionally mantling her wings in yearning when one of the men or dragons were struck; of course she was a dragon of no great age, and all instinct would have driven her to the battlefield. There were men hovering around her flanks, and others running back and forth to the company gathered before the fortress walls, with orders. Laurence could not see if the prince was by her side.

The city itself had been left untouched: the castle alone bore the attack, although the streets had nevertheless been deserted. Some large boulders lay also strewn in the corners, bloodstained, and others trailing behind them a line of smashed bricks, red under their yellow paint. The soldiers were mostly on the walls, sweating as they worked the guns, and a great crowd of settlers, men and women and children together, huddled in the shelter of the barracks waiting for the boats to return.

Mrs. Erasmus sprang almost at once from Temeraire's back when they had landed, scarcely a hand to the harness; General Grey, hurrying to greet them, looked with astonishment as she went past him without a word.

"She has gone for her children," Laurence said, sliding down himself. "Sir, we must bring you off, at once; the *Allegiance* cannot hold the harbor long."

"But who the devil is she?" Grey said, and Laurence realized she must have been quite unrecognizable to him, still in her native dress. "And damn the bloody savages, yes; we cannot hit a one of those beasts, as high as they are keeping, even with pepper-shot; they will have the walls down soon if the place does not catch, first. This has not been built to hold against three companies of dragons. Where have they all come from?"

He was already turning, giving orders, his aides running to organize the withdrawal: an orderly, formal retreat, the men spiking their own guns before abandoning them, only a few gun-crews at a time, and hurling into the moat the barrels of powder. Mr. Fellowes had already gone, with the ground crew, for the dragons' battle-gear: still where it had been stowed, fortunately, in the smithy. They came running with the belly-netting, and all the spare carabiner straps which they had. "The armor, sir, we can't manage, without he come and lift it himself," he said, panting, as they began in haste to rig Temeraire's belly-netting again, and Lily's; Dulcia had gone aloft again, her riflemen armed now with pepper-shot, to keep the enemy off their heads at least a little while.

"Leave it," Laurence said; this would be no prolonged struggle, but a quick dash for safety, and back again for more of the men; they needed speed more than the protection of the armor, when the enemy had no guns.

Temeraire crouched for the first group of soldiers to

climb into the netting: the men stumbling, some pale and sweating with fear, driven by their officers, and others dazed with the noise and smoke. Laurence now bitterly regretted he had not asked Fellowes, back in England, to rig up some of the Chinese silk carrying-harnesses which would now have allowed them to take many more than the normally allotted number for retreat; thirty for a heavy-weight, when by weight Temeraire could have managed two hundred or more at a run.

They crammed some fifty men in, regardless, and hoped the netting would hold for the short flight. "We will—" Laurence began, meaning to say they would return; he was cut short by a shrieked warning from Dulcia, and Temeraire sprang aloft only in time: three of the enemy, using a netting made of the metal hawsers, had brought overhead an enormous boulder roughly the size of an elephant and let fly. It smashed the delicate cup of the bell-tower with a sour, ringing clang, and came down through the short passage of the entryway, brick and mortared stone crumbling everywhere, and the portcullis moaned and sagged open to the ground.

Temeraire sped to the *Allegiance,* to let the men down onto the dragondeck, and as quick hastened back to the shore. The spearmen were coming in through the rubble of the narrow passageway, charging with yells into the teeth of the musket-fire Grey had mustered, flooding by and up towards the guns. In parties they were encircling the emplacements yet manned and stabbing the gun-crews to death with quick, short, jerking motions, their spearheads wet and red with blood; one after another the cannon-roars silenced, and the dragons overhead began circling like ominous crows, waiting for the last to be stifled so they might descend.

Temeraire reared up onto the roof and knocked flat a dozen of the attackers with a swipe of his foreleg, snarling. "Temeraire, the guns," Laurence called. "Smash the guns they have taken—"

The attackers had seized now three cannon not yet spiked, and were trying to turn the first to bring it to bear on the courtyard, where they could fire at Temeraire and Lily. Temeraire simply put his forehand on the housing and thrust the cannon and the six men clinging onto it through the notched brick battlements; it plunged down and into the moat with a terrific splash, the men undaunted letting go and swimming up through the water.

Lily, landing behind them to take on more of the retreat, spat: the second cannon began to hiss and smoke, the barrel thumping to the ground as the wooden housing dissolved quicker than the metal, and went rolling free like a deadly ninepin, knocking men down and spreading the acid everywhere, so splatters hissed upon the brick and dirt.

The earth beneath them shook so violently Temeraire stumbled and dropped back to all four legs in the courtyard: another massive boulder had dropped, and smashed a section of the outer walls, at the far and undefended end of the courtyard. A fresh wave of men came surging through, quicker than Grey's men could turn to meet them, and charged those still defending the ruined entryway of the castle. The riflemen ranged across Temeraire's back set up a quick irregular fire into the onrushing mass; then the spearmen were in and grappling furiously with the soldiers and their bayonets, and a strange quiet descended. The guns were scarcely firing anymore, and only a scattering of occasional musket- and pistol-shot broke the soft grunting noise of panting, struggling men, the groans of the wounded and the dying.

All the yard was a great confusion; with no clear avenue of retreat or line of battle, men ran in all directions, now trying to evade, now trying to seek combat, crowded by frightened and bellowing livestock, horses and cows and sheep. These had been brought into the castle, against a siege expected to last longer, and penned in the smaller second courtyard: maddened by the noise of battle and the dragons wild overhead, they had got loose and now went careening indiscriminately through the grounds, a flock of hens crying around their feet, until they broke their legs or necks in flight, or found their way by chance outside the castle grounds.

In the crowd, Laurence caught sight to his surprise of Demane, clinging with grim desperation to the collar of the heifer he had been promised, which plunged and bellowed madly against his slight weight; she was dragging him out into the melee, while the calf tried to follow moaning. Sipho hung back in the archway which allowed communication between the two courtyards of the castle, gnawing upon his small bunched fist, his face wrenched with terror, and then with sudden decision dashed out after his brother, his hand reaching for the lead-rope which straggled out behind the cow.

A pair of soldiers were bayoneting one of the enemy to death savagely, as the cow went dragging by; one straightened and wiped blood across his mouth, panting, and shouted, "Fucking little thief, couldn't wait till we're cold—"

Demane saw, let go the cow and lunged; Sipho went down beneath his protective weight; the bayonet flashed down towards them. There was not even time to call out a protest: the tide of the battle drew the soldiers away in another moment, and left the two small bodies huddled on the ground, bloody. The cow stumbled away over the rubble, picking her way out of the courtyard through the open gap in the walls, the calf trotting after her.

"Mr. Martin," Laurence said, very low. Martin nodded, and tapped Harley on the shoulder; they let themselves down the harness and dashed out across the field. They carried the boys back to be lifted into the netting; Demane limp, Sipho weeping softly against Harley's shoulder, sticky with his brother's blood.

A handful of the spearmen had got in among the settlers congregated in the barracks, and a terrible confused slaughter was under way: the women and children were pushed aside, the attackers sometimes bodily setting them against the walls to put them out of the way, but with no compunction went on laying the men out at their feet, while the settlers fired their muskets and rifles wildly, striking friend and foe alike. The emptied boats were coming back for more passengers, but the sailors at the oars hesitated to pull in, despite the furious swearing of the coxs'n, his profanities carrying across the water.

"Mr. Ferris," Laurence shouted, "Mr. Riggs, clear them some space there, if you please," and himself slid down, to take charge of the loading of the retreating soldiers in Ferris's place. Someone handed him a pistol and a cartridge box, still sticky with the blood of the corpse from which they had come; Laurence slung it quickly over his shoulder, and tore open the paper cartridge with his teeth. He had the pistol loaded, and drew out his sword; a spearman came running at him, but he had no opportunity to shoot. Temeraire, catching sight of the threat, cried out his name and lunged to slash the man violently down, dislodging as he did so three of the wavering soldiers trying to get into his netting.

Laurence clenched his jaw, and permitted himself to be concealed behind the closed ranks of his ground crew; he handed the pistol forward to Mr. Fellowes, and instead went to speed aboard the now-desperate men, harried on all sides, into the stretching leather of the netting.

Lily, who could not take as many, had been loaded already; she lifted away and spat at the flood of men coming in through the ruined wall, filling the empty space with smoking, hideously twisted corpses. But she had to go towards the ship, and the survivors behind at once began to knock down more of the rubble from the walls to bury the remnants of acid.

"Sir," Ferris said, panting as he came back; his hand was tucked into his belt, and a gash brilliant cerise through his shirt, running the length of his arm, "we have embarked them all, I think; the settlers, I mean, those left."

They had cleared the courtyard, and Temeraire with more savage work had killed those manning the guns; although only a few gun-crews still labored, their irregular fire all that still kept off the dragons. The ship's boats were dashing away over the sea, the sailors pulling on the oars with frantic back-straining haste; the barracks were awash with blood, bodies of black men and white rising and lowering together in the pink-stained froth where the waves were coming in upon the strand.

"Get the general aboard," Laurence said, "and signal *all retreat,* if you please, Mr. Turner." Turning he offered Mrs. Erasmus his hand to climb aboard; Ferris had escorted her back, and her daughters in their pinafores, dirty and marked with soot, were clinging to her skirts.

"No, Captain, thank you," she said. He did not understand, at first, and wondered if she were injured; if she did not realize the boats had left. She shook her head. "Kefentse is coming. I told him that I would find my daughters, and wait for him here in the castle: that is why he let me go."

He stared, bewildered. "Ma'am," he said, "he cannot pursue us, not long, not from shore; if you fear his capturing you again—"

"No," she said again, simply. "We are staying. Do not be afraid for us," she added. "The men will not hurt us. It is dishonor to stain their spears with a woman's blood, and anyway I am sure Kefentse will be here soon."

The *Allegiance* was already weighing anchor, her guns roaring in fresh vigor to clear her skies to make sail. On the battlements, the last working gun-crews had abandoned their posts, and were running madly for escape: to Temeraire, to the last boats waiting.

"Laurence, we must go," Temeraire said, very low and resonant, his head craning from side to side: his ruff was stretched to its full extent, and even on the ground he was instinctively breathing in long, deep draughts, his chest expanding. "Lily cannot hold so many of them, all alone; I must go help her." She was all their shelter from the enemy beasts, who were cautious of her acid having seen its effects now at close range, but they would encircle her and have her down in a moment; or draw her too far aloft, so that some of their number could plunge down upon Temeraire while he remained vulnerable upon the ground.

More of the men had come pouring into the courtyard through the yielded ground; they were keeping beyond Temeraire's reach, but spreading out along the far wall in a half-circle. Individually they could do no great harm, but by rushing together with their spears might drive Temeraire aloft; and above Laurence could see some of the dragons skillfully maneuvering around Lily and into lower positions, ready to receive him onto their claws. There was no time to persuade her; in any case Laurence did not think, looking at her face, that she would be easily persuaded. "Ma'am," he said, "your husband—"

"My husband is dead," she said, with finality, "and my daughters will be raised proud children of the Tswana here, not as beggars in England."

He could not answer: she was a widow, and beholden to no one but herself; he had not the right to compel her. He looked at the children holding on to her, their faces gaunt and hollow, too exhausted by extremity even to be afraid any longer. "Sir, that's everyone," Ferris said at his shoulder, looking anxiously between them.

She nodded her farewell to Laurence's silence, and then bending lifted up the little girl onto her hip; with a hand on the older girl's shoulder, she guided them towards the shelter of the raised covered porch of the governor's residence, oddly decorous where it rose out of the bloody wreckage of the battle scattered all around it, and picked her way over the corpses sprawled upon the curving steps.

Laurence said, "Very well," and turning pulled himself aboard; there was no more time. Temeraire reared up onto his haunches, and roaring sprang aloft: the dragons scattered in alarm before the divine wind, the nearest crying out shrilly in pain as they fell away, and Lily and Dulcia fell in with him as together they bent away towards the *Allegiance,* a broad spread of sail white against the ocean, already carrying out of the harbor into the Atlantic.

In the courtyard, the dragons began to land in the

ruins to pillage among the cattle running free; Mrs. Erasmus was standing straight-backed at the top of the steps, the little girl clasped in her arms, their faces turned up, and Kefentse was arrowing already across the water towards them, calling loud in a joyful voice.

III

Chapter 13

❧

"$\mathcal{P}$RAY AM I disturbing you?" Riley said awkwardly; he could not knock, because there was no door. There were a great many women aboard, refugee, to the service of whose meager comfort nearly all the cabins and bulkheads had gone, and a little ragged sailcloth was all which presently divided Laurence's berth from Chenery's, on one side, and from Berkley's on the other. "May I ask you to take a turn with me, on the dragondeck?"

They had already spoken, of course, from necessity, in those first distracted hours, all the officers united in the effort to make some sense of seven dragons, wailing children, wounded men, several hundred inconvenient passengers, and all the confusion which might be expected on a ship three times the size of a first-rate, launched with no preparation directly into a brutal headwind, with a lee-shore ready to receive her at any time, and her deck still littered with the large metal-shod stones which had served the enemy for missiles.

In the melee Laurence had nevertheless seen Riley looking anxiously over the newly arrived company; an anxiety visibly relieved by the sight of Harcourt calling orders to her crew. But another few chances of observation altered his looks of relief to puzzlement, and then to suspicion. Riley had at last come up to the dragondeck, on the excuse of requesting the dragons to shift their places to bring the ship a little more by the stern, and so obtained a better view of Catherine's condition. It was just as well that Laurence had understood what he meant to achieve, for the request as Riley conveyed it to them became a confused scheme of putting Maximus at the head of the deck, with Lily apparently on his back, and Temeraire stretched along the port rail, which would likely have ended with half the dragons in the water, and the ship turning in stately circles.

"Very willing," Laurence now pronounced himself, and they went above in silence: necessary silence, to some extent, as Laurence had to follow Riley single-file through the narrow lanes that were all that was left of navigable space inside, and up the ladders. The crammed-in passengers having been given the liberty of the quarterdeck, for light and exercise, the dragondeck afforded more privacy than was to be had anywhere else on the ship; so long as one did not mind an interested audience of dragons.

These were in any case for the moment mostly inanimate; Temeraire and Lily and Dulcia worn-out, by their long and desperate flight as well as the excitement at its end, and Maximus making the forestay hum with the resonance of his deep, sonorous snores. It was just as well they were tired enough to sleep without eating, as there was little to be had, nor would be again until the ship could put in at some port for resupply; when they woke they would have to fish for their supper.

"I am afraid," Riley said diffidently, breaking their silence as they walked along the railing, "that we may have to water at Benguela; I regret it very much, if it should give you any pain. I am considering whether we ought not to try for St. Helena instead."

St. Helena was not a slave port, and out of their way. Laurence was deeply sensible of the degree of apology embodied in this offer, and immediately said, "I do not think it can be recommended. We could easily find ourselves blown to Rio on the easterlies, and even though both the cure and word of the loss of the Cape must precede us home, our formation must still be needed urgently back in England."

Riley as gratefully received this gesture in return, and they walked several passes up and down the deck much more comfortably together. "Of course we cannot lose a moment," Riley said, "and for my own part I have reason enough to wish us home again, as quickly as we might go, or thought I did, until I realized she meant to be obstinate; but, Laurence, I beg you will forgive me for speaking freely: I would be grateful for a headwind all the way, if it meant we should not arrive before she has married me."

The other aviators had already begun referring, in uncharitable terms, to what they viewed as Riley's quixotic behavior, Chenery going so far as to say, "If he will not leave off harassing poor Harcourt, one will have to do *something*; but how is he to be worked on?"

Laurence had rather more sympathy for Riley's plight; he was a little shocked by Catherine's refusal to marry rather than burn, when the plain choice was put before her, and he was forcibly reminded to regret Reverend Erasmus, for the lack of what he was sure would have been that gentleman's warm and forceful counsel in favor of the marriage. Mr. Britten, Riley's official chaplain, assigned by the Admiralty, could not have brought a moral argument to bear on anyone, even if he were made sober long enough to do so.

"But at least he is ordained," Riley said, "so there would be no difficulty about the thing whatsoever;

everything would be quite legal. But she will not hear of it. And she cannot say, in fairness," he added half-defiantly, "that it is because I am some sort of scoundrel, because I did not try to speak before; it was not as though—*I* was not the one who—" then cutting himself off hastily, instead ended more plaintively by saying, "and, I did not know how to begin. Laurence, has she no family, who might prevail on her?"

"No; quite alone in the world," Laurence said. "And, Tom, you must know that she cannot leave the service: Lily cannot be spared."

"Well," Riley said reluctantly, "if no one else can be found to take the beast on," a notion of which Laurence did not bother to try and disabuse him, "but it does not matter: I am not such an outrageous scrub as to abandon her. And the governor was kind enough to tell me that Mrs. Grey is perfectly willing to receive her: generous beyond what anyone might expect, and it would surely make everything easy for her in England; they have a large acquaintance, in the best circles; but of course not until we are married, and she will not listen to reason."

"Perhaps she fears the disapproval of your family," Laurence said, more from a motive of consolation than conviction; he was sure Catherine had not given a thought to the feelings of Riley's family, nor would have, if she had determined on the marriage.

"I have already promised her that they would do all that is proper, and so they would," Riley said. "I do not mean to say it is the sort of match they would have looked out for me; but I have my capital, and can marry to please myself without any accusation of *imprudence,* at least. I dare say that my father at least will not care two pins, if only it is a boy; my brother's wife has not managed anything but girls, the last four years ago, and everything entailed," he finished, very nearly flinging up his hands.

"But it is all nonsense, Laurence," Catherine said, equally exasperated, when he approached her. "He expects me to resign the service."

"I believe," Laurence said, "that I have conveyed to him the impossibility of such a thing, and he is reconciled to the necessity, if not pleased by it; and you must see," he added, "the very material importance of the circumstance of the entailment."

"I do not see, at all," she said. "It is something to do with his father's estate? What has it to do with me, or the child? He has an older brother, has he not, with children?"

Laurence, who had not so much been instructed in the legal structures of inheritance and entailment as absorbed them through the skin, stared; and then he hastily made her understand that the estate would descend in the male line, and her child, if a boy, stood to inherit after his uncle. "If you refuse, you deny him his patrimony," Laurence said, "which I believe likely to be substantial, and entailed in default on a distant relation who would care nothing for the interest of Riley's nieces."

"It is a stupid way of going on," she said, "but I do see; and I suppose it would be hard luck on the poor creature, if he grew up knowing what might have been. But all I am hoping for is not a boy at all, but a girl; and then what use is she to him, or I?" She sighed, and rubbed the back of her hand across her brow, and finally said, "Oh, bother; I suppose he can always divorce me. Very well: but if it is a girl, she will be a Harcourt," she added with decision.

* * *

The marriage was briefly postponed for want of anything suitable to make a wedding-feast, until they had managed some resupply. Already extremity had driven them to shore on several occasions: there was no safe harbor on their charts, along the southern coastline, where the *Allegiance* might have safely put in; so instead the empty water-casks were roped together and draped upon the dragons, who daily flew in the twenty miles of open water which Riley's caution left between them and the coast, and tried to find some nameless river emptying into the sea.

Drawing near Benguela, they passed a pair of tattered ships on the fifteenth of June, with blackened sides and makeshift slovenly sails a pirate would have been ashamed to rig, which they took for fellow refugees from the Cape, choosing to make east for St. Helena. The *Allegiance* did not offer to heave-to; they had no water or food to spare of their own, and in any case the smaller ships ran away from them, likely fearing to be pressed either for supplies or men, not without cause. "I would give a good deal for ten able seamen," Riley said soberly, watching them go hull-up over the horizon; he did not speak of what he would give for a proper dole of clean water. The dragons were already licking the sails in the morning, for the dew, all the company having been put on half-rations.

They saw the smoke first, still rising, from a long way off: a steady ongoing smoulder of damp wood piled into massive bonfires, which as they drew nearer the harbor resolved themselves into the overturned hulks of ships, which had been dragged from the ocean onto the beach. Little more than the stout keels and futtocks remained, like the rib cages of beached leviathans who had flung themselves onto the sands to die. The fortifications of the Dutch factory had been reduced to rubble.

There was no sign of life. With all the gunports open, and the dragons roused and alive to the least warning of danger, the ship's boats went to the shore full of empty water-casks. They came back again, pulling more quickly despite their heavier load; in Riley's cabin, Lieutenant Wells reported uneasily. "More than a week, sir, I should say," he said. "There was food rotting, in some of the houses, and all that is left of the fort is perfectly cold. We found a large grave dug in the field behind the port; there must have been at least a hundred dead."

"It cannot have been the same band who came on us in Capetown," Riley said, when he had done. "It cannot; could dragons have flown here, so quickly?"

"Fourteen hundred miles, in less than a week's time? Not if they meant to fight at the end of it, and very likely not at all," Catherine said, measuring upon the map with her fingers; she had the chair, as Riley had managed to carry the point of giving her the large stern-cabin for the journey home. "They needn't have, at any rate; there were dragons enough at the falls to make another raiding party of the same size, or another ten, for that matter."

"Well, and I am sorry to sound like a damned ill-wishing crow," Chenery said, "but I don't see a blessed reason why they shouldn't have gone for Louanda, while they were at it."

Another day's sailing brought them in range of the second port; Dulcia and Nitidus set off, beating urgently before the wind, and some eight hours later returned again, finding the *Allegiance* in the dark by the beacons lit in the tops.

"Burnt to the ground, the whole place," Chenery said, tipping back the cup of grog which had been given him, thirstily. "Not a soul to be seen, and all the wells full of dragonshit; beg your pardon."

The magnitude of the disaster began gradually to dawn upon them all: not only Capetown lost, but two of the largest ports in Africa besides. If the enemy's purpose had been to seize control of the ports, all the intervening territory must have first been conquered; but if simple destruction were all their desire, no such long, drawn-out labor was required. Without aerial forces to oppose them, the dragons could overfly with ease any defenses or mustered force, and go directly to their target, carrying their light infantry with them; and then expend all their energy upon the hapless town which had incurred their wrath.

"The guns were all gone," Warren said quietly. "And the shot; we found the empty caissons where they had been stored. I would imagine they took the powder also; certainly we did not see any left behind."

All the long homeward journey along the coast was attended by the clouds of smoke and ruin, and preceded by their harbingers the scorched and tattered ships, full of survivors, making their limping way back to safe harbor. The *Allegiance* did not attempt again to put in, relying instead on the dragons' short flights to the coast to bring them fresh water, until two weeks more brought them to Cape Coast: Riley felt it their duty to at least make an accounting of the dead, at the British port, and they hoped that the fortifications, older and more extensive than those in the other ports, might have preserved some survivors.

The castle which served as headquarters for the port, built in stone, remained largely intact but for the gaping and scorched roof; the guns, which had been useless to defend her, fixed as they were outward to sea, were all gone, as were the heaped piles of round-shot from the courtyard. The *Allegiance*, being subject to the vicissitudes of the wind and current, could not keep the regular pace of dragons, and had moved more slowly than the wave of attacks; three weeks at least had passed since the assault.

While Riley organized the ship's crew in the sad work of exhuming and making a count of the dead from their mass grave, Laurence and his fellow captains divided amongst themselves the richly forested slopes north and surrounding the wreckage of the town, in hopes of ensuring enough game for them all: fresh meat was badly needed, the ship's supplies of salt pork growing rapidly thin, and the dragons always hungry. Temeraire alone among them was really satisfied with fish, and even he had wistfully expressed the desire for "a few tender antelope, for variety's sake; or an elephant would be beyond anything: they are so very rich."

In the event, he was able to satisfy his own hunger with a couple of smallish, red-furred buffalo, while the riflemen shot another half-a-dozen, as many as he could conveniently carry back to the ship in his foreclaws. "A little gamy, but not at all unpleasant; perhaps Gong Su can try stewing one with a little dried fruit," Temeraire said thoughtfully, rattling the horns in his mouth in a horrible fashion to pick his teeth, before he fastidiously deposited them upon the ground. Then he pricked up his ruff. "Someone is coming, I think."

"For God's sake are you white men?" the cry came a little faintly, from the forest, and shortly a handful of dirty, exhausted men staggered into their clearing, and received with many pitiful expressions of gratitude their canteens of grog and brandy. "We scarcely dared to hope, when we heard your rifles," said their chief, a Mr. George Case of Liverpool, who with his partner David Miles, and their handful of assistants, had not been able to escape the disaster in time.

"We have been hiding in the forest ever since the monsters descended," Miles said. "They took up all the ships that had not fled quick enough, and broke or burnt them, before they left again; and us out here with scarcely any bullets left. We have been ready to despair: I suppose they would all have starved, in another week."

Laurence did not understand, until Miles brought them to the makeshift pen, concealed in the woods, where their last string of some two hundred slaves remained. "Bought and paid for, and in another day we should had them loaded aboard," Miles said, and spat with philosophical disgust upon the ground, while one of the gaunt and starving slaves, his lips badly cracked, turned his head inside the enclosure and made a pleading motion with his hand for water.

The smell of filth was dreadful. The slaves had made some attempt, before weakness had overcome them, to dig small necessary-pits within their enclosure, but they were shackled ankle-to-ankle, and unable to move far from one another. There was a running stream which emptied into the sea, some quarter-of-a-mile distant; Case and his men did not look thirsty, or very hungry themselves; there was the remnant of an antelope over a spit, not twenty feet from the enclosure.

Case added, "If you will take credit for our passage, we will make it good in Madeira; or," with an air of great generosity, "you are welcome to buy them outright if you prefer: we will give you a good price, you may be sure."

Laurence struggled to answer; he would have liked to knock the man down. Temeraire did not suffer any similar pangs; he simply seized the gate in his foreclaws and without a word tore it entirely from its setting, and threw it down on the ground, panting over it in anger.

"Mr. Blythe," Laurence said, grimly, "strike these men's irons, if you please."

"Yes, sir," Blythe said, and fetched his tools; the slavers gaped. "My God, what are you about?" Miles said, and Case cried out that they should sue, they should certainly sue; until Laurence turning on them said low and coldly, "Shall I leave you here, to discuss the matter with these gentlemen?" which shut their mouths at once. It was a long and unhappy process: the men were shackled one to another, with iron fetters, and in groups of four were fastened about the necks with rope; a handful with their ankles cuffed to thick billets of wood, which had rendered it nearly impossible for them to even stand.

Temeraire tried to speak to the slaves as Blythe freed them, but they spoke a wholly different language, and shrank from his lowered head in fear; they were not men of the Tswana, but of some local tribe, which did not have similar relations with dragons. "Give them the meat," Laurence said quietly, to Fellowes; this gesture required no translation, and at once the stronger among the former captives began to arrange cooking-fires, and prop up the weaker to gnaw upon the biscuit which Emily and Dyer distributed among them, with the help of Sipho. Many of the slaves preferred to flee at once, despite their obvious weakness; before the meat was on the spit, nearly half of them had vanished into the forest, to make their way home as best they could, Laurence supposed; there was no way of knowing how far they had been brought, or from what direction.

Temeraire sat stiff with disgust as the slavers were put aboard him; and when they continued to murmur turned his head to snap his teeth towards them, and say in dangerous tones, "Speak of Laurence so again, and I will leave you here myself; you should be ashamed of yourselves, and if you have not enough sense to be, then you may at least be quiet." The crew also regarded them with great disapproval. "Ungrateful sods" was the muttered opinion of Bell, as he rigged out makeshift straps for them.

Laurence was glad to unload them again, on deck, and see them disappear among the rest of the *Allegiance*'s passengers. The other dragons had returned with better luck from their hunting, and Maximus triumphantly deposited on the deck a pair of smallish elephants, of which he had already eaten three; he pronounced them very good eating, and Temeraire sighed a little, but they were earmarked at once for the celebration; which though necessarily muted by their larger circumstances, could not be much longer delayed and yet leave the bride in a state convenient to walking the deck of a rolling ship.

It was a rather muddled occasion, although Chenery, with his usual fine disdain of any notion of polite manners, had ensured the sobriety of the officiant, by taking Britten by the ear and dragging him up onto the dragondeck, the night before, and instructing Dulcia not to let him stir an inch. The minister was thoroughly sober and petrified by morning, and Harcourt's runners brought him his clean shirt and his breakfast on the dragondeck, and brushed his coat for him on the spot, so he could not slip away and fortify himself back into insensibility.

But Catherine had not thought at all of providing herself with a dress, and Riley had not thought at all that she would *not* have done so, with the result that she had to be married in her trousers and coat; giving the ceremony a very strange appearance, and putting poor Mrs. Grey to the blush, and several other of the respectable Capetown matrons who had attended. Britten himself looked very confused, without the comforting haze of liquor, and stuttered rather more than less over his phrases. To crown the event, when he invited onlookers to express any objections, Lily, despite Harcourt's many reassuring conversations on the subject, put her head over the lip of the dragondeck to the alarm of the assembled guests and said, "Mayn't I?"

"No, you may not!" Catherine said, and Lily heaved a disgruntled sigh, and turning her lurid orange eye on Riley said, "Very well, then; but if you are unpleasant to Catherine, I will throw you in the ocean."

It was perhaps not a very propitious entry to the state of matrimony, but the elephant meat was indeed delicious.

The lookout saw the light off Lizard Point the tenth of August as they came at last into the Channel, the dark mass of England off their port bow, and he caught sight also of a few lights running past them to the east: not ships of the blockade. Riley ordered their own lights doused, and put her on a south-east heading, with careful attention to his maps, and when morning came, they had the mingled pain and pleasure of bringing up directly behind a convoy of some eight ships bound unmistakably for Le Havre: six merchantmen, and a couple of frigates escorting them, all lawful prizes, any of which would certainly have struck at once if only they had been in range. But they were a good sixty miles away, and catching sight of the *Allegiance* they hurriedly pressed on more sail and immediately began to run clear away.

Laurence leaned on the rail beside Riley watching them go, wistfully. The *Allegiance* had not been scraped properly clean since leaving England, and her bottom was unspeakably foul; in any event, at her best point of sailing she did not make eight knots, and even the frigate at the rear of the convoy was certainly running at eleven.

Temeraire's ruff was quivering as he sat up to watch them. "I am sure *we* could catch them," he said. "We could certainly catch them; at least by afternoon."

"There are her studdingsails," Riley said, watching through the glass. The sluggish frigate leapt forward, evidently having only waited until her charges had pulled ahead.

"Not with this wind," Laurence said. "Or you might; but not the others, and we have no armor. In any case, we could not take them: the *Allegiance* would be quite out of sight until after dark, and without prize-crews they would all run away from us in the night."

Temeraire sighed and put his head down again on his forelegs. Riley shut up his glass. "Mr. Wells, let us have a heading north-northeast, if you please."

"Yes, sir," Wells said sadly, and turned to make the arrangements; but abruptly, the frigate in the lead checked her way, and bent her course sharply southward, with much frantic activity in the rigging visible through the glass. The convoy all were turning, as if they meant to make now for Granville, past the Jersey Islands; rather a poorer risk, and Laurence could not imagine what they meant by it, unless perhaps they had caught sight of some ship of the blockade. Indeed, Laurence wondered that they should *not* have seen any such ship before now, unless all the blockade had lately been driven up the Channel by a gale.

The *Allegiance* had now the advantage of sailing to head them off, rather than directly in their train. Riley said, "We may as well keep on them a little while longer," with studied calm, and put the ship after them, much to the unspoken but evident satisfaction of the crew: if only the other ship, which as yet they could not see, were fast enough! Even a single frigate might do, imbued by the near and awful presence of the *Allegiance* with greater force, and so long as the *Allegiance* was on the horizon at the climax of the chase, she should have a share in any prize taken.

They searched the ocean anxiously, sweeping with their glasses, without success; until Nitidus, who had been jumping aloft at intervals, landed and said breathlessly, "It is not a ship; it is dragons."

They strained to see, but the oncoming specks were lost among the clouds, nearly all the time. But they were certainly coming fast, and before the hour had closed, the convoy had altered their course yet again: they were now trying only to get under cover of some French gun emplacement along the coast, risking the danger of running for a lee-shore with the wind behind them. The *Allegiance* had closed the distance to some thirty miles.

"*Now* may we go?" Temeraire said, looking around; all the dragons were thoroughly roused, and though crouched to keep from checking the ship's way, they had their heads craned up on their necks, fixed intently upon the chase.

Laurence closed up his glass and turning said, "Mr. Ferris, the fighting crew to go aboard, if you please." Emily held out her hand for the glass, to carry it away; Laurence looked down at her and said, "When you are finished, Roland, I hope you and Dyer may be of use to Lieutenant Ferris, on the lookouts."

"Yes, sir," she said, in almost a breathless squeak, and dashed to stow the glass; Calloway gave her and Dyer each a pistol, and Fellowes their harnesses a tug, before the two of them scrambled aboard.

"I do not see why I must go last," Maximus said petulantly, while Temeraire and Lily's crews scrambled aboard; Dulcia and Nitidus already aloft, Messoria and Immortalis to make ready next.

"Because you are a great mumping lummox and there

is no damned room to rig you out until the deck is cleared away," Berkley said. "Sit quiet and they will be off all the sooner."

"Pray do not finish all the fighting until I am there," Maximus called after them, his deep bellow receding and growing faint with the thunder of their passage; Temeraire was stretching himself, outdistancing the others, and for once Laurence did not mean to check him. With support so near at hand, there was every reason to take advantage of his speed; they needed only to harry and delay the convoy a little while in order to bring up all the pursuit, which should certainly make the enemy shipping strike.

But Temeraire had only just reached the convoy when the clouds above the leading frigate went abruptly boiling away in a sudden blazing eruption like cannon-fire, and through the unearthly ochre glow, Iskierka came diving down, her spikes dragging ragged shreds of mist and smoke along behind her, and shot a flamboyant billowing arc of flame directly across the ship's bows. Arkady and the ferals came pouring after her, yowling fit for a nuisance of cats, and went streaking up and down the length of the convoy, hooting and shrilling, quite in range of the ships' guns; but what looked like recklessness was not so, for they were going by so swiftly that only the very merest chance could have allowed a hit, and the force of their wings set all the sails to shivering.

"Oh," Temeraire said doubtfully, as they went dashing crazily past him, and paused to hover. Iskierka meanwhile was flying in coiled circles over the frigate, yelling down at them to strike, to strike, or she would burn them all up to a tinder, only see if she would not; and she jetted off another burst of flame for emphasis, directly into the water, which set up a monstrous hissing pillar of steam.

The colors came promptly down, and meekly the rest of the convoy followed suit. Where Laurence would have expected the lack of prize-crews to pose many difficulties, there were none: the ferals at once busily and in a practiced manner set about herding the prizes as skillfully as sheepdogs tending their flock, snapping at the wheelmen, and nudging them by the bows to encourage them to turn their heads for England. The littlest of the ferals, like Gherni and Lester, landed on the ships directly, terrifying the poor sailors almost mortally.

"Oh, it is all her own notion," Granby said ruefully, shaking Laurence's hand, on the bow of the *Allegiance*; when that vessel had met them halfway and traveling now in company they had resumed their course for Dover. "She refused to see why the Navy ought to get all the prizes; and I am afraid she has suborned those damned ferals. I am sure she has them secretly flying the Channel at night looking for prizes, without reporting them, and when they tell her of one, she pretends she has just taken it into her head to go in such and such a direction. They are as good as any prize-crew ever was; the sailors are all as meek as maids, with one of them aboard."

The remainder of the ferals were aloft, singing lustily together in their foreign tongue, and larking about with satisfaction. Iskierka however had crammed herself in among the formation, and in particular had seized the place along the starboard rail where Temeraire preferred to nap. She was no small addition: having gained her full growth in the intervening months since they had seen her, she was now enormously long and sprawling, the heavy coils of her serpentine body at least as long as Temeraire, and draped over anything which happened to be in her way, most inconveniently.

"There is not enough room for you," Temeraire said

ungraciously, nosing away the coil which she had deposited upon his back, and picking up his foot out of the other which was slithering around it. "I do not see why you cannot fly back to Dover."

"*You* may fly to Dover if you like," Iskierka said, flicking the tip of her tail dismissively. "I have flown all morning, and anyway I am going to stay with my prizes. Look how many of them there are," she added, exultant.

"They are all our prizes," Temeraire said.

"As it is the rule, I suppose we must share with you," she said, with an air of condescension, "but you did nothing except come late, and watch," a remark which Temeraire rather instinctively felt the justice of, than disputed, and he hunched down to sulk over the situation in silence.

Iskierka nudged him. "Look how fine my captain is," she added, to heap on coals of fire; and much to poor Granby's embarrassment: he was indeed a little ridiculously fine, gold-buttoned and -beringed, and the sword at his waist also hilted in gold, with a great absurd diamond at the pommel, which he did his best to conceal with his hand.

"She fusses for days, if I will not, every time she takes another prize," Granby muttered, crimson to the ears.

"How many has she taken?" Laurence said, rather dubiously.

"Oh—five, since she set about it in earnest, some of them strings like this one," Granby said. "They strike to her right off, as soon as she gives them a bit of flame; and we have not a great deal of competition for them: I do not suppose you know, we have not been able to hold the blockade."

They exclaimed over this news with alarm. "It is the French patrols," Granby said. "I don't know how, but I would swear they have another hundred dragons more than they ought, on the coast; we cannot account for them. They only wait until we are out of sight, and then they go for the ships on blockade: dropping bombs, and as we haven't enough dragons well yet to guard at all hours, the Navy must stand ship-and-ship, to fend them off. It is a damned good thing you have come home."

"*Five* prizes," Temeraire said, very low, and his temper was not improved when they reached Dover, where upon a jutting promontory above the cliffs Iskierka now had a large pavilion made of blackened stone, sweating from the exhalations of her spines and surely over-warm in the summer heat. Temeraire nevertheless regarded it with outrage, particularly after she had smugly arranged herself upon the threshold, her coils of vivid red and violet displayed to advantage against the stone, and informed him that he was very welcome to sleep there, if he should feel at all uncomfortable in his clearing.

He swelled up and said very coolly, "No, I thank you," and retreating to his own clearing did not even resort to the usual consolation, of polishing his breastplate, but only curled his head beneath his wing and sulked.

Chapter 14

❧

HIDEOUS SLAUGHTER AT THE CAPE
Thousands Slain! Cape Coast Destroyed!
Louanda and Benguela Burnt!

It will require yet some time before a complete Accounting will render final all the worst fears of Kin and Creditors alike, throughout these Isles, as to the extent of the Disaster, which has certainly encompassed the Wreck of several of our foremost citizens, for the destruction of many of their Interests, and left us to mourn without certain knowledge the likely Fate of our brave Adventurers and our noble Missionaries. Despite the territorial Questions, associated with the War with France, which lately made us Enemies, the deepest Sympathies must be extended now across the Channel to those bereaved Families, in the Kingdom of Holland, who in the Settlers at the Cape Colony have lost in some cases all their nearest Relations. All voices must be united in lamenting the most hideous and unprovoked Assault imaginable, by a Horde of violent and savage Beasts, egged on by the Jealousy of the native Tribesmen, resentful of the rewards of honest Christian labor . . .

*L*AURENCE FOLDED THE paper, from Bristol, and threw it beside the coffee-pot, with the caricature facing downwards: a bloated and snaggle-toothed creature labeled *Africa*, evidently meant to be a dragon, and several unclothed natives of grinning black visage prodding with spears a small knot of women and children into its open maw, while the pitiful victims uplifted their hands in prayer and cried *O Have You No Pity* in a long banner issuing from their mouths.

"I must go see Jane," he said. "I expect we will be bound for London, this afternoon; if you are not too tired."

Temeraire was still toying with his last bullock, not quite sure if he wanted it or not; he had taken three, greedy after the short commons of their voyage. "I do not mind going," he said, "and perhaps we may go a little early, and see *our* pavilion; there can be no reason not to go near the quarantine-grounds now, surely."

If they did not bring the first intelligence of the wholesale disaster in Africa, having been preceded in their flight by many a swifter vessel, certainly they carried the best: before their arrival, no-one in England had any notion of the identity of the mysterious and implacable foe who had so comprehensively swept clean the African coast. Laurence and Harcourt and Chenery had of course written dispatches, describing their experiences, and handed them on to a frigate which had passed them off Sierra Leone, and to another in Madeira; but in the end, these had only anticipated their arrival by a few days. In any case, formal dispatches, even the lengthy ones produced over the leisure of a month at sea, were by no means calculated to satisfy the clamoring demands of Government for information on so comprehensive a disaster.

Jane at least did not waste their time with a recounting of the facts. "I am sure you will have enough of that before their Lordships," she said. "You will both have to come, and Chenery also; although perhaps I can beg you off, Harcourt, if you like: under the circumstances."

"No, sir, thank you," Catherine said, flushing. "I should prefer no special treatment."

"Oh, I will take all the special treatment we can get, with both hands," Jane said. "At least it will make them give us chairs, I expect; you look wretched."

Jane herself was much improved, from when Laurence had left her; her hair was shot more thoroughly with silver, but her face, better fleshed, showed all the effects of cares lightened and a return to flying: a healthier wind-burnt color in the cheek, and lips a little chapped. She frowned at Catherine, who despite a perpetual lobsterish color from the sun managed still to look faintly bluish under the eyes, and pallid. "Are you still being taken ill?"

"Not *very* often," Catherine said, without perfect candor; Laurence—indeed, all the ship's company—had been witness to her regular visits to the rail, aboard ship. "And I am sure that I will be better now we are not at sea."

Jane shook her head disapprovingly. "At seven months I was as well as ever I have been in my life. You have not put on nearly enough weight. It is an engagement like any other, Harcourt, and we must be sure you are up to the mark."

"Tom wishes me to see a physician, in London," Catherine said.

"Nonsense," Jane said. "A sensible midwife is what you need; I think my own is still in harness, here in

Dover. I will find her direction for you. I was damned glad of her, I will tell you. Twenty-nine hours' labor," she added, with the same dreadful reminiscent satisfaction as a veteran of the wars.

"Oh," Catherine said.

"Tell me, do you find—" Jane began, and shortly Laurence sprang up, and went to interest himself in the map of the Channel which was laid out on Jane's desk, striving rather desperately not to hear the rest of their conversation.

The map was not as distressing in the visceral sense, although this was perhaps rather a sign of improper sensibility on his part, as the circumstances it depicted were as unfortunate as could be imagined. All the French coastline of the Channel was now littered with markers, blue representing companies of men, white for the individual dragons: clustered around Brest there were fifty thousand men at least, and another fifty at Cherbourg; at Calais a force half that number again; and scattered among these positions some two hundred dragons.

"Are these figures certain?" Laurence asked, when they had finished their exchange, and joined him at the table.

"No, more's the pity," Jane said. "He has more; dragons, at any rate. Those are only the official estimates. Powys insists he cannot be feeding so many beasts, so close together, when we have the ports blockaded; but I know they are there, damn them. I get too many reports from the scouts, more dragons than they ought to be seeing at a time; and the Navy tell me they cannot get a smell of fish but they catch it themselves, the price of meat has gone so dear across the way. Our own fishermen are rowing over to sell their catches.

"But let us be grateful," she added. "If the situation were not so damned dire, I am sure they would keep you in Whitehall a month, answering questions about this business in Africa; as it is, I will be able to extract you without much more than a day or two of agony."

Laurence lingered, when Catherine had left; Jane filled his glass again. "And you would do as well with a month at the seashore yourself, to look at you," she said. "You have had rather a dreadful time of it, I find, Laurence. Will you stay to dinner?"

"I beg your pardon," he said. "Temeraire wishes to go up to London while it is still light out." He thought perhaps he ought to excuse himself; he rather felt that he wished to talk to her, more than knew what he wanted to say, and he could not be standing there stupidly.

She rescued him, though, saying, "I am very grateful to you, by the bye, for the compliment to Emily. I have sent on to Powys at Aerial Command to confirm her and Dyer in rank as ensign, just so there should be nothing havey-cavey about the business; but there shan't be any trouble about that. I don't suppose you have any likely boys in mind for their places?"

"I do," he said, steeling himself, "if you please: the ones I brought from Africa."

Demane had passed the weeks after their escape from Capetown deep in delirium, with his side, where the bayonet had gone in, swelled out beneath the small scabbed cut as if an inflated bladder had sat beneath the skin; and Sipho, too distressed even to speak, refusing to leave the sickbed except to creep away and fetch water or gruel, which he patiently fed his brother spoon by spoon. The southern coast had slipped rapidly away to starboard, taking with it any hope of kin to whom they might have been returned, long before the ship's surgeon had informed Laurence that the boy would make a recovery. "It is to your credit, sir," Laurence had said, even while wondering whatever was to be done with the boys now; by then the *Allegiance* had seen Benguela, and there could be no question of turning back.

"It is no such thing," Mr. Raclef had retorted, "a wound in the vitals of this sort is invariably fatal, or ought to be; there was nothing to be done but make him comfortable," and he went away again muttering, vaguely offended at having so obvious a diagnosis defied.

The patient persisted in his defiance, making good proofs of the resilience of youth, and very shortly had reacquired the two stone of weight lost in his illness, and another for good measure. Demane was dismissed the sick-bay before they had crossed the equator, and the two were installed in the passenger quarters together, in a tiny curtained-off compartment scarcely large enough to sling their one small hammock: the older boy's wariness would not permit them to sleep at the same time, and he insisted alternating watches.

He was not without justification nervous of the general crowd of refugees from the Cape, who regarded the boys with simmering anger as representatives of the "kaffirs" they blamed for the destruction of their homes. It was useless to try and explain to the settlers that Demane and Sipho were of a wholly different nation than the one which had attacked them, and there was great indignation that the boys should be housed among them, particularly from the elderly shopkeeper and the farmhand whose respective nooks had each been shortened by the width of seven inches for their sake.

A few quiet belowdecks scuffles with the settler boys predictably followed. These ceased quickly, it becoming rapidly evident that a boy, even lately ill, who had been for several years entirely dependent for his survival upon his own hunting skills, and by necessity forced to contend against lions and hyenas for his supper, was not an advisable opponent for boys whose experience ended at schoolyard squabbling. They resorted instead to the petty torments of smaller children, covert pinching and prodding, small malicious traps of slush or filth left just beside the hammock, and the ingenious use of weevils. The third time Laurence found the boys sleeping on the dragondeck, tucked up against Temeraire's side, he did not send them back to their small compartment below.

Temeraire, being nearly their solitary point of familiarity and the only one left among the company who had any grasp of their language whatsoever, quickly lost whatever lingering horrors he had possessed for them; the more so, as they were sure, in his company, to avoid their tormentors. The boys were soon as apt to be clambering over his back, in their games, as any of the younger officers, and through his tutelage acquiring a reasonable command of English, so that a little while after they had left Cape Coast, Demane might come to Laurence and ask, in a steady voice betrayed only by his hand clutching tightly at the railing, "Are we your slaves now?"

Laurence stared, shocked, and the boy added, "I will not let you sell Sipho away from me," defiantly, but with a note of such desperation as showed his understanding that he had not much power, to defend himself or his brother from such a fate.

"No," Laurence said, at once; it was a dreadful blow, to find himself regarded as a kidnapper. "Certainly not; you are—" but he was here stopped by the uncomfortable lack of any position to name, and forced to conclude, lamely, "you are by no means slaves. You have my word you shall not be parted," he added; Demane did not look much comforted.

"Of course you are not slaves," Temeraire said, in dismissive tones, to rather better effect, "you are of my

crew," an assumption springing from his native posses-
siveness, which serenely made them his own in spite of
all the obvious impracticality of such an arrangement,
and forced Laurence to recognize he could see no other
solution, which should give them the respectability they
might have earned, among their own tribe, for the services which they had performed.

No one could have called them gentleman-like, in
birth or in education, and Laurence was dismally aware
that while Sipho was a biddable, good-natured child,
Demane was too independent, and more likely to be obstinate as a pig, if not belligerent, towards anyone wishing to effect an alteration in his manners. But difficulty
alone could not be permitted to stand in the way: he had
taken them from home, from all the relations which they
might have, and robbed them of all standing in the
world. If, at the end, there had been no practical way to
restore them, he could not escape responsibility for the
situation having arisen; he had willfully contributed to
it, to the material benefit of the Corps and his mission.

"Captains can choose whom they like; that has always been the way of it," Jane said, "but I will not say
there shan't be a noise about it: you may be sure that as
soon as the promotions are posted in the *Gazette*, I will
be hearing from a dozen families. At present we have
more likely boys trained up than places for them, and
you have got yourself the reputation of a proper school-
master, even if they did not like to see their sprouts on a
heavy-weight: it is a pretty sure road to making lieutenant, if they do not cut straps before then."

"I must surely give the greater weight," he said, "to
those who have given so much in our service; and
Temeraire already counts them as his own crew."

"Yes; but the carpers will say you ought to take them
as personal servants, or at best ground crew," she said.

"But damn them all; you shall have the boys, and if any-one complains of their birth, you may always declare them princes in their native country, without any fear of being proven false. Anyway," she added, "I will put them on the books, quietly, and we will hope they slip past. Will you let me give you a third? Temeraire's complement allows for it."

He assented, of course; and she nodded. "Good: I will send you Admiral Gordon's youngest grandson, and that will make him your best advocate, instead of your loudest critic: no one has as much time for writing letters and making noise as a retired admiral, I assure you."

Sipho was very willing to be pleased, when informed of their elevation; Demane said a little suspiciously, "We take messages? And ride the dragon?"

"And other errands," Laurence said, and was then puzzled how to explain errands, until Temeraire said, "Those are small boring things, which no one very much likes to do," which did not reduce the suspicion.

"When will I have time to hunt?" the boy demanded.

"I do not suppose you will," Laurence said, taken aback, and only after a little more exchange gathered the boy did not realize that they would be fed and clothed: at Laurence's expense, of course, as they had no family sponsoring them; cadets drew no pay. "You cannot think we would let you starve; what have you been eating so far?"

"Rats," Demane said succinctly, explaining belatedly to Laurence's satisfaction the unusual lack of those delights more civilly referred to as millers, which had been much lamented among the midshipmen whose traditional prey they were, "but now we are on land again, I took two of those small things last night," and gestured to make long ears.

"Not from the grounds of Dover Castle?" Laurence said; certainly there would not have been many of them nearer-by, with the smell of so many dragons about. "You must not, again; you will be taken up for poaching."

He was not perfectly sure Demane was convinced, but at last Laurence declared a private victory and detailed the two of them to Roland and Dyer's supervision, to be led through their tasks a while.

It was a short flight only to the quarantine-grounds, and the pavilion established to good effect in a sheltered valley, sacrificing prospect for a windbreak. It was not empty: two rather thin and exhausted Yellow Reapers were sleeping inside, still coughing occasionally, and a limp little Greyling: not Volly, but Celoxia, and her captain Meeks. "On the Gibraltar route, I think," Meeks said, to their inquiry, "if *he* has not been broken-down again," rather bitterly. "I don't mean to carp at you, Laurence; God knows *you* have done all you might, and more. But they seem to think at the Admiralty that it is like putting the wheel back on a cart, and they want us flying all the old routes again at once. Halifax and back, by way of Greenland and a transport, anchored in the middle of the north fifties, with ice-water coming over the bow with every wave; of course she is coughing again." He stroked the little dragon's muzzle; she sneezed plaintively.

The floor was very comfortably warm, at least, and if the wood-fire was a little smoky, worming up through the square stone slabs of the floor, the open plan blew the fumes away. It was a simple, practical building, not at all elegant or ornate, and Temeraire might have slept in it, but it could not have been called spacious, on his scale. He regarded it with brooding disappointment, and was not disposed to linger; the crew did not even have the opportunity to dismount before he wished to be off again, putting the pavilion at his back, and flying with rather a drooping ruff.

Laurence tried to console him by remarking on the sick dragons yet sheltering there, even in the summer's heat. "Jane tells me that they would pile them in ten at a time," he said, "during the winter, so wet and cold; and the surgeons are quite certain it saved a dozen lives."

Temeraire only muttered, "Well, I am glad it has been useful," ungraciously; such distant triumphs, achieved out of his sight and several months before, were not quite satisfactory. "That is an ugly hill," he added, "and that one, also; I do not like them," inclined to be displeased even with the landscape, when ordinarily he was mad for anything out of the common way, and would point out anything of the most meager interest to Laurence's attention, with delight.

The hills *were* odd; irregular and richly covered with grass, they drew the eye queerly as they went overhead. "Oh," said Emily suddenly, on the forward lookout, craning her head over Temeraire's shoulder to look down at them, and shut her mouth hurriedly in embarrassment at the solecism of having spoken without a warning to give. Temeraire's wingbeats slowed. "Oh," he said.

The valley was full of them: not hills but barrow-mounds, raised over the dragon-corpses where they had breathed their last. Here and there an outthrust horn or spike came jutting from the sod; or a little fall of dirt had bared the white curve of a jaw-bone. No one spoke; Laurence saw Allen reach down and close his hands around the jingle of his carabiners, where they hooked on to the harness. They flew on silently, above the verdant deserted green, Temeraire's shadow flowing and rippling over the spines and hollows of the dead.

They were still quiet when Temeraire came in to the London covert, and the little unpacking necessary carried on subdued: the men carried the bundles to be stacked at the side of the clearing, and went back for others; the harness-men had none of their usual cheerful squabbling over who was to manage the belly-netting, but in silence Winston and Porter went to it together. "Mr. Ferris," Laurence said, voice deliberately raised, "when we are in reasonable order, you may give a general leave, through tomorrow dinner; barring any pressing duties."

"Yes, sir; thank you," Ferris said, trying to match his tone; it did not quite take, but the work went a little more briskly, and Laurence was confident a night's revelry would soon finish the work of rousing the men out of the sense of oppression.

He went and stood at Temeraire's head, putting his hand comfortingly on his muzzle. "I *am* glad it was useful," Temeraire said, low, and slumped more deeply to the ground.

"Come; I would have you eat something," Laurence said. "A little dinner; and then I will read to you, if you like."

Temeraire did not find much consolation in philosophy, or even mathematics; and he picked at his food until, pricking up his ruff, he raised his head and put a protective forehand over his cow, and Volly came tumbling into the clearing, kicking up a furious hovering cloud of dust behind him.

"Temrer," Volly said happily, and butted him in the shoulder, then immediately cast a wistful eye on the cow.

"Don't be taken in," James said, sliding down from

his back. "Fed not a quarter-of-an-hour ago, while I was waiting for the mails in Hyde Park, and a perfectly handsome sheep, too. How are you, Laurence? Tolerably brown, I find. Here's for you, if you please."

Laurence gladly accepted the parcel of letters for his crew, with one on top, to his personal direction. "Mr. Ferris," he said, handing the packet over, to be distributed. "Thank you, James; I hope we find you well?"

Volly did not look so bad as Meeks's report might have made Laurence fear, if with a degree of rough scarring around the nostrils, and a slightly raspy voice. It did not inhibit him from rambling happily on to Temeraire, with an enumeration of the sheep and goats which he had lately eaten, and a recounting of his triumph at having sired, early in the recent disaster, an *egg*, himself. "Why, that is very good," Temeraire said. "When will it hatch?"

"Novembrer," Volly said delightedly.

"He will say so," James said, "although the surgeons have no notion; it hasn't hardened a tick yet, and it would be early. But the blessed creatures do seem to know, sometimes, so they are looking out a likely boy for the thing."

They were bound for India, "Tomorrow, or the day after, maybe; if the weather keeps fair," James said airily.

Temeraire cocked his head. "Captain James, do you suppose that you might carry a letter for me? To China," he added.

James scratched his head to receive such a request; Temeraire was unique among British dragons, so far as Laurence knew, in writing letters; indeed, not many aviators managed the habit themselves. "I can take it to Bombay," he said, "and I suppose some merchantman is bound to be going on; but they'll only go to Canton."

"I am sure if they give it to the Chinese governor there, he will see it delivered," Temeraire said with justifiable confidence; the governor was likely to consider it an Imperial charge.

"But surely we ought not delay you, for personal correspondence," Laurence said a little guiltily; if James did seem a little careless of his schedule.

"Oh, don't trouble yourself," James said. "I don't quite like the sound of his chest yet, and the surgeons don't, either; as their Lordships ain't disposed to worry about it, so neither am I, about being quite on time. I'm happy enough to linger in port a few days, and let him fatten himself up and sleep a while." He slapped Volly on his flank, and led him away to another clearing, the small Greyling following on his heels almost like an eager hound, if a hound were imagined the size of a moderate elephant.

The letter was from his mother, but it had been franked: a small but valuable sign of his father's approval, of its having been sent, with replies to his last letter:

> We are very shocked by the News you send us from Africa, which in many respects exceeds that appearing in the Papers, and pray for the Solace of those Christian souls caught in the Wrack, but we do not repudiate some Sentiment, which the Abhorrence of such dreadful Violence cannot wholly silence, that the Wages of Sin are not always held in Arrears to be paid off on the Day of Reckoning, but Malefactors by God's Will may be held to account even in this earthly life; Lord Allendale considers it a Judgment upon the failure of the Vote. He is much satisfied by your Account, that the Tswana (if I have it correctly) might perhaps have been appeased, by the Ban; and we have hopes that this necessary Period, to that evil trade,

may soon lead to a better and more humane Condition for those poor Wretches who yet suffer under the Yoke.

She concluded more unfortunately by saying,

> . . . and I have taken the Liberty of enclosing a small Trinket, which amused me to buy, but for which I have no Use, as your Father has mentioned to me that you have taken an Interest in the Education of a Young Lady, who I hope may find it suitable.

It was a fine string of garnets, set in gold; his mother had only one granddaughter, a child of five, out of three sons and now five grandsons, and there was a wistful note to be read between the closely written lines. "That is very nice," Temeraire said, peering over at it with an appraising and covetous eye, although it would not have gone once around one of his talons.

"Yes," Laurence said sadly, and called Emily over to deliver the necklace to her. "My mother sends it you."

"That is very kind of her," Emily said, pleased, and if a little perplexed, quite happy to forgo that sentiment in favor of enjoyment of her present. She admired it, over her hands, and then thought a moment, and a little tentatively inquired, "Ought I write to her?"

"Perhaps I will just express your thanks, in my reply," Laurence said; his mother might not dislike receiving the letter, but it would only have encouraged the misunderstanding, and his father would certainly look with disfavor on any such gesture as suggesting expectations of a formal acknowledgment, no part of his sense of the responsibilities towards an illegitimate child; and there was no easy way to explain to him the perfect lack of foundation for such a concern.

Laurence was sadly puzzled how to write, even in his own letter, to avoid adding to the confusion, as he could not in civility omit the barest facts: that he had delivered the gift, seen it received, and heard thanks; all of which alone revealed that he had seen Emily very lately and, by the speed of his reply, it would seem regularly. He wondered how he might explain the situation to Jane: he had the vague and slightly lowering thought that she would find it highly amusing, nothing to be taken seriously; that she would not at all mind being taken for—and here his pen stuttered and halted, with his thoughts, because of course, she *was* the mother of a child, out of wedlock; she was not a respectable woman, and it was not only the secret of the Corps which would have prevented him ever making her known to his mother.

Chapter 15

❧

"*J*ANE," LAURENCE SAID, "will you marry me?"
"Why, no, dear fellow," she said, looking up in surprise from the chair where she was drawing on her
boots. "It would be a puzzle to give you orders, you
know, if I had vowed to obey; it could hardly be comfortable. But it is very handsome of you to have offered," she added, and standing up kissed him heartily,
before she put on her coat.

A timid knock at the door prevented anything more
he might have said: one of Jane's runners, come to tell
her the carriage was ready at the gates of the covert, and
they had perforce to go. "I will be glad when we are
back in Dover; what a miserable swamp," Jane said, already blotting her forehead on her sleeve as she left the
small barracks-house: the London setting added, to the
attractions of stifling heat and the heavy moisture-laden
air, all the city's unrivaled stench, and the mingling of
barnyard scents with the acrid stink of the small covert's
presently overburdened dragon-middens.

Laurence said something or other about the heat, and
offered her his handkerchief mechanically. He did not
know how to feel. The offer had come from some deeper
impulse than conscious decision; he had not meant to
speak, and certainly not yet, not in such a manner. An

absurd moment to raise the question, almost as if he wished to be refused; but he was not relieved, he was by no means relieved.

"I suppose they will keep us past dinner-time," Jane said, meaning their Lordships, an opinion which seemed to Laurence rather optimistic; he thought it very likely they should be kept for days, if Bonaparte were not so obliging as to invade, with no warning. "So I must look in on Excidium before we go: he ate nothing at all, last night; nothing, and I must try and rouse him up to do better today."

"I do not need to be scolded," Excidium murmured, without opening his eyes, "I am very hungry," but he was scarcely able to rouse himself from his somnolence even to nudge briefly at her hand. Though naturally one of those earliest dosed with the supply of mushroom sent on by frigate from Capetown, he was by no means yet fully recovered from his ordeal; the disease had been well advanced in his case by the time the cure had arrived, and only in the last few weeks had it been judged safe for him to leave the uncomfortable sand-pits which had made his home for more than a year. Nevertheless he had insisted on managing the flight to London, instead of letting Temeraire carry Jane with Laurence, and was now paying for his pride with near-prostration; he had done nothing but sleep since their arrival, the afternoon before.

"Then try and take a little while I am here, for my comfort," Jane said, and stepped back to the clearing's edge to keep her best coat and trousers from being spattered by the fresh-butchered sheep carried hurriedly over by the covert herdsmen, and hacked apart directly in front of Excidium's jaws, which ground methodically away at the joints of meat as they were put in his mouth. Laurence took the opportunity of escaping her company for a moment, and went to the neighboring clearing where Temeraire was busily engaged, despite the early hour, with his two sand-tables, upon the letter. He was working upon an account of the disease, and its treatment, which he meant to send to his mother in China, with Mr. Hammond as his proxy, against the danger that a similar outbreak might one day there occur. "You have made that *Lung* look more like *Chi,*" he said severely, casting an eye over the work of his coterie of secretaries: Emily and Dyer, who had been disgruntled to learn that their promotion to the exalted rank of ensign had not relieved them of all responsibility of schoolwork, and with them Demane and Sipho, who were at least at no greater disadvantage learning Chinese script than anyone else would have been.

Laurence thought, abruptly, he might have asked her the other day, after they had disposed of the fate of the boys. They had been closeted alone together, without interruption, nearly an hour; that, at any rate, would have been a more opportune moment to speak, barring any scruple at introducing a subject so intimate in the precincts of her office. Or he might have spoken yesterday night, when they had left the dragons sleeping and retired together to the barracks-house; or, better still, he ought to have waited some weeks, until the settling of this first furious bustle of activity after their arrival: hindsight serving powerfully to show him how he might better have forwarded the suit he had not wholly intended to make.

Her rejection had been too practical, too quick, to give him much encouragement to renew his addresses, under any future circumstances. In the ordinary way, he should have considered it as forming a necessary end to their relations, but the mode of her refusal made it seem mere petulance to be wounded, or to insist on some sort of moralizing line. Yet he was conscious of a lowering unhappiness; perhaps in turning Catherine's advocate towards the state of matrimony, he had become his own, and without quite knowing had set his heart upon it, or at any rate his convictions.

Temeraire finished his present line upon the sand-table, and lifting his foreleg away to let Emily carefully exchange it with the second, caught sight of Laurence. "Are you going?" he inquired. "Will you be very late?"

"Yes," he said, and Temeraire lowered his head and peered at him searchingly. "Never mind," Laurence said, putting his hand on Temeraire's muzzle. "It is nothing; I will tell you later."

"Perhaps you had better not go," Temeraire suggested.

"There can be no question of that," Laurence said. "Mr. Roland, perhaps you will go and sit with Excidium this afternoon, and see if you can convince him to take a little more food, if you please."

"Yes, sir. May I take the children?" Emily said, from the advanced age of twelve, meaning Demane and Sipho, the older of whom lifted his head indignantly at the name. "I have been teaching them how to read and write in English, in the afternoons," she added importantly, which filled Laurence with anticipatory horror at the results of this endeavor, as Emily's penmanship most often resembled nothing more than snarled thread.

"Very good," he said, consigning them to their fate, "if Temeraire does not need them."

"No; we are almost finished, and then Dyer may read to me," Temeraire said. "Laurence, do you suppose we have enough mushroom to spare, that we may send a sample with my letter?"

"I hope so; Dorset tells me that they have managed to find a way to cultivate the thing, in some caves in Scotland, so what remains need not all be preserved against future need," Laurence said.

The carriage was old and not very comfortable, close and hot and rattling horribly over the streets, which were in any case none to the good this close to the covert. Chenery, so ordinarily irrepressible, was sweating and silent; Harcourt very pale, although this had a more prosaic cause than anxiety, and halfway along she was obliged in a choked voice to request they stop, so she might vomit into the street.

"There, I feel better," she said, leaning back in, and looked only a little shaky when she stepped down from the carriage and refused Laurence's arm for the short walk through the courtyard into the offices.

"A glass of wine, perhaps, before we go in?" Laurence said to her softly, but she shook her head. "No; I will just take a touch of brandy," she said, and moistened her lips from the flask which she carried.

They were received in the boardroom, by the new First Lord and the other commissioners: the Government had changed again in their absence, over the question of Catholic emancipation, Laurence gathered; and the Tories were in once more: Lord Mulgrave sat now at the head of the table, a little heavy by the jowls, with a serious expression and pulling a little at the end of his nose; the Tories did not think much of the Corps, under any circumstances.

But Nelson was there, also; and quite in defiance of the general atmosphere he rose as soon as they had entered, and remained standing, until in some embarrassment the other gentlemen at the table struggled to their feet; then coming forward he shook Laurence's hand, in the handsomest manner, and asked to be presented.

"I am filled with admiration," he declared, on being

named to Catherine, and making her a noble leg, "and indeed humbled, Captain Harcourt, on having read your account; I have been accustomed," he added, smiling, "to think a little well of myself, and to like a little praise: I will be the first to admit it! but your courage stands above any example which I can easily recollect, in a lifetime of service. Now, we are keeping you standing; and you must have something to drink."

"Oh—no, nothing," Catherine said, so mortally crimson her freckles stood out as pale spots. "Nothing, thank you, sir; and it was nothing, I assure you, nothing which anyone else would not have done; which my fellow-officers did not do," she added, confusing her refusals of both refreshment and praise.

Lord Mulgrave did not look entirely satisfied to have his precedence thus usurped. A chair had of course to be offered her, and perforce them all; some shuffling ensued so they were ranged together in a close row along the farther side of the table, with the naval lords facing them along the other, but still it did not quite have the court-martial quality of standing for interrogation.

They went first through a tedious summation of events, and a reconcilement of the accounts: Chenery had set down ten days, for the flight which had carried them prisoner to the falls; Laurence had made it twelve, Catherine eleven; which difference consumed nearly an hour, and required several maps to be dug out by the secretaries, none of which precisely agreed with one another on the scale of the interior. "Sir, we would do better to apply to the dragons, for our facts," Laurence said finally, raising his head from the fourth of these, when they had only been able to agree conclusively that there had been a desert somewhere in the middle, and it had not been less than nine-days' flying. "I will vouch that Temeraire is well able to judge distances, in flight, and while they did not follow directly in our course, I am certain at least he can tell us where the borders of the desert are, which we crossed, and the larger of the rivers."

"Hm," Mulgrave said, not encouragingly, stirring the report before him with a forefinger. "Well, put it aside; let us move to the matter of insubordination. I understand correctly, I believe, that all three beasts disregarded Captain Sutton's orders, to return to Capetown."

"Why, if you like to call it insubordination," Jane said. "It is a good deal more to the point, that all three of them listened at all; and that they did not go haring off wild into the interior at once, when they knew their captains stolen: remarkable discipline, I assure you, and more than I would have looked for under the circumstances."

"Then I should like to know what else it is to be called," Lord Palmerston said, from his seat further down. "A direct order disobeyed—"

"Oh—" Jane made half an impatient gesture with her hand, aborted. "A dragon of twenty tons is not to be called to account by any means other than persuasion, that I know of, and if they did not value their captains enough to disobey for them, they would not ever obey at all; so it is no use complaining. We might as well say that a ship is insubordinate, because it will not go forward when there is no wind: you can command the first as easily as the latter."

Laurence looked down at the table. He had seen dragons enough in China, who without any captain or handler whatsoever behaved with perfect discipline, to know her defense was flawed. He did not know a better name for it than insubordination, himself, and was not inclined to dismiss it so lightly; it in some wise seemed to him more insulting than otherwise, to suggest that the dragons did not know better. That Temeraire had known where his duty lay, Laurence was quite certain; that Temeraire had disobeyed Sutton's orders willfully, only because he did not like to follow them, was also certain. He as surely had considered that disobedience justified and natural, not even requiring of explanation, and would have been surprised to find anything else *truly* expected of him; but he would never have denied the responsibility.

To draw such a fine point, however, before a hostile audience, perhaps inducing them to demand an irrational punishment, Laurence did not deem prudent; even if he had been inclined to contradict Jane in such a setting. He was silent, while a brief wrestling over the question ensued; finished unresolved, when Jane had said, "I am quite willing to lecture them on the subject, if you should like it, my Lords; or put them to a court-martial, if that seems to you sensible; and the best use of our time at present."

"For my part, gentlemen," Nelson said, "I think it cannot come as a surprise to those here, when I say that victory is the best of all justifications, and to answer it with reproaches looks to me very ill. The success of the expedition proves its merit."

"A very fine success," Admiral Gambier said sourly, "which has left a crucial colony not merely lost but in ruins, and seen the destruction of every port along the coast of Africa; most notably meritorious."

"No-one could have expected a company of seven dragons to hold the African continent against a plague of hundreds, under any circumstances," Jane said, "and we had better be grateful to have, instead, what intelligence we have gained from the successful recovery of our officers."

Gambier did not contradict her directly, but snorted and went on to inquire about another small discrepancy, in the reports; but as the session dragged on, it became gradually clear through his line of questioning, and Lord Palmerston's, that they meant to suspect that the prisoners had provoked the invasion deliberately, and subsequently had colluded to conceal the act. How they had gone about it, was not to be specified; nor their motives, until at last Gambier added, in an ironical tone, "And of course, it is the slave trade to which they objected so violently; although as everyone knows, the natives of the continent have made a practice of it from time immemorial, long preceding the arrival of Europeans on their shore; or perhaps I should say, of course it is *they*, who objected to the trade. I believe, Captain Laurence, that you have strong views on the subject; I cannot be speaking out of turn to say so."

Laurence said only, "No, sir; you are not." He offered no further remark; he would not dignify the insinuation with a defense.

"Have we nothing more pressing," Jane said, "that we must spend our time on the possibility, that a large company of officers arranged to have themselves abducted, and a dozen good men killed, so they could go and be offensive enough, among a foreign nation where they did not speak a word, to provoke them into assembling a dozen wings for immediate assault? Which, I suppose, should have been accomplished overnight, for Heaven knows there are no difficulties in providing support, to a hundred dragons."

The questioning, with its grinding focus on minutiae, was sullenly given up in another hour, when it had not provoked confession. There were no official grounds for court-martial, as no dragon had been lost, and if their Lordships meant to seek a trial for the loss of the Cape,

it would have to be General Grey who faced it, and
there was certainly no public sympathy for such an
inquest. There was nothing left for them but to be
deeply dissatisfied; and nothing left for Laurence and his
fellow-captains but to sit and listen to their complaints.

Several measures of recapturing the ports were proposed which had not the least chance of success, Jane
forced to recall to their Lordships, with poorly concealed exasperation, the parade of failures which had
been occasioned by all the attempts to establish colonies
in the face of organized aerial hostilities: by Spain, in the
New World; the total destruction of Roanoke; the disas-
ters in Mysore. "You should need enough ships to throw
twenty tons of metal, and six formations, to take the
Cape long enough to secure the fort again, if they have
not ripped it all down," she said, "and when you were
done, you should have to leave two of those formations
behind with a first-rate's worth of guns, and I hardly like
to think how many soldiers; and somehow supply them
monthly, if the enemy did not have the bright notion of
attacking the supply-ships farther north."

The proposals subsided. "My Lords, you are already
aware, that I see no grounds to quarrel with Admiral
Roland's figures," Nelson said, "if I am perhaps, not so
pessimistic of our chances to succeed, where the attempts of a previous century had failed. But even half
such a force cannot be easily mustered, and certainly not
unobserved; nor could it be transported from any civi-
lized port, to any province of Africa, without the knowledge of the Navy, and indeed without its complaisance
in the matter: I will stand surety for it.

"If we cannot retake the Cape, therefore, or re-
establish a foothold upon the continent, we may nevertheless satisfy ourselves that no other nation may do so.
France, certainly, cannot aspire to it. I will not say that

Napoleon may not conquer anyplace in the world from Calais to Peking, so long as he can walk to it; but if he must put to sea, he is at our mercy.

"Indeed," he added, "I will go further. Without in any way ceasing to lament the dreadful loss we have suffered, in property and lives, from the savagery of this unprovoked assault, I will as a question of *strategy* declare myself heartily content to exchange all the convenience of our possession of the Cape, for the lack of any need to defend that position, henceforth. We have spoken before, gentlemen, in these halls, of all the expense and difficulty of improving the fortifications and patrolling the vast coastline against French incursion: an expense and difficulty which will now be borne instead by our erstwhile enemies."

Laurence was by no means disposed to argue with him, but he could not comprehend at first, why the Admiralty should have feared such an incursion at all. The French had never shown the least ambition to seize the Cape, which if a valuable port in general was unnecessary to them, holding as they did the Île de France, off the eastern coast of Africa, and certainly a difficult nut to crack; they had enough to do to hold what maritime possessions they already had.

Mulgrave pulled at his nose a little, without comment. "Admiral Roland," he said at last reluctantly, as if he did not like to pronounce her title, "what is our present strength at the Channel, if you please?"

"From Falmouth to Middlesbrough, eighty-three I put at fighting strength," she said, "and another twenty who could rise to the occasion. Seventeen of those heavy-weight, and three Longwings, besides the Kazilik and the Celestial. At Loch Laggan we have another fourteen, hatchlings, in training but old enough to bring up; and more, of course, along the North Sea coast. We would be hard-put to feed them, for an action of more than a day, but they would make a good relief."

"What is your estimation of our chances, should he make another attempt to invade by means of airships, such as he used at the battle of Dover?" Nelson asked.

"If he don't mind leaving half of them on the ocean floor, he might be able to land the rest, but I shouldn't recommend it him," Jane said. "The militia will set them on fire as quick as they can come in past us. No; I asked for a year, and it has not been so long, but the cure makes up for all that, and having back Lily and Temeraire in fighting trim: the French cannot come by air."

"Yes, the cure," Nelson said. "It is I trust secured? There is no chance it might be stolen? I believe I heard of an incident—"

"Why, I beg you will not blame the poor fellow," Jane said. "He is a lad of fourteen, and his Winchester was in a bad way. There were some sorry rumors, I am afraid to say, that there was not enough of the cure to go about, because we began a little slowly, to see how small the dose might be kept before we ran around pouring it down their gullets. There was no harm done, and he confessed it all himself, quite rightly, when I put it to all the captains. We put a guard on the supply, afterwards, to keep anyone else from temptation, and no one has gone poking about."

"But if another attempt should be made?" Nelson said. "Might the guard be easily increased, and perhaps some fortification arranged?"

"After feeding every blessed dragon in Britain and the colonies on the stuff, there is precious little of it left to steal, if anyone should want to," Jane said, "except what the gentlemen of the Royal Society have managed to persuade to take root up at Loch Laggan; and as for that, if anyone likes to try and take it from the middle of a covert, they are welcome."

"Very good; so, gentlemen," Nelson said, turning to the other commissioners, "you see that as a result of these events, deplorable as they may be in themselves, we may now be quite certain in our control of the cure: at least as certain as our own efforts could have made us."

"I beg your pardon," Laurence said, making sense at last he thought of the preoccupation, and with dismay, "is there reason to believe the disease has been communicated to the Continent? Are the French dragons taken ill?"

"We hope so," Nelson said, "although we yet lack confirmation upon the point; but the spy-courier, the Plein-Vite whom we captured, was sent over to them two days ago, and we hope any day to receive word that they have been inoculated with the disease."

"The only damned silver lining to the bloody mess," Gambier said, to a general murmur of agreement. "It will be some reparation to see the Corsican's face, when his own beasts are all coughing blood."

"Sir," Laurence managed; beside him Catherine was sickly-wan with horror, the back of her hand pressed to her mouth. "Sir, I must protest against—" He felt as though he were choking. He remembered little Sauvignon, who had kept Temeraire company that long dreadful week when they thought all hope was lost; when Laurence had expected to see *his* dragon coughing blood, at any moment.

"I should damned well hope so," Jane said, standing up. "This is why you had her sent to Eastbourne, I suppose, and none of closing the quarantine-grounds at all; a splendid creeping business. Will we be driving a plague-ship into their harbor, next, pray tell me, or poisoning their convoys of grain? Like a parcel of damned scrubs—"

Mulgrave, straightening outraged in his chair, snapped, "Ma'am, you are out of order," and Admiral Gambier said, "This is what comes of—"

"Why damn you, Gambier, come around here and say so," she said, putting her hand to her sword, and the room devolved very quickly to shouting and scorn, so even the Marines outside the door put in their heads timidly.

"You cannot mean to do this," Laurence said. "Your Grace, *you* have met Temeraire, spoken to him; you cannot imagine they are not thinking creatures, beasts to be put to the slaughter—"

Palmerston said, "Tenderhearted womanish folly—" seconded by Gambier, and Ward; "—the enemy," Nelson said, over the noise, trying to reply, "and we must seize the opportunity which has been offered us, to level the distinction between our aerial forces and theirs—"

The sly, underhanded way it had all been managed, proved well enough that the commissioners had expected opposition, and chosen to avoid it; they were not more ready to be harangued after the fact, and when Jane had shortly grown a little louder, they had reached the limits of their tolerance. "—and this," Jane was shouting, "is how I am told, days past the event; when the stupidest scuttling crab might conceive that, as soon as Bonaparte knows what has happened, as soon as he sees his beasts growing sick, he will come across at once; at once, if he is not a gawping fool—and you drag me here to Dover, with two Longwings and our Celestial, and the damned Channel hanging open like Rotten Row—" when Mulgrave rising beckoned to the guards, to stand open the door.

"Then we must not keep you," he said, rather icily,

and added, when Jane would have gone on, "You are dismissed, madam," holding out the formal orders for the defense of the Channel, the papers crumpling savagely in Jane's fist as she stormed out from the room.

Catherine leaned heavily on Chenery's arm as they left, pale with her lip bitten to dark red. Nelson, following, stopped Laurence in the hall before he could go far after them, with a hand to his arm; and spoke to him at length: about what, Laurence did not entirely follow; a cutting-out expedition which he proposed to make, to Copenhagen, the Danish fleet to be seized there. "I would be glad to have you, Captain," he finished, "and Temeraire, if you can be spared from the defense of the Channel, at least for a week's time."

Laurence stared at him, feeling heavy and stupid, baffled at Nelson's easy manner: he had met Temeraire, had spoken with him; *he* could not plead ignorance. He might not have been the prime mover of this experiment; but he was no opponent of it, whose opposition might have been everything, would have been everything, surely.

The silence grew strained, then oppressive. Nelson paused, said, with a little more hauteur, "You are fresh from a long voyage, and I am sure tired from all this questioning; I have considered it an unnecessary waste, from the first. We will speak again tomorrow; I will come to the covert in the morning, before you must return."

Laurence touched his hat; there was nothing he could say.

Out of the building and into the street, sick to his heart and wretched, seeing nothing; the touch on his elbow made him startle, and he stared at the small, shabby man standing next to him. The expression Laurence wore must have shown some sign of what he felt;

the small man bared a mouthful of wooden teeth in an attempt at a placating smile, thrust into Laurence's hand a packet of papers, and touching his own forelock dashed away, without a word spoken.

Mechanically Laurence unfolded it: a suit for damages in the amount of ten thousand three hundred pounds, two hundred six slaves valued at fifty pounds a head.

Temeraire was asleep in the lingering, slanted light; dappled. Laurence did not wake him, but sat down on the rough-hewn log bench beneath the shelter of the pine-trees, facing him, and silently bent his head: in his hands he turned over the neat roll of crisp rice paper, the seal in red ink already affixed, which Dyer had handed him. The letter could not be allowed to go, he supposed; too much chance of interception, or that the intelligence might find its way back somehow to Lien, if she yet retained any allies in the Chinese court.

The clearing was empty: the men still out on their leave. From the small forge, past the trees, Blythe's hammer steadily rang on the harness-buckles, a thin metallic sound exactly like the odd voice of the African bird, calling along the river, and Laurence found the dust of the clearing suddenly thick in his nostrils, the new-copper smell of blood and dirt vividly recalled, of sour vomit. He had the strong sensation of rope, pressing into the skin of his face, and he rubbed his hand uneasily over his cheek as if he might find a mark there, though they had all faded; there was nothing more than a little roughness, perhaps, an impression of the corded rope left upon the skin.

Jane joined him after a little while, her fine coat discarded and her neckcloth also; there were bloodstains on her shirt. She sat down on the bench and leaned forward mannish with her elbows braced against her knees, her hair still plaited back but the finer strands about the face wisping free.

"May I beg a day's leave of you?" Laurence asked, eventually. "I must see my solicitors, in the City. I know it cannot be long."

"A day," she said. She chafed her hands together absently, though it was not cold in the least, even with the sun making its last farewells behind the barracks-house. "Not longer."

"Surely they will keep her quarantined?" Laurence said, low. "Her captain saw our own quarantine-grounds; he must have realized she was taken ill, as soon as he saw her. He would never expose the other dragons."

"Oh, they thought it out with both hands; never fear," Jane said. "I have had the account of it, now. He was sent home by boat; she was let to see him off, from a distance, and told that he had been sent to the covert outside of Paris, where the mail-couriers nest. I dare say she flung herself directly into their ranks. O, what a filthy business. By now it has been well-spread, I am sure: the couriers go every quarter-of-an-hour, and new come in, as often."

"Jane," Laurence said, "Napoleon's couriers go to Vienna. They go to Russia and to Spain, and all through Prussia—the Prussian dragons themselves are penned in French breeding grounds; our allies whom we deserted, in their hour of need—they go even to Istanbul, and from there, where will the disease *not* be carried?"

"Yes, it is very clever," she said, smiling, with a parchment thinness to the corners of her mouth. "The strategy is very sound; no one could argue with it. At a stroke we go from very nearly the weakest aerial force, in Europe, to the strongest."

"By murder," Laurence said. "It can be called nothing else; wholesale murder." Nor was there any reason why the devastation should end in Europe. All the maps over which he had labored, through their half-year's journey home from China, unfolded again for him without any need for their physical presence; the wavering course of their journey now made a track for slow creeping death to run along in reverse. Strategy, *strategy*, would call it a victory to see the Chinese aerial legions decimated: without them, the Chinese infantry and cavalry could hardly stand against British artillery. The distant corners of India brought under control, Japan humbled; perhaps a sick beast might be delivered to the Inca, and the fabled cities of gold flung open at last.

"I am sure they will find a prettier name for it, in the history books," Jane said. "It is only dragons, you know; we ought think nothing more of it, than if we were to set fire to a few dozen ships in their harbor, which we would gladly enough do."

He bowed his head. "And this is how wars should be fought."

"No," she said tiredly. "This is how they are won." She put her hands on her knees, and pushed herself standing. "I cannot stay, I must take the courier for Dover at once; I have persuaded Excidium to let me go. I will need you by tomorrow night." She rested her hand on his shoulder a moment, and left him.

He did not move, a long while, and when he at last raised his head, Temeraire was awake and watching him, the slit-pupiled eyes a faint gleam in the dark. "What has happened?" Temeraire asked quietly, and quietly Laurence told him.

Temeraire was not angry, precisely; he listened, and grew rather intent than savage, crouched low; when

Laurence had done, he said, simply, "What are we to do?"

Laurence wavered uncertainly—he did not understand; he had expected some other response, something more than this—and said at last, "We are to go to Dover—" He stopped.

Temeraire had drawn back his head. "No," he said, after a moment's strange stillness. "No; that is not what I meant, at all."

Silence. "There is nothing to—no protest which— She is already sent," Laurence said, finally; he felt thick-tongued, helpless. "The invasion is to be expected at any moment, we are to stand guard at the Channel—"

"No," Temeraire said loudly. There was a terrible resonance in his voice; the trees murmured back with it, shivering. "No," he repeated. "We must take them the cure. How can we come at it? We can go back to Africa, if we must—"

"You are speaking treason," Laurence said, without feeling, oddly calm; the words only a recitation of fact, distant.

"Very well," Temeraire said, "if I am an animal, and may be poisoned off like an inconvenient rat, I cannot be expected to care; and I do not. You cannot tell me I should obey; *you* cannot tell me I should stand idle—"

"It is treason!" Laurence said.

Temeraire stopped, and looked at him only. Laurence said, low and exhausted, "It is treason. Not disobedience, not insubordination; it cannot—there is no other name which it can bear. This Government is not of my party; my King is ill and mad; but still I am his subject. You have sworn no oath, but I have." He paused. "I have given my word."

They were silent again. There was a clamor back in the trees; some of the ground-crew men returning from their day's leave, noisy with liquor; a snatch of raised song—*that saucy little trim-rigged doxy*—and roar of laughter, as they went into the barracks-house, their lanterns vanishing.

"Then I must go alone," Temeraire said wretchedly, so softly that for once there was real difficulty in making out the words. "I will go alone."

Laurence breathed once more; hearing it, said aloud, made everything quite clear. He was grateful, it occurred to him, that Jane had refused; that he had not that pain to give. "No," he said, and stepped forward, to put his hand on Temeraire's side.

Chapter 16

❧

LAURENCE WROTE TO Jane, the merest word; no apology could suffice, and he would not insult her, by asking her to sympathize, adding only:

> . . . and I wish to make clear, that I have in no wise made my thoughts known to, nor received Aid of, my officers, my crew, or any man; and, neither deserving nor soliciting any excuse for my own Part, do heartily entreat that all blame attaching to these my actions should be laid at my door alone, and not upon those who cannot even be charged, as might on similar occasions be merited, with culpable blindness, my Resolve having been formed bare minutes before setting ink to this Page, and will upon its enclosure be immediately carried out.
>
> I will not trespass further upon the Patience which I fear I have already tried past all hope of endurance, and beg you only to believe me, in despite of the present Circumstances,
>
> Yr obdt Svt, &c.

He folded it over twice, sealed it with especial care, and laid it flat upon his neatly made cot, the address faced upwards; and left his small quarters, walking between the narrow rows of snoring men to go outside again. "You may be dismissed, Mr. Portis," he said to the officer of the watch, who was nodding at the edge of the clearing. "I will take Temeraire up for a turn; we will not have a quiet flight again in some time."

"Very good, sir," Portis said, barely concealing a bloodshot yawn, and did not stay to be persuaded further: not quite drunk, but his gait a little shambling as he went back to the barracks-house.

It was not nine. In an hour, at most two, Laurence supposed, they should be missed; he relied on scruple to forbid Ferris's opening the letter, addressed to Jane, until he began to suffer a greater degree of anxiety, which might save another hour; but then the pursuit would be furious. There were some five couriers in the covert sleeping now; more by Parliament; some of the fastest flyers in all Britain. They had not only to outrun them to Loch Laggan, but after to the coast: every covert, every shore battery from Dover to Edinburgh would be roused to bar their passage.

Temeraire was waiting, ruff pricked, agitated and crouched small to conceal it. He put Laurence upon his neck, and launched quickly; London falling away, a collection of lamps and lanterns and the bitter smoke of ten thousand chimneys, ships' lights moving gently down the Thames, and only the rushing hollow sound of wind. Laurence shut his eyes, until they had grown accustomed, then looked at his compass to give Temeraire the direction: four hundred miles, north by north-west, into the dark.

It was strange to be all alone on Temeraire's back again, not merely for a pleasure-flight; the ordinary round of duty did not often allow it. Unburdened but by the triviality of Laurence's weight and the barest harness, Temeraire stretched himself and drove high aloft, to the margins where the air grew thin; pale clouds passing beneath them over the dark ground, fellow sailors in the air. His ruff was flattened down, and the wind came whistling hard over his back, cold at these heights even in the midst of August; Laurence drew his leather coat more snugly close, and put his hands beneath his arms. Temeraire was going very fast; his wings beating a full, cupped stroke, and the world beneath blurred when Laurence looked over his shoulder.

Close towards dawn, Laurence saw to the distant west faintly an eerie glow which illuminated the curve of the earth, as if the sun meant to rise the wrong way round; a color broken, now and again, by belching smoke: Manchester, and its mills, he guessed, so they had gone some hundred and sixty miles, in less than seven hours. Twenty knots, twenty-five.

A little after dawn, Temeraire stooped, without a word, and came to ground at the shores of a small lake to drink deeply, his head thrust partway beneath the water, with the gulps traveling convulsively down his throat; he stopped, and panted, and drank some more. "Oh, no; I am not tired; not *very* tired, only I was so thirsty," he said a little thickly, turning his head back: despite his brave words he shook himself all over, and blinked away a dazed expression before he asked, in a more normal tone, "Shall I set you down a moment?"

"No; I am very well," Laurence said; he had his grog-flask with him, and in his pocket a little biscuit, which he had not touched. He wanted nothing; his stomach was closed. "You are making a good time, my dear."

"Yes, I know," Temeraire said complacently. "Oh! It is more pleasant than anything, to go so quickly, in pleasant weather, only the two of us; I should like it above all, if only," he added, looking round sorrowfully, "I did not fear that you were unhappy, dear Laurence."

Laurence would have liked to reassure him; he could not. They had passed over Nottinghamshire during the night; they might have passed over his home, his father's house. He rubbed his hand upon the neck-scales, and said quietly, "We had better be off; we are more visible, in the day."

Temeraire drooped, and did not answer, but launched himself aloft again.

They came in over Loch Laggan after seven hours more, at the dinner-hour; Temeraire without even the pretense of courtesy or warning dived directly into the feeding grounds, and not waiting for the herdsmen seized two surprised cows out of the pen: his descent too swift even for them to bellow. Alighting with them on the ledge which overlooked the training flights, he crammed them one after another down his throat, not pausing even to swallow all the first before he began upon the second. He gave a relieved sigh, afterwards, and belched replete; then daintily began to lick clean his talons before he made a guilty start: they were observed.

Celeritas was lying in the waning sun, upon the ledge, his eyes half-lidded. He looked aged, as he had not during their training, so long ago and yet scarcely three years gone; the luster of his pale jade-colored markings had faded, as cloth washed in too-hot water, and the yellow darkened to a bronzey tone. He coughed a little hoarsely. "You have put on some length, I see."

"Yes, I am as long as Maximus," Temeraire said, "or anyway, not *much* shorter; and also I am a Celestial," he added smugly: they had left off their training under the pressure of the last threat of invasion, in the year five, at the time unaware of Temeraire's real breed or his particular curious ability of the divine wind and thinking him instead an Imperial: still a most valuable breed, but not as vanishingly rare.

"So I had heard," Celeritas said. "Why are you here?"

"Oh," Temeraire said. "Well—"

Laurence let himself down and stepped forward. "I beg your pardon, sir; we are here from London, for some of the mushrooms: may I ask where they are kept?" They had resolved on this brazen frontal assault, as offering the best chance of success; even if Temeraire might look daunted now.

Celeritas snorted. "They are nursing the things like eggs: downstairs, in the baths," he said. "You will find Captain Wexler at table, I believe; he is commander of the fort now," and turned to Temeraire inquisitively, while Temeraire went hunching steadily down. Laurence did not like to leave him alone, to face all the pain of lying in the face of the friendly, unwary curiosity of his old training master, but there was no time: Celeritas would soon begin to wonder, at the absence of their crew, and the most hardened liar could scarcely have concealed this treachery for long.

It was strange to walk the corridors again, now familiar instead of alien; the cheerful roar of the communal dining-tables, which he could hear around the corners, like the blurred continuous noise of a distant cataract: welcoming, and yet closed to him utterly; he felt himself already set apart. There were no servants in the halls, likely all of them busy with the dinner service, but for one small lad running by with a stack of clean napkins, who did not give him a second glance.

Laurence did not go to Captain Wexler: his excuse

could not withstand the absence of orders, of any real
explanation; instead he went directly to the narrow,
humid stairway which led down to the baths, and in the
dressing room put off swiftly his boots, his coat, flung
down upon the shelves with his sword laid down beside
them; his trousers and shirt he left on, and taking with
him a towel went into the great tiled steam room. He
could see dimly a few somnolent forms drowsing, but in
the clouds no faces could be easily made out, and he
moved on with quick purpose; no one spoke to him,
until he had nearly reached the far door, then a fellow
lying with a towel over his face lifted it off. Laurence
did not know him: an older lieutenant perhaps, or a
younger captain, with a thick bristling mustache dripping water off its corners. "Beg pardon," he said.

"Yes?" Laurence said, stiffening.

"Be a good fellow and shut the door quick, if you
mean to go through," the man said, and putting himself
down covered his face again.

Laurence did not understand, until he had opened the
door to the large bathing-room beyond and the thick
miasmic stench of the mushrooms assaulted him, mingled with the pungent smell of a dragon-midden. He
pulled the door to behind him quickly, and put his hand
over his face, breathing deep through his mouth. The
room was deserted, nearly; the dragon eggs sat gleaming
wetly in their niches, safe behind the wrought-iron fence
along the back of the room, and beneath them on the
floor great tubs of black fertile soil, speckled reddish
brown with dragon waste for fertilizer, and mushrooms
like round buttons poking from the dirt.

There were two young Marines, undoubtedly without
much seniority, standing guard: very unhappy, and
nearly red enough in the face to match their coats from

the room's intense heat; their white trousers were stained with lines of running dye. They looked at Laurence rather hopefully as, if nothing else, a distraction; he nodded to them and said, "I am come from Dover, for more of the mushrooms; pray bring out one of those tubs."

They looked dubious, and hesitated; the older ventured, "Sir, we aren't supposed to, unless the commander says so, himself."

"Then I beg your pardon for the irregularity; my orders said nothing of the sort," Laurence said. "Be so kind as to send and confirm them, with him, if you please; I will wait here," he said to the younger soldier, who did not stay to be invited again, much to the poorly stifled outrage of the older man: but he had the key, hanging from the chain on his belt, so he could not be allowed to go.

Laurence waited as the metal door swung to again; waited; the ship turning slowly through the wind, her broadside coming to bear, the enemy's stern in sight; the clang sounded, as a bell, and he struck the Marine a heavy blow, just below the ear, as the man gazed scowling after his fellow.

The man fell staggering to one knee, his face turning up in surprise, his mouth opening; Laurence struck him again, hard, his knuckles bursting and leaving smears of blood along the Marine's cheekbone and jaw; the soldier fell heavily and was still. Laurence found that he was breathing raggedly. He had to steady his hands before he could unlatch the key.

The tubs were of varied sizes, half-barrels of wood filled with dirt, most of them large and unwieldy; Laurence seized the smallest, and threw over it the towel he had brought, hot and damp already only from the moist air of the baths. He went out by the far door, walking quickly through the rest of the circuit, back to the dressing rooms: still deserted, but dinner would by now be far advanced, and men left the tables as they pleased. He could expect interruption at any moment; sooner if the Marine were more inclined to be dutiful than dawdling, and reached the commander. Laurence flung on his boots and coat haphazardly over his wet things, and went up the stairs with the tub balanced on his shoulder, his other hand gripping tight to the rail: not recklessly; he did not mean to do this much, and fail. He burst out into the hall, and went hurriedly around a corner to straighten his clothes: if he were not so plainly disordered, he would not make a spectacle enough to draw conscious attention, he hoped, despite the odd burden of the tub. The stench was not wholly muffled by the covering linen, but it wafted behind him rather than before.

The noise of the dining hall was indeed already less; he heard voices, nearer, in the corridors; and passed a pair of servants laden down with dirty dishes. Looking down another corridor which crossed his own, he saw a couple of young midwingmen go racing across from one door to the next, shouting like boys, gleefully; in another moment he heard more running footsteps, boots falling heavily, fresh shouting: but the tone was very different.

He abandoned circumspection and ran, clumsy with the tub and shifting it every moment, until he burst out onto the ledge. Celeritas looked over at him with his dark green eyes perplexed and doubtful; Temeraire said in a sudden rush, "Pray forgive me, it is all a hum, we are taking them to France so all the dragons there do not die, and tell them Laurence did not like to do it, at all,

only I insisted upon it," not a pause for breath or punc-
tuation, and snatching Laurence with the tub up in his
talons, he flung himself away into the air.

They went rushing away bare moments before five
men charged out after them; bells were ringing madly,
and Temeraire had not settled Laurence back upon his
neck before the beacon-fire went alight and dragons
came pouring out of the castle grounds like smoke.

"Are you safe?" Temeraire cried.

"Go, go at once," Laurence shouted for an answer,
lashing harness-straps around the tub to hold it down
before him, and Temeraire whipped himself straight and
flew, flew; the pursuit was hot upon them. Not dragons
whom Laurence knew: there was one gangly-looking
Anglewing, nearly in the lead, and a few Winchesters
gaining on them: not to much purpose, but perhaps able
to interfere a little with their flight, and delay them for
the others. Temeraire said, "Laurence, I must go higher;
are you warm enough?"

He was soaked through, and chilled to the skin
already by their flight, despite the overhanging sun.
"Yes," he said, and pulled his coat closer about him. A
bank of clouds pressed down upon the crowns of the
mountains, and Temeraire pushed into them, the clinging mist springing up in fat droplets on the buckles, the
waxed and oiled leather of the harness, Temeraire's
glossy scales. The dragons chasing called to one another,
roaring, and plunged in after them, distant obscure
shadows in the fog, their voices echoing and muffled at
odd alternate turns, so he was scaling upwards through
a strange and formless landscape without direction,
haunted by their ghostly images.

He burst clear just short of a towering white mountain-
face, stark against the open blue, and Temeraire roared

as he came: a hammer-blow against the solid-packed ice and snow; Laurence clung to the harness, shivering involuntarily, as Temeraire pulled up nearly vertical, climbing along the face of the mountain, and the pursuit came chasing out of the clouds only to recoil from the thundering, rolling, steady roar of avalanche, coming down upon them like a week's snowstorm compressed into a heartbeat: the Winchesters all squalling alarmed, and scattering away from it like a flock of sparrows.

"South, due south," Laurence said, calling forward to Temeraire, pointing him the way as they came over the peak and broke away, losing the more distant followers. But Laurence could see the beacons going up already down the long line to the coast: the beacons which ordinarily would have warned of invasion, instead now carrying the warning in the other direction and ahead of them. Every covert, every dragon would be alert, even without knowing what was the matter precisely, and would try to stop them in their flight. They could not fly in any direction which would bring them upon a covert, and see them headed off and caught between two forces; their only hope for an escape lay along the more sparsely guarded North Sea coast, short of Edinburgh. Yet they had also to be near enough to make it across to the Continent; with Temeraire already tired.

Night would come, soon; three hours more would give them the safety of dark. Three hours; Laurence wiped his face against his sleeve, and huddled down.

Temeraire came at last exhausted to ground, in darkness, six hours later; his pace had slackened, little by little, the slow measured flap of his wings like a timepiece winding down, until Laurence looking over had seen not a single flickering light; not a shepherd's bonfire, not a torch, as far as his sight could reach, and said at last, "Down, my dear; you must have some rest."

He thought they were in Scotland still, or perhaps Northumberland; he was not certain. They were well south of Edinburgh and Glasgow, somewhere in a shallow valley; he could hear water trickling nearby, but they were too tired to go find it. He ate all his biscuit, ravenous suddenly, and took the last of his grog, huddled up against the curve of Temeraire's neck: it sprawled out untidily from his body, his draggled wings; he slept as he had landed.

Laurence stripped to the skin, and laid his wet things out on Temeraire's side, to let the native heat of the dragon's body do what it might to dry them; then rolled himself in his coat to sleep. The wind was cool enough, among the mountains, to keep the chill upon his skin. Temeraire gave a low rumbling murmur, somewhere in his belly, and twitched; there was distantly a hurried rustling, a clatter of frightened small hooves; but Temeraire did not wake.

The next he knew it was morning, and Temeraire was feasting red-mouthed upon a deer, with another lying dead beside it; he swallowed down his meal and looked at Laurence anxiously. "It is quite nice raw, too, and I can tear it up for you small; or perhaps you can use your sword?" he suggested.

"No; I pray you eat it all. I have not been at hard labor as have you: I can stand to be parted from my dinner a little longer," Laurence said, getting up to scrub his face in the small trickling creek, some ten paces only from where they had collapsed, and to put back on his clothes. Temeraire had attempted to spread them out upon a warm sunny rock, with his claws: they were not very damp anymore, but a little mauled about; at least the tears did not show much, under the long coat.

After Temeraire had finished his breakfast, Laurence sketched out the line of the North Sea coastline, and the Continent. "We cannot risk going much south of York," Laurence said. "Once past the mountains the country is too settled; we will be seen at once by day and perhaps by night also. We must make for the mountains on the coast near Scarborough, pass there the night, and make Holland our final mark across the sea: the country there is unsettled enough I hope we need not fear immediate challenge. Then along the coastline to France; and we shall hope they do not shoot us down without a word."

He put his tattered shirt upon a stick, in the end, to make a ragged flag of parley; and waved it mightily against the side of Temeraire's neck, while they came in over Dunkirk. Beneath them in the harbor, nevertheless, a frantic alarum set up aboard the French ships, when they saw Temeraire coming, to show that the fame of his sinking of the *Valérie* had spread this far, and many useless attempts were made, at firing cannon at him, although he was considerably too high aloft to be in range.

The French dragons came charging in a determined cloud: already some of them were coughing, and they were none of them in a mood to converse, until Temeraire roared out like thunder in their faces, and took them all aback, then loudly said, *"Ârret! Je ne vous ai pas attaqué; il faut que vous m'écouter: nous sommes venus pour vous apporter du médicament."*

As the first handful were mulling this over, flying circles around them, another party came flying fresh from the covert roaring their own defiance; the two groups grew rapidly more confused, captains shouting at one another over their speaking-trumpets, until at last signals were issued, and they were escorted to the ground by a wary honor-guard, six dragons on either side and more preceding them and behind. When they had been brought down, in a wide and pleasant meadow, there was a good deal of shuffling and edging back, not frightened but wary, and anxious murmurs from the dragons as their officers descended.

Laurence unstrapped the tub, and unlatched his own carabiners: men were already swarming up the sides of Temeraire's harness, and there were pistols leveled at him before he stood. "You will surrender," a young lieutenant said, narrow-eyed and thickly accented.

"We already have," Laurence said tiredly, and held out to him the wooden tub; the young man looked at it, perplexed, wincing away from the stench. "They are to cure the cough," Laurence said, *"la grippe, des dragonnes,"* and pointed to one of the coughing dragons.

It was taken from him with much suspicion, but passed down, if not as the priceless treasure it was, at least with some degree of care. The tub vanished from his sight, at any rate, and so beyond his concern; a great sinking weariness was spreading through him, and he fumbled with more awkwardness even than usual at the harness-straps, climbing down, until he slipped and fell the last five feet to the ground.

"Laurence," Temeraire cried urgently, leaning towards him; another French officer sprang forward and seizing Laurence by the arm dragged him up and put the muzzle of a pistol, cold and gritty with powder-grains, to his neck.

"I am well," Laurence said, restraining with an effort a cough; he did not wish to jar the pistol. "I am well, Temeraire, you do not need to—"

He was permitted to say no more; there were many

hands upon him, and the officers gathering tight around him like a knot; he was half-carried across the meadow towards the tense and waiting line of French dragons, a prisoner, and Temeraire made a low wordless cry of protest as he was dragged away.

Chapter 17

❦

$\mathcal{L}$AURENCE SPENT THE night in a solitary uncomfortable cell, in the bowels of the covert headquarters: clammy and hot, without a breath of air; the narrow barred window at the top of wall looked out on a barren parade-ground, and let in only dust. They gave him a little thin porridge and a little water; a little straw on the floor for a bed; but there was none of that humane self-interest which would have let him buy greater comfort, though he had a little money in his pockets.

They did not rob him, but his hints were ignored: a cold resentful suspicion in their looks, and some muttered colloquial remarks that he thought he was meant to understand better than his limited French would allow. He supposed the news had spread, by now, amongst them: the nature of the disease, the virulence; and he would have been as little forgiving as they were. The guards were all old aviators, former ground crewmen with wooden legs, or missing arms: a sinecure, like the post of cook aboard a ship; although no cook he had ever known would have refused a neat bribe for a cup of his slush, not from the Devil himself.

It did not touch him in a personal way, however; there was no room for that. He only gave up the attempt, and threw himself down on the dirty pallet with his coat wrapped around him, and slept dreamless and long; when he roused with the gaol-keepers' clanging delivery of the morning's porridge, he looked down at the floor, where the window square of sunlight lay divided neatly into its barred sections, and shut his eyes again, without bothering to rise and eat.

He had to be woken in the afternoon by rough shaking, and he was brought afterwards to another room with a handful of grim-faced senior officers arranged before him, along the long side of a table. They interrogated him with some harshness as to the nature of the mushrooms, the disease, his purpose in bringing the cure, if a cure it was. He was forced to repeat himself, and exhorted to speak more quickly when he went slowly in his stumbling French; when he tried for a little more speed, and misspoke, the errors were seized upon, and shaken like a rat-killing dog might, to squeeze all the life there was out of them.

Having been served such a black turn to begin with, they had some right to suspect him the instrument of some further underhanded trick, instead of one acting to prevent it; nevertheless he found it hard to bear up; and when they began to ask him other questions, of the position of ships in the Channel, the strength in the Dover covert, he nearly answered at first, only from fatigue and the habit of replying, before he caught himself up.

"You do know we may hang you as a spy," one of the officers said coldly, when Laurence had flatly refused to speak. "You came in without colors, without uniform—"

"If you wish to object, because I had made my shirt a parley-flag, it would be kind of you at least to arrange for me to have another," Laurence said, wondering with black humor if next they would offer to flog him. "As for the rest, I had rather hang for a British spy, than be a French."

He ate the cold waiting porridge when they had put him back into his cell, mechanically, and went to look out of the window at what nothing there was to see. He was not afraid, only still very tired.

The interrogations went on a week, but eased gradually from suspicion to a wary and bewildered sort of gratitude, in step with the progress of the trial they had made, of one of the mushrooms. Even when they had been convinced the cure was as real as the disease, the officers did not know what to make of Laurence's actions; they came at him with the question in one way and then another, and when he repeated that he had only come to bring the cure, to save the dragons' lives, they said, "Yes, but *why?*"

As he could give them no better answer, they settled for thinking him quixotic, with which he could not argue, and his keepers grew sufficiently mellow to let him buy some bread and the occasional stewed fowl. At the end of the week, they put a fetter on his leg, and took him out to see Temeraire, established in respectful state in the covert, and under guard only by one unhappy Petit Chevalier, not much smaller than he, whose nose dripped continuously upon the ground. One small tub of course would not do, to cure all those infected, and although it had evidently been delivered successfully to the charge of several expert Brêton mushroom-farmers, many of the sick dragons would have to suffer for several months more before there was enough of the cure to go around. Where the disease might spread further, Laurence could only hope that with the cure established in England and France, the quarrel of the two powers must deliver it to their respective allies also, and cupidity amongst such a widened number of keepers lead to its eventual dispersal.

"I am very well," Temeraire said. "I like their beef

here, and they have been obliging enough to cook it for me, do you know? The dragons *here* at least are perfectly willing to try cooked food, and Validius here," he nodded to the Petit Chevalier, who sneezed to acknowledge it, "had a notion, that they might stew it for us with wine; I have never understood what was so nice about it, that you were always drinking it, but now I do; it has a very nice flavor."

Laurence wondered how many bottles had been sacrificed, to sate the hunger of two very large dragons; perhaps not a very good year, he thought, and hoped they had not yet formed the notion of drinking spirits unadulterated by cooking. "I am glad you are so comfortably situated," he said, and made no complaint of his own accommodations.

"Yes, and," Temeraire added, with not a little smugness, "they would like me to give them *five* eggs, all to very large dragons, and one of them a fire-breather; although I have told them I cannot," he finished wistfully, "because of course they would teach the eggs French, and make them attack our friends, in England; they were surprised that I should mind."

This was of a piece with the questions Laurence had faced: all the worse grief, that he could so naturally be taken for a wholehearted turncoat, judged by his own acts; it was the greater curiosity to all when he did not offer to be a traitor. He was glad to see Temeraire contented, and sincerely so; but he returned to his cell lower in his spirits, conscious that Temeraire would be as happy here, as he was in England; happier, perhaps.

"I would be grateful for a shirt, and trousers," Laurence said, "if my purse can stand it; I want for nothing else."

"The clothing I insist you will permit me to arrange

from my own part," De Guignes said, "and we will see you at once in better accommodations; I am ashamed," he added, with a cold look over his shoulder that made the gaolers edge away from where they were listening and peeping in at the door, "that you should have met with such indignity, monsieur."

Laurence bowed his head. "You are very kind, sir; I have no complaint to make of my treatment, and I am very sensible of the honor which you do in coming so far to see me," he said quietly.

They had last met under very different circumstances: at a banquet in China, De Guignes there at the head of Napoleon's envoy, and Laurence with the King's. Although their political enemy, he had been impossible to dislike; and Laurence without knowing it had already endeared himself to the gentleman, some time before, by taking some pains to preserve the life of his nephew, taken prisoner in a failed boarding attempt; so the encounter had been, so far as personal matters went, a friendly one.

That he had come all this way was, however, a marked kindness; Laurence knew himself a prisoner of no great importance or rank, except as surety for Temeraire's good behavior, and De Guignes must have been thoroughly occupied. While his embassy had failed in its original designs, De Guignes had succeeded in one marked particular: seducing Lien to Napoleon's cause, and bringing her back with him to France. He had been promoted for it, Laurence vaguely thought, to some higher office in the foreign service; he had heard something of it, interested more in the name than in the rank; certainly De Guignes now showed all the signs of prosperity and position, in his handsome rings and in the elegance of his silk-and-linen coat.

"It is little enough amends for what you have suffered," De Guignes said, "and I am here not only in my own person, but to bear you all the assurances of His Majesty that you will soon better feel the gratitude of France, which you have so richly earned."

Laurence said nothing; he would have preferred to remain in his cell, starved, stripped naked, and fettered with iron, than be rewarded for his actions. But Temeraire's fate stopped his mouth: there was one at least in France, who far from feeling any sentiments of gratitude had all cause in the world to hate and wish them ill: Lien herself, who at least in rumor had Napoleon's confidence, and would gladly have seen Temeraire suffering the torments of the damned. Laurence would not disdain what protection from her malice the public avowals of imperial gratitude might provide.

It had certainly a more immediate effect: De Guignes had scarcely left the room before Laurence was shifted to a handsome chamber upstairs, appointed plainly but with some eye to comfort; a pleasant view of the open harbor, gaily stocked with sails, outside his window. The shirt and trousers materialized by morning: of very fine linen and wool, with silk thread, and with them clean stockings and linen; in the afternoon arrived a notable coat to replace his own much-battered and -stained article: cut of black leather, with skirts lower than the tops of his boots, and buttons in gold so pure they were already no longer quite circular.

Temeraire admired the results, very much, when in the morning they were reunited to be transferred to Paris; and barring an inclination to complain that Laurence was not permitted to ride upon *him,* for the journey, was perfectly satisfied with their change of venue. He did glare ferociously at the small and quailing Pou-de-Ciel who would serve as transport, as if he suspected her of planning to carry Laurence off for some nefarious ends. But the precaution would have been wise even if Laurence had given their parole, as without it he would have set a pace impossible for his escort to match; even as it was, they were hard-pressed. Temeraire outdistanced them, except in fits and starts, when he doubled back to come alongside the Pou-de-Ciel and call out remarks to Laurence; so the other dragons, most of them showing early signs of the illness, were rather exhausted when they came in sight of the Seine.

Laurence had not been to Paris since the year one, in the last peace, and had never before seen it from the dragon-heights; but even with so little familiarity, he could scarcely have failed to notice transformation on such a scale. A broad avenue, still more than half raw dirt, had been driven straight through the heart of the city, smashing through all the old medieval alley-ways. Extending from the Tuileries towards the Bastille, it continued the line of the Champs-Élysées, but dwarfed that into a pleasant country lane: the new avenue perhaps half as wide as that massive square of Peking, which stood before the Forbidden City, and much longer; with dragons hovering over and lowering great stacks of paving-stones into the street.

A triumphal arch of monumental scale was going up, in the Place de l'Étoile, half still presently mocked up in wood, and new embankments upon the Seine; more prosaically, in other places the ground had been opened up to a great depth, and new sewers were being laid in mortared cobblestones. On the city's border an enormous bank of slaughterhouses stood behind a newly raised wall, with a plaza open beside them, and a handful of cows on spits roasting; a dragon was sitting there eating one, holding it on the spit like an ear of corn.

Below them directly, the gardens of the Tuileries had

been widened, out from the banks of the Seine nearly an additional quarter-of-a-mile in the opposite direction, swallowing up the Place Vendôme into their boundaries; and overlooking the riverbank, at right corners to the palace, a great pavilion in stone and marble was going up: an edifice in the Roman style, but on a different scale. In the grassy courtyard already laid down beside it, Lien lay drowsily coiled in the shade, a thin white garden-snake seen from so far aloft, easy to make out among the other dragons who were scattered at decorous distance around her.

They were brought down in those gardens: not where Lien slept, but in another plaza before the palace, with a makeshift pavilion of wood and sailcloth hastily erected in their honor. Laurence had scarcely time to see Temeraire established, before De Guignes took his arm and smiling invited him inside; smiling, but with a firm grip, and the guards gripped their muskets tightly: still honored guest and prisoner both.

The apartments where they conducted him would have befitted a prince; he might have wandered blindfold through the room for five minutes together without knocking into a wall. Used as he was to cramped quarters, Laurence found their scale irritating rather than luxurious: the walk from the chamberpot to the dressing-table a nuisance, and the bed too soft and overburdened with hangings for the hot weather; standing alone under the high and muraled ceiling, he felt an actor in a bad play, with eyes and mockery upon him.

He sat down at the writing-table in the corner, to have somewhere to put himself, and pushed up the cover: paper aplenty, and good pens, and ink, fresh and liquid when he opened the jar; he closed it slowly again. He owed six letters; they would never be written.

Outside it grew dark; from his window he could see

the pavilion on the riverbank, illuminated with many colorful lanterns. The workers had gone away; Lien was now lying across the top of the stairway, her wings folded to her back, watching the light on the water: a silhouette more than a shape. She turned her head, and Laurence saw a man come walking down the broad path towards her, and ascend into the pavilion: lanterns shone red on the uniforms of his guard, which he had left at the foot of the stair.

De Guignes came the next morning after breakfast, all renewals of kindness and generous sentiments, and took him walking down to see Temeraire, with only a moderate guard. Temeraire was awake and by the lashing of his tail in a state of near-agitation; "She has sent me an invitation," he said plaintively, as soon as Laurence had sat down. "I do not know what she means by it; I am not going to go and talk to her, at all."

The invitation was a handsomely calligraphed scroll, in Chinese characters, tied with a tassel of red and gold; it was not long, and merely requested the pleasure of the company of Lung Tien Xiang at the Pavilion of the Seven Pillars for drinking tea and restful repose, in the heat of the day. "There is nothing evidently insincere in it; perhaps she means it as a gesture of reconciliation," Laurence said, though he did not think much of the chances.

"No, she does not," Temeraire said darkly. "I am sure if I go, the tea will be very unpleasant, at least *my* tea will be, and I will have to drink it or look ill-mannered; or she will make remarks which do not seem offensive, until I have gone away and thought them over; or she will try and have you murdered while I am not there: you are not to go anywhere without a guard, and if anyone tries to murder you, you must call for me very loud," he added. "I am sure I could knock down a wall of that palace, if I had to, to reach you," a remark which left De Guignes with a peculiar rigid expression; he could not forbear a glance at the substantial stone wall of the Tuileries, overlooking the pavilion.

"I assure you from my heart," he said, recovering his aplomb, "that no one could be more sensible of the generosity which you have shown to France; Madame Lien has been among the first, to receive the cure which you have delivered us—"

"Oh," Temeraire said, disgruntled.

"—and, as all of the nation, welcomes you with open arms," De Guignes carried on manfully.

"Stuff," Temeraire said. "I do not believe it at all; and I do not like her anyway, even if she does mean it, so she may keep her invitations and her tea; and her pavilion, too," he added, low, with an envious twitch of his tail.

De Guignes coughed, and did not attempt further to persuade him; instead he said, "I will make your regrets, then; in any event, you may be occupied with preparations, as tomorrow morning His Majesty wishes to meet you, and to convey to you all the thanks of the nation. He wishes you to know it grieves him very much that the formalities of war should attend such a meeting; and that for his part, he welcomes you as brothers, and not as prisoners at all," he added, with a look at once tactful and significant: a delicate hinting that they need not be prisoners for *their* part, either, if they chose.

The whole speech, his earnest manner, had a vaguely mercenary quality, which, to do justice to the man's humanity, he gave with a very faint, dismissive air; so to accept would have needed only a nod. Laurence looked away instead; to hide his expression of distaste; but Temeraire said, "If he does not like us to be prisoners, it seems to me he is the Emperor, and can let us go if he likes. We are not going to fight for you against our own friends back in England, if that is what you mean."

De Guignes smiled without any sign of offense. "His Majesty would never invite you to any dishonorable act." A pretty sentiment, and one which Laurence was inclined to trust from Bonaparte as much as from the Lords of the Admiralty: less. De Guignes rose gracefully and said, "I hope you will excuse me now to my other duties: Sergeant Lasalle and his men will escort you to your quarters for dinner, Captain, when you have finished your conversation," and so quitted them strategically, to let them contemplate his vague suggestions alone.

They did not say anything a while; Temeraire scratched at the ground. "I suppose we cannot stay," he muttered, half-ashamedly, "even if we did not fight? I thought we would go back to China, but then we have still left everything in Europe as it is. I am sure I can protect you from Lien, and perhaps I might help work upon that road; or I might write books. It seems very nice here," he added. "One could go walking, here in the gardens, or in the road, and meet people."

Laurence looked down at his hands, which held no answer. He did not mean to grieve Temeraire, or to distress him, but he had known his own fate since first they had embarked upon this adventure; and at last he said quietly, "My dear, I hope you will stay, and have whatever profession you desire; or that Bonaparte will give you passage back to China if you prefer it. But I must go home to England."

Temeraire paused, and then he said uncertainly, "But they will hang you—"

"Yes," Laurence said.

"I will not, I will never let them," Temeraire said. "Laurence—"

"I have committed treason," Laurence said. "I will not now add cowardice to that crime, nor let you shield me from its consequences." He looked away; Temeraire was silent and trembling, and it was painful to look at him. "I do not regret what we have done," he said quietly. "I would not have undertaken the act, if I were not willing to die for it; but I do not mean to live a traitor."

Temeraire shuddered, and drew himself back onto his haunches, staring blindly out into the gardens; motionless. "And if we stay," he said, eventually, "they will say it was all self-interest—that we brought the cure for a reward, so that we should have a pleasant life, here or in China; or perhaps that we were cowards, and thought Napoleon would win the war, and we did not want to fight. They will never admit that *they* were in the wrong; and that we have sacrificed our own happiness, to repair what never ought have been done, in the first place."

Laurence had not so articulated his instinctive decision; he did not need to, to know what he must do. For his own part, he did not care what should be thought of it, and said so. "What will be *thought* of it, I already know, and I do not suppose anything now will alter those sentiments; if that were of any importance, we should not have gone. I am not returning to make a political gesture, but because it must be done; if there is any honor to be preserved after such an act."

"Well, I would not give a button for honor," Temeraire said. "But I do care about the lives of our friends, and that those lords should learn to be ashamed of what they have done; which I suppose *they* will never do, but others might, if they were not given so convenient an excuse to dismiss the whole matter." He bowed his head. "Very well; we will tell him no, and if he will not set us free, we can escape and return, on our own."

"No," Laurence said, recoiling. "My dear, there is no

sense in it; you had much better go back to China. They will only throw you in the breeding grounds."

"Oh! certainly! that I should run away, but not you, when you have done it for me, you never thought of it but for me?" Temeraire heaped scorn upon the notion. "No; if they mean to put you to death, they will have to put *me* to death also; I am as guilty or more, and I will certainly not let you be killed while I am alive. And if they do not like to execute me, I will go lie down in front of Parliament, until they have changed their minds."

They were escorted across the gardens to the great pavilion, together; Laurence marched in a company of Imperial Guards, splendid and sweating in their tall black shakos and blue coats. Lien was lying upon the riverbank, observing benevolently the traffic which went up and down the Seine before her, and turned her head when they came, inclining it politely; Temeraire went very stiff, and rumbled, deep in his throat.

She shook her head disapprovingly at his manners. "You needn't shake your head at me," Temeraire retorted, "because I do not care to pretend that we are friendly; it is only that I am not deceitful: so there."

"How is it deceitful, when you know we are not friendly, and so do I," Lien pointed out, "and all who are in our confidence? There is no-one deceived, who has any right to know, but those who prefer to take no notice of it; except with your boorish behavior, no one about can avoid knowing, and being made to feel awkward."

Temeraire subsided muttering, and crowded up as close as he could to the nervous guards, trying to hover protectively near Laurence; a dish of tea was brought him, which he sniffed suspiciously and then disdained, and a glass of cold sillery, which Laurence did not; a

slight cooling breeze came off the water and the greenery of the park, and the vast marbled space was pleasant, with somewhere hidden a running gurgle of water
over stone, but the day was still very hot, even with the
morning not yet far advanced.

The soldiers went to attention; and then Bonaparte
was coming down the walk, trailing guards and secretaries, one of whom was writing desperately even as
they came: taking down a letter. The valedictions were
added as they came up the steps, then Bonaparte turned
away, came through the two files of guards hastily shuffling out of his way, and seizing Laurence by the shoulders kissed him on both cheeks.

"Your Majesty," Laurence said, rather faintly. He had
seen the emperor once before, briefly and from conceal-
ment, while Bonaparte had been overlooking the field of
Jena; and had been impressed at that time with the intensity and the nearly cruel anticipation in his expression, the remote eye, the hawk about to stoop. There
was no less intensity now, but perhaps some softening;
the emperor looked stouter, his face a little more
rounded, than on that peak.

"Come, walk with me," Bonaparte said, and drew
him by the arm down to the water, where Laurence was
not himself required to walk, but rather to stand and let
the emperor pace before him, gesturing, with a restless
energy. "What do you think of what I have done with
Paris?" he asked, waving his hand towards the sparrow-
cloud of dragons visible, working on the new road.
"Few men have had the opportunity to see my designs,
as you have, from the air."

"An extraordinary work, Your Majesty," Laurence
said, sorry to be so sincere; it was the kind of work
which only tyranny, he supposed unhappily, could
achieve, and characteristic of all Napoleon's works,

smashing through tradition with a kind of heedless forward motion; he would have preferred to find it ugly, and ill-reasoned. "It will expand all the character of the city."

Bonaparte nodded, satisfied with this remark, and said, "It is only a mirror held up to the expansion of the *national* character, however, that I am going to achieve. I will not allow men to fear dragons: if cowardice, it is dishonorable; if superstition, distasteful; and there are no rational objections. It is only habit, and habit which can and must be broken. Why should Peking be superior to Paris? I will have this the most beautiful city of the world, of men and dragons both."

"It is a noble ambition," Laurence said, low.

"But you do not agree with it," Bonaparte said, pouncing; Laurence twitched before the sudden assault, very nearly of palpable force. "But you will not stay, and see it done, though you have already been given proof of the perfidy, the dishonorable measures to which a government of oligarchs will stoop: it can never be otherwise," he added; more declaration than an attempt to convince, "when money becomes the driving force of the state: there must be some moral power beneath, some ambition, that is not only for wealth and safety."

Laurence did not think very much of Bonaparte's method, which substituted an insatiable hunger for glory and power, at the cost of men's lives and liberty; but he did not try to argue. It would have been hard indeed, he thought, to marshal any argument in the face of the monologue, which Bonaparte did not mind continuing in the absence of opposition or even response; he ranged widely across philosophy and economics, the useless folly of government by clerks, the differences, which he detailed minutely on philosophical grounds quite beyond Laurence's comprehension, between the despotism of the Bourbons and his own imperial state: *they* had been tyrants, parasites, holding power through superstition and for their own personal pleasure, lacking in merit; *he* was the defender of the Republic, and the servant of the nation.

Laurence only withstood, as a small rock in a deluge; and the gale past said simply, "Your Majesty, I am a soldier, not a statesman; and I have no great philosophy but that I love my country. I came because it was my duty as a Christian and a man; now it is my duty to return."

Bonaparte regarded him, frowning, displeased, a tyrant's lowering look; but it flitted quickly away, then he stepped closer, and gripped Laurence by the arm, persuasive. "You mistake your duty. You would throw away your life: all right, you might say, but it is not yours alone. You have a young dragon, who has devoted himself to your interest, and who has given you all his love and confidence. What can a man not accomplish, with such a friend, such a councilor, free from any trace of envy or self-interest? It has made you who you are. Think where would you now be, without the stroke of fortune that put his heart into your keeping?"

At sea, like as not, or at home: a small estate in England perhaps, married, by now his first child here; Edith Woolvey, née Galman, had been delivered of her first four months before. Marching steadily up the post-list towards flag-rank; he would probably have been sitting presently on blockade, beating up and down off Brest or Calais, a tedious but necessary routine. A prosperous and an honest life, and if no great chance of glory, as far from treason as from the moon; he had never asked for anything else, or expected it.

The vision stood at a distance almost bewildering, now; mythical, softened by a comfortable blind innocence. He might have regretted it; he did regret it, now, except there was no room in the gardens of that house for a dragon to be sleeping in the sun.

Bonaparte said, "You do not suffer from the disease of ambition—so much the better. Let me give you an honorable retirement. I won't insult you by offering you a fortune, only his keep and yours. A house in the country, a cattle-herd. Nothing will be asked of you that you do not want to give." His hand tightened, when Laurence would have drawn away. "Will your conscience be more clear when you have delivered him into captivity? Into a long captivity," he added sharply. "—they will not tell him when they put you to death."

Laurence flinched; and through the grip Bonaparte felt it and pursued, as a breach in his lines. "Do you think they would hesitate to forge your name to letters? You know they will not, and in any case the messages will only be read aloud. A few words—you are well, you think of him, you hope that he is obedient—and he will be imprisoned by them better than iron bars. He will wait and linger and hope for many years, starved and cold and neglected, long after you have swung from a gibbet. Can you be satisfied to condemn him to it?"

Laurence knew all this sprang from a selfish concern: if Bonaparte could not have Temeraire's active complaisance, even in the matter of breeding, he would still have been glad at least to deny him to the British; and he probably had hopes of persuading them, in time, to do more. That knowledge, cold and impersonal, gave Laurence no comfort; it did not matter to him that Bonaparte was interested, when he was very likely also right.

"Sir," Laurence said unevenly, "I wish you may persuade him to stay. —I must go back."

The words had to be forced. He spoke past a constriction, as one who has been running a race uphill, for a long time: since that moment in the clearing, since they had left London behind. But now the hill was past; he had reached the summit, and he stood there breathing hard; there was nothing more he had to say or bear; his answer was fixed. He looked over at Temeraire, waiting anxiously inside the open pavilion. He thought he would try and put himself in Temeraire's hands, at least, rather than be marched back to prison; if he was killed in the attempt, it did not make much difference.

Bonaparte recognized it; he let go Laurence's arm, and turned away from him to pace frowning up and down; but at last he turned. "God forbid I should alter such a resolve. Your choice is the choice of Regulus, and I honor you for it. You will have your liberty—you must have your liberty," he said, "and more: a troop of my Old Guard will escort you to Calais; Accendare's formation see you across the Channel, under flag of truce: and all the world will know that France at least can recognize a man of honor."

The covert at Calais was busy: fourteen dragons were not easily put in order, and Accendare herself was inclined to snap and be difficult, irritable and weary with coughing. Laurence turned away from the confusion, and wished only, dully, to be gone; to have done with everything, all the hollow ceremony: eagles and flags, polished buckles, the fresh pressed blue of the French uniforms. The wind was fair for England; their party was expected, letters having traveled across and back to arrange the parley. There would be dragons and chains to meet them: perhaps even Jane, or Granby, or strangers who knew nothing more of him than his crime. By now his family surely would know all.

De Guignes was rolling up the map of Africa from the table; Laurence had shown him the valley where they had found the mushroom supply. It was nothing materially more than he had already done; the mushrooms were growing, but Bonaparte did not care to wait, Laurence supposed, or risk a failure of the harvest. They meant at once to send an expedition, which was even now outfitting in the harbor: two sleek frigates, and he believed another three going from La Rochelle, in hopes that at least one would evade the blockade and reach their destination, and by stealth or negotiation acquire an immediately useful supply. Laurence hoped only they should not all be taken prisoner, but even if they were, he supposed it could not matter; the cure was established and would spread; no more dragons would die. It was a small satisfaction, at least, if a dry and tasteless one.

He had feared some last attempt at bribery or seduction, but De Guignes did not even ask him to say anything, with a great sensitivity, but brought out a dusty bottle of brandy, and poured him a generous glass. "To the hope of peace between our people," he proposed; Laurence moistened his lips, polite, and left the cold collation untouched; and when it had been cleared, he went outside to Temeraire.

Temeraire was not embroiled in the general clamor; he was sitting quietly hunched on one side, looking out to sea over the straits: the white cliffs were plainly visible, from their perch. Laurence leaned against his side and shut his eyes, the steady heartbeat beneath like the rushing tide in a conch shell. "I beg you will stay," Laurence said. "You serve me not at all, nor your own cause; it will only be thought blind loyalty."

Temeraire said, after a moment, "If I do, will you tell them that I carried you away, against your will, and made you do it?"

"Never, good God," Laurence said, straightening,

and wounded even to be asked; too late he realized he had been led up to the mark.

"Napoleon said that if I stayed, you might tell them so if you liked," Temeraire said, "and then they might spare you. But I said you would never say such a thing at all, so it was no use; and so you may stop trying to persuade *me*. I will never stay here, while they try to hang you."

Laurence bowed his head, and felt the justice of it; he did not think Temeraire *ought* to stay, but only wished that he would, and be happy. "You will promise me not to stay forever in the breeding grounds," he said, low. "Not past the New Year, unless they let me visit you in the flesh." He was very certain they would execute him by Michaelmas.

Extracts from
The Tswana Kingdom
A BRIEF HISTORY

By
Sipho Tsuluka Dlamini
[1838]

IN THREE VOLUMES

LONDON, CHAPMAN & HALL
LIMITED

Being a history of the Tswana Kingdom from its origins to the present day, and a complete geographical survey of its territories, with particular reference to the capital at Mosi oa Tunya, and several interesting remarks on the native customs.

THE GRADUAL PROCESS of consolidation of the Tswana and Sotho peoples brought together a loose confederation of tribal kingdoms, founded originally, according to tribal historians, throughout the southern part of the continent towards the end of the first millennium, by a general but undeliberate southerly and eastern migration, whose impetus has been lost to us: perhaps a search for fresh hunting grounds, and new territory, by an expanding population both human and dragon.

The first vague beginnings of elephant-farming are believed to have developed shortly after this vast migration was mostly complete, and the pressures of hunger might no longer be relieved by further nomadic progress; a study of the art of the ivory-carvers gives testament to the success of the breeding project that rendered the domesticated beasts more bovine-docile, and considerably larger than their wild counterparts: a succession of tusks held at the capital, each pair the largest harvested within a generation, carved elaborately and presented to the (then largely ceremonial) king. . . .

These tribes, previously united only by distant ties of blood, mutually intelligible dialect, and certain shared customs and religious observances, most notable among these of course the practice of dragon-rebirth, first began to collaborate more closely for the joint administration of the elephant herds, which demanded more labour than could be organised by a single tribe. . . . [A] centralisation further encouraged from the seventeenth century onwards by the increasing demand for ivory and gold, which penetrated to the African interior for several decades before the hunger for slaves was risen to a sufficient pitch to overcome the reluctance of the more aggressive slave-taking tribes to venture into dragon-territory; and spurring, from the middle of the eighteenth century, the rapid development of gold-mining (a venture that the Tswana authorities indicate is most productively pursued through the co-operation of at least ten dragons, more than belong to nearly any individual tribe), and of the ivory trade, which by the open of the present century was sending some sixty thousand pounds a year to the coast without any suspicion on the part of the European traders, who carried the elephant teeth away, that these were obtained by, and not in despite of, the dragons who barred any further entry to the interior. . . .

On Mosi oa Tunya

THE FALLS AT Mosi oa Tunya, so justly celebrated by all who have beheld them, were, despite their beauty, as a settlement inconvenient to men alone, who could not easily navigate the gorges, and in their natural state offered no real haven to feral dragons; admired and occasionally visited, either for mere scenic pleasure or religious observation, they were yet undeveloped and uninhabited when the first Sotho-Tswana peoples moved into the region, and quickly made them their ceremonial capital, a further centralising tie among the tribes. . . . [T]he desire of the dragon-ancestors for more comfortable shelter impelled the first attempts at cave-drilling, the relics of which may yet be seen at the falls, in the holiest and roughest chambers, low in the cliff-side . . . and which later were to prove the foundation of the efficient gold-mining operations. . . .

The practice of rebirth here requires a few words, to expand upon the treatment it has received in the British press, at the hands of well-meaning missionary reporters, who in their zeal have too easily disposed of it as a matter of pure pagan superstition, urgently to be eradicated in favor of Christianity. . . . It will not be found that anyone of the Tswana imagines that the human is *naturally* reborn, in the manner espoused, for instance, by the Buddhist or the Hindu, and if one should propose leaving a selected dragon egg alone in the wilderness, in accordance with the suggestion of Mr. Dennis, to snatch such an egg "to demonstrate to the heathen the wild fancy of their custom," by proving that the resulting hatchling would have no recollection of its former life, no tribesman would dispute this as the natural consequence, but merely abuse the bad husbandry and irreligiosity united, which should so waste a dragon-egg, and insult the spirit of the dead ancestor.

That the feral dragon in the wilderness is no more a reborn human than is a cow is perfectly understood by them, and viewed as no contradiction to their practice. Careful coaxing and ritual are necessary, besides a suitable housing, to induce an ancestral spirit to take up residence again in material form; the article of faith is to believe, *once* this has been achieved, that the dragon is certainly the human reborn, a belief much harder to dislodge, by its being firmly held not only by the men but the dragons, and of so much practical importance within the tribe.

The dragon-ancestors at once serve as a substantial source of labor and military power, and as repositories of tribal history and legend, compensating for the neglect of the written word. Furthermore, each tribe will consider carefully the disposal of the eggs of their own dragon-ancestors, common tribal property, which may be used to reincarnate one of their own, should there be one of sufficient standing to merit the honor, or, far more commonly, traded to a remote tribe in more urgent need, through a complex network of communications sure to bring the news of a suitable egg to those seeking the same, this network serving to knit together tribes that might otherwise have grown more distinct, left to act in isolation. Nor are these dragon bloodlines ignored, as might be expected by one who imagines a sort of simplistic literal belief; rather, such an exchange of eggs is held to establish a kind of distant familial relation between the receiving tribe and the donor, much like state marriages, further strengthening ties. . . .

Mokhachane I *(h)*, a Sotho chieftain, carved out a relatively minor territory that proved notable for its position on the extremes of the Sotho-Tswana tribal regions, touching upon Xhosa territory to the south, and thus indirectly receiving at least vague intelligence of the growing Dutch settlements at the Cape, and having some communication with the beleaguered Monomotapa kingdoms on the East African coast, the descendants of the zimbabwe-builders.

Broader relations were established with this latter power near the turn of the century under the urging of his son, Moshueshue I *(h)*, demonstrating from his youth that wisdom for which his name was to become a byword, which relations were to have great significance after Mokhachane's *(h)* death in raiding during the year 1798, when Moshueshue was able to negotiate the acquisition of a large dragon egg of the Monomotapa royal lines, for his father's rebirth; the Monomotapa government by this time fracturing under increasing pressure from the Portuguese gold-hunters along the eastern coast, and in need of the gold and the military reinforcements that Moshueshue could provide, as a result of negotiations with neighboring Tswana tribes. . . .

The acquisition of so powerful a dragon, in conjunction with Moshueshue's coming of age, which eliminated the last barriers to his being received as an equal by other tribal chieftains, very shortly vaulted the tribe to pre-eminence in the southernmost regions of the Tswana lands. Mokhachane I *(d)* easily established dominance over the dragon-ancestors of neighboring tribes, in joint raiding that Moshueshue organized, and together they were soon able to establish several new mines, both of gold and of precious stones, in the formerly unexploited region; and with the steady increase in wealth and respect soon acquired a primacy that enabled them, in the year 1804, to claim the central seat, at Mosi oa Tunya, and the title of king.

The depredations of the slave-takers had by this time for several years been making systematic inroads into the Tswana territories, as more than isolated incidents, and were a not inconsiderable factor in the willingness of the smaller kingdoms to submit formally to central leadership, in hopes of making a united answer to those raids, and repulsing them decisively, an argument that Moshueshue did not fail of making, in his careful solicitations of fealty from his fellow tribal chieftains, who might otherwise have resisted from pride. The practical as well as ceremonial reign of Mokhachane I was confirmed by the conquest of Capetown and the Slave Coast raids of 1807, and the Tswana themselves date the founding of their kingdom from this year. . . .

Acknowledgements

AMONG MANY WORKS, Basil Davidson's survey of primary sources, *African Civilization Revisited*, stands out as a priceless resource, as does UNESCO's *General History of Africa*, for illuminating the history of the continent outside colonization. I am also deeply indebted to the guides at the Ker & Downey camps in the Okovango Delta of Botswana for sharing their expertise and tolerating endless questions, with particular thanks to our brilliant camp manager at Okuti, Paul Moloseng.

Empire of Ivory has been in some ways the most difficult of the Temeraire books to write so far, and I have to give deep and heartfelt thanks to all my beta readers for heroic work under the gun, as I hardly gave them a weekend for comment on the draft before I was tearing onward into revisions: Holly Benton, Sara Booth, Alison Feeney, Shelley Mitchell, Georgina Paterson, Meredith Rosser, L. Salom, Kellie Takenaka, and Rebecca Tushnet. And much gratitude to Betsy Mitchell, Emma Coode, and Jane Johnson, my wonderful editors, and to my agent, Cynthia Manson.

And always, always, both gratitude and love to Charles, my first and best and most beloved reader.

NAPOLEON
INVADES ENGLAND!!!

**Can't wait to find
out what happens next?**

**Subscribe to the Naomi Novik
e-newsletter and read the first
chapter of Naomi Novik's next
Temeraire novel!**

VICTORY OF EAGLES

**at
www.temeraire.org**